# TORTUGAS

The man stared at Spaulding. The elevator buzzer was incessant now; voices could be heard from above and below.

"I'd prefer not to have to kill you but I will. *Where is Tortugas?*"

Suddenly a loud male voice, no more than ten feet from the enclosure, on the sixth floor, shouted:

"*It's up here! It's stuck!* Are you all *right* up there?"

The man blinked, the shouting had unnerved him. It was the instant Spaulding was waiting for. He lashed his right hand out in a diagonal thrust and gripped the man's forearm, hammering it against the metal door. He slammed his body into the man's chest and brought his knee up in a single, crushing assault against the groin. The man screamed in agony; the body went limp, the revolver fell to the floor, and the man slid downward against the wall.

Spaulding kicked the weapon away and gripped the man's neck with both hands, shaking the head back and forth to keep him conscious.

"Now you tell *me*, you son of a bitch! What *is* 'Tortugas'?"

# THE RHINEMANN EXCHANGE

## ROBERT LUDLUM

BANTAM BOOKS
NEW YORK • TORONTO • LONDON • SYDNEY • AUCKLAND

For Norma and
Ed Marcum—For
So Many Things,
My Thanks

THE RHINEMANN EXCHANGE

*A Bantam Book / published by arrangement with
the author*

*PRINTING HISTORY*
*Doubleday edition published 1974*
*Bantam edition / August 1989*

ISBN 0-553-28063-5

*Published simultaneously in the United States and Canada*

---

*Bantam Books are published by Bantam Books, a division of
Bantam Doubleday Dell Publishing Group, Inc. Its trademark,
consisting of the words "Bantam Books" and the portrayal
of a rooster, is Registered in U.S. Patent and Trademark Office
and in other countries. Marca Registrada. Bantam Books,
666 Fifth Avenue, New York, New York 10103.*

---

PRINTED IN THE UNITED STATES OF AMERICA

KR     0 9 8 7 6 5 4

# PREFACE

"David?"

The girl came into the room and stood silently for a moment, watching the tall army officer as he stared out the hotel window. The March rain fell through a March chill, creating pockets of wind and mist over the Washington skyline.

Spaulding turned, aware of her presence, not of her voice. "I'm sorry. Did you say something?" He saw that she held his raincoat. He saw, too, the concern in her eyes—and the fear she tried to conceal.

"It's over," she said softly.

"It's over," he replied. "Or will be in an hour from now."

"Will they all be there?" she asked as she approached him, holding the coat in front of her as though it were a shield.

"Yes. They have no choice. . . . I have no choice." Spaulding's left shoulder was encased in bandages under his tunic, the arm in a wide, black sling. "Help me on with that, will you? The rain's not going to let up."

Jean Cameron unfolded the coat reluctantly and opened it.

She stopped, her eyes fixed on the collar of his army shirt. Then on the lapels of his uniform.

All the insignia had been removed.

There were only slight discolorations in the cloth where the emblems had been.

There was no rank, no identifying brass or silver. Not even the gold initials of the country he served.

Had served.

He saw that she had seen.

"It's the way I began," he said quietly. "No name, no rank, no history. Only a number. Followed by a letter. I want them to remember that."

The girl stood motionless, gripping the coat. "They'll kill you, David." Her words were barely audible.

"That's the one thing they won't do," he said calmly. "There'll be no assassins, no accidents, no sudden orders flying me out to Burma or Dar es Salaam. That's finished. . . . They can't know what I've done."

He smiled gently and touched her face. Her lovely face. She breathed deeply and imposed a control on herself he knew she did not feel. She slipped the raincoat carefully over his left shoulder as he reached around for the right sleeve. She pressed her face briefly against his back; he could feel the slight trembling as she spoke.

"I won't be afraid. I promised you that."

He walked out the glass entrance of the Shoreham Hotel and shook his head at the doorman under the canopy. He did not want a taxi; he wanted to walk. To let the dying fires of rage finally subside and burn themselves out. A long walk.

It would be the last hour of his life that he would wear the uniform.

The uniform now with no insignia, no identification.

He would walk through the second set of doors at the War Department and give his name to the military police.

David Spaulding.

That's all he would say. It would be enough; no one would stop him, none would interfere.

Orders would be left by unnamed commanders—divisional recognition only—that would allow him to proceed down the grey corridors to an unmarked room.

Those orders would be at that security desk because another order had been given. An order no one could trace. No one comprehended. . . .

They claimed. In outrage.

But none with an outrage matching his.

They knew that, too, the unknown commanders.

Names meaning nothing to him only months ago would

be in the unmarked room. Names that now were symbols of an abyss of deceit that so revolted him, he honestly believed he had lost his mind.

Howard Oliver.

Jonathan Craft.

Walter Kendall.

The names were innocuous sounding in themselves. They could belong to untold hundreds of thousands. There was something so . . . American about them.

Yet these names, these men, had brought him to the brink of insanity.

They would be there in the unmarked room, and he would remind them of those who were absent.

Erich Rhinemann. Buenos Aires.

Alan Swanson. Washington.

Franz Altmüller. Berlin.

Other symbols. Other threads. . . .

The abyss of deceit into which he had been plunged by . . . enemies.

How in God's name had it *happened?*

How *could* it have happened?

But it did happen. And he had written down the facts as he knew them.

Written them down and placed . . . the document in an archive case inside a deposit box within a bank vault in Colorado.

Untraceable. Locked in the earth for a millennium . . . for it was better that way.

Unless the men in the unmarked room forced him to do otherwise.

If they did . . . if they forced him . . . the sanities of millions would be tested. The revulsion would not acknowledge national boundaries or the cause of any global tribe.

The leaders would become pariahs.

As he was a pariah now.

A number followed by a letter.

He reached the steps of the War Department; the tan stone pillars did not signify strength to him now. Only the appearance of light brown paste.

No longer substance.

He walked through the sets of double doors up to the

security desk, manned by a middle-aged lieutenant colonel
flanked by two sergeants.

"Spaulding, David," he said quietly.

"Your I.D. . . ." the lieutenant colonel looked at the
shoulders of the raincoat, then at the collar, "Spaulding. . . ."

"My name is David Spaulding. My source is Fairfax,"
repeated David softly. "Check your papers, soldier."

The lieutenant colonel's head snapped up in anger,
gradually replaced by bewilderment as he looked at
Spaulding. For David had not spoken harshly, or even
impolitely. Just factually.

The sergeant to the left of the lieutenant colonel shoved
a page of paper in front of the officer without interrupting. The lieutenant colonel looked at it.

He glanced back up at David—briefly—and waved him
through.

As he walked down the grey corridor, his raincoat over
his arm, Spaulding could feel the eyes on him, scanning
the uniform devoid of rank or identification. Several
salutes were rendered hesitantly.

None was acknowledged.

Men turned; others stared from doorways.

This was the . . . officer, their looks were telling him.
They'd heard the rumors, spoken in whispers, in hushed
voices in out-of-the-way corners. This was the man.

An order had been given. . . .

The *man*.

# PROLOGUE

## ONE

### *SEPTEMBER 8, 1939, NEW YORK CITY*

The two army officers, their uniforms creased into steel, their hats removed, watched the group of informally dressed men and women through the glass partition. The room in which the officers sat was dark.

A red light flashed; the sounds of an organ thundered out of the two webbed boxes at each corner of the glass-fronted, lightless cubicle. There followed the distant howling of dogs—large, rapacious dogs—and then a voice—deep, clear, forbidding—spoke over the interweaving sounds of the organ and the animals.

> Wherever madness exists, wherever the cries of the helpless can be heard, there you will find the tall figure of Jonathan Tyne—waiting, watching in shadows, prepared to do battle with the forces of hell. The seen and the unseen. . . .

Suddenly there was a piercing, mind-splitting scream. "Eeaagh!" Inside the lighted, inner room an obese woman winked at the short man in thick glasses who had been reading from a typed script and walked away from the microphone, chewing her gum rapidly.

The deep voice continued.

> Tonight we find Jonathan Tyne coming to the aid of the terror-stricken Lady Ashcroft, whose husband disappeared into the misty Scottish moors at precisely midnight three weeks ago. And each night at precisely midnight, the howls of unknown dogs bay across the

darkened fields. They seem to be challenging the very
man who now walks stealthily into the enveloping
mist. Jonathan Tyne. The seeker of evil; the nemesis
of Lucifer. The champion of the helpless victims of
darkness. . . .

The organ music swelled once more to a crescendo; the
sound of the baying dogs grew more vicious.

The older officer, a colonel, glanced at his companion,
a first lieutenant. The younger man, his eyes betraying his
concern, was staring at the group of nonchalant actors
inside the lighted studio.

The colonel winced.

"Interesting, isn't it?" he said.

"What? . . . Oh, yes, sir. Yes, sir; very interesting.
Which one is he?"

"The tall fellow over in the corner. The one reading a
newspaper."

"Does he play Tyne?"

"Who? Oh, no, lieutenant. He has a small role, I think.
In a Spanish dialect."

"A small role . . . in a Spanish dialect." The lieutenant
repeated the colonel's words, his voice hesitant, his look
bewildered. "Forgive me, sir, I'm confused. I'm not sure
what we're *doing* here; what *he's* doing here. I thought he
was a construction engineer."

"He is."

The organ music subsided to a pianissimo; the sound
of the howling dogs faded away. Now another voice—
this one lighter, friendlier, with no undercurrent of
impending drama—came out of the two webbed boxes.

Pilgrim. The soap with the scent of flowers in May;
the Mayflower soap. Pilgrim brings you once again
. . . "The Adventures of Jonathan Tyne."

The thick corked door of the dark cubicle opened and
a balding man, erect, dressed in a conservative business
suit, entered. He carried a manila envelope in his left
hand; he reached over and extended his right hand to the
colonel. He spoke quietly, but not in a whisper. "Hello,
Ed. Nice to see you again. I don't have to tell you your
call was a surprise."

"I guess it was. How are you, Jack? . . . Lieutenant, meet Mr. John Ryan; formerly Major John N. M. I. Ryan of Six Corps."

The officer rose to his feet.

"Sit down, lieutenant," said Ryan, shaking the young man's hand.

"Nice to meet you, sir. Thank you, sir."

Ryan edged his way around the rows of black leather armchairs and sat down next to the colonel in front of the glass partition. The organ music once more swelled, matching the reintroduced sounds of the howling dogs. Several actors and actresses crowded around two microphones, all watching a man behind a panel in another glass booth—this one lighted—on the other side of the studio.

"How's Jane?" asked Ryan. "And the children?"

"She hates Washington; so does the boy. They'd rather be back in Oahu. Cynthia loves it, though. She's eighteen, now; all those D.C. dances."

A hand signal was given by the man in the lighted booth across the way. The actors began their dialogue.

Ryan continued. "How about you? 'Washington' looks good on the roster sheet."

"I suppose it does, but nobody knows I'm there. That won't help me."

"Oh?"

"G-2."

"You look as though you are thriving, Jack."

"Yes, I gathered that."

Ryan smiled a little awkwardly. "No sweat. Ten other guys in the agency could do what I'm doing . . . better. But they don't have the Point on their résumés. I'm an agency symbol, strong-integrity version. The clients sort of fall in for muster."

The colonel laughed. "Horseshit. You were always good with the beady-bags. Even the high brass used to turn the congressmen over to you."

"You flatter me. At least I *think* you're flattering me."

"Eeaagh!" The obese actress, still chewing her gum, had screeched into the second microphone. She backed away, goosing a thin, effeminate-looking actor who was about to speak.

"There's a lot of screaming, isn't there." The colonel wasn't really asking a question.

"And dogs barking and off-key organ music and a hell of a lot of groaning and heavy breathing. 'Tyne's' the most popular program we have."

"I admit I've listened to it. The whole family has; since we've been back."

"You wouldn't believe it if I told you who writes most of the scripts."

"What do you mean?"

"A Pulitzer poet. Under another name, of course."

"That seems strange."

"Not at all. Survival. We pay. Poetry doesn't."

"Is that why *he's* on?" The colonel gestured with a nod of his head toward the tall, dark-haired man who had put down the newspaper but still remained in the corner of the studio, away from the other actors, leaning against the white corked wall.

"Beats the hell out of me. I mean, I didn't know who he was—that is, I knew who he *was,* but I didn't know anything about him—until you called." Ryan handed the colonel the manila envelope. "Here's a list of the shows and the agencies he's worked for. I called around; implied that we were considering him for a running lead. The Hammerts use him a lot. . . ."

"The who?"

"They're packagers. They've got about fifteen programs; daytime serials and evening shows. They say he's reliable; no sauce problems. He's used exclusively for dialects, it seems. And language fluency when it's called for."

"German and Spanish." It was a statement.

"That's right. . . ."

"Only it's not Spanish, it's Portuguese."

"Who can tell the difference? You know who his parents are." Another statement, only agreement anticipated.

"Richard and Margo Spaulding. Concert pianists, very big in England and the Continent. Current status: semi-retirement in Costa del Santiago, Portugal."

"They're American, though, aren't they?"

"Very. Made sure their son was born here. Sent him to American settlement schools wherever they lived. Shipped him back here for his final two years in prep school and college."

"How come Portugal, then?"

"Who knows? They had their first successes in Europe

and decided to stay there. A fact I *think* we're going to be grateful for. They only return here for tours; which aren't very frequent anymore. . . . Did you know that he's a construction engineer?"

"No, I didn't. That's interesting."

"Interesting? Just 'interesting'?"

Ryan smiled; there was a trace of sadness in his eyes. "Well, during the last six years or so there hasn't been a lot of building, has there? I mean, there's no great call for engineers . . . outside of the CCC and the NRA." He lifted his right hand and waved it laterally in front of him, encompassing the group of men and women inside the studio. "Do you know what's in there? A trial lawyer whose clients—when he can get a few—can't pay him; a Rolls-Royce executive who's been laid off since thirty-eight; and a former state senator whose campaign a few years ago not only cost him his job but also a lot of potential employers. They think he's a Red. Don't fool yourself, Ed. You've got it good. The Depression isn't over by a long shot. These people are the lucky ones. They found avocations they've turned into careers. . . . As long as they last."

"If I do *my* job, *his* career won't last any longer than a month from now."

"I figured it was something like that. The storm's building, isn't it? We'll be in it pretty soon. And I'll be back, too. . . . Where do you want to use him?"

"Lisbon."

David Spaulding pushed himself away from the white studio wall. He held up the pages of his script as he approached the microphone, preparing for his cue.

Pace watched him through the glass partition, wondering how Spaulding's voice would sound. He noticed that as Spaulding came closer to the group of actors clustered around the microphone, there was a conscious—or it seemed conscious—parting of bodies, as if the new participant was in some way a stranger. Perhaps it was only normal courtesy, allowing the new performer a chance to position himself, but the colonel didn't think so. There were no smiles, no looks, no indications of familiarity as there seemed to be among the others.

No one winked. Even the obese woman who screamed

and chewed gum and goosed her fellow actors just stood
and watched Spaulding, her gum immobile in her mouth.

And then it happened; a curious moment.

Spaulding grinned, and the others, even the thin, effeminate man who was in the middle of a monologue,
responded with bright smiles and nods. The obese woman
winked.

A curious moment, thought Colonel Pace.

Spaulding's voice—mid-deep, incisive, heavily accented
—came through the webbed boxes. His role was that of a
mad doctor and bordered on the comic. It *would* have
been comic, thought Pace, except for the authority
Spaulding gave the writer's words. Pace didn't know anything about acting, but he knew when a man was being
convincing. Spaulding was convincing.

That would be necessary in Lisbon.

In a few minutes Spaulding's role was obviously over.
The obese woman screamed again; Spaulding retreated to
the corner and quietly, making sure the pages did not
rustle, picked up his folded newspaper. He leaned against
the wall and withdrew a pencil from his pocket. He
appeared to be doing *The New York Times* crossword
puzzle.

Pace couldn't take his eyes off Spaulding. It was important for him to observe closely any subject with whom he
had to make contact whenever possible. Observe the small
things: the way a man walked; the way he held his head;
the steadiness or lack of it in his eyes. The clothes, the
watch, the cuff links; whether the shoes were shined, if
the heels were worn down; the quality—or lack of quality—in a man's posture.

Pace tried to match the human being leaning against
the wall, writing on the newspaper, with the dossier in his
Washington office.

His name first surfaced from the files of the Army
Corps of Engineers. David Spaulding had inquired about
the possibilities of a commission—not volunteered: what
would his opportunities be? were there any challenging
construction projects? what about the length-of-service
commitment? The sort of questions thousands of men—
skilled men—were asking, knowing that the Selective Service Act would become law within a week or two. If
enlistment meant a shorter commitment and/or the con-

tinued practice of their professional skills, then better an enlistment than be drafted with the mobs.

Spaulding had filled out all the appropriate forms and had been told the army would contact him. That had been six weeks ago and no one had done so. Not that the Corps wasn't interested; it was. The word from the Roosevelt men was that the draft law would be passed by Congress any day now, and the projected expansion of the army camps was so enormous, so incredibly massive that an engineer—especially a *construction* engineer of Spaulding's qualifications—was target material.

But those high up in the Corps of Engineers were aware of the search being conducted by the Intelligence Division of the Joint Chiefs of Staff and the War Department.

Quietly, slowly. No mistakes could be made.

So they passed along David Spaulding's forms to G-2 and were told in turn to stay away from him.

The man ID was seeking had to have three basic qualifications. Once these were established, the rest of the portrait could be microscopically scrutinized to see if the whole being possessed the other desirable requirements. The three basics were difficult enough in themselves: the first was fluency in the Portuguese language; the second, an equal mastery of German; the third, sufficient professional experience in structural engineering to enable swift and accurate understanding of blueprints, photographs— even verbal descriptions—of the widest variety of industrial designs. From bridges and factories to warehousing and railroad complexes.

The man in Lisbon would need each of these basic requirements. He would employ them throughout the war that was to be; the war that the United States inevitably would have to fight.

The man in Lisbon would be responsible for developing an Intelligence network primarily concerned with the destruction of the enemy's installations deep within its own territories.

Certain men—and women—traveled back and forth through hostile territories, basing their undefined activities in neutral countries. These were the people the man in Lisbon would use . . . before others used them.

These plus those he would train for infiltration. Espionage units. Teams of bi- and trilingual agents he would

send up through France into the borders of Germany. To
bring back their observations; eventually to inflict destruction themselves.

The English agreed that such an American was needed
in Lisbon. British Intelligence admitted its Portuguese
weakness; they had simply been around too long, too
obviously. And there were current, very serious lapses of
security in London. MI-5 had been infiltrated.

Lisbon would become an American project.

If such an American could be found.

David Spaulding's preapplication forms listed the
primary requisites. He spoke three languages, had spoken
them since he was a child. His parents, the renowned
Richard and Margo Spaulding, maintained three residences: a small, elegant Belgravia flat in London; a winter retreat in Germany's Baden-Baden; and a sprawling
oceanside house in the artists' colony of Costa del Santiago in Portugal. Spaulding had grown up in these envi-
rons. When he was sixteen, his father—over the objections
of his mother—insisted that he complete his secondary
education in the United States and enter an American
university.

Andover in Massachusetts; Dartmouth in New Hamp-
shire; finally Carnegie Institute in Pennsylvania.

Of course, the Intelligence Division hadn't discovered
*all* of the above information from Spaulding's application forms. These supplementary facts—and a great deal
more—were revealed by a man named Aaron Mandel in
New York.

Pace, his eyes still riveted on the tall, lean man who
had put down his newspaper and was now watching the
actors around the microphones with detached amusement,
recalled his single meeting with Mandel. Again, he
matched Mandel's information with the man he saw before
him.

Mandel had been listed on the application under "References." *Power-of-attorney, parents' concert manager.* An
address was given: a suite of rooms in the Chrysler Building. Mandel was a very successful artists' representative, a
Russian Jew who rivaled Sol Hurok for clients, though
not as prone to attract attention, or as desirous of it.

"David has been as a son to me," Mandel told Pace.
"But I must presume you know that."

"Why must you? I know only what I've read on his application forms. And some scattered information; academic records, employment references."

"Let's say I've been expecting you. Or someone like you."

"I beg your pardon?"

"Oh, come. David spent a great many years in Germany; you might say he almost grew up there."

"His application . . . as a matter of fact his passport information, also includes family residences in London and a place called Costa del Santiago in Portugal."

"I said almost. He converses easily in the German language."

"Also Portuguese, I understand."

"Equally so. And its sister tongue, Spanish. . . . I wasn't aware that a man's enlistment in the army engineers called for a full colonel's interest. And passport research." Mandel, the flesh creased around his eyes, smiled.

"I wasn't prepared for you." The colonel's reply had been stated simply. "Most people take this sort of thing as routine. Or they convince themselves it's routine . . . with a little help."

"Most people did not live as Jews in tsarist Kiev. . . . What do you want from me?"

"To begin with, did you tell Spaulding you expected us? Or someone. . . ."

"Of course not," Mandel interrupted gently. "I told you, he is as a son to me. I wouldn't care to give him such ideas."

"I'm relieved. Nothing may come of it anyway."

"However, you hope it will."

"Frankly, yes. But there are questions we need answered. His background isn't just unusual, it seems filled with contradictions. To begin with, you don't expect the son of well-known musicians . . . I mean . . ."

"Concert artists." Mandel had supplied the term Pace sought.

"Yes, concert artists. You don't expect the children of such people to become engineers. Or accountants, if you know what I mean. And then—and I'm sure you'll understand this—it seems highly illogical that once that fact is accepted, the son *is* an engineer, we find that the major portion of his income is currently earned as a . . . as a

radio performer. The pattern indicates a degree of insta-
bility. Perhaps more than a degree."

"You suffer from the American mania for consistency.
I don't say this unkindly. I would be less than adequate
as a neurosurgeon; you may play the piano quite well, but
I doubt that I'd represent you at Covent Garden. . . . The
questions you raise are easily answered. And, perhaps, the
word *stability* can be found at the core. . . . Have you any
idea, any *conception*, of what the world of the concert
stage is like? *Madness*. . . . David lived in this world for
nearly twenty years; I suspect . . . no, I don't suspect, I
know . . . he found it quite distasteful. . . . And so often
people overlook certain fundamental characteristics of
musicianship. Characteristics easily inherited. A great
musician is often, in his own way, an exceptional mathe-
matician. Take Bach. A genius at mathematics. . . ."

According to Aaron Mandel, David Spaulding found
his future profession while in his second year in college.
The solidity, the permanence of structural creation combined with the precision of engineering detail were at once
his answer to and escape from the mercurial world of the
"concert stage." But there were other inherited characteristics equally at work inside him. Spaulding had an
ego, a sense of independence. He needed approval, wanted
recognition. And such rewards were not easily come by
for a junior engineer, just out of graduate school, in a
large New York firm during the late thirties. There simply
wasn't that much to do; or the capital to do it with.

"He left the New York firm," Mandel continued, "to
accept a number of individual construction projects
where he believed the money would grow faster, the jobs
be his own. He had no ties; he could travel. Several in the
Midwest, one . . . no, two, in Central America; four in
Canada, I think. He got the first few right out of the
newspapers; they led to the others. He returned to New
York about eighteen months ago. The money didn't really
grow, as I told him it wouldn't. The projects were not his
own; provincial . . . local interference."

"And somehow this led to the radio work?"

Mandel had laughed and leaned back in his chair. "As
you may know, Colonel Pace, I've diversified. The concert
stage and a European war—soon to reach these shores,
as we all realize—do not go well together. These last

few years my clients have gone into other performing areas, including the highly paid radio field. David quickly saw opportunities for himself and I agreed. He's done extremely well, you know."

"But he's not a trained professional."

"No, he's not. He has something else, however. . . . Think. Most children of well-known performers, or leading politicians, or the immensely rich, for that matter, have it. It's a public confidence, an assurance, if you will; no matter their private insecurities. After all, they've generally been on display since the time they could walk and talk. David certainly has it. And he has a good ear; as do both of his parents, obviously. An aural memory for musical or linguistic rhythms. . . . He doesn't act, he *reads*. Almost exclusively in the dialects or the foreign languages he knows fluently. . . ."

David Spaulding's excursion into the "highly paid radio field" was solely motivated by money; he was used to living well. At a time when owners of engineering companies found it difficult to guarantee themselves a hundred dollars a week, Spaulding was earning three or four hundred from his "radio work" alone.

"As you may have surmised," said Mandel, "David's immediate objective is to bank sufficient monies to start his own company. Immediate, that is, unless otherwise shaped by world or national conditions. He's not blind; anyone who can read a newspaper sees that we are being drawn into the war."

"Do you think we should be?"

"I'm a Jew. As far as I'm concerned, we're late."

"This Spaulding. You've described what seems to me a very resourceful man."

"I've described only what you could have found out from any number of sources. And *you* have described the conclusion you have drawn from that surface information. It's not the whole picture." At this point, Pace recalled, Mandel had gotten out of his chair, avoiding any eye contact, and walked about his office. He was searching for negatives; he was trying to find the words that would disqualify "his son" from the government's interests. And Pace had been aware of it. "What certainly must have struck you—from what I've told you—is David's preoccupation with himself, with his comforts, if

you wish. Now, in a business sense this might be
applauded; therefore, I disabused you of your concerns
for stability. However, I would not be candid if I didn't
tell you that David is abnormally headstrong. He operates
—I think—quite poorly under authority. In a word, he's
a selfish man, not given to discipline. It pains me to say
this; I love him dearly. . . ."

And the more Mandel had talked, the more indelibly did
Pace imprint the word *affirmative* on Spaulding's file. Not
that he believed for a minute the extremes of behavior
Mandel suddenly ascribed to David Spaulding—no man
could function as "stably" as Spaulding had if it were true.
But if it were only half true, it was no detriment; it was
an asset.

The last of the requirements.

For if there were any soldier in the United States Army
—in or out of uniform—who would be called upon to
operate solely on his own, without the comfort of the
chain of command, without the knowledge that difficult
decisions could be made by his superiors, it was the Intelligence officer in Portugal.

The man in Lisbon.

## OCTOBER 8, 1939, FAIRFAX, VIRGINIA

There were no names.
Only numbers and letters.
Numbers followed by letters.
Two-Six-B. Three-Five-Y. Five-One-C.

There were no personal histories, no individual back-
grounds . . . no references to wives, children, fathers,
mothers . . . no countries, cities, hometowns, schools, uni-
versities; there were only bodies and minds and separate,
specific, reacting intelligences.

The location was deep in the Virginia hunt country, 220
acres of fields and hills and mountain streams. There
were sections of dense forest bordering stretches of flat
grasslands. Swamps—dangerous with body-sucking earth
and hostile inhabitants, reptile and insect—were but feet
from sudden masses of Virginia boulders fronting abrupt
inclines.

The area had been selected with care, with precision.

It was bordered by a fifteen-foot-high hurricane fence through which a paralyzing—not lethal—electrical current flowed continuously; and every twelve feet there was a forbidding sign that warned observers that this particular section of the land . . . forest, swamp, grassland and hill . . . was the exclusive property of the United States government. Trespassers were duly informed that entry was not only prohibited, it was exceedingly dangerous. Titles and sections of the specific laws pertaining to the exclusivity were spelled out along with the voltage in the fence.

The terrain was as diverse as could be found within a reasonable distance from Washington. In one way or another—one place or another—it conformed remarkably to the topography of the locations projected for those training inside the enormous compound.

The numbers followed by the letters.

No names.

There was a single gate at the center of the north perimeter, reached by a back country road. Over the gate, between the opposing guard houses, was a metal sign. In block letters it read:

FIELD DIVISON HEADQUARTERS—FAIRFAX.

No other description was given, no purpose identified.

On the front of each guard house were identical signs, duplicates of the warnings placed every twelve feet in the fence, proclaiming the exclusivity, the laws and the voltage.

No room for error.

David Spaulding was assigned an identity—his Fairfax identity. He was Two-Five-L.

No name. Only a number followed by a letter.

*Two—Five—L.*

Translation: his training was to be completed by the fifth day of the second month. His destination: Lisbon.

It was incredible. In the space of four months a new way of life—of *living*—was to be absorbed with such totality that it strained acceptance.

"You probably won't make it," said Colonel Edmund Pace.

"I'm not sure I want to," had been Spaulding's reply.

But part of the training was motivation. Deep, solid, ingrained beyond doubt . . . but not beyond the psychological reality as perceived by the candidate.

With Two-Five-L, the United States government did not wave flags and roar espousals of patriotic causes. Such methods would not be meaningful; the candidate had spent his formative years outside the country in a sophisticated, international environment. He spoke the language of the enemy-to-be; he knew them as people—taxi drivers, grocers, bankers, lawyers—and the vast majority of those he knew were not the Germans fictionalized by the propaganda machines. Instead—and this was Fairfax's legitimate hook—they were goddamned fools being led by psychopathic criminals. The leaders were, indeed, fanatics, and the overwhelming evidence clearly established their crimes beyond doubt. Those crimes included wanton, indiscriminate murder, torture and genocide.

Beyond doubt.

Criminals.

Psychopaths.

Too, there was Adolf Hitler.

Adolf Hitler killed Jews. By the thousands—soon to be millions if his *final solutions* were read accurately.

Aaron Mandel was a Jew. His other "father" was a Jew; the "father" he loved more than the parent. And the goddamned fools tolerated an exclamation point after the word *Juden!*

David Spaulding could bring himself to hate the goddamned fools—the taxi drivers, the grocers, the bankers, the lawyers—without much compunction under the circumstances.

Beyond this very rational approach, Fairfax utilized a secondary psychological "weapon" that was standard in the compound; for some more than others, but it was never absent.

The trainees at Fairfax had a common gift—or flaw— depending on one's approach. None was accepted without it.

A highly developed sense of competition; a thrust to win.

There was no question about it; arrogance was not a despised commodity at Fairfax.

With David Spaulding's psychological profile—a dossier increasingly accepted by the Intelligence Division—the Fairfax commanders recognized that the candidate-in-training for Lisbon had a soft core which the field might harden—undoubtedly *would* harden if he lived that long—but whatever advances could be made in the compound, so much the better. Especially for the subject.

Spaulding was confident, independent, extremely versatile in his surroundings . . . all to the very good; but Two-Five-L had a weakness. There was within his psyche a slowness to take immediate advantage, a hesitancy to spring to the kill when the odds were his. Both verbally and physically.

Colonel Edmund Pace saw this inadequacy by the third week of training. Two-Five-L's abstract code of fairness would never do in Lisbon. And Colonel Pace knew the answer.

The mental adjustment would be made through the physical processes.

"Seizures, Holds and Releases" was the insipid title of the course. It disguised the most arduous physical training at Fairfax: hand-to-hand combat. Knife, chain, wire, needle, rope, fingers, knees, elbows . . . never a gun.

*Reaction, reaction, reaction.*

Except when one initiated the assault.

Two-Five-L had progressed nicely. He was a large man but possessed the quick coordination usually associated with a more compact person. Therefore his progress had to be stymied; the man himself humiliated. He would learn the practical advantages of the odds.

From smaller, more arrogant men.

Colonel Edmund Pace "borrowed" from the British commando units the best they had in uniform. They were flown over by the Bomber Ferry Command; three bewildered "specialists" who were subtly introduced to the Fairfax compound and given their instructions.

"Kick the shit out of Two-Five-L."

They did. For many weeks of sessions.

And then they could not do so with impunity any longer.

David Spaulding would not accept the humiliation; he was becoming as good as the "specialists."

The man for Lisbon was progressing.

Colonel Edmund Pace received the reports in his War Department office.

Everything was on schedule.

The weeks became months. Every known portable offensive and defensive weapon, every sabotage device, every conceivable method of ingress and egress—apparent and covert—was exhaustively studied by the Fairfax trainees. Codes and variations became fluent languages; instant fabrications second nature. And Two-Five-L continued to advance. Whenever there appeared a slackening, harsher instructions were given to the "specialists" in "Seizures, Holds and Releases." The psychological key was in the observable, physical humiliation.

Until it was no longer viable. The commandos were bested.

Everything on schedule.

"You may make it after all," said the colonel.

"I'm not sure what I've made," replied David in his first lieutenant's uniform, over a drink in the Mayflower Cocktail Lounge. And then he laughed quietly. "I suppose if they gave degrees in Advanced Criminal Activities, I'd probably qualify."

Two-Five-L's training would be completed in ten days. His twenty-four-hour pass was an irregularity, but Pace had demanded it. He had to talk with Spaulding.

"Does it bother you?" asked Pace.

Spaulding looked across the small table at the colonel. "If I had time to think about it, I'm sure it would. Doesn't it bother you?"

"No. . . . Because I understand the reasons."

"O.K. Then so do I."

"They'll become clearer in the field."

"Sure," agreed David tersely.

Pace watched Spaulding closely. As was to be expected, the young man had changed. Gone was the slightly soft, slightly pampered grace of inflection and gesture. These had been replaced by a tautness, a conciseness of movement and speech. The transformation was not complete, but it was well in progress.

The patina of the professional was beginning to show through. Lisbon would harden it further.

"Are you impressed by the fact that Fairfax skips you a rank? It took me eighteen months to get that silver bar."

"Again, time. I haven't had time to react. I haven't worn a uniform before today; I think it's uncomfortable." Spaulding flicked his hand over his tunic.

"Good. Don't get used to it."

"That's a strange thing to say. . . ."

"How do you feel?" said Pace, interrupting.

David looked at the colonel. For a moment or two, the grace, the softness—even the wry humor—returned. "I'm not sure. . . . As though I'd been manufactured on a very fast assembly line. A sort of high-speed treadmill, if you know what I mean."

"In some ways that's an accurate description. Except that you brought a lot to the factory."

Spaulding revolved his glass slowly. He stared at the floating cubes, then up at Pace. "I wish I could accept that as a compliment," he said softly. "I don't think I can. I know the people I've been training with. They're quite a collection."

"They're highly motivated."

"The Europeans are as crazy as those they want to fight. They've got their reasons; I can't question them. . . ."

"Well," interrupted the colonel, "we don't have that many Americans. Not yet."

"Those you do are two steps from a penitentiary."

"They're not army."

"I didn't know that," said Spaulding quickly, adding the obvious with a smile. "Naturally."

Pace was annoyed with himself. The indiscretion was minor but still an indiscretion. "It's not important. In ten days you'll be finished in Virginia. The uniform comes off then. To tell you the truth, it was a mistake to issue you one in the first place. We're still new at this kind of thing; rules of requisition and supply are hard to change." Pace drank and avoided Spaulding's eyes.

"I thought I was supposed to be a military attaché at the embassy. One of several."

"For the record, yes. They'll build a file on you. But there's a difference; it's part of the cover. You're not partial to uniforms. We don't think you should wear one. Ever." Pace put down his glass and looked at David. "You hustled yourself a very safe, very comfortable job because of the languages, your residences and your family connections. In a nutshell, you ran as fast as you could when you thought there was a chance your pretty neck might be in the real army."

Spaulding thought for a moment. "That sounds logical. Why does it bother you?"

"Because only one man at the embassy will know the truth. He'll identify himself. . . . After a while others may suspect—after a long while. But they won't know. Not the ambassador, not the staff. . . . What I'm trying to tell you is, you won't be very popular."

David laughed quietly. "I trust you'll rotate me before I'm lynched."

Pace's reply was swift and quiet, almost curt. "Others will be rotated. Not you."

Spaulding was silent as he responded to the colonel's look. "I don't understand."

"I'm not sure I can be clear about it." Pace put down his drink on the small cocktail table. "You'll have to start slowly, with extreme caution. British MI-5 has given us a few names—not many but something to start with. You'll have to build up your own network, however. People who will maintain contact only with you, no one else. This will entail a great deal of traveling. We think you'll gravitate to the north country, across the borders into Spain. Basque country . . . by and large anti-Falangist. We think those areas south of the Pyrenees will become the data and escape routes. . . . We're not kidding ourselves: the Maginot won't hold. France will fall. . . ."

"*Jesus,*" interrupted David softly. "You've done a lot of projecting."

"That's almost *all* we do. It's the reason for Fairfax."

Spaulding leaned back in the chair, once more revolving his glass. "I understand about the network; in one form or another it's what the compound's training all of us for. This is the first I've heard about the north of Spain, the Basque areas. I know that country."

"We could be wrong. It's only a theory. You might find the water routes . . . Mediterranean, Málaga, or Biscay, or the Portuguese coast . . . more feasible. That's for you to decide. And develop."

"All right. I understand. . . . What's that got to do with rotation?"

Pace smiled. "You haven't reached your post. Are you angling for a leave already?"

"You brought it up. Sort of abruptly, I think."

"Yes, I did." The colonel shifted his position in the small chair. Spaulding was very quick; he locked in on words and used brief time spans to maximize their effectiveness. He would be good in interrogations. Quick, harsh inquiries. In the field. "We've decided that you're to remain in Portugal for the duration. Whatever normal and 'abnormal' leaves you take should be spent in the south. There's a string of colonies along the coast. . . ."

"Costa del Santiago among them," interjected Spaulding under his breath. "Retreats for the international rich."

"That's right. Develop covers down there. Be seen with your parents. Become a fixture." Pace smiled again; the smile was hesitant. "I could think of worse duty."

"You don't know those colonies. . . . If I read you—as we say in Fairfax—Candidate Two-Five-L had better take a good, hard look at the streets of Washington and New York because he's not going to see them again for a very long time."

"We can't risk bringing you back once you've developed a network, assuming you *do* develop one. If, for whatever reason, you flew out of Lisbon to Allied territory, there'd be an enemy scramble to microscopically trace every movement you made for months. It would jeopardize everything. *You're* safest—*our interests* are safest—if you remain permanent. The British taught us this. Some of their operatives have been local fixtures for years."

"That's not very comforting."

"You're not in MI-5. Your tour is for the duration. The war won't last forever."

It was Spaulding's turn to smile; the smile of a man caught in a matrix he had not defined. "There's something insane about that statement. . . . 'The war won't last forever.' . . ."

"Why?"

"We're not in it yet."

"You are," Pace said.

TWO

## SEPTEMBER 8, 1943, PEENEMÜNDE, GERMANY

The man in the pinstriped suit, styled by tailors in Alte Strasse, stared in disbelief at the three men across the table. He would have objected strenuously had the three laboratory experts not worn the square red metal insignias on the lapels of their starched white laboratory jackets, badges that said these three scientists were permitted to walk through passageways forbidden to all but the elite of Peenemünde. He, too, had such a badge attached to his pinstriped lapel; it was a temporary clearance he was not sure he wanted.

Certainly he did not want it now.

"I can't accept your evaluation," he said quietly. "It's preposterous."

"Come with us," replied the scientist in the center, nodding to his companion on the right.

"There's no point procrastinating," added the third man.

The four men got out of their chairs and approached the steel door that was the single entrance to the room. Each man in succession unclipped his red badge and pressed it against a grey plate in the wall. At the instant of contact, a small white bulb was lighted, remained so for two seconds and then went off; a photograph had been taken. The last man—one of the Peenemünde personnel—then opened the door and each went into the hallway.

Had only three men gone out, or five, or any number not corresponding to the photographs, alarms would have been triggered.

They walked in silence down the long, starched-white corridor, the Berliner in front with the scientist who sat between the other two at the table, and was obviously the spokesman; his companions were behind.

They reached a bank of elevators and once more went through the ritual of the red tags, the grey plate and the tiny white light that went on for precisely two seconds. Below the plate a number was also lighted.

Six.

From elevator number six there was the sound of a single muted bell as the thick steel panel slid open. One by one each man walked inside.

The elevator descended eight stories, four below the surface of the earth, to the deepest levels of Peenemünde. As the four men emerged into yet another white corridor, they were met by a tall man in tight-fitting green coveralls, an outsized holster in his wide brown belt. The holster held a Lüger Sternlicht, a specially designed arm pistol with a telescopic sight. As the man's visor cap indicated, such weapons were made for the Gestapo.

The Gestapo officer obviously recognized the three scientists. He smiled perfunctorily and turned his attention to the man in the pinstriped suit. He held out his hand, motioning the Berliner to remove the red badge.

The Berliner did so. The Gestapo man took it, walked over to a telephone on the corridor wall and pushed a combination of buttons. He spoke the Berliner's name and waited, perhaps ten seconds.

He replaced the phone and crossed back to the man in the pinstriped suit. Gone was the arrogance he had displayed moments ago.

"I apologize for the delay, Herr Strasser. I should have realized. . . ." He gave the Berliner his badge.

"No need for apologies, Herr Oberleutnant. They would be necessary only if you overlooked your duties."

"*Danke*," said the Gestapo man, gesturing the four men beyond his point of security.

They proceeded toward a set of double doors; clicks could be heard as locks were released. Small white bulbs were lighted above the moldings; again photographs were taken of those going through the double doors.

They turned right into a bisecting corridor—this one not white, but instead, brownish black; so dark that Strasser's eyes took several seconds to adjust from the pristine brightness of the main halls to the sudden night quality of the passageway. Tiny ceiling lights gave what illumination there was.

"You've not been here before," said the scientist-spokesman to the Berliner. "This hallway was designed by an optics engineer. It supposedly prepares the eyes for the high-intensity microscope lights. Most of us think it was a waste."

There was a steel door at the end of the long, dark tunnel. Strasser reached for his red metal insignia automatically; the scientist shook his head and spoke with a slight wave of his hand.

"Insufficient light for photographs. The guard inside has been alerted."

The door opened and the four men entered a large laboratory. Along the right wall was a row of stools, each in front of a powerful microscope, all the microscopes equidistant from one another on top of a built-in workbench. Behind each microscope was a high-intensity light, projected and shaded on a goose-necked stem coming out of the immaculate white surface. The left wall was a variation of the right. There were no stools, however, and fewer microscopes. The work shelf was higher; it was obviously used for conferences, where many pairs of eyes peered through the same sets of lenses; stools would only interfere, men stood as they conferred over magnified particles.

At the far end of the room was another door; not an entrance. A vault. A seven-foot-high, four-foot-wide, heavy steel vault. It was black; the two levers and the combination wheel were in glistening silver.

The spokesman-scientist approached it.

"We have fifteen minutes before the timer seals the panel and the drawers. I've requested closure for a week. I'll need your counterauthorization, of course."

"And you're sure I'll give it, aren't you?"

"I am." The scientist spun the wheel right and left for the desired locations. "The numbers change automatically every twenty-four hours," he said as he held the wheel steady at its final mark and reached for the silver levers. He pulled the top one down to the accompaniment of a barely audible whirring sound, and seconds later, pulled the lower one up.

The whirring stopped, metallic clicks could be heard and the scientist pulled open the thick steel door. He turned to Strasser. "These are the tools for Peenemünde. See for yourself."

Strasser approached the vault. Inside were five rows of removable glass trays, top to bottom; each row had a total of one hundred trays, five hundred in all.

The trays that were empty were marked with a white

strip across the facing glass, the word *Auffüllen* printed clearly.

The trays that were full were so designated by strips of black across their fronts.

There were four and a half rows of white trays. Empty.

Strasser looked closely, pulled open several trays, shut them and stared at the Peenemünde scientist.

"This is the sole repository?" he asked quietly.

"It is. We have six thousand casings completed; God knows how many will go in experimentation. Estimate for yourself how much further we can proceed."

Strasser held the scientist's eyes with his own. "Do you realize what you're saying?"

"I do. We'll deliver only a fraction of the required schedules. Nowhere near enough. Peenemünde is a disaster."

## SEPTEMBER 9, 1943, THE NORTH SEA

The fleet of B-17 bombers had aborted the primary target of Essen due to cloud cover. The squadron commander, over the objections of his fellow pilots, ordered the secondary mission into operation: the shipyards north of Bremerhaven. No one liked the Bremerhaven run; Messerschmitt and Stuka interceptor wings were devastating. They were called the Luftwaffe suicide squads, maniacal young Nazis who might as easily collide with enemy aircraft as fire at them. Not necessarily due to outrageous bravery; often it was merely inexperience or worse: poor training.

Bremerhaven-north was a terrible secondary. When it was a primary objective, the Eighth Air Force fighter escorts took the sting out of the run; they were not there when Bremerhaven was a secondary.

The squadron commander, however, was a hardnose. Worse, he was West Point; the secondary would not only be hit, it would be hit at an altitude that guaranteed maximum accuracy. He did not tolerate the very vocal criticism of his second-in-command aboard the flanking aircraft, who made it clear that such an altitude was barely logical *with* fighter escorts; *without* them, considering the heavy ack-ack fire, it was ridiculous. The squadron commander had replied with a terse recital of the new navigational headings and termination of radio contact.

Once they were into the Bremerhaven corridors, the German interceptors came from all points; the antiaircraft guns were murderous. And the squadron commander took his lead plane directly down into maximum-accuracy altitude and was blown out of the sky.

The second-in-command valued life and the price of aircraft more than his West Point superior. He ordered the squadron to scramble altitudes, telling his bombardiers to unload on anything below but for-God's-sake-release-the-goddamn-weight so all planes could reach their maximum heights and reduce antiaircraft and interceptor fire.

In several instances it was too late. One bomber caught fire and went into a spin; only three chutes emerged from it. Two aircraft were riddled so badly both planes began immediate descents. Pilots and crew bailed out. Most of them.

The remainder kept climbing; the Messerschmitts climbed with them. They went higher and still higher, past the safe altitude range. Oxygen masks were ordered; not all functioned.

But in four minutes, what was left of the squadron was in the middle of the clear midnight sky, made stunningly clearer by the substratosphere absence of air particles. The stars were extraordinary in their flickering brightness, the moon more a bombers' moon than ever before.

Escape was in these regions.

"Chart man!" said the exhausted, relieved second-in-command into his radio, "give us headings! Back to Lakenheath, if you'd be so kind."

The reply on the radio soured the moment of relief. It came from an aerial gunner aft of navigation. "He's dead, colonel. Nelson's dead."

There was no time in the air for comment. "Take it, aircraft three. It's your chart," said the colonel in aircraft two.

The headings were given. The formation grouped and, as it descended into safe altitude with cloud cover above, sped toward the North Sea.

The minutes reached five, then seven, then twelve. Finally twenty. There was relatively little cloud cover below; the coast of England should have come into sighting range at least two minutes ago. A number of pilots were concerned. Several said so.

"Did you give accurate headings, aircraft three?" asked the now squadron commander.

"Affirmative, colonel," was the radioed answer.

"Any of you chart men disagree?"

A variety of negatives was heard from the remaining aircraft.

"No sweat on the headings, colonel," came the voice of the captain of aircraft five. "I fault your execution, though."

"What the hell are you talking about?"

"You pointed two-three-niner by my reading. I figured my equipment was shot up. . . ."

Suddenly there were interruptions from every pilot in the decimated squadron.

"I read one-seven. . . ."

"My heading was a goddamned two-niner-two. We took a direct hit on . . ."

"*Jesus!* I had sixer-four. . . ."

"Most of our middle took a load. I discounted my readings totally!"

And then there was silence. All understood.

Or understood what they could not comprehend.

"Stay off all frequencies," said the squadron commander. "I'll try to reach base."

The cloud cover above broke; not for long, but long enough. The voice over the radio was the captain of aircraft three.

"A quick judgment, colonel, says we're heading due northwest."

Silence again.

After a few moments, the commander spoke. "I'll reach somebody. Do all your gauges read as mine? Fuel for roughly ten to fifteen minutes?"

"It's been a long haul, colonel," said aircraft seven. "No more than that, it's for sure."

"I figured we'd be circling, if we had to, five minutes ago," said aircraft eight.

"We're not," said aircraft four.

The colonel in aircraft two raised Lakenheath on an emergency frequency.

"As near as we can determine," came the strained, agitated, yet controlled English voice, "and by that I mean open lines throughout the coastal defense areas—water and land—you're approaching the Dunbar sector. That's the Scottish border, colonel. What in blazes are you doing there?"

"For Christ's sake, I don't *know!* Are there any fields?"

"Not for *your* aircraft. Certainly not a formation; perhaps one or two. . . ."

"I don't want to hear that, you son of a bitch! Give me emergency instructions!"

"We're really quite unprepared. . . ."

"Do you *read me?!* I have what's left of a very chopped-up squadron! We have less than six minutes' fuel! Now you *give!*"

The silence lasted precisely four seconds. Lakenheath conferred swiftly. With finality.

"We believe you'll sight the coast, probably Scotland. Put your aircraft down at sea. . . . We'll do our best, lads."

"We're eleven *bombers,* Lakenheath! We're not a bunch of ducks!"

"There isn't time, squadron leader. . . . The logistics are insurmountable. After all, we didn't guide you there. Put down at sea. We'll do our best. . . . Godspeed."

# PART
# 1

# 1

## SEPTEMBER 10, 1943, BERLIN, GERMANY

Reichsminister of Armaments Albert Speer raced up the steps of the Air Ministry on the Tiergarten. He did not feel the harsh, diagonal sheets of rain that plummeted down from the grey sky; he did not notice that his raincoat —unbuttoned—had fallen away, exposing his tunic and shirt to the inundation of the September storm. The pitch of his fury swept everything but the immediate crisis out of his mind.

Insanity! Sheer, unmitigated, unforgivable insanity!

The industrial reserves of all Germany were about exhausted; but he could handle that immense problem. Handle it by properly utilizing the manufacturing potential of the occupied countries; reverse the unmanageable practices of importing the labor forces. Labor forces? Slaves!

Productivity disastrous; sabotage continuous, unending. What did they expect?

It was a time for sacrifice! Hitler could not continue to be all things to all people! He could not provide outsized Mercedeses and grand operas and populated restaurants; he had to provide, instead, tanks, munitions, ships, aircraft! *These* were the priorities!

But the Führer could never erase the memory of the 1918 revolution.

How totally inconsistent! The sole man whose will was shaping history, who was close to the preposterous dream of a thousand-year Reich, was petrified of a long-ago memory of unruly mobs, of unsatisfied masses.

Speer wondered if future historians would record the

fact. If they would comprehend just how weak Hitler really was when it came to his own countrymen. How he buckled in fear when consumer production fell below anticipated schedules.

Insanity!

But still *he*, the Reichsminister of Armaments, could control this calamitous inconsistency as long as he was convinced it was just a question of time. A few months; perhaps six at the outside.

For there was Peenemünde.

The rockets.

Everything reduced itself to Peenemünde!

Peenemünde was irresistible. Peenemünde would cause the collapse of London and Washington. Both governments would see the futility of continuing the exercise of whole-sale annihilation.

Reasonable men could then sit down and create reasonable treaties.

Even if it meant the silencing of *un*reasonable men. Silencing Hitler.

Speer knew there were others who thought that way, too. The Führer was manifestly beginning to show unhealthy signs of pressure—fatigue. He now surrounded himself with mediocrity—an ill-disguised desire to remain in the comfortable company of his intellectual equals. But it went too far when the Reich itself was affected. A wine merchant, the foreign minister! A third-rate party propagandizer, the minister of eastern affairs! An erstwhile fighter pilot, the overseer of the *entire economy!*

Even himself. Even the quiet, shy architect; now the minister of armaments.

All that would change with Peenemünde.

Even himself. Thank *God!*

But first there *had* to be Peenemünde. There could be no *question* of its operational success. For without Peenemünde, the war was lost.

And now they were telling him there *was* a question. A flaw that might well be the precursor of Germany's defeat.

A vacuous-looking corporal opened the door of the cabinet room. Speer walked in and saw that the long conference table was about two-thirds filled, the chairs in cliquish separation, as if the groups were suspect of one another. As, indeed, they were in these times of progressively sharpened rivalries within the Reich.

He walked to the head of the table, where—to his right —sat the only man in the room he could trust. Franz Altmüller.

Altmüller was a forty-two-year-old cynic. Tall, blond, aristocratic; the vision of the Third Reich Aryan who did not, for a minute, subscribe to the racial nonsense proclaimed by the Third Reich. He did, however, subscribe to the theory of acquiring whatever benefits came his way by pretending to agree with anyone who might do him some good.

In public.

In private, among his *very* close associates, he told the truth.

When that truth might also benefit him.

Speer was not only Altmüller's associate, he was his friend. Their families had been more than neighbors; the two fathers had often gone into joint merchandising ventures; the mothers had been school chums.

Altmüller had taken after his father. He was an extremely capable businessman; his expertise was in production administration.

"Good morning," said Altmüller, flicking an imaginary thread off his tunic lapel. He wore his party uniform far more often than was necessary, preferring to err on the side of the archangel.

"That seems unlikely," replied Speer, sitting down rapidly. The groups—and they were groups—around the table kept talking among themselves but the voices were perceptibly quieter. Eyes kept darting over in Speer's direction, then swiftly away; everyone was prepared for immediate silence yet none wished to appear apprehensive, guilty.

Silence would come when either Altmüller or Speer himself rose from his chair to address the gathering. That would be the signal. Not before. To render attention before that movement might give the appearance of fear. Fear was equivalent to an admission of error. No one at the conference table could afford that.

Altmüller opened a brown manila folder and placed it in front of Speer. It was a list of those summoned to the meeting. There were essentially three distinct factions with subdivisions within each, and each with its spokesman. Speer read the names and unobtrusively—he thought— looked up to ascertain the presence and location of the three leaders.

At the far end of the table, resplendent in his general's uniform, his tunic a field of decorations going back thirty years, sat Ernst Leeb, Chief of the Army Ordnance Office. He was of medium height but excessively muscular, a condition he maintained well into his sixties. He smoked his cigarette through an ivory holder which he used to cut off his various subordinates' conversations at will. In some ways Leeb was a caricature, yet still a powerful one. Hitler liked him, as much for his imperious military bearing as for his abilities.

At the midpoint of the table, on the left, sat Albert Vögler, the sharp, aggressive general manager of Reich's Industry. Vögler was a stout man, the image of a burgomaster; the soft flesh of his face constantly creased into a questioning scowl. He laughed a great deal, but his laughter was hard; a device, not an enjoyment. He was well suited to his position. Vögler liked nothing better than hammering out negotiations between industrial adversaries. He was a superb mediator because all parties were usually frightened of him.

Across from Vögler and slightly to the right, toward Altmüller and Speer, was Wilhelm Zangen, the Reich official of the German Industrial Association. Zangen was thin-lipped, painfully slender, humorless; a fleshed-out skeleton happiest over his charts and graphs. A precise man who was given to perspiring at the edge of his receding hairline and below the nostrils and on his chin when nervous. He was perspiring now, and continuously brought his handkerchief up to blot the embarrassing moisture. Somewhat in contradiction to his appearance, however, Zangen was a persuasive debater. For he never argued without the facts.

They were all persuasive, thought Speer. And if it were not for his anger, he knew such men could—probably would—intimidate him. Albert Speer was honest in self-assessment; he realized that he had no substantial sense of authority. He found it difficult to express his thoughts forthrightly among such potentially hostile men. But now the potentially hostile men were in a defensive position. He could not allow his anger to cause them to panic, to seek only absolution for themselves.

They needed a remedy. Germany needed a remedy.

Peenemünde had to be saved.

"How would you suggest we begin?" Speer asked Altmüller, shading his voice so no one else at the table could hear him.

"I don't think it makes a particle of difference. It will take an hour of very loud, very boring, very obtuse explanations before we reach anything concrete."

"I'm not interested in explanations. . . ."

"Excuses, then."

"Least of all, excuses. I want a solution."

"If it's to be found at this table—which, frankly, I doubt—you'll have to sit through the excess verbiage. Perhaps something will come of it. Again, I doubt it."

"Would you care to explain that?"

Altmüller looked directly into Speer's eyes. "Ultimately, I'm not sure there is a solution. But if there is, I don't think it's at this table. . . . Perhaps I'm wrong. Why don't we listen first?"

"All right. Would you please open with the summary you prepared? I'm afraid I'd lose my temper midway through."

"May I suggest," Altmüller whispered, "that it will be necessary for you to lose your temper at some point during this meeting. I don't see how you can avoid it."

"I understand."

Altmüller pushed back his chair and stood up. Grouping by grouping the voices trailed off around the table.

"Gentlemen. This emergency session was called for reasons of which we assume you are aware. At least you should be aware of them. Apparently it is only the Reichsminister of Armaments and his staff who were not informed; a fact which the Reichsminister and his staff find appalling. . . . In short words, the Peenemünde operation faces a crisis of unparalleled severity. In spite of the millions poured into this most vital weaponry development, in spite of the assurances consistently offered by your respective departments, we now learn that production may be brought to a complete halt within a matter of weeks. Several months prior to the *agreed-upon* date for the first operational rockets. That date has never been questioned.

It has been the keystone for whole military strategies; entire armies have been maneuvered to coordinate with it. Germany's victory is predicated on it. . . . But now Peenemünde is threatened; Germany is threatened. . . . If the projections the Reichsminister's staff have compiled—*unearthed* and compiled—are valid, the Peenemünde complex will exhaust its supply of industrial diamonds in less than ninety days. Without industrial diamonds the precision tooling in Peenemünde cannot continue."

The babble of voices—excited, guttural, vying for attention—erupted the second Altmüller sat down. General Leeb's cigarette holder slashed the air in front of him as though it were a saber; Albert Vögler scowled and wrinkled his flesh-puffed eyes, placed his bulky hands on the table and spoke harshly in a loud monotone; Wilhelm Zangen's handkerchief was working furiously around his face and his neck, his high-pitched voice in conflict with the more masculine tones around him.

Franz Altmüller leaned toward Speer. "You've seen cages of angry ocelots in the zoo? The zookeeper can't let them hurl themselves into the bars. I suggest you lose your benign temper far earlier than we discussed. Perhaps now."

"That is not the way."

"Don't let them think you are cowed. . . ."

"Nor that I am cowering." Speer interrupted his friend, the slightest trace of a smile on his lips. He stood up. "Gentlemen."

The voices trailed off.

"Herr Altmüller speaks harshly; he does so, I'm sure, because I spoke harshly with him. That was this morning, very early this morning. There is greater perspective now; it is no time for recriminations. This is not to lessen the critical aspects of the situation, for they are great. But anger will solve nothing. And we need solutions. . . . Therefore, I propose to seek your assistance—the assistance of the finest industrial and military minds in the Reich. First, of course, we need to know the specifics. I shall start with Herr Vögler. As manager of Reich's Industry, would you give us your estimate?"

Vögler was upset; he didn't wish to be the first called. "I'm not sure I can be of much enlightenment, Herr

Reichsminister. I, too, am subject to the reports given me. They have been optimistic; until the other week there was no suggestion of difficulty."

"How do you mean, optimistic?" asked Speer.

"The quantities of bortz and carbonado diamonds were said to be sufficient. Beyond this there are the continuing experiments with lithicum, carbon and paraffin. Our intelligence tells us that the Englishman Storey at the British Museum reverified the Hannay-Moissan theories. Diamonds *were* produced in this fashion."

"Who verified the Englishman?" Franz Altmüller did not speak kindly. "Had it occurred to you that such data was meant to be passed?"

"Such verification is a matter for Intelligence. I am not with Intelligence, Herr Altmüller."

"Go on," said Speer quickly. "What else?"

"There is an Anglo-American experiment under the supervision of the Bridgemann team. They are subjecting graphite to pressures in excess of six million pounds per square inch. So far there is no word of success."

"Is there word of failure?" Altmüller raised his aristocratic eyebrows, his tone polite.

"I remind you again, I am not with Intelligence. I have received no word whatsoever."

"Food for thought, isn't it," said Altmüller, without asking a question.

"Nevertheless," interrupted Speer before Vögler could respond, "you had reason to assume that the quantities of bortz and carbonado were sufficient. Is that not so?"

"Sufficient. Or at least obtainable, Herr Reichsminister."

"How so obtainable?"

"I believe General Leeb might be more knowledgeable on that subject."

Leeb nearly dropped his ivory cigarette holder. Altmüller noted his surprise and cut in swiftly. "Why would the army ordnance officer have that information, Herr Vögler? I ask merely for my own curiosity."

"The reports, once more. It is my understanding that the Ordnance Office is responsible for evaluating the industrial, agricultural and mineral potentials of occupied territories. Or those territories so projected."

Ernst Leeb was not entirely unprepared. He *was* unpre-

pared for Vögler's insinuations, not for the subject. He
turned to an aide, who shuffled papers top to bottom as
Speer inquired.

"The Ordnance Office is under enormous pressure these
days; as is your department, of course, Herr Vögler. I
wonder if General Leeb has had the time . . ."

"We *made* the time," said Leeb, his sharp military
bearing pitted in counterpoint to Vögler's burgomaster
gruffness. "When we received word—from Herr Vögler's
subordinates—that a crisis was imminent—not upon us,
but imminent—we immediately researched the possibilities
for extrication."

Franz Altmüller brought his hand to his mouth to cover
an involuntary smile. He looked at Speer, who was too
annoyed to find any humor in the situation.

"I'm relieved the Ordnance Office is so confident, general," said Speer. The Reichsminister of Armaments had
*little* confidence in the military and had difficulty disguising
it. "Please, your extrication?"

"I said *possibilities*, Herr Speer. To arrive at practical
solutions *will* take more time than we've been given."

"Very well. Your possibilities?"

"There is an immediate remedy with historical precedent." Leeb paused to remove his cigarette, crushing it out,
aware that everyone around the table watched him
intently. "I have taken the liberty of recommending preliminary studies to the General Staff. It involves an
expeditionary force of less than four battalions. . . . Africa.
The diamond mines east of Tanganyika."

*"What?"* Altmüller leaned forward; he obviously could
not help himself. "You're not serious."

"Please!" Speer would not allow his friend to interrupt.
If Leeb had even conceived of such drastic action, it
might have merit. No military man, knowing the thin line
of combat strength—chewed up on the Eastern Front,
under murderous assault by the Allies in Italy—could suggest such an absurdity unless he had a realistic hope of
success. "Go ahead, general."

"The Williamson Mines at Mwadui. Between the districts of Tanganyika and Zanzibar in the central sector.
The mines at Mwadui produce over a million carats of the
carbonado diamond annually. Intelligence—the intelligence
that is forwarded regularly to me at my insistence—

informs us that there are supplies going back several months. Our agents in Dar es Salaam are convinced such an incursion would be successful."

Franz Altmüller passed a sheet of paper to Speer. On it he had scribbled: "He's lost his senses!"

"What is the historical precedent to which you refer?" asked Speer, holding his hand over Altmüller's paper.

"All of the districts east of Dar es Salaam rightfully belong to the Third Reich, German West Africa. They were taken from the fatherland after the Great War. The Führer himself made that clear four years ago."

There was silence around the table. An embarrassed silence. The eyes of even his aides avoided the old soldier. Finally Speer spoke quietly.

"That is justification, not precedent, general. The world cares little for our justifications, and although I question the logistics of moving battalions halfway around the globe, you may have raised a valid point. Where else nearer . . . in *East* Africa, perhaps, can the bortz or the carbonado be found?"

Leeb looked to his aides; Wilhelm Zangen lifted his handkerchief to his nostrils and bowed his thin head in the direction of the general. He spoke as if exhaling, his high voice irritating.

"I'll answer you, Herr Reichsminister. And then, I believe, you will see how fruitless this discussion is. . . . Sixty per cent of the world's crushing-bortz diamonds are in the Belgian Congo. The two principal deposits are in the Kasai and Bakwanga fields, between the Kanshi and the Bushimaie rivers. The district's governor-general is Pierre Ryckmans; he is devoted to the Belgian government in exile in London. I can assure Leeb that the Congo's allegiances to Belgium are far greater than ours ever were in Dar es Salaam."

Leeb lit a cigarette angrily. Speer leaned back in his chair and addressed Zangen.

"All right. Sixty per cent crushing-bortz; what of carbonado and the rest?"

"French Equatorial: totally allied to de Gaulle's Free French. Ghana and Sierra Leone: the tightest of British controls. Angola: Portuguese domination and their neutrality's inviolate; we know that beyond doubt. French West Africa: not only under Free French mandate but

with Allied forces manning the outposts. . . . Here, there
was only one possibility and we lost it a year and a half
ago. Vichy abandoned the Ivory Coast. . . . There is no
access in Africa, Reichsminister. None of a military
nature."

"I see." Speer doodled on top of the paper Altmüller
had passed to him. "You are recommending a nonmilitary
solution?"

"There is no other. The question is what."

Speer turned to Franz Altmüller. His tall, blond associate was staring at them all. Their faces were blank.
Baffled.

# 2

Brigadier General Alan Swanson got out of the taxi and
looked up at the huge oak door of the Georgetown residence. The ride over the cobblestone streets had seemed
like a continuous roll of hammering drums.

Prelude to execution.

Up those steps, inside that door, somewhere within that
five-story brownstone and brick aristocratic home, was a
large room. And inside that room thousands of executions
would be pronounced, unrelated to any around the table
within that room.

Prelude to annihilation.

*If* the schedules were kept. And it was inconceivable
that they would be altered.

Wholesale murder.

In line with his orders he glanced up and down the street
to make sure he hadn't been followed. Asinine! CIC had
all of them under constant surveillance. Which of the
pedestrians or slowly moving automobiles had him in their
sights? It didn't matter; the choice of the meeting place
was asinine, too. Did they really believe they could keep
the crisis a secret? Did they think that holding conferences
in secluded Georgetown houses would help?

Asses!

He was oblivious to the rain; it came down steadily, in
straight lines. An autumn rainstorm in Washington. His
raincoat was open, the jacket of his uniform damp and
wrinkled. He didn't give a damn about such things; he
couldn't think about them.

The only thing he could think about was packaged in a metal casing no more than seven inches wide, five high, and perhaps a foot long. It was designed for those dimensions; it had the appearance of sophisticated technology; it was tooled to operate on the fundamental properties of inertia and precision.

And it wasn't functional; it didn't work.

It failed test after test.

Ten thousand high-altitude B-17 bomber aircraft were emerging from production lines across the country. Without high-altitude, radio-beam gyroscopes to guide them, they might as well stay on the ground!

And without those aircraft, Operation Overlord was in serious jeopardy. The invasion of Europe would extract a price so great as to be obscene.

Yet to send the aircraft up on massive, round-the-clock, night and day bombing strikes throughout Germany without the cover of higher altitudes was to consign the majority to destruction, their crews to death. Examples were constant reminders . . . whenever the big planes soared too high. The labels of pilot error, enemy fire and instrument fatigue were not so. It was the higher altitudes. . . . Only twenty-four hours ago a squadron of bombers on the Bremerhaven run had scrambled out of the strike, exacting the maximum from their aircraft, and regrouped far above oxygen levels. From what could be determined, the guidance systems went crazy; the squadron ended up in the Dunbar sector near the Scottish border. All but one plane crashed into the sea. Three survivors were picked up by coastal patrols. Three out of God knows how many that had made it out of Bremerhaven. The one aircraft that attempted a ground landing had blown up on the outskirts of a town. . . . No survivors.

Germany was in the curve of inevitable defeat, but it would not die easily. It was ready for counterstrike. The Russian lesson had been learned; Hitler's generals were prepared. They realized that ultimately their only hope for any surrender other than *unconditional* lay in their ability to make the cost of an Allied victory so high it would stagger imagination and sicken the conscience of humanity.

Accommodation would then be reached.

And *that* was unacceptable to the Allies. *Unconditional surrender* was now a tripartite policy; the absolute had been so inculcated that it dared not be tampered with. The fever of total victory had swept the lands; the leaders had shaped that, too. And at this pitch of frenzy, the leaders stared into blank walls seeing nothing others could see and said heroically that losses would be tolerated.

Swanson walked up the steps of the Georgetown house. As if on cue, the door opened, a major saluted and Swanson was admitted quickly. Inside the hallway were four noncommissioned officers in paratroop leggings standing at ready-at-ease; Swanson recognized the shoulder patches of the Ranger battalions. The War Department had set the scene effectively.

A sergeant ushered Swanson into a small, brass-grilled elevator. Two stories up the elevator stopped and Swanson stepped out into the corridor. He recognized the face of the colonel who stood by a closed door at the end of the short hallway. He could not recall his name, however. The man worked in Clandestine Operations and was never much in evidence. The colonel stepped forward, saluting.

"General Swanson? Colonel Pace."

Swanson nodded his salute, offering his hand instead. "Oh, yes. Ed Pace, right?"

"Yes, sir."

"So they pulled you out of the cellars. I didn't know this was your territory."

"It's not, sir. Just that I've had occasion to meet the men you're seeing. Security clearances."

"And with you here they know we're serious." Swanson smiled.

"I'm sure we are, but I don't know what we're serious about."

"You're lucky. Who's inside?"

"Howard Oliver from Meridian. Jonathan Craft from Packard. And the lab man, Spinelli, from ATCO."

"They'll make my day; I can't wait. Who's presiding? Christ, there should be *one* person on our side."

"Vandamm."

Swanson's lips formed a quiet whistle; the colonel nodded in agreement. Frederic Vandamm was Undersecretary of State and rumored to be Cordell Hull's closest associate. If one wanted to reach Roosevelt, the best way was through Hull; if that avenue was closed, one pursued Vandamm.

"That's impressive artillery," Swanson said.

"When they saw him, I think he scared the hell out of Craft and Oliver. Spinelli's in a perpetual daze. He'd figure Patton for a doorman."

"I don't know Spinelli, except by rep. He's supposed to be the best gyro man in the labs. . . . Oliver and Craft I know *too* well. I wish to hell you boys had never cleared them for road maps."

"Not much you can do when they own the roads, sir." The colonel shrugged. It was obvious he agreed with Swanson's estimate.

"I'll give you a clue, Pace. Craft's a social-register flunky. Oliver's the bad meat."

"He's got a lot of it on him," replied the colonel, laughing softly.

Swanson took off his raincoat. "If you hear gunfire, colonel, it's only me fooling around. Walk the other way."

"I accept that as an order, general. I'm deaf," answered Pace as he reached for the handle and opened the door swiftly for his superior.

Swanson walked rapidly into the room. It was a library with the furniture pushed back against the walls and a conference table placed in the center. At the head of the table sat the white-haired, aristocratic Frederic Vandamm. On his left was the obese, balding Howard Oliver, a sheaf of notes in front of him. Opposite Oliver were Craft and a short, dark, bespectacled man Swanson assumed was Gian Spinelli.

The empty chair at the end of the table, facing Vandamm, was obviously for him. It was good positioning on Vandamm's part.

"I'm sorry to be late, Mr. Undersecretary. A staff car would have prevented it. A taxi wasn't the easiest thing to find. . . . Gentlemen?"

The trio of corporate men nodded; Craft and Oliver each uttered a muted "General." Spinelli just stared from behind the thick lenses of his glasses.

"I apologize, General Swanson," said Vandamm in the precise, Anglicized speech that bespoke a background of wealth. "For obvious reasons we did not want this conference to take place in a government office, nor, if known, did we wish any significance attached to the meeting itself. These gentlemen represent War Department gossip, I don't have to tell you that. The absence of urgency was desirable. Staff cars speeding through Washington—don't ask me why, but they never seem to slow down—have a tendency to arouse concern. Do you see?"

Swanson returned the old gentleman's veiled look. Vandamm was a smart one, he thought. It was an impetuous gamble referring to the taxi, but Vandamm had understood. He'd picked it up and used it well, even impartially.

The three corporate men were on notice. At this conference, they were the enemy.

"I've been discreet, Mr. Undersecretary."

"I'm sure you have. Shall we get down to points? Mr. Oliver has asked that he be permitted to open with a general statement of Meridian Aircraft's position."

Swanson watched the heavy-jowled Oliver sort out his notes. He disliked Oliver intensely; there was a fundamental gluttony about him. He was a manipulator; there were so many of them these days. They were everywhere in Washington, piling up huge sums of money from the war; proclaiming the power of the deal, the price of the deal, the price of the power—which they held.

Oliver's rough voice shot out from his thick lips. "Thank you. It's our feeling at Meridian that the . . . *assumed* gravity of the present situation has obscured the real advancements that *have* been made. The aircraft in question has proved beyond doubt its superior capabilities. The new, improved Fortress is ready for operational combat; it's merely a question of desired altitudes."

Oliver abruptly stopped and put his obese hands in front of him, over his papers. He had finished his statement; Craft nodded in agreement. Both men looked noncommittally at Vandamm. Gian Spinelli simply stared at Oliver, his brown eyes magnified by his glasses.

Alan Swanson was astounded. Not necessarily by the brevity of the statement but by the ingenuousness of the lie.

"If that's a position statement, I find it wholly unacceptable. The aircraft in question has *not* proved its capabilities until it's operational at the altitudes specified in the government contracts."

"It's operational," replied Oliver curtly.

"Operational. Not functional, Mr. Oliver. It is not functional until it can be guided from point A to point B at the altitudes called for in the specifications."

"*Specified* as 'intended maximum,' General Swanson," shot back Oliver, smiling an obsequious smile that conveyed anything but courtesy.

"What the hell does that mean?" Swanson looked at Undersecretary Vandamm.

"Mr. Oliver is concerned with a contractual interpretation."

"I'm *not*."

"I *have* to be," replied Oliver. "The War Department has refused payment to Meridian Aircraft Corporation. We have a contract. . . ."

"Take the goddamned contract up with someone else!"

"Anger won't solve anything." Vandamm spoke harshly.

"I'm sorry, Mr. Undersecretary, but I'm not here to discuss *contractual interpretations.*"

"I'm afraid you'll have to, General Swanson." Vandamm now spoke calmly. "The Disbursement Office has withheld payment to Meridian on *your* negative authorization. You haven't cleared it."

"Why should I? The aircraft can't do the job we expected."

"It *can* do the job you contracted for," said Oliver, moving his thick neck from Vandamm to the brigadier general. "Rest assured, general, our best efforts are being poured into the *intended* maximum guidance system. We're expending all our resources. We'll reach a breakthrough, we're convinced of that. But until we do, we expect the contracts to be honored. We've met the guarantees."

"Are you suggesting that we take the aircraft *as is?*"

"It's the finest bomber in the air." Jonathan Craft spoke. His soft, high voice was a weak exclamation that floated to a stop. He pressed his delicate fingers together in what he believed was emphasis.

Swanson disregarded Craft and stared at the small face and magnified eyes of the ATCO scientist, Gian Spinelli. "What about the *gyros?* Can you give me an answer, Mr. Spinelli?"

Howard Oliver intruded bluntly. "Use the existing systems. Get the aircraft into combat."

"*No!*" Swanson could not help himself. His was the roar of disgust, let Undersecretary Vandamm say what he liked. "Our strategies call for round-the-clock strikes into the deepest regions of Germany. From all points—known and unknown. Fields in England, Italy, Greece . . . yes, even unlisted bases in Turkey and Yugoslavia; carriers in the Mediterranean and, goddamn it, the Black Sea! Thousands and thousands of planes crowding the air corridors for space. We need the extra altitude! We need the guidance systems to operate at those altitudes! Anything less is unthinkable! . . . I'm sorry, Mr. Vandamm. I believe I'm justifiably upset."

"I understand," said the white-haired Undersecretary of State. "That's why we're here this afternoon. To look for solutions . . . as well as money." The old gentleman shifted his gaze to Craft. "Can you add to Mr. Oliver's remarks, from Packard's vantage point?"

Craft disengaged his lean, manicured fingers and took a deep breath through his nostrils as if he were about to deliver essential wisdom. The executive font of knowledge, thought Alan Swanson, jockeying for a chairman's approval.

"Of course, Mr. Undersecretary. As the major subcontractor for Meridian, we've been as disturbed as the general over the lack of guidance results. We've spared nothing to accommodate. Mr. Spinelli's presence is proof of that. After all, we're the ones who brought in ATCO. . . ." Here Craft smiled heroically, a touch sadly. "As we all know, ATCO is the finest—and most costly. We've spared *nothing.*"

"You brought in ATCO," said Swanson wearily, "because your own laboratories couldn't do the job. You submitted cost overruns to Meridian which were passed on to us. I don't see that you spared a hell of a lot."

"Good Lord, general!" exclaimed Craft with very little conviction. "The *time*, the *negotiations* . . . time is money, sir; make no mistake about *that*. I could show you. . . ."

"The general asked *me* a question. I should like to answer him."

The words, spoken with a trace of dialect, came from the tiny scientist, who was either dismissing Craft's nonsense, or oblivious to it, or, somehow, both.

"I'd be grateful, Mr. Spinelli."

"Our progress has been consistent, steady if you like. Not rapid. The problems are great. We believe the distortion of the radio beams beyond certain altitudes varies with temperatures and land-mass curvatures. The solutions lie in alternating compensations. Our experiments continuously narrow that field. . . . Our rate of progress would be more rapid were it not for constant interferences."

Gian Spinelli stopped and shifted his grotesquely magnified eyes to Howard Oliver, whose thick neck and jowled face were suddenly flushed with anger.

"You've had no interference from *us!*"

"And certainly not from Packard!" chimed in Craft. "We've stayed in almost daily contact. Our concerns have never flagged!"

Spinelli turned to Craft. "Your concerns . . . as those of Meridian . . . have been exclusively budgetary, as far as I can see."

"That's preposterous! Whatever financial inquiries were made, were made at the request of the . . . contractor's audit division. . . ."

"And totally necessary!" Oliver could not conceal his fury at the small Italian. "You *laboratory* . . . people don't reconcile! You're *children!*"

For the next thirty seconds the three agitated men babbled excitedly in counterpoint. Swanson looked over at Vandamm. Their eyes met in understanding.

Oliver was the first to recognize the trap. He held up his hand . . . a corporate command, thought Swanson.

"Mr. Undersecretary." Oliver spoke, stifling the pitch of his anger. "Don't let our squabbling convey the wrong impression. We turn out the products."

"You're not turning out this one," said Swanson. "I recall vividly the projections in your bids for the contract. You had everything *turned out then.*"

When Oliver looked at him, Alan Swanson instinctively felt he should reach for a weapon to protect himself. The Meridian executive was close to exploding.

"We relied on subordinates' evaluations," said Oliver slowly, with hostility. "I think the military has had its share of staff errors."

"Subordinates don't plan major strategies."

Vandamm raised his voice. "Mr. Oliver. Suppose Gen-

eral Swanson were convinced it served no purpose withholding funds. What kind of time limits could you *now*
guarantee?"

Oliver looked at Spinelli. "What would you estimate?"
he asked coldly.

Spinelli's large eyes swept the ceiling. "In candor, I
cannot give you an answer. We *could* solve it next week.
Or next year."

Swanson quickly reached into his tunic pocket and
withdrew a folded page of paper. He spread it out in front
of him and spoke swiftly. "According to this memorandum
. . . our last communication from ATCO . . . once the
guidance system *is* perfected, you state you need six
weeks of inflight experimentation. The Montana Proving
Grounds."

"That's correct, general. I dictated that myself," said
Spinelli.

"Six weeks from next week. Or next year. And assuming
the Montana experiments are positive, another month to
equip the fleets."

"Yes."

Swanson looked over at Vandamm. "In light of this,
Mr. Undersecretary, there's no other course but to alter
immediate priorities. Or at least the projections. We can't
meet the logistics."

"Unacceptable, General Swanson. We have to meet
them."

Swanson stared at the old man. Each knew precisely
what the other referred to.

*Overlord.* The invasion of Europe.

"We must postpone, sir."

"Impossible. That's the word, general."

Swanson looked at the three men around the table.
The enemy.

"We'll be in touch, gentlemen," he said.

# 3

David Spaulding waited in the shadows of the thick, gnarled tree on the rocky slope above the ravine. It was Basque country and the air was damp and cold. The late afternoon sun washed over the hills; his back was to it. He had years ago—it seemed a millennium but it wasn't —learned the advantage of catching the reflections of the sun off the steel of small weapons. His own rifle was dulled with burnt, crushed cork.

Four.

Strange, but the number *four* kept coming to mind as he scanned the distance.

*Four.*

Four years and four days ago exactly. And this after-noon's contract was scheduled for precisely four o'clock in the afternoon.

Four years and four days ago he had first seen the creased brown uniforms behind the thick glass partition in the radio studio in New York. Four years and four days ago since he had walked toward that glass wall to pick up his raincoat off the back of a chair and realized that the eyes of the older officer were looking at him. Steadily. Coldly. The younger man avoided him, as if guilty of intrusion, but not his superior, not the lieutenant colonel.

The lieutenant colonel had been studying him.

That was the beginning.

He wondered now—as he watched the ravine for signs of movement—when it would end. Would he be alive to see it end?

He intended to be.

He had called it a treadmill once. Over a drink at the Mayflower in Washington. Fairfax had *been* a treadmill; still, he had not known at the time how completely accurate that word would continue to be: a racing treadmill that never stopped.

It slowed down occasionally. The physical and mental pressures demanded deceleration at certain recognizable times—recognizable to him. Times when he realized he was getting careless . . . or too sure of himself. Or too absolute with regard to decisions that took human life.

Or might take his.

They were often too easily arrived at. And sometimes that frightened him. Profoundly.

During such times he would take himself away. He would travel south along the Portuguese coast where the enclaves of the temporarily inconvenienced rich denied the existence of war. Or he would stay in Costa del Santiago —with his perplexed parents. Or he would remain within the confines of the embassy in Lisbon and engross himself in the meaningless chores of neutral diplomacy. A minor military attaché who did not wear a uniform. It was not expected in the streets; it was inside the "territory." He did not wear one, however; no one cared. He was not liked very much. He socialized too frequently, had too many prewar friends. By and large, he was ignored . . . with a certain disdain.

At such times he rested. Forced his mind to go blank; to recharge itself.

Four years and four days ago such thoughts would have been inconceivable.

Now they consumed him. When he had the time for such thoughts.

Which he did not have now.

There was still no movement in the ravine. Something was wrong. He checked his watch; the team from San Sebastián was too far behind schedule. It was an abnormal delay. Only six hours ago the French underground had radioed that everything was secure; there were no complications, the team had started out.

The runners from San Sebastián were bringing out photographs of the German airfield installations north of Mont-de-Marsan. The strategists in London had been

screaming for them for months. Those photographs had
cost the lives of four . . . again, that goddamned number
. . . four underground agents.

If anything, the team should have been early; the runners should have been waiting for the man from Lisbon.

Then he saw it in the distance; perhaps a half a mile
away, it was difficult to tell. Over the ravine, beyond the
opposite slope, from one of the miniature hills. A flashing.

An intermittent but rhythmic flashing. The measured
spacing was a mark of intent, not accident.

They were being signaled. *He* was being signaled by
someone who knew his methods of operation well; perhaps
someone he had trained. It was a warning.

Spaulding slung the rifle over his shoulder and pulled
the strap taut, then tighter still so that it became a fixed
but flexible appendage to his upper body. He felt the hasp
of his belt holster; it was in place, the weapon secure. He
pushed himself away from the trunk of the old tree and,
in a crouching position, scrambled up the remainder of
the rock-hewn slope.

On the ridge he ran to his left, into the tall grass toward
the remains of a dying pear orchard. Two men in mud-
caked clothes, rifles at their sides, were sitting on the
ground playing trick knife, passing the time in silence.
They snapped their heads up, their hands reaching for their
guns.

Spaulding gestured to them to remain on the ground.
He approached and spoke quietly in Spanish.

"Do either of you know who's on the team coming in?"

"Bergeron, I think," said the man on the right. "And
probably Chivier. That old man has a way with patrols;
forty years he's peddled across the border."

"Then it's Bergeron," said Spaulding.

"What is?" asked the second man.

"We're being signaled. They're late and someone is using
what's left of the sun to get our attention."

"Perhaps to tell you they're on their way." The first
man put the knife back in his scabbard as he spoke.

"Possible but not likely. We wouldn't go anywhere. Not
for a couple of hours yet." Spaulding raised himself partially off the ground and looked eastward. "Come on!
We'll head down past the rim of the orchard. We can get
a cross view there."

The three men in single file, separated but within hearing of each other, raced across the field below the high ground for nearly four hundred yards. Spaulding positioned himself behind a low rock that jutted over the edge of the ravine. He waited for the other two. The waters below were about a hundred feet straight down, he judged. The team from San Sebastián would cross them approximately two hundred yards west, through the shallow, narrow passage they always used.

The two other men arrived within seconds of each other.

"The old tree where you stood was the mark, wasn't it?" asked the first man.

"Yes," answered Spaulding, removing his binoculars from a case opposite his belt holster. They were powerful, with Zeiss Ikon lenses, the best Germany produced. Taken from a dead German at the Tejo River.

"Then why come down here? If there's a problem, your line of vision was best where you were. It's more direct."

"If there's a problem, they'll know that. They'll flank to their left. East. To the west the ravine heads *away* from the mark. Maybe it's nothing. Perhaps you were right; they just want us to know they're coming."

A little more than two hundred yards away, just west of the shallow passage, two men came into view. The Spaniard who knelt on Spaulding's left touched the American's shoulder.

"It's Bergeron and Chivier," he said quietly.

Spaulding held up his hand for silence and scanned the area with the binoculars. Abruptly he fixed them in one position. With his left hand he directed the attention of his subordinates to the spot.

Below them, perhaps fifty yards, four soldiers in Wehrmacht uniforms were struggling with the foliage, approaching the waters of the ravine.

Spaulding moved his binoculars back to the two Frenchmen, now crossing the water. He held the glasses steady against the rock until he could see in the woods behind the two men what he knew was there.

A fifth German, an officer, was half concealed in the tangled mass of weeds and low branches. He held a rifle on the two Frenchmen crossing the ravine.

Spaulding passed the binoculars quickly to the first Spaniard. He whispered, "Behind Chivier."

The man looked, then gave the glasses to his countryman.

Each knew what had to be done; even the methods were clear. It was merely a question of timing, precision. From a scabbard behind his right hip, Spaulding withdrew a short carbine bayonet, shortened further by grinding. His two associates did the same. Each peered over the rock at the Wehrmacht men below.

The four Germans, faced with waters waist high and a current—though not excessively strong, nevertheless considerable—strapped their rifles across their shoulders laterally and separated in a downstream column. The lead man started across, testing the depths as he did so.

Spaulding and the two Spaniards came from behind the rock swiftly and slid down the incline, concealed by the foliage, their sounds muffled by the rushing water. In less than half a minute they were within thirty feet of the Wehrmacht men, hidden by fallen tree limbs and overgrowth. David entered the water, hugging the embankment. He was relieved to see that the fourth man—now only fifteen feet in front of him—was having the most difficulty keeping his balance on the slippery rocks. The other three, spaced about ten yards apart, were concentrating on the Frenchmen upstream. Concentrating intently.

The Nazi saw him; the fear, the bewilderment was in the German's eyes. The split second he took to assimilate the shock was the time David needed. Covered by the sounds of the water, Spaulding leaped on the man, his knife penetrating the Wehrmacht throat, the head pushed violently under the surface, the blood mingling with the rushing stream.

There was no time, no second to waste. David released the lifeless form and saw that the two Spaniards were parallel with him on the embankment. The first man, crouched and hidden, gestured toward the lead soldier; the second nodded his head toward the next man. And David knew that the third Wehrmacht soldier was his.

It took no more than the time necessary for Bergeron and Chivier to reach the south bank. The three soldiers were dispatched, their blood-soaked bodies floating downstream, careening off rocks, filling the waters with streaks of magenta.

Spaulding signaled the Spaniards to cross the water to the north embankment. The first man pulled himself up beside David, his right hand bloodied from a deep cut across his palm.

"Are you all right?" whispered Spaulding.

"The blade slipped. I lost my knife." The man swore.

"Get out of the area," said David. "Get the wound dressed at the Valdero farm."

"I can put on a tight bandage. I'll be fine."

The second Spaniard joined them. He winced at the sight of his countryman's hand, an action Spaulding thought inconsistent for a guerrilla who had just minutes ago plunged a blade into the neck of a man, slicing most of his head off.

"That looks bad," he said.

"You can't function," added Spaulding, "and we don't have time to argue."

"I can. . . ."

"You *can't*." David spoke peremptorily. "Go back to Valdero's. I'll see you in a week or two. Get going and stay out of sight!"

"Very well." The Spaniard was upset but it was apparent that he would not, could not, disobey the American's commands. He started to crawl into the woods to the east.

Spaulding called quietly, just above the rush of the water. "Thank you. Fine work today."

The Spaniard grinned and raced into the forest, holding his wrist.

Just as swiftly, David touched the arm of the second man, beckoning him to follow. They sidestepped their way along the bank upstream. Spaulding stopped by a fallen tree whose trunk dipped down into the ravine waters. He turned and crouched, ordering the Spaniard to do the same. He spoke quietly.

"I want him alive. I want to question him."

"I'll get him."

"No, I will. I just don't want you to fire. There could be a backup patrol." Spaulding realized as he whispered that the man couldn't help but smile. He knew why: his Spanish had the soft lilt of Castilian, a foreigner's Castilian at that. It was out of place in Basque country.

As he was out of place, really.

"As you wish, good friend," said the man. "Shall I cross farther back and reach Bergeron? He's probably sick to his stomach by now."

"No, not yet. Wait'll we're secure over here. He and the old man will just keep walking." David raised his head over the fallen tree trunk and estimated distances. The German officer was about sixty yards away, hidden in the woods. "I'll head in there, get behind him. I'll see if I can spot any signs of another patrol. If I do, I'll come back and we'll get out. If not, I'll try to grab him. . . . If anything goes wrong, if he hears me, he'll probably head for the water. Take him."

The Spaniard nodded. Spaulding checked the tautness of his rifle strap, giving it a last-second hitch. He gave his subordinate a tentative smile and saw that the man's hands —huge, calloused—were spread on the ground like claws. If the Wehrmacht officer headed this way, he'd never get by those hands, thought David.

He crept swiftly, silently into the woods, his arms and feet working like a primitive hunter's, warding off branches, sidestepping rocks and tangled foliage.

In less than three minutes he had gone thirty yards behind the German on the Nazi's left flank. He stood immobile and withdrew his binoculars. He scanned the forest and the trail. There were no other patrols. He doubled back cautiously, blending every movement of his body with his surroundings.

When he was within ten feet of the German, who was kneeling on the ground, David silently unlatched his holster and withdrew his pistol. He spoke sharply, though not impolitely, in German.

"Stay where you are or I'll blow your head off."

The Nazi whipped around and awkwardly fumbled for his weapon. Spaulding took several rapid steps and kicked it out of his hands. The man started to rise, and David brought his heavy leather boot up into the side of the German's head. The officer's visor hat fell to the ground; blood poured out of the man's temple, spreading throughout the hairline, streaking down across his face. He was unconscious.

Spaulding reached down and tore at the Nazi's tunic. Strapped across the Oberleutnant's chest was a traveling pouch. David pulled the steel zipper laterally over the waterproofed canvas and found what he was sure he would find.

The photographs of the hidden Luftwaffe installations north of Mont-de-Marsan. Along with the photographs were amateurish drawings that were, in essence, basic blueprints. At least, schematics. Taken from Bergeron, who had then led the German into the trap.

If he could make sense out of them—along with the photographs—he would alert London that sabotage units could inflict the necessary destruction, immobilizing the Luftwaffe complex. He would send in the units himself.

The Allied air strategists were manic when it came to bombing runs. The planes dove from the skies, reducing to rubble and crater everything that was—and was not—a target, taking as much innocent life as enemy. If Spaulding could prevent air strikes north of Mont-de-Marsan, it might somehow . . . abstractly . . . make up for the decision he now had to face.

There were no prisoners of war in the Galician hills, no internment centers in the Basque country.

The Wehrmacht lieutenant, who was so ineffectual in his role of the hunter . . . who might have had a life in some peaceful German town in a peaceful world . . . had to die. And he, the man from Lisbon, would be the executioner. He would revive the young officer, interrogate him at the point of a knife to learn how deeply the Nazis had penetrated the underground in San Sebastián. Then kill him.

For the Wehrmacht officer had seen the man from Lisbon; he could identify that man as David Spaulding.

The fact that the execution would be mercifully quick —unlike a death in partisan hands—was of small comfort to David. He knew that at the instant he pulled the trigger, the world would spin insanely for a moment or two. He would be sick to his stomach and want to vomit, his whole being in a state of revulsion.

But he would not show these things. He would say nothing, indicate nothing . . . silence. And so the legend would continue to grow. For that was part of the treadmill.

The man in Lisbon was a killer.

# 4

## SEPTEMBER 20, 1943, MANNHEIM, GERMANY

Wilhelm Zangen brought the handkerchief to his chin, and then to the skin beneath his nostrils, and finally to the border of his receding hairline. The sweat was profuse; a rash had formed in the cleft below his lips, aggravated by the daily necessity to shave and the continuous pressure.

His whole face was stinging, his embarrassment compounded by Franz Altmüller's final words:

"Really, Wilhelm, you should see a doctor. It's most unattractive."

With that objective solicitousness, Altmüller had gotten up from the table and walked out the door. Slowly, deliberately, his briefcase—the briefcase containing the reports—held down at arm's length as though it had been some diseased appendage.

They had been alone. Altmüller had dismissed the group of scientists without acknowledging any progress whatsoever. He had not even allowed him, the Reich official of German Industry, to thank them for their contributions. Altmüller knew that these were the finest scientific minds in Germany, but he had no understanding of how to handle them. They were sensitive, they were volatile in their own quiet way; they needed praise constantly. He had no patience for tact.

And there *had* been progress.

The Krupp laboratories were convinced that the answer lay in the graphite experiments. Essen had worked around the clock for nearly a month, its managers undergoing one sleepless night after another. They had actually *produced carbon particles* in sealed iron tubes and were convinced these carbons held all the properties required for precision tooling. It was merely a question of time; time to create larger particles, sufficient for tolerance placement within existing machinery.

Franz Altmüller had listened to the Krupp team without the slightest indication of enthusiasm, although enthusiasm certainly had been called for under the circumstances. Instead, when the Krupp spokesman had finished his summary, Altmüller had asked one question. Asked it with the most bored expression imaginable!

"Have these . . . particles been subjected to the pressure of operational tooling?"

Of course they hadn't! How could they have been? They *had* been subjected to artificial, substitute pressures; it was all that was possible at the moment.

That answer had been unacceptable; Altmüller dismissed the most scientifically creative minds in the Reich without a single sentence of appreciation, only ill-disguised hostility.

"Gentlemen, you've brought me words. We don't need words, we need diamonds. We need them, we *must have* them within weeks. Two months at the outside. I suggest you return to your laboratories and consider our problem once again. Good day, gentlemen."

Altmüller was impossible!

After the scientists had left, Altmüller had become even more abrasive.

"Wilhelm," he had said with a voice bordering on contempt, "was *this* the nonmilitary solution of which you spoke to the minister of armaments?"

Why hadn't he used Speer's name? Was it necessary to threaten with the use of titles?

"Of course. Certainly more realistic than that insane march into the Congo. The mines at the Bushimaie River! Madness!"

"The comparison is odious. I overestimated you; I gave you more credit than you deserve. You understand, of course, that you failed." It was not a question.

"I disagree. The results aren't in yet. You can't make such a judgment."

"I can and I have!" Altmüller had slammed the flat of his hand against the tabletop; a crack of soft flesh against hard wood. An intolerable insult. "We have no time! We can't waste weeks while your laboratory misfits play with their bunsen burners, creating little stones that could fall apart at the first contact with steel! We need the *product!*"

"You'll have it!" The surface of Zangen's chin became an oily mixture of sweat and stubble. "The finest minds in all Germany are . . ."

"Are *experimenting*." Altmüller had interrupted quietly, with scornful emphasis. "Get us the *product*. That's my order to you. Our powerful companies have long histories that go back many years. Certainly one of them can find an old friend."

Wilhelm Zangen had blotted his chin; the rash was agonizing. "We've covered those areas. Impossible."

"Cover them again." Altmüller had pointed an elegant finger at Zangen's handkerchief. "Really, Wilhelm, you should see a doctor. It's most unattractive."

## *SEPTEMBER 24, 1943, NEW YORK CITY*

Jonathan Craft walked up Park Avenue and checked his wristwatch under the spill of a streetlamp. His long, thin fingers trembled; the last vestige of too many martinis, which he had stopped drinking twenty-four hours ago in Ann Arbor. Unfortunately, he had been drunk for the previous three days. He had not been to the office. The office reminded him of General Alan Swanson; he could not bear that memory. Now he had to.

It was a quarter to nine; another fifteen minutes and he would walk into 800 Park Avenue, smile at the doorman and go to the elevator. He did not want to be early, dared not be late. He had been inside the apartment house exactly seven times, and each occasion had been traumatic for him. Always for the same reason: he was the bearer of bad news.

But they needed him. He was the impeccable man. His family was old, fine money; he had been to the right schools, the best cotillions. He had access into areas— social and institutional—the *merchants* would never possess. No matter he was stuck in Ann Arbor; it was a temporary situation, a wartime inconvenience. A sacrifice.

He would be back in New York on the Exchange as soon as the damn thing was over.

He had to keep these thoughts in mind tonight because in a few minutes he would have to repeat the words Swanson had screamed at him in his Packard office. He had written a confidential report of the conversation . . . the *unbelievable* conversation . . . and sent it to Howard Oliver at Meridian.

*If you've done what I think you've done, it falls under the heading of treasonable acts! And we're at war!*

Swanson.

Madness.

He wondered how many would be there, in the apartment. It was always better if there were quite a few, say a dozen. Then they argued among themselves; he was almost forgotten. Except for his information.

He walked around the block, breathing deeply, calming himself . . . killing ten minutes.

*Treasonable acts!*

*And we're at war!*

His watch read five minutes to nine. He entered the building, smiled at the doorman, gave the floor to the elevator operator and, when the brass grill opened, he walked into the private foyer of the penthouse.

A butler took his overcoat and ushered him across the hall, through the door and down three steps into the huge sunken living room.

There were only two men in the room. Craft felt an immediate sharp pain in his stomach. It was an instinctive reaction partly brought on by the fact that there were only two other people for this extremely vital conference, but mainly caused by the sight of Walter Kendall.

Kendall was a man in shadows, a manipulator of figures who was kept out of sight. He was fiftyish, medium-sized, with thinning, unwashed hair, a rasping voice and an undistinguished—shoddy—appearance. His eyes darted continuously, almost never returning another man's look. It was said his mind concentrated incessantly on schemes and counterschemes; his whole purpose in life was apparently to outmaneuver other human beings—friend or enemy, it made no difference to Kendall, for he did not categorize people with such labels.

All were vague opponents.

But Walter Kendall was brilliant at what he did. As long as he could be kept in the background, his manipulations

served his clients. And made him a great deal of money—
which he hoarded, attested to by ill-fitting suits that
bagged at the knees and sagged below the buttocks. But
he was always kept out of sight; his presence signified
crisis.

Jonathan Craft despised Kendall because he was frightened by him.

The second man was to be expected under the circumstances. He was Howard Oliver, Meridian Aircraft's obese
debater of War Department contracts.

"You're on time," said Walter Kendall curtly, sitting
down in an armchair, reaching for papers in an open,
filthy briefcase at his feet.

"Hello, Jon." Oliver approached and offered a short,
neutral handshake.

"Where are the others?" asked Craft.

"No one wanted to be here," answered Kendall with a
furtive glance at Oliver. "Howard has to be, and I'm paid
to be. You had one hell of a meeting with this Swanson."

"You've read my report?"

"He's read it," said Oliver, crossing to a copper-topped
wheel-cart in the corner on which there were bottles and
glasses. "He's got questions."

"I made everything perfectly clear. . . ."

"Those aren't the questions," interrupted Kendall while
squeezing the tip of a cigarette before inserting it into his
mouth. As he struck a match, Craft walked to a large
velvet chair across from the accountant and sat down.
Oliver had poured himself a whisky and remained standing.

"If you want a drink, Jon, it's over here," said Oliver.

At the mention of alcohol, Kendall glanced up at him
from his papers with ferret-like eyes. "No, thank you,"
Craft replied. "I'd like to get this over with as soon as
possible."

"Suit yourself." Oliver looked at the accountant. "Ask
your questions."

Kendall, sucking on his cigarette, spoke as the smoke
curled around his nostrils. "This Spinelli over at ATCO.
Have you talked to him since you saw Swanson?"

"No. There was nothing to say; nothing *I* could say . . .
without instructions. As you know, I spoke with Howard
on the phone. He told me to wait; write a report and do
nothing."

"Craft's the funnel to ATCO," said Oliver. "I didn't want him running scared, trying to smooth things over. It'd look like we were hiding something."

"We are." Kendall removed his cigarette, the ash falling on his trousers. He continued while slowly shuffling the papers on his lap. "Let's go over Spinelli's complaints. As Swanson brought them up."

The accountant touched briefly, concisely on each point raised. They covered Spinelli's statements regarding delayed deliveries, personnel transfers, blueprint holdups, a dozen other minor grievances. Craft replied with equal brevity, answering when he could, stating ignorance when he could not. There was no reason to hide anything.

He had been carrying out instructions, not issuing them.

"Can Spinelli substantiate these charges? And don't kid yourselves, these are charges, not complaints."

"What *charges?*" Oliver spat out the words. "That guinea bastard's fucked up everything! Who's he to make charges?"

"Get off it," said Kendall in his rasping voice. "Don't play games. Save them for a congressional committee, unless I can figure something."

At Kendall's words the sharp pain returned to Craft's stomach. The prospects of disgrace—even remotely associated—could ruin his life. The life he expected to lead back in New York. The financial boors, the *merchants*, could never understand. "That's going a little far. . . ."

Kendall looked over at Craft. "Maybe you didn't *hear* Swanson. It's not going far enough. You got the Fortress contracts because your *projections* said you could do the job."

"Just a minute!" yelled Oliver. "We . . ."

"*Screw* the legal crap!" countered Kendall, shouting over Oliver's interruption. "My firm . . . *me, I* . . . squared those projections. I know what they say, what they implied. You left the other companies at the gate. They wouldn't *say* what you said. Not Douglas, not Boeing, not Lockheed. You were hungry and you got the meat and now you're not delivering. . . . So what else is new? Let's go back: can Spinelli substantiate?"

"*Shit,*" exploded Oliver, heading for the bar.

"How do you mean . . . substantiate?" asked Jonathan Craft, his stomach in agony.

"Are there any memorandums floating around," Kendall tapped the pages in his hand, "that bear on any of this?"

"Well . . ." Craft hesitated; he couldn't stand the pain in his stomach. "When personnel transfers were expedited, they were put into interoffice. . . ."

"The answer's yes," interrupted Oliver in disgust, pouring himself a drink.

"What about financial cutbacks?"

Oliver once again replied. "We obscured those. Spinelli's requisitions just got lost in the paper shuffle."

"Didn't he scream? Didn't *he* shoot off memos?"

"That's Craft's department," answered Oliver, drinking most of his whisky in one swallow. "Spinelli was his little guinea boy."

"Well?" Kendall looked at Craft.

"Well . . . he sent numerous communications." Craft leaned forward in the chair, as much to relieve the pain as to appear confidential. "I removed everything from the files," he said softly.

"*Christ*," exploded Kendall quietly. "I don't give a *shit* what *you* removed. He's got copies. Dates."

"Well, I couldn't say. . . ."

"He didn't type the goddamned things *himself*, did he? You didn't take away the fucking secretaries, *too*, did you?"

"There's no call to be offensive. . . ."

"*Offensive!* You're a funny man! Maybe they've got fancy stripes for you in Leavenworth." The accountant snorted and turned his attention to Howard Oliver. "Swanson's got a case; he'll hang you. Nobody has to be a lawyer to see that. You held back. *You figured to use the existing guidance systems.*"

"Only because the new gyroscopes couldn't be developed! Because that guinea bastard fell so far behind he couldn't catch up!"

"Also it saved you a couple of hundred million. . . . You should have primed the pumps, not cut off the water. You're big ducks in a short gallery; a blind man could knock you off."

Oliver put his glass down and spoke slowly. "We don't pay you for that kind of judgment, Walter. You'd better have something else."

Kendall crushed out his mutilated cigarette, his dirty fingernails covered with ash. "I do," he said. "You need company; you're in the middle of a very emotional issue. It'll cost you but you don't have a choice. You've got to make deals; ring in everybody. Get hold of Sperry Rand, GM, Chrysler, Lockheed, Douglas, Rolls-Royce, if you have to . . . every son of a bitch with an engineering laboratory. A patriotic crash program. Cross-reference your data, open up everything you've got."

"They'll steal us blind!" roared Oliver. "Millions!"

"Cost you more if you don't. . . . I'll prepare supplementary financial stats. I'll pack the sheets with so much ice, it'll take ten years to thaw. That'll cost you, too." Kendall smirked, baring soiled teeth.

Howard Oliver stared at the unkempt accountant. "It's crazy," he said quietly. "We'll be giving away fortunes for something that can't be bought because it doesn't exist."

"But you said it *did* exist. You told Swanson it existed —at least a hell of a lot more confidently than anybody else. You sold your great industrial know-how, and when you couldn't deliver, you covered up. Swanson's right. You're a menace to the war effort. Maybe you *should* be shot."

Jonathan Craft watched the filthy, grinning bookkeeper with bad teeth and wanted to vomit. But he was their only hope.

# 5

## SEPTEMBER 25, 1943, STUTTGART, GERMANY

Wilhelm Zangen stood by the window overlooking Stuttgart's Reichssieg Platz, holding a handkerchief against his inflamed, perspiring chin. This outlying section of the city had been spared the bombing; it was residential, even peaceful. The Neckar River could be seen in the distance, its waters rolling calmly, oblivious to the destruction that had been wrought on the other side of the city.

Zangen realized he was expected to speak, to answer von Schnitzler, who spoke for all of I. G. Farben. The two other men were as anxious to hear his words as was von Schnitzler. There was no point in procrastinating. He had to carry out Altmüller's orders.

"The Krupp laboratories have failed. No matter what Essen says, there is no time for experimentation. The Ministry of Armaments has made that clear; Altmüller is resolute. He speaks for Speer." Zangen turned and looked at the three men. "He holds you responsible."

"How can that be?" asked von Schnitzler, his guttural lisp pronounced, his voice angry. "How can we be responsible for something we know nothing about? It's illogical. Ridiculous!"

"Would you wish me to convey that judgment to the ministry?"

"I'll convey it myself, thank you," replied von Schnitzler. "Farben is not involved."

"We are all involved," said Zangen quietly.

"How can *our* company be?" asked Heinrich Krepps, Direktor of Schreibwaren, the largest printing complex in

Germany. "Our work with Peenemünde has been practically nothing; and what there was, obscured to the point of foolishness. Secrecy is one thing; lying to ourselves, something else again. Do not include us, Herr Zangen."

"You *are* included."

"I reject your conclusion. I've studied our communications with Peenemünde."

"Perhaps you were not cleared for all the facts."

"Asinine!"

"Quite possibly. Nevertheless . . ."

"Such a condition would hardly apply to *me*, Herr Reich official," said Johann Dietricht, the middle-aged, effeminate son of the Dietricht Fabriken empire. Dietricht's family had contributed heavily to Hitler's National Socialist coffers; when the father and uncle had died, Johann Dietricht was allowed to continue the management—more in name than in fact. "Nothing occurs at Dietricht of which I am unaware. We've had nothing to do with Peenemünde!"

Johann Dietricht smiled, his fat lips curling, his blinking eyes betraying an excess of alcohol, his partially plucked eyebrows his sexual proclivity—excess, again. Zangen couldn't stand Dietricht; the man—although no man— was a disgrace, his life-style an insult to German industry. Again, felt Zangen, there was no point in procrastinating. The information would come as no surprise to von Schnitzler and Krepps.

"There are many aspects of the Dietricht Fabriken of which you know *nothing*. Your own laboratories have worked consistently with Peenemünde in the field of chemical detonation."

Dietricht blanched; Krepps interrupted.

"What is your purpose, Herr Reich official? You call us here only to insult us? You tell us, directors, that we are not the masters of our own companies? I don't know Herr Dietricht so well, but I can assure you that von Schnitzler and myself are not puppets."

Von Schnitzler had been watching Zangen closely, observing the Reich official's use of his handkerchief. Zangen kept blotting his chin nervously. "I presume you have specific information—such as you've just delivered to Herr Dietricht—that will confirm your statements."

"I have."

"Then you're saying that isolated operations—within our own factories—were withheld from us."

"I am."

"Then how can we be held responsible? These are insane accusations."

"They are made for practical reasons."

"Now you're talking in circles!" shouted Dietricht, barely recovered from Zangen's insult.

"I must agree," said Krepps, as if agreement with the obvious homosexual was distasteful, yet mandatory.

"Come, gentlemen. Must I draw pictures? These are *your companies*. Farben has supplied eighty-three per cent of all chemicals for the rockets; Schreibwaren has processed every blueprint; Dietricht, the majority of detonating compounds for the casing explosives. We're in a crisis. If we don't overcome that crisis, no protestations of ignorance will serve you. I might go so far as to say that there are those in the ministry and elsewhere who will deny that anything was withheld. You simply buried your collective heads. I'm not even sure myself that such a judgment is in error."

"Lies!" screamed Dietricht.

"Absurd!" added Krepps.

"But obscenely practical," concluded von Schnitzler slowly, staring at Zangen. "So this is what you're telling us, isn't it? What Altmüller tells us. We either employ our resources to find a solution—to come to the aid of our industrial *Schwachling*—or we face equilateral disposition in the eyes of the ministry."

"And in the eyes of the Führer; the judgment of the Reich itself."

"But *how?*" asked the frightened Johann Dietricht.

Zangen remembered Altmüller's words precisely. "Your companies have long histories that go back many years. Corporate and individual. From the Baltic to the Mediterranean, from New York to Rio de Janeiro, from Saudi Arabia to Johannesburg."

"And from Shanghai down through Malaysia to the ports in Australia and the Tasman Sea," said von Schnitzler quietly.

"They don't concern us."

"I thought not."

"Are you suggesting, Herr Reich official, that the solution for Peenemünde lies in our past associations?" Von Schnitzler leaned forward in his chair, his hands and eyes on the table.

"It's a crisis. No avenues can be overlooked. Communications can be expedited."

"No doubt. What makes you think they'd be exchanged?" continued the head of I. G. Farben.

"Profits," replied Zangen.

"Difficult to spend facing a firing squad." Von Schnitzler shifted his large bulk and looked up at the window, his expression pensive.

"You assume the commission of specific transactions. I refer more to acts of *omission*."

"Clarify that, please," Krepps's eyes remained on the tabletop.

"There are perhaps twenty-five acceptable sources for the bortz and carbonado diamonds—acceptable in the sense that sufficient quantities can be obtained in a single purchase. Africa and South America; one or two locations in Central America. These mines are run by companies under fiat security conditions: British, American, Free French, Belgian . . . you know them. Shipments are controlled, destinations cleared. . . . We are suggesting that shipments can be sidetracked, destinations altered in neutral territories. By the expedient of omitting normal security precautions. Acts of incompetence, if you will; human error, not betrayal."

"Extraordinarily profitable mistakes," summed up von Schnitzler.

"Precisely," said Wilhelm Zangen.

"Where do you find such men?" asked Johann Dietricht in his high-pitched voice.

"Everywhere," replied Heinrich Krepps.

Zangen blotted his chin with his handkerchief.

# 6

## NOVEMBER 29, 1943,
## BASQUE COUNTRY, SPAIN

Spaulding raced across the foot of the hill until he saw
the converging limbs of the two trees. They were the
mark. He turned right and started up the steep incline,
counting off an approximate 125 yards; the second mark.
He turned left and walked slowly around to the west
slope, his body low, his eyes darting constantly in all
directions; he gripped his pistol firmly.

On the west slope he looked for a single rock—one
among so many on the rock-strewn Galician hill—that
had been chipped on its downward side. Chipped carefully with three indentations. It was the third and final
mark.

He found it, spotting first the bent reeds of the stiff hill
grass. He knelt down and looked at his watch: two forty-
five.

He was fifteen minutes early, as he had planned to be.
In fifteen minutes he would walk down the west slope,
directly in front of the chipped rock. There he would find
a pile of branches. Underneath the branches would be a
short-walled cave; in that cave—if all went as planned—
would be three men. One was a member of an infiltration
team. The other two were *Wissenschaftler*—German
scientists who had been attached to the Kindorf laboratories in the Ruhr Valley. Their defections—escape—had
been an objective of long planning.

The obstacles were always the same.

Gestapo.

The Gestapo had broken an underground agent and

was on to the *Wissenschaftler*. But, typical of the SS
elite, it kept its knowledge to itself, looking for bigger
game than two disaffected laboratory men. Gestapo
*Agenten* had given the scientists wide latitude; surveillance
dismissed, laboratory patrols relaxed to the point of ineffi-
ciency, routine interrogation disregarded.

Contradictions.

The Gestapo was neither inefficient nor careless. The
SS was setting a trap.

Spaulding's instructions to the underground had been
terse, simple: let the trap be sprung. With no quarry in
its net.

Word was leaked that the scientists, granted a weekend
leave to Stuttgart, were in reality heading due north
through underground routing to Bremerhaven. There contact was being made with a high-ranking defecting German naval officer who had commandeered a small craft
and would make a dramatic run to the Allies. It was
common knowledge that the German navy was rife with
unrest. It was a recruiting ground for the anti-Hitler
factions springing up throughout the Reich.

The *word* would give everyone something to think
about, reasoned Spaulding. And the Gestapo would be
following two men it assumed were the *Wissenschaftler*
from Kindorf, when actually they were two middle-aged
Wehrmacht security patrols sent on a false surveillance.

Games and countergames.

So much, so alien. The expanded interests of the man
in Lisbon.

This afternoon was a concession. Demanded by the
German underground. He was to make the final contact
alone. The underground claimed the man in Lisbon had
created too many complications; there was too much
room for error and counterinfiltration. There wasn't,
thought David, but if a solo run would calm the nervous
stomachs of the anti-Reichists, it was little enough to
grant them.

He had his own Valdero team a half mile away in the
upper hills. Two shots and they would come to his help on
the fastest horses Castilian money could buy.

It was time. He could start toward the cave for the
final contact.

He slid down the hard surface, his heels digging into the

earth and rocks of the steep incline until he was above the pile of branches and limbs that signified the hideout's opening. He picked up a handful of loose dirt and threw it down into the broken foliage.

The response was as instructed: a momentary thrashing of a stick against the piled branches. The fluttering of bird's wings, driven from the bush.

Spaulding quickly sidestepped his way to the base of the enclosure and stood by the camouflage.

*"Alles in Ordnung. Kommen Sie,"* he said quietly but firmly. "There isn't much traveling time left."

*"Halt!"* was the unexpected shout from the cave.

David spun around, pressed his back into the hill and raised his Colt. The voice from inside spoke again. In English.

"Are you . . . Lisbon?"

"For God's sake, yes! Don't *do* that! You'll get your head shot off!" *Christ*, thought Spaulding, the infiltration team must have used a child, or an imbecile, or both as its runner. "Come on out."

"I am with apologies, Lisbon," said the voice, as the branches were separated and the pile dislodged. "We've had a bad time of it."

The runner emerged. He was obviously not anyone David had trained. He was short, very muscular, no more than twenty-five or twenty-six; nervous fear was in his eyes.

"In the future," said Spaulding, "don't acknowledge signals, then question the signaler at the last moment. Unless you intend to kill him. *Es ist Schwarztuch-chiffre.*"

*"Was ist das?* Black . . ."

"Black Drape, friend. Before our time. It means . . . confirm and terminate. Never mind, just don't do it again. Where are the others?"

"Inside. They are all right; very tired and very afraid, but not injured." The runner turned and pulled off more branches. "Come out. It's the man from Lisbon."

The two frightened, middle-aged scientists crawled out of the cave cautiously, blinking at the hot, harsh sun. They looked gratefully at David; the taller one spoke in halting English.

"This is a . . . minute we have waited for. Our very much thanks."

Spaulding smiled. "Well, we're not out of the woods, yet. *Frei.* Both terms apply. You're brave men. We'll do all we can for you."

"There was . . . *nichts* . . . remaining," said the shorter laboratory man. "My friend's socialist . . . *Politik* . . . was unpopular. My late wife was . . . *eine Jüdin.*"

"No children?"

"*Nein,*" answered the man. "*Gott seli dank.*"

"I have one son," said the taller scientist coldly. "*Er ist . . . Gestapo.*"

There was no more to be said, thought Spaulding. He turned to the runner, who was scanning the hill and the forests below. "I'll take over now. Get back to Base Four as soon as you can. We've got a large contingent coming in from Koblenz in a few days. We'll need everyone. Get some rest."

The runner hesitated; David had seen his expression before . . . so often. The man was now going to travel alone. No company, pleasant or unpleasant. Just alone.

"That is not my understanding, Lisbon. I am to stay with you. . . ."

"Why?" interrupted Spaulding.

"My instructions. . . ."

"From whom?"

"From those in San Sebastián. Herr Bergeron and his men. Weren't you informed?"

David looked at the runner. The man's fear was making him a poor liar, thought Spaulding. Or he was something else. Something completely unexpected because it was not logical; it was not, at this point, even remotely to be considered. Unless . . .

David gave the runner's frayed young nerves the benefit of the doubt. A benefit, not an exoneration. That would come later.

"No, I wasn't told," he said. "Come on. We'll head to Beta camp. We'll stay there until morning." Spaulding gestured and they started across the foot of the slope.

"I haven't worked this far south," said the runner, positioning himself behind David. "Don't you travel at night, Lisbon?"

"Sometimes," answered Spaulding, looking back at the scientists, who were walking side by side. "Not if we can help it. The Basques shoot indiscriminately at night. They have too many dogs off their leashes at night."

"I see."

"Let's walk single file. Flank our guests," said David to the runner.

The four traveled several miles east. Spaulding kept up a rapid pace; the middle-aged scientists did not complain but they obviously found the going difficult. A number of times David told the others to remain where they were while he entered the woods at various sections of the forest and returned minutes later. Each time he did so, the older men rested, grateful for the pauses. The runner did not. He appeared frightened—as if the American might not come back. Spaulding did not encourage conversation, but after one such disappearance, the young German could not restrain himself.

"What are you *doing?*" he asked.

David looked at the *Widerstandskämpfer* and smiled. "Picking up messages."

"Messages?"

"These are drops. Along our route. We establish marks for leaving off information we don't want sent by radio. Too dangerous if intercepted."

They continued along a narrow path at the edge of the woods until there was a break in the Basque forest. It was a grazing field, a lower plateau centered beneath the surrounding hills. The *Wissenschaftler* were perspiring heavily, their breaths short, their legs aching.

"We'll rest here for a while," said Spaulding, to the obvious relief of the older men. "It's time I made contact anyway."

*"Was ist los?"* asked the young runner. "Contact?"

"Zeroing our position," replied David, taking out a small metal mirror from his field jacket. "The scouts can relax if they know where we are. . . . If you're going to work the north country—what you call south—you'd better remember all this."

"I shall, I shall."

David caught the reflection of the sun on the mirror and beamed it up to a northern hill. He made a series of motions with his wrist, and the metal plate moved back and forth in rhythmic precision.

Seconds later there was a reply from halfway up the

highest hill in the north. Flashes of light shafted out of an infinitesimal spot in the brackish green distance. Spaulding turned to the others.

"We're not going to Beta," he said. "Falangist patrols are in the area. We'll stay here until we're given clearance. You can relax."

The heavyset Basque put down the knapsack mirror. His companion still focused his binoculars on the field several miles below, where the American and his three charges were now seated on the ground.

"He says they are being followed. We are to take up counterpositions and stay out of sight," said the man with the metal mirror. "We go down for the scientists tomorrow night. He will signal us."

"What's *he* going to do?"

"I don't know. He says to get word to Lisbon. He's going to stay in the hills."

"He's a cold one," the Basque said.

## DECEMBER 2, 1943, WASHINGTON, D.C.

Alan Swanson sat in the back of the army car trying his best to remain calm. He looked out the window; the late morning traffic was slight. The immense Washington labor force was at its appointed destinations; machines were humming, telephones ringing, men were shouting and whispering and, in too many places, having the first drink of the day. The exhilaration that was apparent during the first hours of the working day faded as noon approached. By eleven thirty a great many people thought the war was dull and were bored by their mechanical chores, the unending duplicates, triplicates and quadruplicates. They could not understand the necessity of painstaking logistics, of disseminating information to innumerable chains of command.

They could not understand because they could not be given whole pictures, only fragments, repetitious statistics. Of course they were bored.

They were weary. As he had been weary fourteen hours ago in Pasadena, California.

Everything had failed.

Meridian Aircraft had initiated—was *forced* to initiate

—a crash program, but the finest scientific minds in the country could not eliminate the errors inside the small box that was the guidance system. The tiny, whirling spheroid discs would not spin true at maximum altitudes. They were erratic; absolute one second, deviant the next.

The most infinitesimal deviation could result in the midair collision of giant aircraft. And with the numbers projected for the saturation bombing prior to Overlord—scheduled to commence in less than four months—collisons *would* occur.

But this morning everything was different.

*Could* be different, if there was substance to what he had been told. He hadn't been able to sleep on the plane, hardly been able to eat. Upon landing at Andrews, he had hurried to his Washington apartment, showered, shaved, changed uniforms and called his wife in Scarsdale, where she was staying with a sister. He didn't remember the conversation between them; the usual endearments were absent, the questions perfunctory. He had no time for her.

The army car entered the Virginia highway and accelerated. They were going to Fairfax; they'd be there in twenty minutes or so. In less than a half hour he would find out if the impossible was, conversely, entirely possible. The news had come as a last-minute stay of execution; the cavalry in the distant hills—the sounds of muted bugles signaling reprieve.

Muted, indeed, thought Swanson as the army car veered off the highway onto a back Virginia road. In Fairfax, covering some two hundred acres in the middle of the hunt country, was a fenced-off area housing Quonset huts beside huge radar screens and radio signal towers that sprang from the ground like giant steel malformities. It was the Field Division Headquarters of Clandestine Operations; next to the underground rooms at the White House, the most sensitive processing location of the Allied Intelligence services.

Late yesterday afternoon, FDHQ-Fairfax had received confirmation of an Intelligence probe long since abandoned as negative. It came out of Johannesburg, South Africa. It had not been proved out, but there was sufficient evidence to believe that it could be.

High-altitude directional gyroscopes had been perfected. Their designs could be had.

## DECEMBER 2, 1943, BERLIN, GERMANY

Altmüller sped out of Berlin on the Spandau highway toward Falkensee in the open Duesenberg. It was early in the morning and the air was cold and that was good.

He was so exhilarated that he forgave the theatrically secretive ploys of the Nachrichtendienst, code name for a select unit of the espionage service known to only a few of the upper-echelon ministers, not to many of the High Command itself. A Gehlen specialty.

For this reason it never held conferences within Berlin proper; always outside the city, always in some remote, secluded area or town and even then in private surroundings, away from the potentially curious.

The location this morning was Falkensee, twenty-odd miles northwest of Berlin. The meeting was to take place in a guest house on the estate belonging to Gregor Strasser.

Altmüller would have flown to Stalingrad itself if what he'd been led to believe was true.

The Nachrichtendienst had found the solution for Peenemünde!

The solution *was true*; it was up to others to expedite it.

The solution that had eluded teams of "negotiators" sent to all parts of the world to explore—unearth—prewar "relationships." Capetown, Dar es Salaam, Johannesburg, Buenos Aires. . . .

Failure.

No company, no individual would touch German negotiations. Germany was in the beginning of a death struggle. It would go down to defeat.

That was the opinion in Zürich. And what Zürich held to be true, international business did not debate.

But the Nachrichtendienst had found another truth.

So he was told.

The Duesenberg's powerful engine hummed; the car reached high speed; the passing autumn foliage blurred.

The stone gates of Strasser's estate came into view on the left, Wehrmacht eagles in bronze above each post. He swung into the long, winding drive and stopped at the gate guarded by two soldiers and snarling shepherd dogs. Altmüller thrust his papers at the first guard, who obviously expected him.

"Good morning, Herr Unterstaatssekretär. Please follow the drive to the right beyond the main house."

"Have the others arrived?"

"They are waiting, sir."

Altmüller maneuvered the car past the main house, reached the sloping drive and slowed down. Beyond the wooded bend was the guest cottage; it looked more like a hunting lodge than a residence. Heavy dark-brown beams everywhere; a part of the forest.

In the graveled area were four limousines. He parked and got out, pulling his tunic down, checking his lapels for lint. He stood erect and started toward the path to the door.

No names were ever used during a Nachrichtendienst conference; if identities were known—and certainly they had to be—they were never referred to in a meeting. One simply addressed his peer by looking at him, the group by gesture.

There was no long conference table as Altmüller had expected; no formal seating arrangement by some hidden protocol. Instead, a half dozen informally dressed men in their fifties and sixties were standing around the small room with the high Bavarian ceiling, chatting calmly, drinking coffee. Altmüller was welcomed as "Herr Unterstaatssekretär" and told that the morning's conference would be short. It would begin with the arrival of the final expected member.

Altmüller accepted a cup of coffee and tried to fall into the casual atmosphere. He was unable to do so; he wanted to roar his disapproval and demand immediate and serious talk. Couldn't they *understand?*

But this was the Nachrichtendienst. One didn't yell; one didn't demand.

Finally, after what seemed an eternity to his churning stomach, Altmüller heard an automobile outside the lodge. A few moments later the door opened; he nearly dropped his cup of coffee. The man who entered was known to him from the few times he had accompanied Speer to Berchtesgaden. He was the Führer's valet, but he had no subservient look of a valet now.

Without announcement, the men fell silent. Several sat in armchairs, others leaned against walls or stayed by the coffee table. An elderly man in a heavy tweed jacket stood in front of the fireplace and spoke. He looked at Franz, who remained by himself behind a leather couch.

"There is no reason for lengthy discussions. We believe we have the information you seek. I say 'believe,' for we gather information, we do not act upon it. The ministry may not care to act."

"That would seem inconceivable to me," said Altmüller.

"Very well. Several questions then. So there is no conflict, no misrepresentation." The old man paused and lit a thick meerschaum pipe. "You have exhausted all normal Intelligence channels? Through Zürich and Lisbon?"

"We have. And in numerous other locations—occupied, enemy and neutral."

"I was referring to the acknowledged conduits, Swiss, Scandinavian and Portuguese, primarily."

"We made no concentrated efforts in the Scandinavian countries. Herr Zangen did not think . . ."

"No names, please. Except in the area of Intelligence confrontation or public knowledge. Use governmental descriptions, if you like. Not individuals."

"The Reichsamt of Industry—which has continuous dealings in the Baltic areas—was convinced there was nothing to be gained there. I assume the reasons were geographical. There are no diamonds in the Baltic."

"Or they've been burnt too often," said a nondescript middle-aged man below Altmüller on the leather sofa. "If you want London and Washington to know what you're doing before you do it, deal with the Scandinavians."

"An accurate analysis," concurred another member of the Nachrichtendienst, this one standing by the coffee table, cup in hand. "I returned from Stockholm last week. We can't trust even those who publicly endorse us."

"Those least of all," said the old man in front of the fireplace, smiling and returning his eyes to Franz. "We gather you've made substantial offers? In Swiss currency, of course."

"Substantial is a modest term for the figures we've spoken of," replied Altmüller. "I'll be frank. No one will touch us. Those who could, subscribe to Zürich's judgment that

we shall be defeated. They fear retribution; they even
speak of postwar bank deposit reclamations."

"If such whispers reach the High Command there'll be
a panic." The statement was made humorously by the
Führer's valet, sitting in an armchair. The spokesman by
the fireplace continued.

"So you must eliminate money as an incentive . . . even
extraordinary sums of money."

"The negotiating teams were not successful. You know
that." Altmüller had to suppress his irritation. Why didn't
they get to the *point?*

"And there are no ideologically motivated defectors on
the horizon. Certainly none who have access to industrial
diamonds."

"Obviously, *mein Herr.*"

"So you must look for another motive. Another incentive."

"I fail to see the point of this. I was told . . ."

"You will," interrupted the old man, tapping his pipe on
the mantel. "You see, we've uncovered a panic as great
as yours. . . . The enemy's panic. We've found the most
logical motive for all concerned. Each side possesses the
other's solution."

Franz Altmüller was suddenly afraid. He could not be
sure he fully understood the spokesman's implications.
"What are you saying?"

"Peenemünde has perfected a high-altitude directional
guidance system, is this correct?"

"Certainly. Indigenous to the basic operation of the
rockets."

"But there'll be no rockets—or at best, a pitiful few—
without shipments of industrial diamonds."

"Obviously."

"There are business interests in the United States who
face insurmountable . . .," the old man paused for precisely one second and continued, "*insurmountable* problems that can only be resolved by the acquisition of functional high-altitude gyroscopes."

"Are you suggesting . . ."

"The Nachrichtendienst does not suggest, Herr Unterstaatssekretär. We say what is." The spokesman removed
the meerschaum from his lips. "When the occasion war-
rants, we transmit concrete information to diverse recipi-

ents. Again, only what is. We did so in Johannesburg. When the man I. G. Farben sent in to purchase diamonds from the Koening mines met with failure, we stepped in and confirmed a long-standing Intelligence probe we knew would be carried back to Washington. Our agents in California had apprised us of the crisis in the aircraft industry. We believe the timing was propitious."

"I'm not sure I understand. . . ."

"Unless we're mistaken, an attempt will be made to reestablish contact with one of the Farben men. We assume contingencies were made for such possibilities."

"Of course. Geneva. The acknowledged conduits."

"Then our business with you is concluded, sir. May we wish you a pleasant drive back to Berlin."

## DECEMBER 2, 1943, FAIRFAX, VIRGINIA

The interior of the Quonset belied its stark outside. To begin with, it was five times larger than the usual Quonset structure, and its metal casing was insulated with a sound-absorbing material that swept seamless down from the high ceiling. The appearance was not so much that of an airplane hangar—as it should have been—as of a huge, windowless shell with substantial walls. All around the immense room were banks of complicated high-frequency radio panels; opposite each panel were glass-enclosed casings with dozens of detailed maps, changeable by the push of a button. Suspended above the maps were delicate, thin steel arms—markers, not unlike polygraph needles—that were manipulated by the radio operators, observed by men holding clipboards. The entire staff was military, army, none below the rank of first lieutenant.

Three-quarters into the building was a floor-to-ceiling wall that obviously was not the end of the structure. There was a single door, centered and closed. The door was made of heavy steel.

Swanson had never been inside this particular building. He had driven down to Field Division, Fairfax, many times—to get briefed on highly classified Intelligence findings, to observe the training of particular insurgence or espionage teams—but for all his brigadier's rank and regardless of the secrets he carried around in his head, he

had not been cleared for this particular building. Those
who were, remained within the two-hundred-acre compound for weeks, months at a time; leaves were rare and
taken only in emergency and with escort.

It was fascinating, thought Swanson, who honestly
believed he had lost all sense of awe. No elevators, no
back staircases, no windows; he could see a washroom
door in the left wall and without going inside, knew it was
machine-ventilated. And there was only a single entrance.
Once inside there was no place for a person to conceal
himself for any length of time, or to exit without being
checked out and scrutinized. Personal items were left at
the entrance; no briefcases, envelopes, papers or materials were removed from the building without signed authorization by Colonel Edmund Pace and with the colonel
personally at the side of the individual in question.

If there was ever total security, it was here.

Swanson approached the steel door; his lieutenant
escort pushed a button. A small red light flashed above a
wall intercom, and the lieutenant spoke.

"General Swanson, colonel."

"Thank you, lieutenant," were the words that came
from the webbed circle below the light. There was a
click in the door's lock and the lieutenant reached for the
knob.

Inside, Pace's office looked like any other Intelligence
headquarters—huge maps on the walls, sharp lighting on
the maps, lights and maps changeable by pushbuttons on
the desk. Teletype machines were equidistant from one
another below printed signs designating theaters of operation—all the usual furnishings. Except the furniture itself.
It was simple to the point of primitiveness. No easy
chairs, no sofas, nothing comfortable. Just plain metal
straight-backed chairs, a desk that was more a table than
a desk, and a rugless hardwood floor. It was a room for
concentrated activity; a man did not relax in such a room.

Edmund Pace, Commander of Field Division, Fairfax,
got up from his chair, came around his table and saluted
Alan Swanson.

There was one other man in the room, a civilian.
Frederic Vandamm, Undersecretary of State.

"General. Good to see you again. The last time was at
Mr. Vandamm's house, if I remember."

"Yes, it was. How are things here?"

"A little isolated."

"I'm sure." Swanson turned to Vandamm. "Mr. Under-secretary? I got back here as soon as I could. I don't have to tell you how anxious I am. It's been a difficult month."

"I'm aware of that," said the aristocratic Vandamm, smiling a cautious smile, shaking Swanson's hand perfunctorily. "We'll get right to it. Colonel Pace, will you brief the general as we discussed?"

"Yes, sir. And then I'll leave." Pace spoke noncommittally; it was the military's way of telegraphing a message to a fellow officer: *be careful.*

Pace crossed to a wall map, presented with markings. It was an enlarged, detailed section of Johannesburg, South Africa. Frederic Vandamm sat in a chair in front of the desk; Swanson followed Pace and stood beside him.

"You never know when a probe will get picked up. Or where." Pace took a wooden pointer from a table and indicated a blue marker on the map. "Or even if the location is important. In this case it *may* be. A week ago a member of the Johannesburg legislature, an attorney and a former director of Koening Mines, Ltd., was contacted by what he believed were two men from the Zürich Staats-Bank. They wanted him to middle man a negotiation with Koening: simple transaction of Swiss francs for diamonds—on a large scale, with the anticipation that the diamond standard would remain more constant than the gold fluctuations." Pace turned to Swanson. "So far, so good. With lend-lease, and monetary systems going up in smoke everywhere, there's a lot of speculation in the diamond market. Postwar killings could be made. When he accepted the contact, you can imagine his shock when he arrived for the meeting and found that one of the 'Swiss' was an old friend—a very old and good friend—from the prewar days. A German he'd gone to school with—the Afrikaner's mother was Austrian; father a Boer. The two men had kept in close touch until thirty-nine. The German worked for I. G. Farben."

"What was the point of the meeting?" Swanson was impatient.

"I'll get to that. This background's important."

"O.K. Go on."

"There was no diamond market speculation involved, no transaction with any Zürich bank. It was a simple purchase. The Farben man wanted to buy large shipments of bortz and carbonado. . . ."

"Industrial diamonds?" interrupted Swanson.

Pace nodded. "He offered a fortune to his old friend if he could pull it off. The Afrikaner refused; but his long-standing friendship with the German kept him from reporting the incident. Until three days ago." Pace put down the pointer and started for his desk. Swanson understood that the colonel had additional information, written information, that he had to refer to; the general crossed to the chair beside Vandamm and sat down.

"Three days ago," continued Pace, standing behind the desk, "the Afrikaner was contacted again. This time there was no attempt to conceal identities. The caller said he was German and had information the Allies wanted; had wanted for a long time."

"The probe?" asked Swanson, whose impatience was carried by his tone of voice.

"Not exactly the probe we expected. . . . The German said he would come to the Afrikaner's office, but he protected himself. He told the lawyer that if any attempt was made to hold him, his old friend at I. G. Farben would be executed back in Germany." Pace picked up a sheet of paper from his desk. He spoke as he leaned across and handed it to Swanson. "This is the information, the report flown in by courier."

Swanson read the typewritten words below the Military Intelligence letterhead; above the large, stamped *Top Secret. Eyes Only. Fairfax 4–0.*

Nov. 28, 1943. Johannesburg: Confirmed by Nachrichtendienst. Substratospheric directional gyroscopes perfected. All tests positive. Peenemünde. Subsequent contact: Geneva. Johannesburg contingent.

Swanson let the information sink in; he read the statement over several times. He asked a question of Edmund Pace with a single word: "Geneva?"

"The conduit. Neutral channel. Unofficial, of course."

"What is this . . . Nachrichtendienst?"

"Intelligence unit. Small, specialized; so rarefied it's above even the most classified crowds. Sometimes we wonder if it takes sides. It often appears more interested in observing than participating; more concerned with after the war than now. We suspect that it's a Gehlen operation. But it's never been wrong. Never misleading."

"I see." Swanson held out the paper for Pace.

The colonel did not take it. Instead, he walked around the desk toward the steel door. "I'll leave you gentlemen. When you're finished, please signify by pushing the white button on my desk." He opened the door and left quickly. The heavy steel frame closed into an airtight position; a subsequent click could be heard in the lock housing.

Frederic Vandamm looked at Swanson. "There is your solution, general. Your gyroscope. In Peenemünde. All you have to do is send a man to Geneva. Someone wants to sell it."

Alan Swanson stared at the paper in his hand.

# 7

## DECEMBER 4, 1943, BERLIN, GERMANY

Altmüller stared at the paper in his hand. It was after midnight, the city in darkness. Berlin had withstood another night of murderous bombardment; it was over now. There would be no further raids until late morning, that was the usual pattern. Still, the black curtains were pulled tight against the windows. As they were everywhere in the ministry.

Speed was everything now. Yet in the swiftness of the planning, mandatory precautions could not be overlooked. The meeting in Geneva with the conduit was only the first step, the prelude, but it had to be handled delicately. Not so much *what* was said but *who* said it. The *what* could be transmitted by anyone with the proper credentials or acknowledged authority. But in the event of Germany's collapse, that *someone* could not represent the Third Reich. Speer had been adamant.

And Altmüller understood: if the war was lost, the label of traitor could not be traced to the Reichsministry. Or to those leaders Germany would need in defeat. In 1918 after Versailles, there had been mass internal recriminations. Polarization ran deep, unchecked, and the nation's paranoia over betrayal from within laid the groundwork for the fanaticism of the twenties. Germany had not been able to accept defeat, could not tolerate the destruction of its identity by traitors.

Excuses, of course.

But the prospects of repetition, no matter how remote, were to be avoided at all costs. Speer was himself fanatic on the subject. The Geneva representative was to be a figure isolated from the High Command. Someone from the ranks of German industry, in no way associated with the rulers of the Third Reich. Someone expendable.

Altmüller tried to point out the inconsistency of Speer's manipulation: high-altitude gyroscopic designs would hardly be given to an expendable mediocrity from German business. Peenemünde was buried—literally buried in the earth; its military security measures absolute.

But Speer would not listen, and Altmüller suddenly grasped the Reichsminister's logic. He was shifting the problem precisely where it belonged: to those whose lies and concealments had brought Peenemünde to the brink of disaster. And as with so much in the wartime Reich—the labor forces, the death camps, the massacres—Albert Speer conveniently looked away. He wanted positive results, but he would not dirty his tunic.

In this particular case, mused Altmüller, Speer was right. If there were to be risks of great disgrace, let German industry take them. Let the German businessman assume complete responsibility.

Geneva was vital only in the sense that it served as an introduction. Cautious words would be spoken that could —or could not—lead to the second stage of the incredible negotiation.

Stage two was geographical: the location of the exchange, should it actually take place.

For the past week, day and night, Altmüller had done little else but concentrate on this. He approached the problem from the enemy's viewpoint as well as his own. His worktable was covered with maps, his desk filled with scores of reports detailing the current political climates of every neutral territory on earth.

For the location had to be neutral; there had to be sufficient safeguards each side could investigate and respect. And perhaps most important of all, it had to be thousands of miles away . . . from either enemy's corridors of power.

Distance.

Remote.

Yet possessing means of instant communication.

South America.

*Buenos Aires.*

An inspired choice, thought Franz Altmüller. The Americans might actually consider it advantageous to them. It was unlikely that they would reject it. Buenos Aires had much each enemy considered its own; both had enormous influence, yet neither controlled with any real authority.

The third stage, as he conceived of it, was concerned with the human factor, defined by the word *Schiedsrichter*.

Referee.

A man who was capable of overseeing the exchange, powerful enough within the neutral territory to engineer the logistics. Someone who had the appearance of impartiality . . . above all, acceptable to the Americans.

Buenos Aires had such a man.

One of Hitler's gargantuan errors.

His name was Erich Rhinemann. A Jew, forced into exile, disgraced by Goebbels's insane propaganda machine, his lands and companies expropriated by the Reich.

Those lands and companies he had not converted before the misplaced thunderbolts struck. A minor percentage of his holdings, sufficient for the manic screams of the anti-Semitic press, but hardly a dent in his immense wealth.

Erich Rhinemann lived in exiled splendor in Buenos Aires, his fortunes secure in Swiss banks, his interests expanding throughout South America. And what few people knew was that Erich Rhinemann was a more dedicated fascist than Hitler's core. He was a supremacist in all things financial and military, an elitist with regard to the human condition. He was an empire builder who remained strangely—stoically—silent.

He had reason to be.

He would be returned to Germany regardless of the outcome of the war. He knew it.

If the Third Reich was victorious, Hitler's asinine edict would be revoked—as, indeed, might be the Führer's powers should he continue to disintegrate. If Germany went down to defeat—as Zürich projected—Rhinemann's expertise and Swiss accounts would be needed to rebuild the nation.

But these things were in the future. It was the present that mattered, and presently Erich Rhinemann was a Jew, forced into exile by his own countrymen, Washington's enemy.

He would be acceptable to the Americans.

And he would look after the Reich's interests in Buenos Aires.

Stages two and three, then, felt Altmüller, had the ring of clarity. But they were meaningless without an accord in Geneva. The prelude had to be successfully played by the minor instruments.

What was needed was a man for Geneva. An individual no one could link to the leaders of the Reich, but still one who had a certain recognition in the market place.

Altmüller continued to stare at the pages under the desk lamp. His eyes were weary, as he was weary, but he knew he could not leave his office or sleep until he had made the decision.

*His* decision; it was his alone. To be approved by Speer in the morning with only a glance. A name. Not discussed; someone instantly acceptable.

He would never know whether it was the letters in Johannesburg or the subconscious process of elimination, but his eyes riveted on one name, and he circled it. He recognized immediately that it was, again, an inspired choice.

Johann Dietricht, the bilious heir of Dietricht Fabriken; the unattractive homosexual given to alcoholic excess and sudden panic. A completely expendable member of the industrial community; even the most cynical would be reluctant to consider him a liaison to the High Command.

An expendable mediocrity.

A messenger.

## DECEMBER 5, 1943, WASHINGTON, D.C.

The bass-toned chimes of the clock on the mantel marked the hour somberly. It was six in the morning and Alan Swanson stared out the window at the dark buildings that were Washington. His apartment was on the twelfth floor, affording a pretty fair view of the capital's skyline, especially from the living room, where he now stood in his bathrobe, no slippers on his feet.

He had been looking at Washington's skyline most of the night . . . most of the hours of the night for the past three days. God knew what sleep he managed was fitful, subject to sudden torments and awakenings; and always there was the damp pillow that absorbed the constant perspiration that seeped from the pores in the back of his neck.

If his wife were with him, she would insist that he turn himself in to Walter Reed for a checkup. She would force the issue with constant repetition until he was nagged into submission. But she was *not* with him; he had been adamant. She was to remain with her sister in Scarsdale. The nature of his current activities was such that his hours were indeterminate. Translation: the army man had no time for his army wife. The army wife understood: there was a severe crisis and her husband could not cope with even her minor demands and the crisis, too. He did not like her to observe him in these situations; he knew she knew that. She would stay in Scarsdale.

*Oh, Christ! It was beyond belief!*

None said the words; perhaps no one allowed himself to think them.

That was it, of course. The few—and there were *very* few—who had access to the data turned their eyes and their minds away from the ultimate judgment. They cut off the transaction at midpoint, refusing to acknowledge the final half of the bargain. That half was for others to contend with. Not them.

As the wily old aristocrat Frederic Vandamm had done.

*There's your solution, general. Your guidance system. In Peenemünde. . . . Someone wants to sell it.*

That's all.

Buy it.

None wanted to know the price. The price was insignificant . . . let others concern themselves with details. Under no circumstances—*no circumstances*—were insignificant details to be brought up for discussion! They were merely to be expedited.

Translation: the chain of command depended upon the execution of general orders. It did not—repeat, *not*—require undue elaboration, clarification or justification. Specifics were an anathema; they consumed time. And by all that was military holy writ, the highest echelons *had* no time. Goddamn it, man, there was a *war on!* We must tend to the great military issues of state!

The garbage will be sorted out by lesser men . . . whose

hands may on occasion reek with the stench of their lesser
duties, but that's what the chain of command is all about.
*Buy it!*

*We have no time. Our eyes are turned. Our minds are
occupied elsewhere.*

Carry out the order on your own initiative as a good
soldier should who understands the chain of command. No
one will be inquisitive; it is the result that matters. We all
know that; the chain of command, old boy.

Insanity.

By the *strangest coincidence* an Intelligence probe is
returned by a man in Johannesburg through which the
purchase of industrial diamonds was sought. A purchase
for which a fortune in Swiss currency was tendered by
Germany's I. G. Farben, the armaments giant of the Third
Reich.

Peenemünde had the guidance system; it could be had.
For a price.

It did not take a major intellect to arrive at that price.

Industrial diamonds.

Insanity.

For reasons beyond inquiry, Germany desperately
needed the diamonds. For reasons all too clear, the Allies
desperately needed the high-altitude guidance system.

An exchange between enemies at the height of the bit-
terest war in the history of mankind.

Insanity. Beyond comprehension.

And so General Alan Swanson removed it from his immediate . . . totality.

The single deep chime of the clock intruded, signifying
the quarter hour. Here and there throughout the maze of
dark concrete outside, lights were being turned on in a
scattering of tiny windows. A greyish purple slowly began
to impose itself on the black sky; vague outlines of cloud
wisps could be discerned above.

In the higher altitudes.

Swanson walked away from the window to the couch
facing the fireplace and sat down. It had been twelve hours
ago . . . eleven hours and forty-five minutes, to be precise
. . . when he had taken the first step of *removal*.

He had placed . . . delegated the insanity where it belonged. To the men who had created the crisis; whose lies

and manipulations had brought Overlord to the precipice
of obscenity.

He had ordered Howard Oliver and Jonathan Craft to be
in his apartment at six o'clock. Twelve hours and fifteen
minutes ago. He had telephoned them on the previous day,
making it clear that he would tolerate no excuses. If transportation were a problem, he would resolve it, but they
were to be in Washington, in his apartment, by six o'clock.

Exposure was a viable alternative.

They had arrived at precisely six, as the somber chimes
of the mantel clock were ringing. At that moment Swanson
knew he was dealing from absolute strength. Men like
Oliver and Craft—especially Oliver—did not adhere to
such punctuality unless they were afraid. It certainly was
not courtesy.

The transference had been made with utter simplicity.

There was a telephone number in Geneva, Switzerland.
There was a man at that number who would respond to a
given code phrase and bring together two disparate parties,
act as an interpreter, if necessary. It was understood that
the second party—for purposes of definition—had access
to a perfected high-altitude guidance system. The first
party, in turn, should have knowledge of . . . perhaps
access to . . . shipments of industrial diamonds. The Koening mines of Johannesburg might be a place to start.

That was all the information they had.

It was recommended that Mr. Oliver and Mr. Craft act
on this information immediately.

If they failed to do so, extremely serious charges involving individual and corporate deceit relative to armaments
contracts would be leveled by the War Department.

There had been a long period of silence. The implications of his statement—with all its ramifications—were accepted gradually by both men.

Alan Swanson then added the subtle confirmation of
their worst projections: whoever was chosen to go to
Geneva, it could *not* be anyone known to him. Or to any
War Department liaison with *any* of their companies. That
was paramount.

The Geneva meeting was exploratory. Whoever went to
Switzerland should be knowledgeable and, if possible, capable of spotting deception. Obviously a man who practiced
deception.

That shouldn't be difficult for them; not in the circles they traveled. Surely they knew such a man.

They did. An accountant named Walter Kendall.

Swanson looked up at the clock on the mantel. It was twenty minutes past six.

Why did the time go so slowly? On the other hand, why didn't it stop? Why didn't everything stop but the sunlight? Why did there have to be the nights to go through?

In another hour he would go to his office and quietly make arrangements for one Walter Kendall to be flown on neutral routes to Geneva, Switzerland. He would bury the orders in a blue pouch along with scores of other transport directives and clearances. There would be no signature on the orders, only the official stamp of Field Division, Fairfax; standard procedure with conduits.

*Oh, Christ!* thought Swanson. If there could be control *... without participation.*

But he knew that was not possible. Sooner or later he would have to face the reality of what he had done.

# 8

*DECEMBER 6, 1943, BASQUE COUNTRY,
SPAIN*

He had been in the north country for eight days. He had
not expected it to be this long, but Spaulding knew it was
necessary . . . an unexpected dividend. What had begun as
a routine escape involving two defecting scientists from the
Ruhr Valley had turned into something else.

The scientists were throwaway bait. Gestapo bait. The
runner who had made their escape possible out of the Ruhr
was not a member of the German underground. He was
Gestapo.

It had taken Spaulding three days to be absolutely sure.
The Gestapo man was one of the best he had ever en-
countered, but his mistakes fell into a pattern: he was *not*
an experienced runner. When David *was* sure, he knew
exactly what had to be done.

For five days he led his "underground" companion
through the hills and mountain passes to the east as far as
Sierra de Guara, nearly a hundred miles from the clandestine escape routes. He entered remote villages and held
"conferences" with men he knew were Falangists—but
who did *not* know him—and then told the Gestapo man
they were partisans. He traveled over primitive roads and
down the Guayardo River and explained that these routes
were the avenues of escape. . . . Contrary to what the
Germans believed, the routes were to the *east*, into the
*Mediterranean, not* the Atlantic. This confusion was the
prime reason for the success of the Pyrenees network. On
two occasions he sent the Nazi into towns for supplies—
both times he followed and observed the Gestapo man

entering buildings that had thick telephone wires sagging into the roofs.

The information was being transmitted back to Germany. That was reason enough for the investment of five additional days. The German interceptors would be tied up for months concentrating on the eastern "routes"; the network to the west would be relatively unencumbered.

But now the game was coming to an end. It was just as well, thought David; he had work to do in Ortegal, on the Biscay coast.

The small campfire was reduced to embers, the night air cold. Spaulding looked at his watch. It was two in the morning. He had ordered the "runner" to stay on guard quite far from the campsite . . . out of the glow of the fire. In darkness. He had given the Gestapo man enough time and isolation to make his move, but the German had *not* made his move; he had remained at his post.

So be it, thought David. Perhaps the man wasn't as expert as he thought he was. Or perhaps the information his own men in the hills had given him was not accurate. There was no squad of German soldiers—suspected Alpine troops—heading down from the mountain borders to take out the Gestapo agent.

And him.

He approached the rock on which the German sat. "Get some rest. I'll take over."

"*Danke*," said the man, getting to his feet. "First, nature calls; I must relieve my bowels. I'll take a spade into the field."

"Use the woods. Animals graze here. The winds carry."

"Of course. You're thorough."

"I try to be," said David.

The German crossed back toward the fire, to his pack. He removed a camp shovel and started for the woods bordering the field. Spaulding watched him, now aware that his first impression was the correct one. The Gestapo agent *was* expert. The Nazi had not forgotten that six days ago the two Ruhr scientists had disappeared during the night—at a moment of the night when he had dozed. David had seen the fury in the German's eyes and knew the Nazi was now remembering the incident.

If Spaulding assessed the current situation accurately, the Gestapo man would wait at least an hour into his watch, to be sure he, David, was not making contact with unseen partisans in the darkness. Only then would the German give the signal that would bring the Alpine troops out of the forest. With rifles leveled.

But the Gestapo man had made a mistake. He had accepted too readily—without comment—Spaulding's statement about the field and the wind and the suggestion that he relieve himself in the woods.

They had reached the field during late daylight; it was barren, the grass was sour, the slope rocky. Nothing would graze here, not even goats.

And there was no wind at all. The night air was cold, but dead.

An experienced runner would have objected, no doubt humorously, and say he'd be damned if he'd take a crap in the pitch-black woods. But the Gestapo agent could not resist the gratuitous opportunity to make his own contact.

If there *was* such a contact to be made, thought Spaulding. He would know in a few minutes.

David waited thirty seconds after the man had disappeared into the forest. Then he swiftly, silently threw himself to the ground and began rolling his body over and over again, away from the rock, at a sharp angle from the point where the runner had entered the forest.

When he had progressed thirty-five to forty feet into the grass, he stood up, crouching, and raced to the border of the woods, judging himself to be about sixty yards away from the German.

He entered the dense foliage and noiselessly closed the distance between them. He could not see the man but he knew he would soon find him.

Then he saw it. The German's signal. A match was struck, cupped, and extinguished swiftly.

Another. This one allowed to burn for several seconds, then snuffed out with a short spit of breath.

From deep in the woods came two separate, brief replies. Two matches struck. In opposite directions.

David estimated the distance to be, perhaps, a hundred feet. The German, unfamiliar with the Basque forest, stayed close to the edge of the field. The men he had signaled were approaching. Spaulding—making no sound that disturbed the hum of the woods—crawled closer.

He heard the voices whispering. Only isolated words were distinguishable. But they were enough.

He made his way rapidly back through the overgrowth to his original point of entry. He raced to his sentry post, the rock. He removed a small flashlight from his field jacket, clamped separated fingers over the glass and aimed it southwest. He pressed the switch five times in rapid succession. He then replaced the instrument in his pocket and waited.

It wouldn't be long now.

It wasn't.

The German came out of the woods carrying the shovel, smoking a cigarette. The night was black, the moon breaking only intermittently through the thick cover of clouds; the darkness was nearly total. David got up from the rock and signaled the German with a short whistle. He approached him.

"What is it, Lisbon?"

Spaulding spoke quietly. Two words.

"Heil Hitler."

And plunged his short bayonet into the Nazi's stomach, ripping it downward, killing the man instantly.

The body fell to the ground, the face contorted; the only sound was a swallow of air, the start of a scream, blocked by rigid fingers thrust into the dead man's mouth, yanked downward, as the knife had been, shorting out the passage of breath.

David raced across the grass to the edge of the woods, to the left of his previous entry. Nearer, but not much, to the point where the Nazi had spoken in whispers to his two confederates. He dove into a cluster of winter fern as the moon suddenly broke through the clouds. He remained immobile for several seconds, listening for sounds of alarm.

There were none. The moon was hidden again, the darkness returned. The corpse in the field had not been spotted in the brief illumination. And that fact revealed to David a very important bit of knowledge.

Whatever Alpine troops were in the woods, they were not on the *edge* of the woods. Or if they were, they were not concentrating on the field.

They were waiting. Concentrating in other directions.

Or just waiting.

He rose to his knees and scrambled rapidly west through the dense underbrush, flexing his body and limbs to every bend in the foliage, making sounds compatible to the forest's tones. He reached the point where the three men had conferred but minutes ago, feeling no presence, seeing nothing.

He took out a box of waterproof matches from his pocket and removed two. He struck the first one, and the instant it flared, he blew it out. He then struck the second match and allowed it to burn for a moment or two before he extinguished it.

About forty feet in the woods there was a responding flash of a match. Directly north.

Almost simultaneously came a second response. This one to the west, perhaps fifty or sixty feet away.

No more.

But enough.

Spaulding quickly crawled into the forest at an angle. Northeast. He went no more than fifteen feet and crouched against the truck of an ant-ridden ceiba tree.

He waited. And while he waited, he removed a thin, short, flexible coil of wire from his field jacket pocket. At each end of the wire was a wooden handle, notched for the human hand.

The German soldier made too much noise for an Alpiner, thought David. He was actually hurrying, anxious to accommodate the unexpected command for rendezvous. That told Spaulding something else; the Gestapo agent he had killed was a demanding man. That meant the remaining troops would stay in position, awaiting orders. There would be a minimum of individual initiative.

There was no time to think of them now. The German soldier was passing the ceiba tree.

David sprang up silently, the coil held high with both hands. The loop fell over the soldier's helmet, the reverse pull so swift and brutally sudden that the wire sliced into the flesh of the neck with complete finality.

There was no sound but the expunging of air again.

David Spaulding had heard that sound so often it no longer mesmerized him. As it once had done.

Silence.

And then the unmistakable breaking of branches; foot-steps crushing the ground cover of an unfamiliar path. Rushing, impatient; as the dead man at his foot had been impatient.

Spaulding put the bloody coil of wire back into his pocket and removed the shortened carbine bayonet from the scabbard on his belt. He knew there was no reason to hurry; the third man would be waiting. Confused, fright-ened perhaps . . . but probably not, if he was an Alpiner. The Alpine troops were rougher than the Gestapo. The rumors were that the Alpiners were chosen primarily for streaks of sadism. Robots who could live in mountain passes and nurture their hostilities in freezing isolation until the orders for attack were given.

There was no question about it, thought David. There was a certain pleasure in killing Alpiners.

*The treadmill.*

He edged his way forward, his knife leveled.

"*Wer? . . . Wer ist dort?*" The figure in darkness whis-pered in agitation.

"*Hier, mein Soldat,*" replied David. His carbine bayonet slashed into the German's chest.


The partisans came down from the hills. There were five men, four Basque and one Catalonian. The leader was a Basque, heavyset and blunt.

"You gave us a wild trip, Lisbon. There were times we thought you were *loco*. Mother of God! We've traveled a hundred miles."

"The Germans will travel many times that, I assure you. What's north?"

"A string of Alpiners. Perhaps twenty. Every six kilo-meters, right to the border. Shall we let them sit in their wastes?"

"No," said Spaulding thoughtfully. "Kill them. . . . All but the last three; harass them back. They'll confirm what we want the Gestapo to believe."

"I don't understand."

"You don't have to." David walked to the dying fire and kicked at the coals. He had to get to Ortegal. It was all he could think about.

Suddenly he realized that the heavyset Basque had followed him. The man stood across the diminished campfire; he wanted to say something. He looked hard at David and spoke over the glow.

"We thought you should know now. We learned how the pigs made the contact. Eight days ago."

"What are you talking about?" Spaulding was irritated. Chains of command in the north country were at best a calculated risk. He would get the written reports; he did not want conversation. He wanted to sleep, wake up, and get to Ortegal. But the Basque seemed hurt; there was no point in that. "Go on, *amigo*."

"We did not tell you before. We thought your anger would cause you to act rashly."

"How so? Why?"

"It was Bergeron."

"I don't believe that. . . ."

"It is so. They took him in San Sebastián. He did not break easily, but they broke him. Ten days of torture . . . wires in the genitals, among other devices, including hypodermics of the drug. We are told he died spitting at them."

David looked at the man. He found himself accepting the information without feeling. *Without feeling.* And that lack of feeling warned him . . . to be on guard. He had trained the man named Bergeron, lived in the hills with him, talked for hours on end about things only isolation produces between men. Bergeron had fought with him, sacrificed for him. Bergeron was the closest friend he had in the north country.

Two years ago such news would have sent him into furious anger. He would have pounded the earth and called for a strike somewhere across the borders, demanding that retribution be made.

A year ago he would have walked away from the bearer of such news and demanded a few minutes to be by himself. A brief silence to consider . . . by himself . . . the whole of the man who had given his life, and the memories that man conjured up.

Yet now he felt nothing.

Nothing at all.

And it was a terrible feeling to feel nothing at all.

"Don't make that mistake again," he said to the Basque. "Tell me next time. I don't act rashly."

# 9

## DECEMBER 13, 1943, BERLIN, GERMANY

Johann Dietrich shifted his immense soft bulk in the
leather chair in front of Altmüller's desk. It was ten thirty
at night and he had not had dinner; there had been no
time. The Messerschmitt flight from Geneva had been
cramped, petrifying; and all things considered, Dietricht
was in a state of aggravated exhaustion. A fact he conveyed a number of times to the Unterstaatssekretär.

"We appreciate everything you've been through, Herr
Dietricht. And the extraordinary service you've rendered to
your country." Altmüller spoke solicitously. "This will take
only a few minutes longer, and then I'll have you driven
anywhere you like."

"A decent restaurant, if you can find one open at this
hour," said Dietricht petulantly.

"We apologize for rushing you away. Perhaps a pleasant
evening; a really good meal. Schnapps, good company.
Heaven knows you deserve it. . . . There's an inn several
miles outside the city. Its patronage is restricted; mostly
young flight lieutenants, graduates in training. The kitchen
is really excellent."

There was no need for Johann Dietricht to return
Altmüller's smiling look; he accepted certain things as indigenous to his life-style. He had been catered to for years.
He was a very important man, and other men were invariably trying to please him. As Herr Altmüller was trying to
please him now.

"That might be most relaxing. It's been a dreadful day.
Days, really."

"Of course, if you've some other . . ."

"No, no. I'll accept your recommendation. . . . Let's get on with it, shall we?"

"Very well. Going back over several points so there's no room for error. . . . The American was not upset with regard to Buenos Aires?"

"He jumped at it. Revolting man; couldn't look you in the eye, but he meant what he said. Simply revolting, though. His clothes, even his fingernails. Dirty fellow!"

"Yes, of course. But you couldn't have misinterpreted?"

"My English is fluent. I understand even the nuances. He was very pleased. I gathered that it served a dual purpose: far removed—thousands of miles away—and in a city nominally controlled by American interests."

"Yes, we anticipated that reaction. Did he have the authority to confirm it?"

"Indeed, yes. There was no question. For all his uncouth manner, he's obviously highly placed, very decisive. Unquestionably devious, but most anxious to make the exchange."

"Did you discuss—even peripherally—either's motives?"

"My word, it was unavoidable! This Kendall was most direct. It was a financial matter, pure and simple. There were no other considerations. And I believe him totally; he talks only figures. He reduces everything to numbers. I doubt he has capacities for anything else. I'm extremely perceptive."

"We counted on that. And Rhinemann? He, too, was acceptable?"

"Immaterial. I pointed out the calculated risk we were taking in an effort to allay suspicions; that Rhinemann was in forced exile. This Kendall was impressed only by Rhinemann's wealth."

"And the time element; we must be thoroughly accurate. Let's go over the projected dates. It would be disastrous if I made any mistake. As I understand you, the American had graduated estimates of carbonado and bortz shipping requirements. . . ."

"Yes, yes," broke in Dietricht, as if enlightening a child. "After all, he had no idea of our needs. I settled on the maximum, of course; there was not that much difference in terms of time. They must divert shipments from points of origin; too great a risk in commandeering existing supplies."

"I'm not sure I understand that. It could be a ploy."

"They're trapped in their own security measures. As of a month ago, every repository of industrial diamonds has excessive controls, dozens of signatures for every kiloweight. To extract our requirements would be massive, lead to exposure."

"The inconvenience of the democratic operation. The underlings are given responsibility. And once given, difficult to divest. Incredible."

"As this Kendall phrased it, there would be too many questions, far too many people would be involved. It would be very sensitive. Their security is filled with Turks."

"We have to accept the condition," said Altmüller with resignation—his own, not for the benefit of Dietricht. "And the anticipated time for these shipment diversions is four to six weeks. It can't be done in less?"

"Certainly. If we are willing to process the ore ourselves."

"Impossible. We could end up with tons of worthless dirt. We must have the finished products, of course."

"Naturally. I made that clear."

"It strikes me as an unnecessary delay. I have to look for inconsistencies, Herr Dietricht. And you said this Kendall was devious."

"But anxious. I said he was anxious, too. He drew an analogy that lends weight to his statements. He said that their problem was no less than that of a man entering the national vaults in the state of Kentucky and walking out with crates of gold bullion. . . . Are we concluded?"

"Just about. The conduit in Geneva will be given the name of the man in Buenos Aires? The man with whom we make contact?"

"Yes. In three or four days. Kendall believed it might be a scientist named Spinelli. An expert in gyroscopics."

"That title could be questioned, I should think. He's Italian?"

"A citizen, however."

"I see. That's to be expected. The designs will be subject to scrutiny, of course. What remains now are the checks and counterchecks each of us employ up to the moment of the exchange. A ritual dance."

"*Ach!* That's for your people. I'm out of it. I have made the initial and, I believe, the most important contribution."

"There's no question about it. And, I assume, you have abided by the Führer's trust in you, conveyed through this office. You have spoken to no one of the Geneva trip?"

"No one. The Führer's trust is not misplaced. He knows that. As my father and his brother, my uncle, the Dietricht loyalty and obedience are unswerving."

"He's mentioned that often. We are finished, *mein Herr*."

"Good! It's been absolutely nerve-wracking! . . . I'll accept your recommendation of the restaurant. If you'll make arrangements, I'll telephone for my car."

"As you wish, but I can easily have my personal driver take you there. As I said, it's somewhat restricted; my chauffeur is a young man who knows his way around." Altmüller glanced at Dietricht. Their eyes met for the briefest instant. "The Führer would be upset if he thought I inconvenienced you."

"Oh, very well. I suppose it *would* be easier. And we don't want the Führer upset." Dietricht struggled out of the chair as Altmüller rose and walked around the desk.

"Thank you, Herr Dietricht," said the Unterstaatssekretär, extending his hand. "When the time comes we will make known your extraordinary contribution. You are a hero of the Reich, *mein Herr*. It is a privilege to know you. The adjutant outside will take you down to the car. The chauffeur is waiting."

"Such a relief! Good evening, Herr Altmüller." Johann Dietricht waddled toward the door as Franz reached over and pushed a button on his desk.

In the morning Dietricht would be dead, the circumstances so embarrassing no one would care to elaborate on them except in whispers.

Dietricht, the misfit, would be eliminated.

And all traces of the Geneva manipulation to the leaders of the Reich canceled with him. Buenos Aires was now in the hands of Erich Rhinemann and his former brothers in German industry.

Except for him—for Franz Altmüller.

The true manipulator.

Swanson disliked the methods he was forced to employ. They were the beginnings, he felt, of an unending string of deceits. And he was not a deceitful man. Perhaps better than most at spotting deceitful men, but that was due to continuous exposure, not intrinsic characteristics.

The methods were distasteful: observing men who did not know they were being watched and listened to; who spoke without the inhibitions they certainly would have experienced had they any idea there were eyes and ears and wire recorders eavesdropping. It all belonged to that other world, Edmund Pace's world.

It had been easy enough to manipulate. Army Intelligence had interrogation rooms all over Washington. In the most unlikely places. Pace had given him a list of locations; he'd chosen one at the Sheraton Hotel. Fourth floor, Suite 4-M; two rooms in evidence and a third room that was not. This unseen room was behind the wall with openings of unidirectional glass in the two rooms of the suite. These observation holes were fronted by impressionist paintings hung permanently in the bedroom and the sitting room. Wire recorders with plug-in jacks were on shelves beneath the openings within the unseen room. Speakers amplified the conversation with minor distortion. The only visual obstructions were the light pastel colors of the paintings.

Not obstructions at all, really.

Neither had it been difficult to maneuver the three men to this room at the Sheraton. Swanson had telephoned Packard's Jonathan Craft and informed him that Walter Kendall was due in on an early afternoon flight from Geneva. The authoritative general also told the frightened civilian that it was possible the military might want to be in telephone communication. Therefore he suggested that Craft reserve a room at a busy, commercial hotel in the center of town. He recommended the Sheraton.

Craft was solicitous; he was running for his life. If the War Department suggested the Sheraton, then the Sheraton it would be. He had booked it without bothering to tell Meridian Aircraft's Howard Oliver.

The front desk took care of the rest.

When Walter Kendall had arrived an hour ago, Swanson was struck by the accountant's disheveled appearance. It was innate untidiness, not the result of traveling. A slovenliness that extended to his gestures, to his constantly darting eyes. He was an outsized rodent in the body of a medium-sized man. It seemed incongruous that men like Oliver and Craft—especially Craft—would associate with a Walter Kendall. Which only pointed up Kendall's value, he supposed. Kendall owned a New York auditing firm. He was a financial analyst, hired by companies to manipulate projections and statistics.

The accountant had not shaken hands with either man. He had gone straight to an easy chair opposite the sofa, sat down, and opened his briefcase. He had begun his report succinctly.

"The son of a bitch was a homo, I swear to Christ!"

As the hour wore on, Kendall described in minute detail everything that had taken place in Geneva. The quantities of bortz and carbonado agreed upon; the quality certifications; Buenos Aires; Gian Spinelli, the gyroscopic designs —*their* certifications and delivery; and the liaison, Erich Rhinemann, exiled Jew. Kendall was an authoritative rodent who was not awkward in the tunnels of negotiated filth. He was, in fact, very much at home.

"How can we be sure they'll bargain in good faith?" asked Craft.

"Good *faith?*" Kendall smirked and winced and grinned at the Packard executive. "You're too goddamned much. Good *faith!*"

"They might not give us the proper designs," continued Craft. "They could pass off substitutes, worthless substitutes!"

"He's got a point," said the jowled Oliver, his lips taut.

"And we could package crates of cut glass. You think that hasn't crossed their minds? . . . But they won't and we won't. For the same shit-eating reason. Our respective necks are on chopping blocks. We've got a common enemy and it's not each other."

Oliver, sitting across from Kendall, stared at the accountant. "Hitler's generals there; the War Department here."

"That's right. We're both lines of supply. For God, country and a dollar or two. And we're both in a lousy position. We don't tell the goddamned generals how to fight a war, and they don't tell us how to keep up production. If they screw up strategy or lose a battle, no screams come from us. But if we're caught short, if we don't deliver, those fuckers go after our necks. It's goddamned unfair. This homo Dietricht, he sees it like I do. We have to protect ourselves."

Craft rose from the couch; it was a nervous action, a gesture of doubt. He spoke softly, hesitantly. "This isn't exactly protecting ourselves in any normal fashion. We're dealing with the enemy."

"Which enemy?" Kendall shuffled papers on his lap; he did not look up at Craft. "But right, again. It's better than 'normal.' No matter who wins, we've each got a little something going when it's over. We agreed on that, too."

There was silence for several moments. Oliver leaned forward in his chair, his eyes still riveted on Kendall. "That's a dividend, Walter. There could be a lot of common sense in that."

"A lot," replied the accountant, allowing a short glance at Oliver. "We're kicking the crap out of their cities, bombing factories right off the map; railroads, highways— they're going up in smoke. It'll get worse. There's going to be a lot of money made putting it all back together. Reconstruction money."

"Suppose Germany wins?" asked Craft, by the window.

"Goddamned unlikely," answered Kendall. "It's just a question of how much damage is done to both sides, and we've got the hardware. The more damage, the more it'll cost to repair. That includes England. If you boys are smart, you'll be prepared to convert and pick up some of the postwar change."

"The diamonds. . . ." Craft turned from the window. "What are they for?"

"What difference does it make?" Kendall separated a page on his lap and wrote on it. "They ran out; their asses are in a sling. Same as yours with the guidance system. . . . By the way, Howard, did you have a preliminary talk with the mines?"

Oliver was deep in thought. He blinked and raised his eyes. "Yes. Koening. New York offices."

"How did you put it?"

"That it was top secret, War Department approval. The authorization would come from Swanson's office but even *he* wasn't cleared."

"They bought that?" The accountant was still writing.

"I said the money would be up front. They stand to make a few million. We met at the Bankers' Club."

"They bought it." A statement.

"Walter . . .," continued Oliver, "you said Spinelli before. I don't like it. He's a bad choice."

Kendall stopped writing and looked up at the Meridian man. "I didn't figure to tell him anything. Just that we were buying; he was to clear everything before we paid, make sure the designs were authentic."

"No good. He wouldn't be taken off the project. Not now; too many questions. Find somebody else."

"I see what you mean." Kendall put down the pencil. He picked his nose; it was a gesture of thought. "Wait a minute. . . . There *is* someone. Right in Pasadena. He's a weird son of a bitch, but he could be perfect." Kendall laughed while breathing through his mouth. "He doesn't even talk; I mean he *can't* talk."

"Is he any good?" asked Oliver.

"He's got problems but he may be better than Spinelli," replied Kendall, writing on a separate piece of paper. "I'll take care of it. . . . It'll cost you."

Oliver shrugged. "Include it in the overruns, you prick. What's next?"

"A contact in Buenos Aires. Someone who can deal with Rhinemann, work out the details of the transfer."

"Who?" asked Craft apprehensively, both hands clasped in front of him.

The accountant grinned, baring his discolored teeth. "You volunteering? You look like a priest."

"Good Lord, no! I was simply . . ."

"How much, Kendall?" interrupted Oliver.

"More than you want to pay but I don't think you've got a choice. I'll pass on what I can to Uncle Sam; I'll save you what I can."

"You do that."

"There's a lot of military down in Buenos Aires. Swanson will have to run some interference."

"He won't touch it," said Oliver quickly. "He was specific. He doesn't want to hear or see your name again."

"I don't give a shit if he does. But this Rhinemann's going to want certain guarantees. I can tell you that right now."

"Swanson will be upset." Craft's voice was high and intense. "We don't *want* him upset."

"Upset, shit! He wants to keep that pretty uniform nice and clean. . . . Tell you what, don't push him now. Give me some time; I've got a lot of things to figure out. Maybe I'll come up with a way to keep his uniform clean after all. Maybe I'll send him a bill."

*He wants to keep that pretty uniform nice and clean. . . .*
So devoutly to be wished, Mr. Kendall, thought Swanson as he approached the bank of elevators.

But not possible now. The uniform had to get dirty. The emergence of a man named Erich Rhinemann made that necessary.

Rhinemann was one of Hitler's fiascos. Berlin knew it; London and Washington knew it. Rhinemann was a man totally committed to power: financial, political, military. For him all authority must emanate from a single source and he would ultimately settle for nothing less than being at the core of that source.

The fact that he was a Jew was incidental. An inconvenience to end with the end of the war.

When the war was over, Erich Rhinemann would be called back. What might be left of German industry would demand it; the world's financial leaders would demand it.

Rhinemann would reenter the international market place with more power than ever before.

Without the Buenos Aires manipulation.
*With* it his leverage would be extraordinary.

His knowledge, his participation in the exchange would provide him with an unparalleled weapon to be used against all sides, all governments.

Especially Washington.

Erich Rhinemann would have to be eliminated.

After the exchange.

And if only for this reason, Washington had to have another man in Buenos Aires.

# 10

conver...

*DECEMBER 16, 1943,*
*WASHINGTON, D.C.*

It was unusual for the ranking officer of Fairfax to leave the compound for any reason, but Colonel Edmund Pace was so ordered.

Pace stood in front of General Swanson's desk and began to understand. Swanson's instructions were brief, but covered more territory than their brevity implied. Intelligence files would have to be culled from dozens of double-locked cabinets, a number examined minutely.

Swanson knew that at first Pace disapproved. The Fairfax commander could not conceal his astonishment—at first. The agent in question had to be fluent in both German and Spanish. He had to have a working knowledge—not expert but certainly more than conversational—of aircraft engineering, including metallurgical dynamics and navigational systems. He had to be a man capable of sustaining a cover perhaps on the embassy level. That meant an individual possessing the necessary graces to function easily in monied circles, in the diplomatic arena.

At this juncture Pace had balked. His knowledge of the Johannesburg probe and the Geneva conduit caused him to object. He interrupted Swanson, only to be told to hold his remarks until his superior had finished.

The last qualification of the man for Buenos Aires—and the general conceded its inconsistency when included with the previous technical qualifications—was that the agent be experienced in "swift dispatch."

The man was to be no stranger to killing. Not combat fire with its adversaries separated, pitched into frenzy by the sights and sounds of battle. But a man who could kill in silence, facing his target. Alone.

This last qualification mollified Pace. His expression conveyed the fact that whatever his superiors were involved in, it was not wholly what he suspected it to be—might be. The War Department did not request such a man if it intended to keep surface agreements.

The ranking officer of Fairfax made no comment. It was understood that he, alone, would make the file search. He asked for a code, a name to which he could refer in any communications.

Swanson had leaned forward in his chair and stared at the map on his desk. The map that had been there for over three hours.

"Call it 'Tortugas,' " he said.

## DECEMBER 18, 1943, BERLIN, GERMANY

Altmüller stared at the unbroken seal on the wide, brown manila envelope. He moved it under his desk lamp and took a magnifying glass from his top drawer. He examined the seal under the magnification; he was satisfied. It had not been tampered with.

The embassy courier had flown in from Buenos Aires— by way of Senegal and Lisbon—and delivered the envelope in person, as instructed. Since the courier was based permanently in Argentina, Altmüller did not want him carrying back gossip, so he indulged the man in innocuous conversation, referring to the communication several times in an offhand, derogatory manner. He implied it was a nuisance—a memorandum concerned with embassy finances and really belonged at the Finanzministerium, but what could he do? The ambassador was reputed to be an old friend of Speer's.

Now that the courier was gone and the door shut, Altmüller riveted his attention on the envelope. It was from Erich Rhinemann.

He sliced open the top edge. The letter was written by hand, in Rhinemann's barely decipherable script.

My Dear Altmüller:

To serve the Reich is a privilege I undertake with enthusiasm. I am, of course, grateful for your assurances that my efforts will be made known to my many old friends. I assumed you would do no less under the circumstances.

You will be pleased to know that in the coastal waters from Punta Delgada north to the Caribbean, my ships are honored under the neutrality of the Paraguayan flag. This convenience may be of service to you. Further, I have a number of vessels, notably small and medium-sized craft converted with high-performance engines. They are capable of traveling swiftly through the coastal waters, and there are refueling depots, thus enabling considerable distances to be traversed rapidly. Certainly no comparison to the airplane, but then the trips are made in utter secrecy, away from the prying eyes that surround all airfields these days. Even we neutrals must constantly outflank the blockades.

This information should answer the curiously obscure questions you raised.

I beg you to be more precise in future communications. Regardless, you may be assured of my commitment to the Reich.

Along these lines, associates in Berne inform me that your Führer is showing marked signs of fatigue. It was to be expected, was it not?

Remember, my dear Franz, the concept is always a greater monument than the man. In the current situation, the concept came *before* the man. *It* is the monument.

I await word from you.

                                        Erich Rhinemann

How delicately unsubtle was Rhinemann! . . . *commitment to the Reich . . . associates in Berne . . . marked signs of fatigue . . . to be expected. . . .*

*. . . a greater monument than the man. . . .*

Rhinemann spelled out his abilities, his financial power, his "legitimate" concerns and his unequivocal commitment to Germany. By including, *juxtaposing* these factors, he elevated himself above even the Führer. And by so doing, condemned Hitler—for the greater glory of the Reich. No doubt Rhinemann had photostats made of his letter; Rhinemann would start a very complete file of the Buenos Aires operation. And one day he would use it to maneuver himself to the top of postwar Germany. Perhaps of all Europe. For he would have the weapon to guarantee his acceptance.

In victory *or* defeat. Unswerving devotion or, conversely, blackmail of such proportions the Allies would tremble at the thought of it.

So be it, thought Altmüller. He had no brief with Rhinemann. Rhinemann was an expert at whatever he entered into. He was methodical to the point of excess; conservative in progress—only in the sense of mastering all details before going forward. Above everything, he was boldly imaginative.

Altmüller's eyes fell on Rhinemann's words:

*I beg you to be more precise in future communications.*

Franz smiled. Rhinemann was right. He *had* been obscure. But for a sound reason: he wasn't sure where he was going; where he was being led, perhaps. He only knew that the crates of carbonado diamonds had to be thoroughly examined, and that would take time. More time than Rhinemann realized if the information he had received from Peenemünde was accurate. According to Peenemünde, it would be a simple matter for the Americans to pack thousands of low-quality bortz that, to the inexperienced eye, would be undetectable. Stones that would crack at the first touch to steel.

If the operation was in the hands of the British, that would be the expected maneuver.

And even the Americans had decent Intelligence manipulators. *If* the Intelligence services were intrinsic to the exchange. Yet Altmüller doubted their active involvement. The Americans were governmentally hypocritical. They would make demands of their industrialists and expect those demands to be met. However, they would close their eyes to the methods; the unsophisticated Puritan streak was given extraordinary lip service in Washington.

Such children. Yet angry, frustrated children were dangerous.

The crates would have to be examined minutely.

In Buenos Aires.

And once accepted, no risks could be taken that the crates would be blown out of the sky or the water. So it seemed logical to ask Rhinemann what avenues of escape were available. For somewhere, somehow, the crates would have to make rendezvous with the most logical method of transportation back to Germany.

Submarine.

Rhinemann would understand; he might even applaud the precision of future communications.

Altmüller got up from his desk and stretched. He walked absently around his office, trying to rid his back of the cramps resulting from sitting too long. He approached the leather armchair in which Johann Dietricht had sat several days ago.

Dietricht was dead. The expendable, misfit messenger had been found in a bloodsoaked bed, the stories of the evening's debauchery so demeaning that it was decided to bury them and the body without delay.

Altmüller wondered if the Americans had the stomach for such decisions.

He doubted it.

## DECEMBER 19, 1943, FAIRFAX, VIRGINIA

Swanson stood silently in front of the heavy steel door inside the Quonset structure. The security lieutenant was on the wall intercom for only the length of time it took for him to give the general's name. The lieutenant nodded, replaced the phone, saluted the general for a second time. The heavy steel door clicked and Swanson knew he could enter.

The Fairfax commander was alone, as Swanson had ordered. He was standing to the right of his table-desk, a file folder in his hand. He saluted his superior.

"Good morning, general."

"Morning. You worked fast; I appreciate it."

"It may not be everything you want but it's the best we can come up with. . . . Sit down, sir. I'll describe the qualifications. If they meet with your approval, the file's yours. If not, it'll go back into the vaults."

Swanson walked to one of the straight-backed chairs in

front of the colonel's desk and sat down. He did so with a touch of annoyance. Ed Pace, as so many of his subordinates in Clandestine Operations, functioned as though he were responsible to no one but God; and even He had to be cleared by Fairfax. It struck Swanson that it would be much simpler if Pace simply gave him the file and let him read it for himself.

On the other hand, Fairfax's indoctrination had at its core the possibility—however remote—that any pair of eyes might be captured by the enemy. A man could be in Washington one week, Anzio or the Solomons the next. There was logic in Pace's methods; a geographical network of underground agents could be exposed with a single break in the security chain.

Still, it was annoying as hell. Pace seemed to enjoy his role; he was humorless, thought Swanson.

"The subject under consideration is a proven field man. He's acted as independently as anyone in one of our touchiest locations. Languages: acceptable fluency. Deportment and cover: extremely flexible. He moves about the civilian spectrum facilely, from embassy teacups to bricklayers' saloons—he's very mobile and convincing."

"You're coming up with a positive print, colonel."

"If I am, I'm sorry. He's valuable where he is. But you haven't heard the rest. You may change your mind."

"Go on."

"On the negative side, he's not army. I don't mean he's a civilian—he holds the rank of captain, as a matter of fact, but I don't think he's ever used it. What I'm saying is that he's never operated within a chain of command. He set up the network; he *is* the command. He has been for nearly four years now."

"Why is that negative?"

"There's no way to tell how he reacts to discipline. Taking orders."

"There won't be much latitude for deviation. It's cut and dried."

"Very well. . . . A second negative; he's not aeronautical. . . ."

"That *is* important!" Swanson spoke harshly; Pace was wasting his time. The man in Buenos Aires had to understand what the hell was going on; perhaps more than understand.

"He's in a related field, sir. One that our people say primes him for crash instructions."

"What is it?"

"He's a construction engineer. With considerable experience in mechanical, electrical and metal design. His background includes full responsibility for whole structures—from foundations through the finished productions. He's a blueprint expert."

Swanson paused, then nodded noncommittally. "All right. Go on."

"The most difficult part of your request was to find someone—someone with these technical qualifications—who had practical experience in 'dispatch.' You even conceded that."

"I know." Swanson felt it was the time to show a little more humanity. Pace looked exhausted; the search had not been easy. "I handed you a tough one. Does your nonmilitary, mobile engineer have any 'dispatches' of record?"

"We try to avoid records, because . . ."

"You know what I mean."

"Yes. He's stationed where it's unavoidable, I'm sorry to say. Except for the men in Burma and India, he's had more occasions to use last-extremity solutions than anyone in the field. To our knowledge, he's never hesitated to implement them."

Swanson started to speak, then hesitated. He creased his brow above his questioning eyes. "You can't help but wonder about such men, can you?"

"They're trained. Like anyone else they do a job . . . for a purpose. He's not a killer by nature. Very few of our really good men are."

"I've never understood your work, Ed. Isn't that strange?"

"Not at all. I couldn't possibly function in your end of the War Department. Those charts and graphs and civilian double-talkers confuse me. . . . How does the subject sound to you?"

"You have no alternates?"

"Several. But with each there's the same negative. Those that have the languages *and* the aeronautical training have no experience in 'dispatch.' No records of . . . extreme prejudice. I worked on the assumption that it was as important as the other factors."

"Your assumption was correct. . . . Tell me, do you know him?"

"Very well. I recruited him, I observed every phase of his training. I've seen him in the field. He's a pro."

"I want one."

"Then maybe he's your man. But before I say it, I'd like to ask you a question. I have to ask it, actually; I'll be asked the same question myself."

"I hope I can give you an answer."

"It's within bounds. It's not specific."

"What is it?"

Pace came to the edge of the desk toward Swanson. He leaned his back against it and folded his arms. It was another army signal: *I'm your subordinate but this puts us on equal footing right now—at this moment.*

"I said the subject was valuable where he is. That's not strong enough. He's *in*valuable, essential. By removing him from his station we jeopardize a very sensitive operation. We can handle it, but the risks are considerable. What I have to know is, does the assignment justify his transfer?"

"Let me put it this way, colonel," said Swanson, the tone of his voice gentle but strong. "The assignment has no priority equal, with the possible exception of the Manhattan Project. You've heard of the Manhattan Project, I assume."

"I have." Pace got off his desk. "And the War Department—through your office—will confirm this priority?"

"It will."

"Then here he is, general." Pace handed Swanson the file folder. "He's one of the best we've got. He's our man in Lisbon. . . . Spaulding. Captain David Spaulding."

# 11

## *DECEMBER 26, 1943, RIBADAVIA, SPAIN*

David sped south on the motorcycle along the dirt road paralleling the Minho River. It was the fastest route to the border, just below Ribadavia. Once across he would swing west to an airfield outside Valença. The flight to Lisbon would take another two hours, if the weather held and if an aircraft was available. Valença didn't expect him for another two days; its planes might all be in use.

His anxiety matched the intensity of the spinning, careening wheels beneath him. It was all so extraordinary; it made no *sense* to him. There was *no one* in *Lisbon* who could issue such orders as he had received from Ortegal!

What had *happened?*

He felt suddenly as though a vitally important part of his existence was being threatened. And then he wondered at his own reaction. He had no love for his temporary world; he took no pleasure in the countless manipulations and countermanipulations. In fact, he despised most of his day-to-day activities, was sick of the constant fear, the unending high-risk factors to be evaluated with every decision.

Yet he recognized what bothered him so: he had grown in his work. He had arrived in Lisbon centuries ago, beginning a new life, and he had mastered it. Somehow it signified all the buildings he wanted to build, all the blueprints he wanted to turn into mortar and steel. There was precision and finality in his work; the results were there every day. Often many times every day. Like the hundreds of details in construction specifications, the information came to him and he put it all together and emerged with reality.

And it was this reality that others depended upon.

Now someone wanted him out of Lisbon! Out of Portugal and Spain! Was it as simple as that? Had his reports angered one general too many? Had a strategy session been nullified because he sent back the truth of a supposedly successful operation? Were the London and Washington brass finally annoyed to the point of removing a critical thorn? It was possible; he had been told often enough that the men in the underground rooms in London's Tower Road had exploded more than once over his assessments. He knew that Washington's Office of Strategic Services felt he was encroaching on their territory; even G-2, ostensibly his own agency, criticized his involvement with the escape teams.

But beyond the complaints there was one evaluation that overrode them all: he was good. He had welded together the best network in Europe.

Which was why David was confused. And not a little disturbed, for a reason he tried not to admit: he needed praise.

There were no buildings of consequence, no extraordinary blueprints turned into more extraordinary edifices. Perhaps there never would be. He would be a middle-aged engineer when it was over. A middle-aged engineer who had not practiced his profession in years, not even in the vast army of the United States, whose Corps of Engineers was the largest construction crew in history.

He tried not to think about it.

He crossed the border at Mendoso, where the guards knew him as a rich, irresponsible expatriate avoiding the risks of war. They accepted his gratuities and waved him over.

The flight from Valença to the tiny airfield outside Lisbon was hampered by heavy rains. It was necessary to put down twice—at Águeda and Pombal—before the final leg. He was met by an embassy vehicle; the driver, a cryptographer named Marshall, was the only man in the embassy who knew his real function.

"Rotten weather, isn't it?" said the code man, settling behind the wheel as David threw his pack in the back seat. "I don't envy you up in a crate like that. Not in this rain."

"Those grass pilots fly so low you could jump down. I worry more about the trees."

"I'd just worry." Marshall started up and drove toward the broken-down pasture gate that served as the field's entrance. On the road he switched on his high beams; it was not yet six o'clock, but the sky was dark, headlights necessary. "I thought you might flatter me and ask why an expert of my standing was acting as chauffeur. I've been here since four. Go on, ask me. It was a hell of a long wait."

Spaulding grinned. "Jesus, Marsh, I just figured you were trying to get in my good graces. So I'd take you north on the next trip. Or have I been made a brigadier?"

"You've been made something, David." Marshall spoke seriously. "I took the D.C. message myself. It was that high up in the codes: eyes-only, senior cryp."

"I'm flattered," said Spaulding softly, relieved that he could talk to someone about the preposterous news of his transfer. "What the hell is it all about?"

"I have no idea what they want you for, of course, but I can spell out one conclusion: they want you yesterday. They've covered all avenues of delay. The orders were to compile a list of your contacts with complete histories of each: motives, dates, repeats, currency, routings, codes . . . everything. Nothing left out. Subsequent order: alert the whole network that you're out of strategy."

"*Out of . . .*" David trailed off the words in disbelief. *Out of strategy* was a phrase used as often for defectors as it was for transfers. Its connotation was final, complete breakoff. "That's insane! This is *my network!*"

"Not anymore. They flew a man in from London this morning. I think he's Cuban; rich, too. Studied architecture in Berlin before the war. He's been holed up in an office studying your files. He's your replacement. . . . I wanted you to know."

David stared at the windshield, streaked with the harsh Lisbon rain. They were on the hard-surface road that led through the Alfama district, with its winding, hilly streets below the cathedral towers of the Moorish St. George and the Gothic Sé. The American embassy was in the Baixa, past the Terreiro do Paço. Another twenty minutes.

So it was really over, thought Spaulding. They were sending him out. A Cuban architect was now the man in

Lisbon. The feeling of being dispossessed took hold of him again. So much was being taken away and under such extraordinary conditions. *Out of strategy* . . .

"Who signed the orders?"

"That's part of the craziness. The use of high codes presumes supreme authority; no one else has access. But no one signed them, either. No name other than yours was in the cable."

"What am I supposed to do?"

"You get on a plane tomorrow. The flight time will be posted by tonight. The bird makes one stop. At Lajes Field on Terceira, the Azores. You pick up your orders there."

# 12

Swanson reached for the tiny lever on his desk intercom and spoke: "Send Mr. Kendall in." He stood up, remaining where he was, waiting for the door to open. He would not walk around his desk to greet the man; he would not offer his hand in even a symbol of welcome. He recalled that Walter Kendall had avoided shaking hands with Craft and Oliver at the Sheraton. The handshake would not be missed; his avoidance of it, however, might be noted.

Kendall entered; the door closed. Swanson saw that the accountant's appearance had changed little since the afternoon conference he had observed from the unseen room eleven days ago. Kendall wore the same suit, conceivably the same soiled shirt. God knew about his underwear; it wasn't a pleasant thought to dwell on. There was the slightest curl on Kendall's upper lip. It did not convey anger or even disdain. It was merely the way the man breathed: mouth and nostrils simultaneously. As an animal might breathe.

"Come in, Mr. Kendall. Sit down."

Kendall did so without comment. His eyes locked briefly with Swanson's but only briefly.

"You're listed on my appointment calendar as being called in to clarify a specific overrun on a Meridian contract," said the general, sitting down promptly. "Not to justify, simply enumerate. As the . . . outside auditing firm you can do that."

"But that's not why I'm here, is it?" Kendall reached into his pocket for a crumpled pack of cigarettes. He squeezed the end before lighting one. Swanson noted that the accountant's fingernails were unkempt, ragged, soiled at the tips. The brigadier began to see—but would not ponder it—that there was a sickness about Walter Kendall, the surface appearance merely one manifestation.

"No, that's not why you're here," he answered curtly. "I want to set up ground rules so neither of us misunderstands. . . . So *you* don't misunderstand, primarily."

"Ground rules mean a game. What's the game we're playing, general?"

"Perhaps . . . 'Clean Uniforms' might be a good name for it. Or how to run some 'Interference in Buenos Aires.' That might strike you as more inclusive."

Kendall, who had been gazing at his cigarette, abruptly shifted his eyes to the general. "So Oliver and Craft couldn't wait. They had to bring their teacher his big fat apple. I didn't think you wanted it."

"Neither Craft nor Howard Oliver has been in touch with this office—or with me—in over a week. Since you left for Geneva."

Kendall paused before speaking. "Then your uniform's pretty goddamned dirty now. . . . The Sheraton. I thought that was a little unritzy for Craft; he's the Waldorf type. . . . So you had the place *wired*. You trapped those fuckers." Kendall's voice was hoarse, not angry, not loud. "Well, you just remember how I got to where I was going. How I got to Geneva. You got that on the wire, too."

"We accommodated a request of the War Production Board; relative to a business negotiation with a firm in Geneva. It's done frequently. However, we often follow up if there's reason to think *anything prejudicial. . . .*"

"Horseshit!"

Swanson exhaled an audible breath. "That reaction is pointless. I don't want to argue with you. The *point* has been *made*. I have an . . . edited spool of wire that could send you straight to the hangman or the electric chair. Oliver, too. . . . Craft might get off with a life sentence. You ridiculed his doubts; you didn't let him talk. . . . The point, however, *has been made*."

Kendall leaned forward and crushed out his cigarette in an ashtray on Swanson's desk. His sudden fear made him look at the general; he was searching. "But you're more interested in Buenos Aires than the electric chair. That's right, isn't it?"

"I'm forced to be. As distasteful as it may be to me. As loathsome. . . ."

"Cut out the horseshit," Kendall interrupted sharply; he was no amateur in such discussions. He knew when to assert himself and his contributions. "As you said, the point's been made. I think you're in the barnyard with the rest of us pigs. . . . So don't play Jesus. Your halo smells."

"Fair enough. But don't you forget, I've got a dozen different pigsties to run to. A great big War Department that could get me to Burma or Sicily in forty-eight hours. You don't. You're right out there . . . in the barnyard. For everyone to see. And I've got a spool of wire that would make you *special*. *That's* the understanding I want you to have clear in your mind. I hope it is."

Kendall squeezed the tip of a second cigarette and lit the opposite end. The smoke drifted over his nostrils; he was about to speak, then stopped, staring at the general, his look a mixture of fear and hostility.

Swanson found himself consciously avoiding Kendall's eyes. To acknowledge the man at that moment was to acknowledge the pact. And then he realized what would make the pact bearable. It was the answer, *his* answer; at least a surface one. He was amazed it had not occurred to him before this moment.

Walter Kendall would have to be eliminated.

As Erich Rhinemann would be eliminated.

When Buenos Aires was in reach of completion, Kendall's death was mandatory.

And then all specific traces to the government of the United States would be covered.

He wondered briefly if the men in Berlin had the foresight for such abrupt decisions. He doubted it.

He looked up at the filthy—sick—accountant and returned his stare in full measure. General Alan Swanson was no longer afraid. Or consumed with guilt.

He was a soldier.

"Shall we continue, Mr. Kendall?"

The accountant's projections for Buenos Aires were well thought out. Swanson found himself fascinated by Walter Kendall's sense of maneuver and countermeasure. The man thought like a sewer rat: instinctively, probing sources of smell and light; his strength in his suspicions, in his constantly varying estimates of his adversaries. He was indeed an animal: predator and evader.

The Germans' prime concerns could be reduced to three: the quality of the bortz and carbonado diamonds; the quantity of the shipment; and finally the methods of safe transport to Germany. Unless these factors could be guaranteed, there would be no delivery of the gyroscopic designs—the guidance system.

Kendall assumed that the shipment of diamonds would be inspected by a team of experts—not one man or even two.

A team, then, three to five men, would be employed; the length of time required might extend to the better part of a week, depending upon the sophistication of the instruments used. This information he had learned from Koening in New York. During this period simultaneous arrangements would be agreed to that allowed an aerophysicist to evaluate the gyroscopic designs brought from Peenemünde. If the Nazis were as cautious as Kendall assumed they would be, the designs would be delivered in stages, timed to the schedule the inspection team considered adequate for its examination of the diamonds. The gyroscope scientist would no doubt be fed step-blueprints in isolation, with no chance of photostat or duplication until the diamond team had completed its work.

Once both sides were satisfied with the deliveries, Kendall anticipated that an ultimate threat would be imposed that guaranteed safe transport to the respective destinations. And it was logical that this "weapon" be identical for each party: threat of exposure. Betrayal of cause and country.

Penalties: death.

The same "weapon" the general held on him, on Walter Kendall.

What else was new?

Did Kendall think it was possible to get the designs and subsequently sabotage or reclaim the diamond shipment?

No. Not as long as it remained a civilian exchange. The threat of exposure was too complete; there was too much proof of contact. Neither crisis could be denied and names were known. The taint of collaboration could ruin men and corporations. "Authenticated" rumors could be circulated easily.

And if the military moved in, the civilians would move

out instantly—the responsibility of delivery no longer theirs.

Swanson should know this; it was precisely the situation he had engineered.

Swanson knew it.

Where would the diamonds be inspected? Where was the most advantageous location?

Kendall's reply was succinct: any location that seemed advantageous to one side would be rejected by the other. He thought the Germans foresaw this accurately and for that reason suggested Buenos Aires. It was on the spool of wire. Didn't Swanson listen?

Powerful men in Argentina were unquestionably, if quietly, pro-Axis, but the government's dependency on Allied economics took precedence. The neutrality essentially was controlled by the economic factors. Each side, therefore, had something: the Germans would find a sympathetic environment, but the Americans were capable of exerting a strong enough influence to counteract that sympathy—without eliminating it.

Kendall respected the men in Berlin who centered in on Buenos Aires. They understood the necessity of balancing the psychological elements, the need to give up, yet still retain spheres of influence. They were good.

Each side would be extremely cautious; the environment demanded it. Timing would be everything.

Swanson knew how the designs would be gotten out: a string of pursuit aircraft flying up the coastal bases under diplomatic cover. This cover would extend to the military. Only *he* would be aware of the operation; no one else in the services or, for that matter, in the government would be apprised. He would make the arrangements and give them to Kendall at the proper time.

What transport would the Germans arrive at? asked the general.

"They've got a bigger problem. They recognize it so they'll probably make some kind of airtight demands. They could ask for a hostage, but I don't think so."

"Why not?"

"Who've we got—that's involved—that's not expendable? Christ! If it was me, you'd be the first to say, 'Shoot the son of a bitch!'" Kendall again locked his eyes briefly with Swanson's. "Of course, you wouldn't know what particular safeguards *I* took; a lot of uniforms would be dirty as hell."

Swanson recognized Kendall's threat for what it was. He also knew he could handle it. It would take some thought, but such considerations could come later. It would be no insurmountable hurdle to prepare for Kendall's dispatch. The isolation would come first; then an elaborate dossier. . . .

"Let's concentrate on how they expect to ship out the bortz and carbonado. There's no point in going after each other," said Swanson.

"We're beyond that, then?"

"I think we are."

"Good. Just don't forget it," said Kendall.

"The diamonds will be brought to Buenos Aires. Have those arrangements been made?"

"They're being made. Delivery date in three, three-and-a-half weeks. Unless there's a fuck-up in the South Atlantic. We don't expect any."

"The inspection team does its work in Buenos Aires. We send the physicist . . . who will it be? Spinelli?"

"No. For both our sakes we ruled him out. But you know that. . . ."

"Yes. Who, then?"

"Man named Lyons. Eugene Lyons. I'll get you a file on him. You'll sweat bullets when you read it, but if there's anyone better than Spinelli, it's him. We wouldn't take any chances. He's in New York now."

Swanson made a note. "What about the German transport? Any ideas?"

"A couple. Neutral cargo plane north to Recife in Brazil, across east to Palmas or someplace in Guinea on the African coast. Then straight up to Lisbon and out. That's the fastest routing. But they may not want to chance the air corridors."

"You sound military."

"When I do a job, it's thorough."

"What else?"

"I think they'll probably settle for a submarine. Maybe two, for diversion purposes. It's slower but the safest."

"Subs can't enter Argentine ports. Our southern patrols would blow them out of the water. If they put in, they're impounded. We're not going to change those rules."

"You may have to."

"Impossible. There has to be another way."

"You may have to find it. Don't forget those clean uniforms."

Swanson looked away. "What about Rhinemann?"

"What about him? He's on his way back. With his kind of money, even Hitler can't freeze him out."

"I don't trust him."

"You'd be a goddamned fool if you did. But the worst he can do is hold out for market concessions—or money—from both sides. So what? He'll deliver. Why wouldn't he?"

"I'm sure he'll deliver; that's the one thing I'm positive about. . . . Which brings me to the main point of this meeting. I want a man in Buenos Aires. At the embassy."

Kendall absorbed Swanson's statement before replying. He reached for the ashtray and put it on the arm of his chair. "One of your men or one of ours? We need someone; we figured you'd have us supply him."

"You figured wrong. I've picked him."

"That could be dangerous. I tell you this with no charge . . . since I already said it."

"If we move in, the civilian contingent moves out?" A question.

"It makes sense. . . ."

"Only if the man I send *knows* about the diamonds. You're to make sure he doesn't." A statement. "Make *very* sure, Kendall. Your life depends on it."

The accountant watched Swanson closely. "What's the point?"

"There are six thousand miles between Buenos Aires and the Meridian Aircraft plants. I want that trip made without any mishaps. I want those designs brought back by a professional."

"You're taking a chance on dirtying up the uniforms, aren't you, general?"

"No. The man will be told that Rhinemann made a deal for the designs out of Peenemünde. We'll say Rhinemann brought in the German underground. For escape routings."

"Full of holes! Since when does the underground work for a price? Why would they go three thousand miles out of their way? Or work with Rhinemann?"

"Because they need him and he needs them. Rhinemann

was exiled as a Jew; it was a mistake. He rivaled Krupp. There are many in German industry still loyal to him; and he maintains offices in Berne. . . . Our crisis in gyroscopics is no secret, we know that. Rhinemann would use that knowledge; make deals in Berne."

"Why even bring in the underground?"

"I have my own reasons. They're not your concern." Swanson spoke curtly, clipping his words. It crossed his mind—fleetingly—that he was getting overtired again. He had to watch that; his strength was hollow when he was tired. And now he had to be convincing. He had to make Kendall obey without question. The important thing was to get Spaulding within reach of Erich Rhinemann. Rhinemann was the target.

The brigadier watched the filthy man in front of him. It sickened him to think that such a human slug was so necessary to the moment. Or was it, he wondered, that he was reduced to using such a man? Using him and then ordering his execution. It made their worlds closer.

"All right, Mr. Kendall, I'll spell it out. . . . The man I've picked for Buenos Aires is one of the best Intelligence agents we've got. He'll bring those designs back. But I don't want to take the slightest chance that he could learn of the diamond transfer. Rhinemann operating alone is suspect; the inclusion of the German underground puts it above suspicion."

Swanson had done his homework; everyone spoke of the French and Balkan undergrounds, but the *German* underground had worked harder and more effectively, with greater sacrifice, than all the others combined. The former man in Lisbon would know that. It would make the Buenos Aires assignment palatable and legitimate.

"Wait a minute. . . . Jesus Christ! *Wait* a minute." Kendall's disagreeable expression abruptly changed. It was as if suddenly—with reluctant enthusiasm—he had found merit in something Swanson said. "That could be a good device."

"What do you mean, *device?*"

"Just that. You say you're going to use it for this agent. The underground's above suspicion and all that shit. . . . O.K., let's go further. You just spelled out the guarantee we have to give."

"What guarantee?"

"That the shipment of Koening diamonds can get *out* of Buenos Aires. It's going to be *the* ball-breaker. . . . Let me ask you a couple of questions. And give me straight answers."

The *sewer rat*, thought Swanson, looking at the excited, disheveled figure-man. "Go ahead."

"This underground. They've gotten a lot of people out of Germany, very important people. I mean everybody knows that."

"They've—it's—been very effective."

"Does it have any hooks into the German *navy?*"

"I imagine so. Allied Central Intelligence would know specifically. . . ."

"But you don't want to go to them. Or do you?"

"Out of the question."

"But it is possible?"

"What?"

"The German *navy*, goddamn it! The submarine fleet!" Kendall was leaning forward, his eyes now boring into Swanson's.

"I would think so. I'm not . . . not primarily an Intelligence man. The German underground has an extensive network. I assume it has contacts in the naval command."

"Then it *is* possible."

"Yes, *anything's* possible." Swanson lowered his voice, turning away from his own words. "This is possible."

Kendall leaned back in the chair and crushed out his cigarette. He grinned his unattractive grin and wagged his forefinger at Swanson. "Then there's your story. Clean as a goddamned whistle and way above any goddamned suspicion. . . . While we're buying those designs, it just so happens that a German submarine is floating around, ready to surface and bring out one—even two, if you like —very important defectors. Courtesy of the underground. What better reason for a submarine to surface in hostile waters? Protected from patrols. . . . Only nobody gets off. Instead, some fresh cargo gets put on board."

Swanson tried to assimilate Kendall's rapidly delivered maneuvers. "There'd be complications. . . ."

"Wrong! It's *isolated. One* has nothing to do with the *other!* It's just talk anyway."

Brigadier General Alan Swanson knew when he had met

a man more capable in the field than himself. "It's possible. Radio blackout; Allied Central instructions."

Kendall rose from his chair; he spoke softly. "Details. I'll work them out. . . . And you'll pay me. Christ, will you pay."

# 13

## DECEMBER 27, 1943, THE AZORES

The island of Terceira in the Azores, 837 miles due west of Lisbon, was a familiar stop to the trans-Atlantic pilots flying the southern route to the United States mainland. As they descended there was always the comfortable feeling that they would encounter minor traffic to be serviced by efficient ground crews who allowed them to be rapidly airborne again. Lajes Field was good duty; those assigned there recognized that and performed well.

Which was why the major in command of the B-17 cargo and personnel carrier which had a Captain David Spaulding as its single passenger couldn't understand the delay. It had begun at descent altitude, fourteen thousand feet. The Lajes tower had interrupted its approach instructions and ordered the pilot to enter a holding pattern. The major had objected; there was no necessity from his point of view. The field was clear. The Lajes tower radioman agreed with the major but said he was only repeating telephone instructions from American headquarters in Ponta Delgada on the adjacent island of São Miguel. Az-Am-HQ gave the orders; apparently it was expecting someone to meet the plane and that someone hadn't arrived. The tower would keep the major posted and, incidentally, was the major carrying some kind of priority cargo? Just curiosity.

Certainly not. There was *no* cargo; only a military attaché named Spaulding from the Lisbon embassy. One of those goddamned diplomatic teaparty boys. The trip was a routine return flight to Norfolk, and why the hell couldn't he land?

The tower would keep the major posted.

The B-17 landed at 1300 hours precisely, its holding pattern lasting twenty-seven minutes.

David got up from the removable seat, held to the deck by clamps, and stretched. The pilot, an aggressive major who looked roughly thirteen years old to Spaulding, emerged from the enclosed cockpit and told him a jeep was outside—or would be outside shortly—to drive the captain off the base.

"I'd like to maintain a decent schedule," said the young pilot, addressing his outranked elder humorlessly. "I realize you diplomatic people have a lot of friends in these social posts, but we've got a long lap to fly. Bear it in mind, please."

"I'll try to keep the polo match down to three chukkers," replied David wearily.

"Yeah, you do that." The major turned and walked to the rear of the cabin, where an air force sergeant had sprung open the cargo hatch used for the aircraft's exit. Spaulding followed, wondering who would meet him outside.

"My name's Ballantyne, captain," said the middle-aged civilian behind the wheel of the jeep, extending his hand to Spaulding. "I'm with Azores-American. Hop in; we'll only be a few minutes. We're driving to the provost's house, a few hundred yards beyond the fence."

David noticed that the guards at the gate did not bother to stop Ballantyne, they just waved him through. The civilian turned right on the road paralleling the field and accelerated. In less time than it took to adequately light a cigarette, the jeep entered the driveway of a one-story Spanish hacienda and proceeded past the house to what could only be described as an out-of-place gazebo.

"Here we are. Come on, captain," said Ballantyne, getting out, indicating the screen door of the screened enclosure. "My associate, Paul Hollander, is waiting for us."

Hollander was another middle-aged civilian. He was nearly bald and wore steel-rimmed spectacles that gave him an appearance beyond his years. As with Ballantyne, there was a look of intelligence about him. Both small and capital *I*. Hollander smiled genuinely.

"This is a distinct pleasure, Spaulding. As so many others, I've admired the work of the man in Lisbon."

Capital *I*, thought David.

"Thank you. I'd like to know why I'm not him any longer."

"I can't answer that. Neither can Ballantyne, I'm afraid."

"Perhaps they thought you deserved a rest," offered Ballantyne. "Good Lord, you've been there—how long is it now? Three years with no break."

"Nearer four," answered David. "And there were plenty of 'breaks.' The Costa Brava beats the hell out of Palm Beach. I was told that you—I assume it's you—have my orders. . . . I don't mean to seem impatient but there's a nasty teenager with a major's rank flying the plane. *He's* impatient."

"Tell him to go to blazes," laughed the man named Hollander. "We *do* have your orders and also a little surprise for you: you're a lieutenant colonel. Tell the major to get his uniform pressed."

"Seems I jumped one."

"Not really. You got your majority last year. Apparently you don't have much use for titles in Lisbon."

"Or military associations," interjected Ballantyne.

"Neither, actually," said David. "At least I wasn't broken. I had premonitions of walking guard duty around latrines."

"Hardly." Hollander sat down in one of the four deck chairs, gesturing David to do the same. It was his way of indicating that their meeting might not be as short as Spaulding had thought. "If it was a time for parades or revelations, I'm sure you'd be honored in the front ranks."

"Thanks," said David, sitting down. "That removes a very real concern. What's this all about?"

"Again, we don't have answers, only ex cathedra instructions. We're to ask you several questions—only one of which could preclude our delivering your orders. Let's get that over with first; I'm sure you'd like to know at least where you're going." Hollander smiled his genuine smile again.

"I would. Go on."

"Since you were relieved of your duties in Lisbon, have you made contact—intentional or otherwise—with *anyone* outside the embassy? I mean by this, even the most innocuous good-bye? Or a settling of a bill—a restaurant, a store; or a chance run-in with an acquaintance at the airport, or on the way to the airport?"

"No. And I had my luggage sent in diplomatic cartons; no suitcases, no traveling gear."

"You're thorough," said Ballantyne, still standing.

"I've had reason to be. Naturally, I had engagements for the week after I returned from the north country. . . ."

"From *where?*" asked Hollander.

"Basque and Navarre. Contact points below the border. I always scheduled engagements right after; it kept a continuity. Not many, just enough to keep in sight. Part of the cover. I had two this week: lunch and cocktails."

"What about them?" Ballantyne sat down next to David.

"I instructed Marshall—he's the cryp who took my orders—to call each just before I was supposed to show up. Say I'd be delayed. That was all."

"Not that you wouldn't *be* there?" Hollander seemed fascinated.

"No. Just delayed. It fit the cover."

"I'll take your word for it," laughed Hollander. "You answered affirmatively and then some. How does New York strike you?"

"As it always has: pleasantly for limited periods."

"I don't know for how long but that's your assignment. And out of uniform, colonel."

"I lived in New York. I know a lot of people there."

"Your new cover is simplicity itself. You've been discharged most honorably after service in Italy. Medical reasons, minor wounds." Hollander took out an envelope from the inside pocket of his jacket and handed it across to David. "It's all here. Terribly simple, papers . . . everything."

"O.K.," said David, accepting the envelope. "I'm a ruptured duck in New York. So far, very nice. You couldn't make it the real thing, could you?"

"The papers are simple, I didn't say authentic. Sorry."

"So am I. What happens then?"

"Someone's very solicitous of you. You have an excellent job; good pay, too. With Meridian Aircraft."

"Meridian?"

"Blueprint Division."

"I thought Meridian was in the Midwest. Illinois or Michigan."

"It has a New York office. Or it does now."

"Aircraft blueprints, I assume."

"I should think so."

"Is it counterespionage?"

"We don't know," answered Ballantyne. "We weren't given any data except the names of the two men you'll report to."

"They're in the envelope?"

"No," said Hollander. "They're verbal and to be committed. Nothing written until you're on the premises."

"Oh, Christ, this all sounds like Ed Pace. He loves this kind of nonsense."

"Sorry, again. It's above Pace."

"What? . . . I didn't think anything was, except maybe Holy Communion. . . . Then how do *you* report? And to whom?"

"Priority courier straight through to an address in Washington. No department listing, but transmission *and* priority cleared through Field Division, Fairfax."

Spaulding emitted a soft, nearly inaudible whistle. "What are the two names?"

"The first is Lyons. Eugene Lyons. He's an aerophysicist. We're to tell you that he's a bit strange, but a goddamned genius."

"In other words, reject the man; accept the genius."

"Something like that. I suppose you're used to it," said Ballantyne.

"Yes," answered Spaulding. "And the other?"

"A man named Kendall." Hollander crossed his legs. "Nothing on him; he's just a name. Walter Kendall. Have no idea what he does."

David pulled the strap across his waist in the removable seat. The B-17's engines were revving at high speed, sending vibrations through the huge fuselage. He looked about in a way he hadn't looked at an airplane before, trying to reduce the spans and the plating to some kind of imaginary blueprint. If Hollander's description of his assignment was accurate—and why shouldn't it be?—he'd be studying aircraft blueprints within a few days.

What struck him as strange were the methods of precaution. In a word, they were unreasonable; they went beyond even abnormal concerns for security. It would have been a simple matter for him to report to Washington, be reassigned, and be given an in-depth briefing. Instead, apparently there would be *no* briefing.

Why not?

Was he to accept open-ended orders from two men he'd never met before? Without the sanction of recognition—even introduction—from any military authority? What the hell was Ed Pace doing?

*Sorry. . . . It's above Pace.*

Those were the words Hollander had used.

*. . . cleared through Field Division, Fairfax.*

Hollander again.

Except for the White House itself, David realized that Fairfax was about as high up as one could go. But Fairfax was still *military*. And he wasn't being instructed by Fairfax, simply "cleared."

Hollander's remaining "questions" had not been questions at all, really. They had been introduced with interrogatory words: *do you, have you, can you*. But not questions; merely further instructions.

"Do you have friends in any of the aircraft companies? On the exective level?"

He didn't know, for God's sake. He'd been out of the country so damned long he wasn't sure he had any friends, period.

Regardless, Hollander had said, he was to avoid any such "friends"—should they exist. Report their names to Walter Kendall, if he ran across them.

"Have you any women in New York who are in the public eye?"

What kind of question was *that?* Silliest goddamned thing he'd ever heard of! What the hell did Hollander mean?

The balding, bespectacled Az-Am agent had clarified succinctly. It was listed in David's file that he had supplemented his civilian income as a radio performer. That meant he knew actresses.

And actors, Spaulding suggested. And so what?

Friendships with well-known actresses could lead to newspaper photographs, Hollander rejoined. Or speculations in columns; his name in print. That, too, was to be avoided.

David recalled that he did know—knew—several girls

who'd done well in pictures since he'd left. He'd had a short-lived affair with an actress who was currently a major star for Warner Brothers. Reluctantly he agreed with Hollander; the agent was right. Such contacts would be avoided.

"Can you absorb quickly, commit to memory, blueprint specifications unrelated to industrial design?"

Given a breakdown key of correlative symbols and material factors, the answer was probably yes.

Then he was to prepare himself—however it was done—for aircraft design.

That, thought Spaulding, was obvious.

That, Hollander had said, was all he could tell him.

The B-17 taxied to the west extreme of the Lajes runway and turned for takeoff. The disagreeable major had made it a point to be standing by the cargo hatch looking at his wristwatch when Spaulding returned. David had climbed out of the jeep, shaken hands with Ballantyne and held up three fingers to the major.

"The timer lost count during the last chukker," he said to the pilot. "You know how it is with these striped-pants boys."

The major had not been amused.

The aircraft gathered speed, the ground beneath hammered against the landing gear with increasing ferocity. In seconds the plane would be airborne. David bent over to pick up an Azores newspaper that Hollander had given him and which he'd placed at his feet when strapping himself in.

Suddenly it happened. An explosion of such force that the removable seat flew out of its clamps and jettisoned into the right wall of the plane, carrying David, bent over, with it. And he'd never know but often speculate on whether that Azores newspaper had saved his life.

Smoke was everywhere; the aircraft careened off the ground and spun laterally. The sound of twisting metal filled the cabin with a continuous, unending scream; steel ribs whipped downward from the top and sides of the fuselage—snapping, contorted, sprung from their mountings.

A second explosion blew out the front cabin; sprays of blood and pieces of flesh spat against the crumbling, spinning walls. A section of human scalp with traces of burnt hairline under the bright, viscous red fluid slapped into Spaulding's forearm. Through the smoke David could see the bright sunlight streaming through the front section of the careening plane.

The aircraft had been severed!

David knew instantly that he had only one chance of survival. The fuel tanks were filled to capacity for the long Atlantic flight; they'd go up in seconds. He reached for the buckle at his waist and ripped at it with all his strength. It was locked; the hurling fall had caused the strap to bunch and crowd the housing with cloth. He tugged and twisted, the snap sprung and he was free.

The plane—what was left of it—began a series of thundering convulsions signifying the final struggle to come to a halt on the rushing, hilly ground beyond the runway. David crashed backward, crawling as best he could toward the rear. Once he was forced to stop and hug the deck, his face covered by his arms, a jagged piece of metal piercing the back of his right shoulder.

The cargo hatch was blown open; the air force sergeant lay half out of the steel frame, dead, his chest ripped open from throat to rib cage.

David judged the distance to the ground as best his panic would allow and hurled himself out of the plane, coiling as he did so for the impact of the fall and the necessary roll away from the onrushing tail assembly.

The earth was hard and filled with rocks, but he was *free*. He kept rolling, rolling, crawling, digging, gripping his bloodied hands into the dry, hard soil until the breath in his lungs was exhausted.

He lay on the ground and heard the screaming sirens far in the distance.

And then the explosion that filled the air and shook the earth.


Priority high-frequency radio messages were sent back and forth between the operations room of Lajes Airfield and Field Division, Fairfax.

David Spaulding was to be airlifted out of Terceira on the next flight to Newfoundland, leaving in less than an hour. At Newfoundland he would be met by a pursuit fighter plane at the air force base and flown directly to Mitchell Field, New York. In light of the fact that Lieutenant Colonel Spaulding had suffered no major physical disability, there would be no change in the orders delivered to him.

The cause of the B-17 explosions and resultant killings was, without question, sabotage. Timed out of Lisbon or set during the refueling process at Lajes. An intensive investigation was implemented immediately.

Hollander and Ballantyne had been with David when he was examined and treated by the British army doctor. Bandages around the sutures in his right shoulder, the cuts on his hands and forearms cleaned, Spaulding pronounced himself shaken but operable. The doctor left after administering an intravenous sedative that would make it possible for David to rest thoroughly on the final legs of his trip to New York.

"I'm sure it will be quite acceptable for you to take a leave for a week or so," said Hollander. "My God, you're lucky to be among us!"

"*Alive* is the word," added Ballantyne.

"Am I a mark?" asked Spaulding. "Was it connected with me?"

"Fairfax doesn't think so," answered the balding Hollander. "They think it's coincidental sabotage."

Spaulding watched the Az-Am agent as he spoke. It seemed to David that Hollander hesitated, as if concealing something.

"Narrow coincidence, isn't it? I *was* the only passenger."

"If the enemy can eliminate a large aircraft and a pilot in the bargain, well, I imagine he considers that progress. And Lisbon security *is* rotten."

"Not where I've been. Not generally."

"Well, perhaps here at Terceira, then. . . . I'm only telling you what Fairfax thinks."

There was a knock on the dispensary door and Ballantyne opened it. A first lieutenant stood erect and spoke gently, addressing David, obviously aware that Spaulding had come very close to death.

"It's preparation time, sir. We should be airborne in twenty minutes. Can I help you with anything?"

"I haven't *got* anything, lieutenant. Whatever I had is in that mass of burnt rubble in the south forty."

"Yes, of course. I'm sorry."

"Don't be. Better it than me. . . . I'll be right with you."

David turned to Ballantyne and Hollander, shaking their hands.

As he said his last good-bye to Hollander, he saw it in the agent's eyes.

Hollander *was* hiding something.

The British naval commander opened the screen door of the gazebo and walked in. Paul Hollander rose from the deck chair.

"Did you bring it?" he asked the officer.

"Yes." The commander placed his attaché case on the single wrought iron table and snapped up the hasps. He took out an envelope and handed it to the American. "The photo lab did a rather fine job. Well lighted, front and rear views. Almost as good as having the real item."

Hollander unwound the string on the envelope's flap and removed a photograph. It was an enlargement of a small medallion, a star with six points.

It was the Star of David.

In the center of the face was the scrolled flow of a Hebrew inscription. On the back was the bas-relief of a knife with a streak of lightning intersecting the blade.

"The Hebrew spells out the name of a prophet named Haggai; he's the symbol of an organization of Jewish fanatics operating out of Palestine. They call themselves the Haganah. Their business, they claim, is vengeance—two thousand years' worth. We anticipate quite a bit of trouble from them in the years to come; they've made that clear, I'm afraid."

"But you say it was welded to the bottom main strut of the rear cabin."

"In such a way as to escape damage from all but a direct explosion. Your aircraft was blown up by the Haganah."

Hollander sat down, staring at the photograph. He looked up at the British commander. "Why? For God's sake, *why?*"

"I can't answer that."

"Neither can Fairfax. I don't think they even want to acknowledge it. They want it buried."

# 14

When the words came over his intercom in the soft, compensating voice of the WAC lieutenant who was his secretary, Swanson knew it was no routine communication.

"Fairfax on line one, sir. It's Colonel Pace. He says to interrupt you."

Since delivering David Spaulding's file, the Fairfax commander had been reluctant to call personally. He hadn't spoken of his reluctance, he simply relegated messages to subordinates. And since they all concerned the progress of getting Spaulding out of Portugal, Pace's point was clear: he would expedite but not personally acknowledge his participation.

Edmund Pace was still not satisfied with the murky "highest priority" explanations regarding his man in Lisbon. He would follow orders once-removed.

"General, there's a radio emergency from Lajes Field in Terceira," said Pace urgently.

"What the hell does that mean? *Where?*"

"Azores. The B-17 carrier with Spaulding on it was sabotaged. Blown up on takeoff."

"Jesus!"

"May I suggest you come out here, sir?"

"Is Spaulding dead?"

"Preliminary reports indicate negative, but I don't want to guarantee anything. Everything's unclear. I wanted to wait till I had further confirmations but I can't now. An unexpected development. Please, come out, general."

"On my way. Get the information on Spaulding!"

Swanson gathered the papers on his desk—the information from Kendall—that had to be clipped together, sealed in a thin metal box and locked in a file cabinet with two combinations and a key.

If there was ever a reason for total security, it was symbolized by those papers.

He spun the two combination wheels, turned the key and then thought for a second that he might reverse the process and take the papers with him. . . . No, that was unsound. They were safer in the cabinet. A file cabinet riveted to the floor was better than a cloth pocket on a man who walked in the street and drove in automobiles. A file cabinet could not have accidents; was not subject to the frailties of a tired, fifty-three-year-old brigadier.

He saluted the guard on duty at the entrance and walked rapidly down the steps to the curb. His driver was waiting, alerted by the WAC secretary, whose efficiency overcame her continuous attempts to be more than an efficient secretary to him. He knew that one day when the pressures became too much, he'd ask her in, lock the door and hump the ass off her on the brown leather couch.

Why was he thinking about his secretary? He didn't give a goddamn about the WAC lieutenant who sat so protectively outside his office door.

He sat back in the seat and removed his hat. He knew why he thought about his secretary: it gave him momentary relief. It postponed thoughts about the complications that may or may not have exploded on a runway in the Azores.

Oh *Christ!* The thought of rebuilding what he'd managed to put together was abhorrent to him. To go back, to reconstruct, to research for the right man was impossible. It was difficult enough for him to go over the details as they now stood.

The details supplied by the sewer rat.

Kendall.

An enigma. An unattractive puzzle even G-2 couldn't piece together. Swanson had run a routine check on him, based on the fact that the accountant was privy to Meridian's aircraft contracts; the Intelligence boys and Hoover's tight-lipped maniacs had returned virtually nothing but names and dates. They'd been instructed *not* to interview Meridian personnel or anyone connected with ATCO or

Packard; orders that apparently made their task close to impossible.

Kendall was forty-six, severely asthmatic and a CPA. He was unmarried, had few if any friends and lived two blocks from his firm, which he solely owned, in mid-Manhattan.

The personal evaluations were fairly uniform: Kendall was a disagreeable, antisocial individualist who happened to be a brilliant statistician.

The dossier might have told a desolate story—paternal abandonment, lack of privilege, the usual—but it didn't. There was no indication of poverty, no record of deprivation or hardship anywhere near that suffered by millions, especially during the Depression years.

No records of depth on anything, for that matter.

An enigma.

But there was nothing enigmatic about Walter Kendall's "details" for Buenos Aires. They were clarity itself. Kendall's sense of manipulation had been triggered; the challenge stimulated his already primed instincts for maneuvering. It was as if he had found the ultimate "deal"—and indeed, thought Swanson, he had.

The operation was divided into three isolated exercises: the arrival and inspection of the diamond shipment; the simultaneous analysis of the gyroscopic blueprints, as they, too, arrived; and the submarine transfer. The crates of bortz and carbonado from the Koening mines would be secretly cordoned off in a warehouse in the Dársena Norte district of the Puerto Nuevo. The Germans assigned to the warehouse would report only to Erich Rhinemann.

The aerophysicist, Eugene Lyons, would be billeted in a guarded apartment in the San Telmo district, an area roughly equivalent to New York's Gramercy Park—rich, secluded, ideal for surveillance. As the step-blueprints were delivered, he would report to Spaulding.

Spaulding would precede Lyons to Buenos Aires and be attached to the embassy on whatever pretext Swanson thought feasible. His assignment—as *Spaulding* thought it to be—was to coordinate the purchase of the gyroscopic designs, and if their authenticity was confirmed, authorize payment. This authorization would be made by a code radioed to Washington that supposedly cleared a transfer of funds to Rhinemann in Switzerland.

Spaulding would then stand by at a mutually agreed-upon airfield, prepared to be flown out of Argentina. He would be given airborne clearance when Rhinemann received word that "payment" had been made.

In reality, the code sent by Spaulding was to be a signal for the German submarine to surface at a prearranged destination at sea and make rendezvous with a small craft carrying the shipment of diamonds. Ocean and air patrols would be kept out of the area; if the order was questioned —and it was unlikely—the cover story of the underground defectors would be employed.

When the transfer at sea was made, the submarine would radio confirmation—Rhinemann's "payment." It would dive and start its journey back to Germany. Spaulding would then be cleared for takeoff to the United States.

These safeguards were the best either side could expect. Kendall was convinced he could sell the operation to Erich Rhinemann. He and Rhinemann possessed a certain objectivity lacking in the others.

Swanson did not dispute the similarity; it was another viable reason for Kendall's death.

The accountant would fly to Buenos Aires in a week and make the final arrangements with the German expatriate. Rhinemann would be made to understand that Spaulding was acting as an experienced courier, a custodian for the eccentric Eugene Lyons—a position Kendall admitted was desirable. But Spaulding was nothing else. He was not part of the diamond transfer; he knew nothing of the submarine. He would provide the codes necessary for the transfer, but he'd never know it. There was no way he could learn of it.

Airtight, ironclad: acceptable.

Swanson had read and reread Kendall's "details"; he could not fault them. The ferret-like accountant had reduced an enormously complicated negotiation to a series of simple procedures and separate motives. In a way Kendall had created an extraordinary deception. Each step had a checkpoint, each move a countermove.

And Swanson would add the last deceit: David Spaulding would kill Erich Rhinemann.

Origin of command: instructions from Allied Central Intelligence. By the nature of Rhinemann's involvement, he was too great a liability to the German underground. The former man in Lisbon could employ whatever methods he thought best. Hire the killers, do it himself; whatever the situation called for. Just make sure it was done.

Spaulding would understand. The shadow world of agents and double agents had been his life for the past several years. David Spaulding—if his dossier was to be believed—would accept the order for what it was: a reasonable, professional solution.

If Spaulding was alive.

*Oh, Christ!* What had *happened?* Where was it? Lapess, Lajes. Some goddamned airfield in the Azores! Sabotage. Blown up on takeoff!

What the hell did it *mean?*

The driver swung off the highway onto the back Virginia road. They were fifteen minutes from the Fairfax compound; Swanson found himself sucking his lower lip between his teeth. He had actually bitten into the soft tissue; he could taste a trickle of blood.


"We have further information," said Colonel Edmund Pace, standing in front of a photograph map frame. The map was the island of Terceira in the Azores. "Spaulding's all right. Shaken up, of course. Minor sutures, bruises; nothing broken, though. I tell you he pulled off a miracle. Pilot, copilot, a crewman: all dead. Only survivors were Spaulding and a rear aerial gunner who probably won't make it."

"Is he mobile? Spaulding?"

"Yes. Hollander and Ballantyne are with him now. I assumed you wanted him out. . . ."

"Jesus, *yes,*" interrupted Swanson.

"I got him on a Newfoundland transfer. Unless you want to switch orders, a coastal patrol flight will pick him up there and bring him south. Mitchell Field."

"When will he get in?"

"Late tonight, weather permitting. Otherwise, early morning. Shall I have him flown down here?"

Swanson hesitated. "No. . . . Have a doctor at Mitchell give him a thorough going-over. But keep him in New York. If he needs a few days' rest, put him up at a hotel. Otherwise, everything remains."

"Well . . ." Pace seemed slightly annoyed with his superior. "Someone's going to have to see him."

"Why?"

"His papers. Everything we prepared went up with the plane. They're a packet of ashes."

"Oh. Yes, of course. I didn't think about that." Swanson walked away from Pace to the chair in front of the stark, plain desk. He sat down.

The colonel watched the brigadier. He was obviously concerned with Swanson's lack of focus, his inadequate concentration. "We can prepare new ones easily enough, that's no problem."

"Good. Do that, will you? Then have someone meet him at Mitchell and give them to him."

"O.K. . . . But it's possible you may want to change your mind." Pace crossed to his desk chair but remained standing.

"Why? About what?"

"Whatever it is. . . . The plane was sabotaged, I told you that. If you recall, I asked you to come out here because of an unexpected development."

Swanson stared up at his subordinate. "I've had a difficult week. And I've told *you* the gravity of this project. Now, don't play Fairfax games with me. I make no claims of expertise in your field. I asked only for assistance; ordered it, if you like. Say what you mean without the preamble, please."

"I've tried to give you that assistance." Pace's tone was rigidly polite. "It's not easy, sir. And I've just bought you twelve hours to consider alternatives. That plane was blown up by the Haganah."

"The *what?*"

Pace explained the Jewish organization operating out of Palestine. He watched Swanson closely as he did so.

"That's insane! It doesn't make sense! How do you know?"

"The first thing an inspection team does at the site of sabotage is to water down, pick over debris, look for evidence that might melt from the heat, or burn, if explosives are used. It's a preliminary check and it's done fast. . . . A Haganah medallion was found riveted to the tail assembly. They wanted full credit."

"Good God! What did you say to the Azores people?"

"I bought you a day, general. I instructed Hollander to minimize any connection, keep it away from Spaulding. Frankly, to imply coincidence if the subject got out of hand. The Haganah is independent, fanatic. Most Zionist organizations won't touch it. They call it a group of savages."

"How could it get out of hand?" Swanson was disturbed on another level.

"I'm sure you're aware that the Azores are under British control. An old Portuguese treaty gives them the right to military installations."

"I know that," said Swanson testily.

"The British found the medallion."

"What will they do?"

"Think about it. Eventually make a report to Allied Central."

"But you know about it *now*."

"Hollander's a good man. He does favors; gets favors in return."

Swanson got out of the chair and walked aimlessly around it. "What do you think, Ed? Was it meant for Spaulding?" He looked at the colonel.

The expression on Pace's face let Swanson know that Pace was beginning to understand his anxiety. Not so much about the project—that was out of bounds and he accepted it—but that a fellow officer was forced to deal in an area he was out-of-sync with; territory he was not trained to cross. At such times a decent army man had sympathy.

"All I can give you are conjectures, very loose, not even good guesses. . . . It could be Spaulding. And even if it was, it doesn't necessarily mean it's connected with *your* project."

"What?"

"I don't know what Spaulding's field activities have been. Not specifically. And the Haganah is filled with psychopaths—deadly variety. They're about as rational as Julius Streicher's units. Spaulding may have had to kill a Portuguese or Spanish Jew. Or use one in a 'cover trap.' In a Catholic country that's all a Haganah cell would need. . . . Or it could be someone else on the plane. An officer or crewman with an anti-Zionist relative, especially a *Jewish* anti-Zionist relative. I'd have to run a check. . . . Unless you'd read the book, you couldn't possibly understand those kikes."

Swanson remained silent for several moments. When he

spoke he did so acknowledging Pace's attitude. "Thank you. . . . But it probably isn't any of those things, is it? I mean, Spanish Jews or 'cover traps' or some pilot's uncle . . . it's Spaulding."

"You don't *know* that. Speculate, sure; don't assume."

"I can't understand *how*." Swanson sat down again, thinking aloud, really. "All things considered . . ." His thought drifted off into silence.

"May I make a suggestion?" Pace went to his chair. It was no time to talk down to a bewildered superior.

"By all means," said Swanson, looking over at the colonel, his eyes conveying gratitude to this hard-nosed, confident Intelligence man.

"I'm not cleared for your project and, let's face it, I don't want to be. It's a DW exercise, and that's where it belongs. I said a few minutes ago that you should consider alternatives . . . maybe you should. But *only* if you see a direct connection. I watched you and you didn't."

"Because there isn't any."

"You're not involved—and even I don't see how, considering what I *do* know from the probe and Johannesburg —with the concentration camps? Auschwitz? Belsen?"

"Not even remotely."

Pace leaned forward, his elbows on the desk. "Those are Haganah concerns. Along with the 'Spanish Jews' and 'cover traps.' . . . Don't make any new decisions now, general. You'd be making them too fast, without supportive cause."

"Sup*port*. . . ." Swanson looked incredulous. "A plane was blown up. Men were killed!"

"And a medallion could be planted on a tail assembly by anyone. It's quite possible you're being tested."

"By *whom?*"

"I couldn't answer that. Warn Spaulding; it'll strike him as funny, he was *on* that aircraft. But let my man at Mitchell Field tell him there could be a recurrence; to be careful. . . . He's been there, general. He'll handle himself properly. . . . And in the meantime, may I also suggest you look for a replacement."

"A replacement?"

"For Spaulding. If there *is* a recurrence, it could be successful. He'd be taken out."

"You mean he'd be killed."

"Yes."

"What kind of world do you people live in?" asked Swanson softly.

"It's complicated," said Pace.

# 15

*DECEMBER 29, 1943, NEW YORK CITY*

Spaulding watched the traffic below from the hotel window overlooking Fifth Avenue and Central Park. The Montgomery was one of those small, elegant hotels his parents had used while in New York, and there was a pleasant sense of nostalgia in his being there again. The old desk clerk had actually wept discreet tears while registering him. Spaulding had forgotten—fortunately he remembered before his signature was dry—that the old man years ago had taken him for walks in the park. Over a quarter of a century ago!

Walks in the park. Governesses. Chauffeurs standing in foyers, prepared to whisk his parents away to a train, a concert, a rehearsal. Music critics. Record company executives. Endless dinner parties where he'd make his usual "appearance" before bedtime and be prompted by his father to tell some guest at what age Mozart composed the Fortieth; dates and facts he was forced to memorize and which he gave not one goddamn about. Arguments. Hysterics over an inadequate conductor or a bad performance or a worse review.

Madness.

And always the figure of Aaron Mandel, soothing, placating—so often fatherly to his overbearing father while his mother faded, waiting in a secondary status that belied her natural strength.

And the quiet times. The Sundays—except for concert Sundays—when his parents would suddenly remember his existence and try to make up in one day the attention they thought they had allocated improperly to governesses, chauffeurs and nice, polite hotel managements. At these

times, the quiet times, he had felt his father's honest yet
artificial attempts; had wanted to tell him it was all right,
he wasn't deprived. They didn't have to spend autumn days
wandering around zoos and museums; the zoos and museums were much better in Europe, anyway. It wasn't
necessary that he be taken to Coney Island or the beaches
of New Jersey in summer. What were they, compared to
the Lido or Costa del Santiago? But whenever they were in
America, there was this parental compulsion to fit into a
mold labeled "An American Father and Mother."

Sad, funny, inconsistent; impossible, really.

And for some buried reason, he had never come back to
this small, elegant hotel during the later years. There was
rarely a need, of course, but he could have made the effort;
the management was genuinely fond of the Spaulding
family. Now it seemed right, somehow. After the years
away he wanted a secure base in a strange land, secure at
least in memories.

Spaulding walked away from the window to the bed
where the bellboy had placed his new suitcase with the new
civilian clothes he had purchased at Rogers Peet. Everything, including the suitcase. Pace had had the foresight to
send money with the major who had brought him duplicates of the papers destroyed in Terceira. He had to sing
for the money, not for the papers; that amused him.

The major who met him at Mitchell Field—on the field
—had escorted him to the base infirmary, where a bored
army doctor pronounced him fit but "run down"; had professionally criticized the sutures implanted by the British
doctor in the Azores but saw no reason to change them;
and suggested that David take two APCs every four hours
and rest.

*Caveat* patient.

The courier-major had played a tune on the Fairfax
piano and told him Field Division was still analyzing the
Lajes sabotage; it could have been aimed at him for misdeeds out of Lisbon. He should be careful and report any
unusual incidents directly to Colonel Pace at Fairfax. Further, Spaulding was to commit the name of Brigadier General Alan Swanson, DW. Swanson was his source control
and would make contact in a matter of days, ten at the
outside.

Why call Pace, then? Regarding any "incidents." Why

not get in touch directly with this Swanson? Since he was the SC.

Pace's instructions, replied the major—until the brigadier took over; just simpler that way.

Or further concealment, thought David, remembering the clouded eyes of Paul Hollander, the Az-Am agent in Terceira.

*Something* was happening. The source control transfer was being handled in a very unorthodox manner. From the unsigned, high-priority codes received in Lisbon to the extraordinary command: out of strategy. From the mid-ocean delivery of papers from Az-Am agents who said they had to question him first, to the strange orders that had him reporting to two civilians in New York without prior briefing.

It was all like a hesitation waltz. It was either very professional or terribly amateur; really, he suspected, a combination of both. It would be interesting to meet this General Swanson. He had never heard of him.

He lay down on the hotel bed. He would rest for an hour and then shower and shave and see New York at night for the first time in over three years. See what the war had done to a Manhattan evening; it had done little or nothing to the daylight hours, from what he'd seen—only the posters. It would be good to have a woman tonight. But if it happened, he'd want it to be comfortable, without struggle or urgency. A happy coincidence would be just right; a likable, really likable interlude. On the other hand, he wasn't about to browse through a telephone directory to create one. Three years and nine months had passed since he last picked up a telephone in New York City. During that time he had learned to be wary of the changes taking place over a matter of days, to say nothing of three years and nine months.

And he recalled pleasantly how the Stateside transfers to the embassy in Lisbon often spoke of the easy accessibility of the women back home. Especially in Washington and New York, where the numbers and the absence of permanency worked in favor of one-night stands. Then he remembered, with a touch of amused resignation, that these same reports usually spoke of the irresistible magnetism of an officer's uniform, especially captain and over.

He had worn a uniform exactly three times in the past

four years: at the Mayflower Hotel lounge with Ed Pace, the day he arrived in Portugal and the day he left Portugal.

He didn't even own one now.

His telephone rang and it startled him. Only Fairfax and, he assumed, this brigadier, Swanson, knew where he was. He had called the Montgomery from the Mitchell Field infirmary and secured the reservation; the major had said to take seventy-two hours. He needed the rest; no one would bother him. Now someone was bothering him.

"Hello?"

"*David!*" It was a girl's voice; low, cultivated at the Plaza. "David *Spaulding!*"

"Who is this?" He wondered for a second if his just-released fantasies were playing tricks on reality.

"*Leslie*, darling! Leslie *Jenner!* My God, it must be nearly *five years!*"

Spaulding's mind raced. Leslie Jenner was part of the New York scene but not the radio world; she was the up-from-college crowd. Meeting under the clock at the Biltmore; late nights at LaRue; the cotillions—which he'd been invited to, not so much from social bloodlines as for the fact that he was the son of the concert Spauldings. Leslie was Miss Porter's, Finch and the Junior League.

Only her name had been changed to something else. She had married a boy from Yale. He didn't remember the name.

"Leslie, this is . . . well, Jesus, a surprise. How did you know I was here?" Spaulding wasn't engaging in idle small talk.

"*Nothing* happens in New York that I don't know about! I have eyes and ears everywhere, darling! A veritable spy network!"

David Spaulding could feel the blood draining from his face; he didn't like the girl's joke. "I'm serious, Leslie. . . . Only because I haven't called anyone. Not even Aaron. How did you find out?"

"If you must know, Cindy Bonner—she was Cindy Tottle, married Paul Bonner—Cindy was exchanging some dreary Christmas gifts for Paul at Rogers Peet and she *swore* she saw you trying on a suit. Well, you know Cindy! Just too shy for *words* . . ."

David *didn't* know Cindy. He couldn't even recall the

name, much less a face. Leslie Jenner went on as he thought about that.

". . . and so she ran to the nearest phone and called me. After all, darling, we *were* a major item!"

If a "major item" described a couple of summer months of weekending at East Hampton and bedding the daughter of the house, then David had to agree. But he didn't subscribe to the definition; it had been damned transient, discreet and before the girl's very social marriage.

"I'd just as soon you kept that information from your husband. . . ."

"Oh, *God*, you poor lamb! It's *Jenner*, darling, not Hawkwood! Didn't even keep the *name*. Damned if I would."

That was it, thought David. She'd married a man named Hawkwood: Roger or Ralph; something like that. A football player, or was it tennis?

"I'm sorry. I didn't know. . . ."

"Richard and I called it quits simply *centuries* ago. It was a *disaster*. The son of a bitch couldn't even keep his hands off my best friends! He's in London now; air corps, but very hush-hush, I think. I'm sure the English girls are getting their fill of him . . . and I do mean fill! I *know!*"

There was a slight stirring in David's groin. Leslie Jenner was proffering an invitation.

"Well, they're allies," said Spaulding humorously. "But you didn't tell me, how did you find me here?"

"It took exactly four telephone calls, my lamb. I tried the usual: Commodore, Biltmore and the Waldorf; and then I remembered that your dad and mum always stopped off at the Montgomery. Very Old World, darling. . . . I thought, with reservations simply *hell*, you might have thought of it."

"You'd make a good detective, Leslie."

"Only when the object of my detecting is worthwhile, lamb. . . . We *did* have fun."

"Yes, we did," said Spaulding, his thoughts on an entirely different subject. "And we can't let your memory prowess go to waste. Dinner?"

"If you hadn't asked, I would have *screamed*."

"Shall I pick you up at your apartment? What's the address?"

Leslie hesitated a fraction of a moment. "Let's meet at a restaurant. We'd never get out of here."

An invitation, indeed.

David named a small Fifty-first Street cafe he remembered. It was on Park. "At seven thirty? Eight?"

"Seven thirty's lovely, but not *there*, darling. It closed simply years ago. Why not the Gallery? It's on Forty-sixth. I'll make reservations; they know me."

"Fine."

"You poor lamb, you've been away so *long*. You don't know *anything*. I'll take you in tow."

"I'd like that. Seven thirty, then."

"Can't wait. And I promise not to cry."

Spaulding replaced the telephone; he was bewildered—on several levels. To begin with, a girl didn't call a former lover after nearly four war years without asking—especially in these times—where he'd been, how he was; at least the length of his stay in town. It wasn't natural, it denied curiosity in these curiosity-prone days.

Another reason was profoundly disturbing.

The last time his parents had been at the Montgomery was in 1934. And he had not returned since then. He'd met the girl in 1936; in October of 1936 in New Haven at the Yale Bowl. He remembered distinctly.

Leslie Jenner couldn't possibly know about the Montgomery Hotel. Not as it was related to his parents.

She was lying.

# 16

*DECEMBER 29, 1943, NEW YORK CITY*

The Gallery was exactly as David thought it would be: a
lot of deep-red velvet with a generous sprinkling of palms
in varying shapes and sizes, reflecting the soft-yellow pools
of light from dozens of wall sconces far enough above the
tables to make the menus unreadable. The clientele was
equally predictable: young, rich, deliberately casual; a pro-
fusion of wrinkled eyebrows and crooked smiles and very
bright teeth. The voices rose and subsided, words running
together, the diction glossy.

Leslie Jenner was there when he arrived. She ran into his
arms in front of the cloak room; she held him fiercely, in
silence, for several minutes—or it seemed like minutes to
Spaulding; at any rate, too long a time. When she tilted her
head back, the tears had formed rivulets on her cheeks.
The tears were genuine, but there was something—was it
the tautness of her full mouth? the eyes themselves?—
something artificial about the girl. Or was it him? The
years away from places like the Gallery and girls like
Leslie Jenner.

In all other respects she was as he remembered her.
Perhaps older, certainly more sensual—the unmistakable
look of experience. Her dark blonde hair was more a light
brown now, her wide brown eyes had added subtlety to her
innate provocativeness, her face was a touch lined but still
sculptured, aristocratic. And he could feel her body against
his; the memories were sharpened by it. Lithe, strong, full
breasted; a body that centered on sex. Shaped by it and for
it.

"God, God, God! Oh, *David!*" She pressed her lips against his ear.

They went to their table; she held his hand firmly, releasing it only to light a cigarette, taking it back again. They talked rapidly. He wasn't sure she listened, but she nodded incessantly and wouldn't take her eyes off him. He repeated the simple outlines of his cover: Italy, minor wounds; they were letting him out to go back into an essential industry where he'd do more good than carrying a rifle. He wasn't sure how long he'd be in New York. (He was honest about that, he thought to himself. He had no idea how long he'd be in town; he wished he did know.) He was glad to see her again.

The dinner was a prelude to bed. They both knew it; neither bothered to conceal the excitement of reviving the most pleasant of experiences: young sex that was taken in shadows, beyond the reprimands of elders. Enjoyed more because it was prohibited, dangerous.

"Your apartment?" he asked.

"No, lamb. I share it with my aunt, mum's younger sister. It's very chic these days to share an apartment; very patriotic."

The reasoning escaped David. "Then my place," he said firmly.

"David?" Leslie squeezed his hand and paused before speaking. "Those old family retainers who run the Montgomery, they know so many in our crowd. For instance, the Allcotts have a suite there, so do the Dewhursts. . . . I have a key to Peggy Webster's place in the Village. Remember Peggy? You were at their wedding. Jack Webster? You know Jack. He's in the navy; she went out to see him in San Diego. Let's go to Peggy's place."

Spaulding watched the girl closely. He hadn't forgotten her odd behavior on the telephone, her lie about the old hotel and his parents. Yet it was possible that his imagination was overworking—the years in Lisbon made one cautious. There could be explanations, memory lapses on his part; but now he was as curious as he was stimulated.

He was very curious. Very stimulated.

"Peggy's place," he said.

If there was anything beyond the sexual objective, it escaped him.

Their coats off, Leslie made drinks in the kitchen while David bunched newspapers beneath the fireplace grill and watched the kindling catch.

Leslie stood in the kitchen doorway looking down at him separating the logs, creating an airflow. She held their drinks and smiled. "In two days it's New Year's Eve. We'll jump and call this ours. Our New Year's. The start of many, I hope."

"Of many," he replied, standing up and going to her. He took both glasses, not the one extended. "I'll put them over here." He carried them to the coffee table in front of the small couch that faced the fireplace. He turned rapidly, politely to watch her eyes. She wasn't looking at the glasses. Or his placement of them.

Instead, she approached the fire and removed her blouse. She dropped it on the floor and turned around, her large breasts accentuated by a tight, transparent brassiere that had webbed stitching at the tips.

"Take off your shirt, David."

He did so and came to her. She winced at his bandages and gently touched them with her fingers. She pressed herself against him, her pelvis firm against his thighs, moving laterally, expertly. He reached around her back and undid the hasps of the brassiere; she hunched slightly as he pulled it away; then she turned, arching her breasts upward into his flesh. He cupped her left breast with his right hand; she reached down, stepping partially away, and undid his trousers.

"The drinks can wait, David. It's New Year's Eve. Ours, anyway."

Still holding her breast, he put his lips to her eyes, her ears. She felt him and moaned.

"Here, David," she said. "Right here on the floor." She sank to her knees, her skirt pulled up to her thighs, the tops of her stockings visible.

He lay down beside her and they kissed.

"I remember," he whispered with a gentle laugh. "The first time; the cottage by the boathouse. The floor. I remember."

"I wondered if you would. I've never forgotten."

It was only one forty-five in the morning when he took her home. They had made love twice, drunk a great deal of

Jack and Peggy Webster's good whisky and spoken of the
"old days" mostly. Leslie had no inhibitions regarding her
marriage. Richard Hawkwood, ex-husband, was simply not
a man who could sustain a permanent relationship. He was
a sexual glutton as long as the sex was spread around; not
much otherwise. He was also a failure—as much as his
family would allow—in the business world. Hawkwood
was a man brought up to enjoy fifty thousand a year with
the ability to make, perhaps, six.

The war was created, she felt, for men like Richard.
They would excel in it, as her ex-husband had done. He
should "go down in flames" somewhere, exiting brilliantly
rather than return to the frustrations of civilian inadequacy. Spaulding thought that was harsh; she claimed
she was being considerate. And they laughed and made
love.

Throughout the evening David kept alert, waiting for
her to say something, reveal something, ask something unusual. Anything to clarify—if nothing else—the reasons
behind her earlier lies about finding him. There was nothing.

He asked her again, claiming incredulity that she would
remember his parents and the Montgomery. She stuck to
her infallible memory, adding only that "love makes any
search more thorough."

She was lying again; he knew that. What they had was
not love.

She left him in the taxi; she didn't want him to come up.
Her aunt would be asleep; it was better this way.

They'd meet again tomorrow. At the Websters'. Ten
o'clock in the evening; she had a dinner date she'd get rid
of early. And she'd break her engagement for the real New
Year's Eve. They'd have the whole day to themselves.

As the doorman let her in and the taxi started up toward
Fifth Avenue, he thought for the first time that Fairfax had
him beginning his assignment at Meridian Aircraft the day
after tomorrow. New Year's Eve. He expected it would be
a half-day.

It was strange. New Year's Eve. Christmas.

He hadn't even thought about Christmas. He'd remembered to send his parents' gifts to Santiago, but he'd done
that before his trip to the north country. To the Basque
Provinces and Navarre.

Christmas had no meaning. The Santa Clauses ringing their clinking bells on the New York streets, the decorations in the store windows—none had meaning for him.

He was sad about that. He had always enjoyed the holidays.

David paid the driver, said hello to the Montgomery night clerk and took the elevator to his floor. He got off and approached his door. Automatically, because his eyes were tired, he flipped his finger above the Do Not Disturb sign beneath the lock.

Then he felt the wood and looked down, punching his cigarette lighter for better vision.

The field thread was gone.

Second nature and the instructions from Fairfax to stay alert had caused him to "thread" his hotel room. Strands of invisible tan and black silk placed in a half-dozen locations, that if missing or broken meant a trespasser.

He carried no weapon and he could not know if anyone was still inside.

He returned to the elevator and pushed the button. He asked the operator if he had a passkey; his door wouldn't open. The man did not; he was taken to the lobby.

The night clerk obliged, ordering the elevator operator to remain at the desk while he went to the aid of Mr. Spaulding and his difficult lock.

As the two men walked out of the elevator and down the corridor, Spaulding heard the distinct sound of a latch being turned, snapped shut quietly but unmistakably. He rapidly turned his head in both directions, up and down the corridor, trying to locate the origin of the sound.

Nothing but closed hotel doors.

The desk clerk had no trouble opening the door. He had more difficulty understanding Mr. Spaulding's arm around his shoulder, ushering him into the single room with him.

David looked around quickly. The bathroom and closet doors were open as he had left them. There were no other places of concealment. He released the desk clerk and tipped him with a five-dollar bill.

"Thank you very much. I'm embarrassed; I'm afraid I had too much to drink."

"Not at all, sir. *Thank* you, sir." The man left, pulling the door shut behind him.

David rapidly began his thread check. In the closet: his jacket breast pocket, leafed out, centered.

No thread.

The bureau: the first and third drawers, inserted.

Both threads out of place. The first inside on top of a handkerchief; the second, wedged between shirts.

The bed: laterally placed along the spread in line with the pattern.

Nowhere. Nothing.

He went to his suitcase, which lay on a luggage rack by the window. He knelt down and inspected the right lock; the thread had been clamped inside the metal hasp up under the tiny hinge. If the suitcase was opened, it had to break.

It was broken, only one half remaining.

The inside of the suitcase housed a single strand at the rear, crossing the elastic flap three fingers from the left side.

It was gone.

David stood up. He crossed to the bedside table and reached underneath for the telephone directory. There was no point in delay; what advantage he had was in surprise. His room had been searched professionally; he was not expected to know.

He would get Leslie Jenner's number, return to her apartment house and find a telephone booth near the entrance—with luck, in sight of it. He would then call her, tell her some wildly incredible story about anything and ask to see her. No mention of the search, nothing of his borne-out suspicions. Throw her off completely and listen acutely to her reaction. If she agreed to see him, all well and good. If she didn't, he'd keep her apartment under surveillance throughout the night, if necessary.

Leslie Jenner had a story to tell and he'd find out what it was. The man in Lisbon had not spent three years in the north provinces without gaining expertise.

There was no Jenner at the address of the apartment building.

There were six Jenners listed in Manhattan.

One by one he gave the hotel switchboard the numbers, and one by one—in varying stages of sleep and anger—the replies were the same.

No Leslie Jenner. None known.

Spaulding hung up. He'd been sitting on the bed; he got up and walked around the room.

He would go to the apartment building and ask the doorman. It was possible the apartment was in the aunt's name but it wasn't plausible. Leslie Jenner would put her name and number in the Yellow Pages, if she could; for her the telephone was an instrument of existence, not convenience. And if he went to the apartment and started asking questions, he would be announcing unreasonable concern. He wasn't prepared to do that.

Who was the girl at Rogers Peet? The one exchanging Christmas gifts. Cynthia? Cindy? . . . Cindy. Cindy Tuttle . . . Tottle. But not Tottle. . . . Bonner. Married to Paul Bonner, exchanging "dreary gifts for Paul."

He crossed to the bed and picked up the telephone directory.

Paul Bonner was listed: 480 Park Avenue. The address was appropriate. He gave the number to the switchboard.

The voice of a girl more asleep than awake answered.

"Yes? . . . Hello?"

"Mrs. Bonner?"

"Yes. What is it? This is Mrs. Bonner."

"I'm David Spaulding. You saw me this afternoon at Rogers Peet; you were exchanging gifts for your husband and I was buying a suit. . . . Forgive me for disturbing you but it's important. I had dinner with Leslie . . . Leslie Jenner; you called her. I just left her at her apartment; we were to meet tomorrow and now I find that I may not be able to. It's foolish but I forgot to get her telephone number, and I can't find it in the book. I wondered . . ."

"Mr. Spaulding." The girl interrupted him, her tone sharp, no longer blurred with sleep. "If this is a joke, I think it's in bad taste. I *do* remember your name. . . . I did *not* see you this afternoon and I wasn't exchanging . . . I wasn't in Rogers Peet. My husband was killed four months ago. In Sicily. . . . I haven't spoken to Leslie Jenner . . . Hawkwood, I think now . . . in over a year. She moved to California. Pasadena, I believe. . . . We haven't been in touch. Nor is it likely we would be."

David heard the abrupt click of the broken connection.

# 17

*DECEMBER 31, 1943, NEW YORK CITY*

It was the morning of New Year's Eve.

His first day of "employment" for Meridian Aircraft,
Blueprint Division.

He had stayed most of the previous day in his hotel
room, going out briefly for lunch and magazines, dinner
through room service, and finally a pointless taxi to Greenwich Village, where he knew he would not find Leslie
Jenner at ten o'clock.

He had remained confined for two reasons. The first
was a confirmation of the Mitchell Field doctor's diag-
nosis: he was exhausted. The second reason was equally
important. Fairfax was running checks on Leslie Jenner
Hawkwood, Cindy Tottle Bonner, and a naval officer
named Jack or John Webster, whose wife was conveniently
in California. David wanted this data before progressing
further, and Ed Pace had promised to be as thorough as
forty-eight hours allowed.

Spaulding had been struck by Cindy Bonner's words
concerning Leslie Jenner.

*She moved to California. Pasadena, I believe. . . .*

And a routine phone call to the Greenwich Village
apartment's superintendent had confirmed that, indeed, the
Websters *did* live there; the husband was in the navy, the
wife was visiting him someplace in California. The superintendent was holding the mail.

Someplace in California.

*She moved to California. . . .*

Was there a connection? Or simple coincidence.

Spaulding looked at his watch. It was eight o'clock. The
morning of New Year's Eve. Tomorrow would be 1944.

*This* morning, however, he was to report to one Walter Kendall and one Eugene Lyons at Meridian's temporary offices on Thirty-eighth Street.

Why would one of the largest aircraft companies in the United States have "temporary" offices?

The telephone rang. David reached for it.

"Spaulding?"

"Hello, Ed."

"I got what I could. It doesn't make a hell of a lot of sense. To begin with, there's no record of a divorce between the Hawkwoods. And he *is* in England. Eighth Air Force, but nothing classified. He's a pilot, Tenth Bomber Command down in Surrey."

"What about her living in California?"

"Eighteen months ago she left New York and moved in with an aunt in Pasadena. Very rich aunt, married to a man named Goldsmith; he's a banker—Social Register, polo set. From what we've learned—and it's sketchy—she just likes California."

"O.K. What about this Webster?"

"Checks out. He's a gunnery officer on the *Saratoga*. It pulled into San Diego for combat repairs. It's scheduled for sea duty in two weeks, and the date holds. Until then there are a lot of forty-eights, seventy-twos; no extended leaves, though. The wife Margaret joined her lieutenant a couple of days ago. She's at the Greenbrier Hotel."

"Anything on the Bonners?"

"Only what you know, except that he was a bona fide hero. Posthumous Silver Star, infantry. Killed on a scout patrol covering an ambush evacuation. Sicily invasion."

"And that's it?"

"That's it. Obviously they all know each other, but I can't find anything to relate to your DW assignment."

"But you're not the control, Ed. You said you didn't know what the assignment was."

"True. But from the fragments I *do* know about, I can't find anything."

"My room was searched. I'm not mistaken about that."

"Maybe theft. Rich soldier in a rich hotel, home from an extended tour. Could be someone figured you were carrying a lot of back pay, discharge money."

"I doubt that. It was too pro."

"A lot of pros work those hotels. They wait for guys to start off on an alcoholic evening and . . ."

Spaulding interrupted. "I want to follow up something."

"What?"

"The Bonner girl said it 'wasn't likely' she'd be in touch with Leslie Jenner, and she wasn't kidding. That's an odd thing to say, isn't it? I'd like to know why she said it."

"Go ahead. It was your hotel room, not mine. . . . You know what I think? And I've thought about it; I've had to."

"What?"

"That New York crowd plays a fast game of musical beds. Now, you didn't elaborate, but isn't it logical the lady was in New York for a few days, perhaps saw you herself, or knew someone who had, and figured, why not? I mean, what the hell, she's headed back to California; probably never see you again. . . ."

"No, it's not logical. She was too complicated; she didn't have to be. She was keeping me away from the hotel."

"Well, you were there. . . ."

"I certainly was. You know, it's funny. According to your major at Mitchell Field, you think the Azores thing was directed at me. . . ."

"I said *might* be," interjected Pace.

"And I don't. Yet here I am, convinced the other night was, and *you* don't. Maybe we're both getting tired."

"Maybe I'm also concerned for your source control. This Swanson, he's very nervous; this isn't his ball park. I don't think he can take many more complications."

"Then let's not give him any. Not now. I'll know if I should."

Spaulding watched the disheveled accountant as he outlined the Buenos Aires operation. He had never met anyone quite like Walter Kendall. The man was positively unclean. His body odor was only partially disguised by liberal doses of bay rum. His shirt collar was dirty, his suit unpressed, and David was fascinated to watch the man breathe simultaneously through his mouth and nostrils. The agent in Terceira had said Eugene Lyons was "odd"; if this Kendall was "normal," he couldn't wait to meet the scientist.

The Buenos Aires operation seemed simple enough, far

less complicated than most of the Lisbon work. So simple, in fact, that it angered him to think he had been removed from Lisbon for it. Had anyone bothered to fill him in a few weeks ago, he could have saved Washington a lot of planning, and probably money. He had been dealing with the German underground since that organization had consolidated its diverse factions and become an effective force. If this Erich Rhinemann was capable of buying the designs, removing them from the Peenemünde complex, he—the man in Lisbon—could have gotten them out of the country. Probably with more security than trying to slip them out of North Sea or Channel ports. Those ports were clamped tight, obsessively patrolled. Had they not been, much of his own work would have been unnecessary. The only really remarkable aspect of the operation was that Rhinemann *could* get blueprints—on *anything*—related to Peenemünde. That *was* extraordinary. Peenemünde was a concrete and steel vault buried in the earth. With the most complex system of safeguards and backups ever devised. It would be easier to get a man out—for any number of invented reasons—than to remove a single page of paper.

Further, Peenemünde kept its laboratories separate, vital stages coordinated by only a handful of elite scientific personnel under Gestapo check. In Buenos Aires terms, this meant that Erich Rhinemann was able to (1) reach and buy diverse laboratory heads in a systematic order; (2) circumvent or buy (impossible) the Gestapo; or (3) enlist the cooperation of those handful of scientists who crossed laboratory lines.

David's experience led him to disqualify the last two possibilities; there was too much room for betrayal. Rhinemann must have concentrated on the laboratory heads; that was dangerous enough but more feasible.

As Kendall talked, David decided to keep his conclusions to himself. He would ask several questions, one or two of which he really wanted answered, but he would not form a partnership with Walter Kendall at this time. It was an easy decision to make. Kendall was one of the least likable men he'd ever met.

"Is there any particular reason why the designs have to be delivered in stages?" Spaulding asked.

"They may not be. But Rhinemann's smuggling them out section by section. Everybody's got a schedule; he says it's safer that way. From his projections, we figure a period of a week."

"All right, that makes sense. . . . And this Lyons fellow can authenticate them?"

"There's no one better. I'll get to him in a few minutes; there are a couple of things you'll have to know. Once in Argentina, he's your property."

"That sounds ominous."

"You can handle him. You'll have help. . . . The point is, as soon as he's cleared those blueprints, you send the codes and Rhinemann gets paid. Not before."

"I don't understand. Why so complicated? If they check out, why not pay him off in Buenos Aires?"

"He doesn't want that money in an Argentine bank."

"It must be a bundle."

"It is."

"From what little I know of this Rhinemann, isn't it unusual for him to be working with the German underground?"

"He's a Jew."

"Don't tell any graduates of Auschwitz. They won't believe you."

"War makes necessary relationships. Look at us. We're working with the Reds. Same thing: common goals, forget the disagreements."

"In this case, that's a little cold-blooded."

"Their problem, not ours."

"I won't pursue it. . . . One obvious question. Since I'm on my way to Buenos Aires, the embassy, why this stop in New York? Wouldn't it have been easier to just rotate from Lisbon to Argentina?"

"A last-minute decision, I'm afraid. Awkward, huh?"

"Not too smooth. Am I on a transfer list?"

"A what?"

"Foreign Service transfer sheet. State Department. Military attaché."

"I don't know. Why?"

"I'd like to find out if it's common knowledge that I left Lisbon. Or could be common knowledge. I didn't think it was supposed to be."

"Then it wasn't. *Why?*"

"So I know how to behave, that's all."

"We thought you should spend a few days getting familiar with everything. Meet Lyons, me; go over the schedule. What we're after, that sort of thing."

"Very considerate." David saw the questioning look on Kendall's face. "No, I mean that. So often we get thrown field problems knowing too little background. I've done it to men myself. . . . Then this discharge, the combat in Italy, they're the cover for my Lisbon activities? For New York only."

"Yeah, I guess that's right." Kendall, who'd been sitting on the edge of his desk, got up and walked around to his chair.

"How far am I to carry it?"

"Carry what?" Kendall avoided looking at David, who was leaning forward on an office couch.

"The cover. The papers mention Fifth Army—that's Clark; Thirty-Fourth Division, One Hundred and Twelfth Battalion, et cetera. Should I bone up? I don't know much about the Italian Theater. Apparently I got hit beyond Salerno; are there circumstances?"

"That's army stuff. As far as I'm concerned you'll be here five, six days, then Swanson will see you and send you down to Buenos Aires."

"All right, I'll wait for General Swanson." David realized there was no point in pursuing G-2 rituals with Kendall. . . . Part professional, part amateur. The hesitation waltz.

"Until you leave you'll spend whatever time you think is necessary with Lyons. In his office."

"Fine. I'd like to meet him." David stood up.

"Sit down, he's not here today. Nobody's here today but the receptionist. Till one o'clock. It's New Year's Eve." Kendall slumped into his chair and took out a cigarette, which he squeezed. "I've got to tell you about Lyons."

"All right." David returned to the couch.

"He's a drunk. He spent four years in jail, in a penitentiary. He can hardly talk because his throat got burned out with raw alcohol. . . . He's also the smartest son of a bitch in aerophysics."

Spaulding stared at Kendall without replying for several moments. When he did speak, he made no attempt to conceal his shock. "That's kind of a contradictory recommendation, isn't it?"

"I said he's smart."

"So are half the lunatics in Bellevue. Can he *function?* Since he's going to be my 'property'—as you put it—I'd like to know what the hell you've given me. And *why,* not incidentally."

"He's the best."

"That doesn't answer my question. Questions."

"You're a soldier. You take orders."

"I give them, too. Don't start that way."

"All right. . . . O.K. You're entitled, I guess."

"I'd say so."

"Eugene Lyons wrote the book on physical aerodynamics; he was the youngest full professor at the Massachusetts Institute of Technology. Maybe he was too young; he went downhill fast. Bum marriage, a lot of drinking, a lot of debts; the debts did it, they usually do. That and too many brains no one wants to pay for."

"Did what?"

"He went out of his skull, a week's bender. When he woke up in a South Side Boston hotel room, the girl he was with was dead. He'd beaten her to death. . . . She was a whore so nobody cared too much; still, he did it. They called it unpremeditated murder and MIT got him a good lawyer. He served four years, got out and nobody would hire him, wouldn't touch him. . . . That was 1936. He gave up; joined the skid row bums. I mean he really joined them." Kendall paused and grinned.

David was disturbed by the accountant's smile; there was nothing funny in the story. "Obviously he didn't stay there." It was all he could think to say.

"Did for damn near three years. Got his throat burned out right down on Houston Street."

"That's very sad."

"Best thing that happened to him. In the hospital ward they took his history and a doctor got interested. He was shipped off to the goddamned CCC, was reasonably rehabilitated, and what with the war coming he got into defense work."

"Then he's all right now." Spaulding made the statement positively. Again, it was all he could think to say.

"You don't clean out a man like that overnight. Or in a couple of years. . . . He has lapses, falls into the booze barrel now and then. Since working on classified stuff he's cooped up with his own personal wardens. For instance, here in New York he's got a room at St. Luke's Hospital. He's taken back and forth just like your socialite drunks. . . . In California, Lockheed's got him in a garden apartment with male nurses round the clock, when he's away from the plant. Actually, he's got it pretty good."

"He must be valuable. That's a lot of trouble. . . ."

"I told you," interrupted Kendall. "He's *the best*. He's just got to be watched."

"What happens when he's on his own? I mean, I've known alcoholics; they can slip away, often ingeniously."

"That's no problem. He'll get liquor—when he wants it; he'll be ingenious about that. But he doesn't go outside by himself. He won't go where there are any people, if you know what I mean."

"I'm not sure I do."

"He doesn't talk. The best he can manage is a hoarse whisper; remember, his throat was boiled out. He stays away from people. . . . Which is fine. When he's not drinking—which is most of the time—he's reading and working. He'll spend days in a laboratory stone sober and never go outside. It's just fine."

"How does he communicate? In the lab? In a meeting?"

"Pad and pencil, a few whispers, his hands. Mostly a pad and pencil. It's just numbers, equations, diagrams. That's his language."

"His entire language?"

"That's right. . . . If you're thinking about holding a conversation with him, forget it. He hasn't had a conversation with anyone in ten years."

# 18

The
close
those
extra

*DECEMBER 31, 1943, NEW YORK CITY*

Spaulding hurried down Madison Avenue to the northeast corner of B. Altman's. There was a light snow falling; taxis rushed past the few pedestrians signaling in the middle of the block. The better fares were at the department store's entrance, carrying last-minute purchases for New Year's Eve. People who shopped at Altman's on the afternoon of New Year's Eve were prime passengers. Why waste gas on less?

David found himself walking faster than he had reason to; he wasn't going anywhere, to any specific place that required his presence at a specific time; he was getting away from Walter Kendall as fast as he could.

Kendall had finished his briefing on Eugene Lyons with the statement that "two hulks" would accompany the scientist to Buenos Aires. There'd be no liquor for the hermit-mute with his throat burned out; the male nurses carried "horse pills" at all times. Eugene Lyons, with no drink available, would spend hours over the work problems. Why not? He didn't do anything *else*. No conversations, David mused.

David turned down Kendall's offer of lunch on the pretext of looking up family friends. After all, it had been over three years. . . . He'd be in the office on January 2.

The truth was that Spaulding just wanted to get away from the man. And there was another reason: Leslie Jenner Hawkwood.

He didn't know where he'd begin, but he had to begin quickly. He had roughly a week to learn the story behind that incredible evening two nights ago. The beginning

would include a widow named Bonner, that much he
knew.

Perhaps Aaron Mandel could help him.

He took a dollar bill from his pocket and approached
the doorman in front of Altman's. A taxi was found in less
than a minute.

The ride uptown was made to the accompanying loqua-
ciousness of the driver, who seemed to have an opinion on
most any subject. David found the man annoying; he
wanted to think and it was difficult. Then suddenly he
was grateful to him.

"I was gonna catch the New Year's Eve crowds, like up
at the Plaza, you know what I mean? There's big tips over
at those war relief things. But the wife said no. She said
come home, drink a little wine, pray to God our boy gets
through the year. Now, I gotta. I mean if anything happened, I'd figure it was the tips I made New Year's Eve.
Superstitions! What the hell, the kid's a typist in Fort Dix."

David had forgotten the obvious. No, not forgotten; he
just hadn't considered the possibilities because they did not
relate to him. Or he to them. He was in New York. On
New Year's Eve. And that meant parties, dances, charity
balls and an infinite variety of war-created celebrations in a
dozen ballrooms and scores of townhouses.

Mrs. Paul Bonner would be at one of those places, at
one of those parties. It had been four months since her
husband had been killed. It was sufficient mourning under
the circumstances, for the times. Friends—other women
like Leslie Jenner, but of course not Leslie Jenner—would
make that clear to her. It was the way social Manhattan
behaved. And quite reasonable, all things considered.

It shouldn't be too difficult to find out where she was
going. And if he found her, he'd find others . . . it was a
place to start.

He tipped the driver and walked rapidly into the Montgomery lobby.

"Oh, Mr. Spaulding!" The old desk clerk's voice echoed
in the marble enclosure. "There's a message for you."

He crossed to the counter. "Thank you." He unfolded
the paper; *Mr. Fairfax had telephoned. Would he return
the call as soon as possible?*

Ed Pace wanted to reach him.

The thread was intact under the door lock. He entered his room and went directly to the telephone.

"We got something in on the Hawkwood girl," Pace said. "Thought you'd want to know."

"What is it?" Why, oh *why*, did Pace *always* start conversations like that? Did he expect him to say, no, I don't want to know anything, and hang up?

"It fits in, I'm afraid, with my opinion of the other night. Your antenna's been working overtime."

"For Christ's sake, Ed, I'll pin a medal on you whenever you like. What *is* it?"

"She plays around. She's got a wide sex life in the Los Angeles area. Discreet but busy. A high-class whore, if I don't offend you."

"You don't offend me. What's the source?"

"Several brother officers to begin with; navy and air force. Then some of the movie people, actors and a couple of studio executives. And the social-industrial crowd: Lockheed, Sperry Rand. She's not the most welcome guest at the Santa Monica Yacht Club."

"Is there a G-2 pattern?"

"First thing we looked for. Negative. No classified personnel in her bed. Just rank: military and civilian. And she *is* in New York. Careful inquiry says she went back to visit her parents for Christmas."

"There are no Jenners listed in the phone book who've ever heard of her."

"In Bernardsville, New Jersey?"

"No," said David wearily. "Manhattan. You *did* say New York."

"Try Bernardsville. If you want to find her. But don't hand in any expense vouchers; you're not on a courier run in the north country."

"No. Bernardsville is hunt country."

"What?"

"Very social territory. Stables and stirrup cups. . . . Thanks, Ed. You just saved me a lot of work."

"Think nothing of it. All you've had is the conduit center of Allied Intelligence solving the problems of your sex life. We try to please our employees."

"I promise to reenlist when it's all over. Thanks again."

"Dave?"

"Yes?"

"I'm not cleared for the Swanson job, so no specifics, but how does it strike you?"

"I'll be damned if I know why you're *not* cleared. It's a simple purchase being handled by some oddballs—at least one . . . no, two that I know about. The one I've met is a winner. It seems to me they've complicated the deal, but that's because they're new at it. . . . We could have done it better."

"Have you met Swanson?"

"Not yet. After the holidays, I'm told. What the hell, we wouldn't want to interfere with the brigadier's Christmas vacation. School doesn't start until the first week in January."

Pace laughed on the other end of the line. "Happy New Year, Dave."

"The same, Ed. And thanks."

Spaulding replaced the receiver. He looked at his watch; it was one fifteen. He could requisition an army vehicle somewhere, he supposed, or borrow a car from Aaron Mandel. Bernardsville was about an hour outside New York, west of the Oranges, if he remembered correctly. It might be best to take Leslie Jenner by surprise, giving her no chance to run. On the other hand, on the premise he had considered before Pace's call, Leslie was probably in New York, preparing for the New Year's Eve she'd promised him. Somewhere, someplace. In an apartment or a brownstone or a hotel room like his own.

Spaulding wondered for a moment whether Pace had a point. Was he trying to find Leslie for reasons quite apart from his suspicions? The lies, the search. . . . It was possible. Why not? But a two- to three-hour drive to west Jersey and back would bring him no closer to either objective, investigatory or Freudian. If she wasn't there.

He asked the Montgomery switchboard to get him the number of the Jenner residence in Bernardsville, New Jersey. Not to place the call, just get the telephone number. And the address. Then he called Aaron Mandel.

He had postponed it for as long as he could; Aaron would be filled with tears and questions and offers of anything under the Manhattan sun and moon. Ed Pace told him he had interviewed the old concert manager four years ago before approaching David for Lisbon; that would mean he could reasonably avoid any lengthy discussions about his work.

And Aaron might be able to help him, should he need the old man's particular kind of assistance. Mandel's New York contacts were damn near inexhaustible. David would know more after he reached Bernardsville; and it would be less awkward to have made his duty call to Aaron before asking favors.

At first Spaulding thought the old man would have a coronary over the telephone. Aaron's voice choked, conveying his shock, his concern . . . and his love. The questions came faster than David could answer them: his mother, his father, his own well-being.

Mandel did not ask him about his work, but neither would he be satisfied that David was as healthy as he claimed. Aaron insisted on a meeting, if not this evening then certainly tomorrow.

David agreed. In the morning, late morning. They would have a drink together, perhaps a light lunch; welcome the New Year together.

"God be praised. You are well. You'll come around tomorrow?"

"I promise," David said.

"And you've never broken a promise to me."

"I won't. Tomorrow. And Aaron . . ."

"Yes?"

"It's possible I may need to find someone tonight. I'm not sure where to look but probably among the Social Register crowd. How are your Park Avenue connections?"

The old man chuckled in the quiet, good-humored, slightly arrogant way David remembered so well. "I'm the only Jew with a Torah stand in St. John the Divine. Everybody wants an artist—for nothing, of course. Red Cross, green cross; debutantes for war bandages, dances for fancy-sounding French medal winners. You name it, Mandel's on the hook for it. I got three coloraturas, two pianists and five Broadway baritones making appearances for 'our boys' tonight. All on the Upper East Side."

"I may call you in a little while. Will you still be at the office?"

"Where else? For soldiers and concert managers, when are the holidays?"

"You haven't changed."

"The main thing is that you're well. . . ."

No sooner had David hung up the phone than it rang.

"I have the telephone number and the address of your party in Bernardsville, Mr. Spaulding."

"May I have them, please?"

The operator gave him the information and he wrote it down on the ever-present stationery next to the phone.

"Shall I put the call through, sir?"

David hesitated, then said, "Yes, please. I'll stay on the line. Ask for a Mrs. Hawkwood, please."

"Mrs. Hawkwood. Very well, sir. But I can call you back when I have the party."

"I'd rather stay on an open circuit. . . ." David caught himself, but not in time. The blunder was minor but confirmed by the operator. She replied in a knowing voice.

"Of course, Mr. Spaulding. I assume if someone other than Mrs. Hawkwood answers, you'll wish to terminate the call?"

"I'll let you know."

The operator, now part of some sexual conspiracy, acted her role with firm efficiency. She dialed the outside operator and in moments a phone could be heard ringing in Bernardsville, New Jersey. A woman answered; it was not Leslie.

"Mrs. Hawkwood, please."

"Mrs. . . ." The voice on the Bernardsville line seemed hesitant.

"Mrs. Hawkwood, please. Long distance calling," said the Montgomery operator, as if she were from the telephone company, expediting a person-to-person call.

"Mrs. Hawkwood isn't here, operator."

"Can you tell me what time she's expected, please?"

"What time? Good heavens, she's not expected. At least, I didn't think she was. . . ."

Not fazed, the Montgomery employee continued, interrupting politely. "Do you have a number where Mrs. Hawkwood can be reached, please?"

"Well . . ." The voice in Bernardsville was now bewildered. "I suppose in California. . . ."

David knew it was time to intercede. "I'll speak to the party on the line, operator."

"Very well, sir." There was a *ther-ump* sound indicating the switchboard's disengagement from the circuit.

"Mrs. Jenner?"

"Yes, this is Mrs. Jenner," answered Bernardsville, obviously relieved with the more familiar name.

"My name is David Spaulding, I'm a friend of Leslie's and . . ." *Jesus!* He'd forgotten the husband's first name. ". . . Captain Hawkwood's. I was given this number. . . ."

"Well, *David Spaulding!* How are you, dear? This is Madge Jenner, you silly boy! Good heavens, it must be eight, ten years ago. How's your father and mother? I hear they're living in London. So very brave!"

Christ! thought Spaulding, it never occurred to him that Leslie's mother would remember two East Hampton months almost a decade ago. "Oh, Mrs. Jenner. . . . They're fine. I'm sorry to disturb you. . . ."

"You could never disturb us, you dear boy. We're just a couple of old stablehands out here. James has doubled our colors; no one wants to keep horses anymore. . . . You thought Leslie was here?"

"Yes, that's what I was told."

"I'm sorry to say she's not. To be quite frank, we rarely hear from her. She moved to California, you know."

"Yes, with her aunt."

"Only half-aunt, dear. My stepsister; we've not gotten along too well, I'm afraid. She married a Jew. He calls himself Goldsmith—hardly a disguise for Goldberg or Goldstein, is it? We're convinced he's in the black market and all that profiteering, if you know what I mean."

"Oh? Yes, I see. . . . Then Leslie didn't come East to visit you for Christmas?"

"Good heavens, no! She barely managed to send us a card. . . ."

He was tempted to call Ed Pace in Fairfax; inform the Intelligence head that California G-2 had come up with a Bernardsville zero. But there was no point. Leslie Jenner Hawkwood was in New York.

He had to find out why.

He called Mandel back and gave him two names: Leslie's and Cindy Tottle Bonner, widow of Paul Bonner, hero. Without saying so, David indicated that his curiosity might well be more professional than personal. Mandel did not question; he went to work.

Spaulding realized that he could easily phone Cindy Bonner, apologize and ask to see her. But he couldn't risk her turning him down; which she probably would do in light of the crude telephone call he had placed two nights ago. There simply wasn't the time. He'd have to see her, trust the personal contact.

And even then she might not be able to tell him anything. Yet there were certain instincts one developed and came to recognize. Inverted, convoluted, irrational. . . . Atavistic.

Twenty minutes passed; it was quarter to three. His telephone rang.

"David? Aaron. This Hawkwood lady, there's absolutely nothing. Everyone says she moved to California and nobody's heard a word. . . . Mrs. Paul Bonner: there's a private party tonight, on Sixty-second Street, name of Warfield. Number 212."

"Thanks. I'll wait outside and crash it with my best manners."

"No need for that. You have an invitation. Personal from the lady of the house. Her name's Andrea and she's delighted to entertain the soldier son of the famous you-know-who. She also wants a soprano in February, but that's my problem."

# 19

THE RHINEMANN EXCHANGE

"I think I believe you."
"You should. It was sick. I'm not sick."
The army lieutenant returned carrying two glasses. He was plainly hostile. As David

## DECEMBER 31, 1943, NEW YORK CITY

The dinner clientele from the Gallery could have moved intact to the Warfield brownstone on Sixty-second Street. David mixed easily. The little gold emblem in his lapel served its purpose; he was accepted more readily, he was also more available. The drinks and buffet were generous, the small Negro jazz combo better than good.

And he found Cindy Bonner in a corner, waiting for her escort—an army lieutenant—to come back from the bar. She was petite, with reddish hair and very light, almost pale skin. Her posture was Vogue, her body slender, supporting very expensive, very subdued clothes. There was a pensive look about her; not sad, however. Not the vision of a hero's widow, not heroic at all. A rich little girl.

"I have a sincere apology to make," he told her. "I hope you'll accept it."

"I can't imagine what for. I don't think we've met." She smiled but not completely, as if his presence triggered a memory she could not define. Spaulding saw the look and understood. It was his voice. The voice that once had made him a good deal of money.

"My name is Spaulding. David . . ."

"You telephoned the other night," interrupted the girl, her eyes angry. "The Christmas gifts for Paul. Leslie . . ."

"That's why I'm apologizing. It was all a terrible misunderstanding. Please forgive me. It's not the sort of joke I'd enter into willingly; I was as angry as you were." He spoke calmly, holding her eyes with his own. It was sufficient; she blinked, trying to understand, her anger fading. She looked briefly at the tiny brass eagle in his lapel, the small insignia that could mean just about anything.

"I think I believe you."

"You should. It was sick; I'm not sick."

The army lieutenant returned carrying two glasses. He was drunk and hostile. Cindy made a short introduction; the lieutenant barely acknowledged the civilian in front of him. He wanted to dance; Cindy did not. The situation—abruptly created—was about to deteriorate.

David spoke with a trace of melancholy. "I served with Mrs. Bonner's husband. I'd like to speak with her for just a few minutes. I'll have to leave shortly, my wife's waiting for me uptown."

The combination of facts—reassurances—bewildered the drunken lieutenant as well as mollified him. His gallantry was called; he bowed tipsily and walked back toward the bar.

"Nicely done," Cindy said. "If there *is* a Mrs. Spaulding uptown, it wouldn't surprise me. You said you were out with Leslie; that's par for her course."

David looked at the girl. *Trust the developed instincts,* he thought to himself. "There is no Mrs. Spaulding. But there was a Mrs. Hawkwood the other night. I gather you're not very fond of her."

"She and my husband were what is politely referred to as 'an item.' A long-standing one. There are some people who say I forced her to move to California."

"Then I'll ask the obvious question. Under the circumstances, I wonder why she used your name? And then disappeared. She'd know I'd try to reach you."

"I think you used the term *sick*. She's sick."

"Or else she was trying to tell me something."

David left the Warfields' shortly before the New Year arrived. He reached the corner of Lexington Avenue and turned south. There was nothing to do but walk, think, try to piece together what he had learned; find a pattern that made sense.

He couldn't. Cindy Bonner was a bitter widow; her husband's death on the battlefield robbed her of any chance to strike back at Leslie. She wanted, according to her, simply to forget. But the hurt had been major. Leslie and Paul Bonner had been more than an "item." They had reached—again, according to Cindy—the stage where the Bonners had mutually sued for divorce. A confrontation between the two women, however, did not confirm Paul Bonner's story; Leslie Jenner Hawkwood had no *intention* of divorcing *her* husband.

It was all a messy, disagreeable Social Register foul-up; Ed Pace's "musical beds."

Why, then, would Leslie use Cindy's name? It was not only provocative and tasteless, it was senseless.

Midnight arrived as he crossed Fifty-second Street. A few horns blared from passing automobiles. In the distance could be heard tower bells and whistles; from inside bars came the shrill bleats of noisemakers and a cacophony of shouting. Three sailors, their uniforms filthy, were singing loudly off key to the amusement of pedestrians.

He walked west toward the string of cafes between Madison and Fifth. He considered stopping in at Shor's or 21 . . . in ten minutes or so. Enough time for the celebrations to have somewhat subsided.

"Happy New Year, Colonel Spaulding."

The voice was sharp and came from a darkened doorway.

"What?" David stopped and looked into the shadows. A tall man in a light grey overcoat, his face obscured by the brim of his hat, stood immobile. "What did you say?"

"I wished you a Happy New Year," said the man. "Needless to say, I've been following you. I overtook you several minutes ago."

The voice was lined with an accent, but David couldn't place it. The English was British tutored, the origin somewhere in Middle Europe. Perhaps the Balkans.

"I find that a very unusual statement and . . . needless to say . . . quite disturbing." Spaulding held his place; he had no weapon and wondered if the man recessed in the doorway was, conversely, armed. He couldn't tell. "What do you want?"

"Welcome you home, to begin with. You've been away a long time."

"Thank you. . . . Now, if you don't mind . . ."

"I mind! Don't move, colonel! Just stand there as if you were talking with an old friend. Don't back away; I'm holding a .45 leveled at your chest."

Several passersby walked around David on the curb side. A couple came out of an apartment entrance ten yards to the right of the shadowed doorway; they were in a hurry and crossed rapidly between Spaulding and the tall man with the unseen gun. David was first tempted to use them, but two considerations prevented him. The first was the grave danger to the couple; the second, the fact that the man with the gun had something to say. If he'd wanted to kill him, he would have done so by now.

"I won't move. . . . What is it?"

"Take two steps forward. Just *two*. No more."

David did so. He could see the face better now, but not clearly. It was a thin face, gaunt and lined. The eyes were deepset with hollows underneath. Tired eyes. The dull finish of the pistol's barrel was the clearest object David could distinguish. The man kept shifting his eyes to his left, behind Spaulding. He was looking for someone. Waiting.

"All right. Two steps. Now no one can walk between us. . . . Are you expecting someone?"

"I'd heard that the main agent in Lisbon was very controlled. You bear that out. Yes, I'm waiting; I'll be picked up shortly."

"Am I to go with you?"

"It won't be necessary. I'm delivering a message, that is all. . . . The incident at Lajes. It is to be regretted, the work of zealots. Nevertheless, accept it as a warning. We can't always control deep angers; surely you must know that. Fairfax should know it. Fairfax *will* know it before this first day of the New Year is over. Perhaps by now. . . . There is my car. Move to my right, your *left*." David did so as the man edged toward the curb, hiding the pistol under the cloth of his coat. "Heed us, colonel. There are to be no negotiations with Franz Altmüller. They are finished!"

"Wait a minute! I don't know what you're talking about. I don't *know* any Altmüller!"

"*Finished!* Heed the lesson of Fairfax!"

A dark brown sedan with bright headlights pulled up to the curb. It stopped, the rear door was thrown open, and the tall man raced across the sidewalk between the pedestrians and climbed in. The car sped away.

David rushed to the curb. The least he could do was get the vehicle's license number.

There was none. The rear license plate was missing.

Instead, above the trunk in the oblong rear window, a face looked back at him. His shock caused him to lose his breath. For the briefest of moments he wondered if his eyes, his senses were playing tricks on him, transporting his imagination back to Lisbon.

He started after the car, running in the street, dodging automobiles and the goddamned New Year's Eve revelers.

The brown sedan turned north on Madison Avenue and sped off. He stood in the street, breathless.

The face in the rear window was a man he had worked with in the most classified operations out of Portugal and Spain.

Marshall. Lisbon's master cryptographer.

The taxi driver accepted David's challenge to get him to the Montgomery in five minutes or less. It took seven, but considering the traffic on Fifth Avenue, Spaulding gave him five dollars and raced into the lobby.

There were no messages.

He hadn't bothered to thread his door lock; a conscious oversight, he considered. In addition to the maid service, if he could have offered an open invitation to those who had searched his room two nights ago, he would have done so. A recurrence might cause carelessness, some clues to identities.

He threw off his coat and went to his dresser, where he kept a bottle of Scotch. Two clean glasses stood on a silver tray next to the liquor. He'd take the necessary seconds to pour himself a drink before calling Fairfax.

"A very Happy New Year," he said slowly as he lifted the glass to his lips.

He crossed to the bed, picked up the telephone and gave the Virginia number to the switchboard. The circuits to the Washington area were crowded; it would take several minutes to get through.

What in God's name did the man mean? *Heed the lesson of Fairfax.* What the hell was he talking about? Who was Altmüller? . . . What was the first name? . . . Franz. Franz Altmüller.

Who was he?

So the Lajes Field "incident" *was* aimed at him. For Christ's sake, what *for*?

And *Marshall*. It *was* Marshall in that rear window! He *hadn't* been mistaken!

"Field Division Headquarters" were the monotoned words from the State of Virginia, County of Fairfax.

"Colonel Edmund Pace, please."

There was a slight pause at the other end of the line. David's ears picked up a tiny rush of air he knew very well.

It was a telephone intercept, usually attached to a wire recorder.

"Who's calling Colonel Pace?"

It was David's turn to hesitate. He did so thinking that perhaps he'd missed the interceptor sound before. It was entirely possible, and Fairfax was, after all . . . well, Fairfax.

"Spaulding. Lieutenant Colonel David Spaulding."

"Can I give the colonel a message, sir? He's in conference."

"No, you may not. You may and can give me the colonel."

"I'm sorry, sir." Fairfax's hesitation was now awkward. "Let me have a telephone number. . . ."

"Look, soldier, my name is Spaulding. My clearance is four-zero and this is a four-zero priority call. If those numbers don't mean anything to you, ask the son of a bitch on your intercept. Now, it's an emergency. Put me through to Colonel Pace!"

There was a loud double click on the line. A deep, hard voice came over the wire.

"And this is Colonel Barden, Colonel Spaulding. I'm also four-zero and any four-zeros will be cleared with this son of a bitch. Now, I'm in no mood for any rank horseshit. What do you want?"

"I like your directness, colonel," said David, smiling in spite of his urgency. "Put me through to Ed. It's really priority. It concerns Fairfax."

"I can't put you through, colonel. We don't have any circuits, and I'm not trying to be funny. Ed Pace is dead. He was shot through the head an hour ago. Some goddamned son of a bitch killed him right here in the compound."

## 20

## JANUARY 1, 1944, FAIRFAX, VIRGINIA

It was four thirty in the morning when the army car carrying Spaulding reached the Fairfax gate.

The guards had been alerted; Spaulding, in civilian clothes, possessing no papers of authorization, was matched against his file photograph and waved through. David had been tempted to ask to see the photograph; to the best of his knowledge, it was four years old. Once inside, the automobile swung left and headed to the south area of the huge compound. About a half mile down the gravel road, past rows of metal Quonset huts, the car pulled up in front of a barracks structure. It was the Fairfax Administration Building.

Two corporals flanked the door. The sergeant driver climbed out of the car and signaled the noncoms to let Spaulding through; he was already in front of them.

David was shown to an office on the second floor. Inside were two men: Colonel Ira Barden and a doctor named McCleod, a captain. Barden was a thick, short man with the build of a football tackle and close-cropped black hair. McCleod was stooped, slender, bespectacled—the essence of the thoughtful academician.

Barden wasted the minimum time with introductions. Completed, he went immediately to the questions at hand.

"We've doubled patrols everywhere, put men with K-9s all along the fences. I'd like to think no one could get out. What bothers us is whether someone got out beforehand."

"How did it happen?"

"Pace had a few people over for New Year's. Twelve, to be exact. Four were from his own Quonset, three from

Records, the rest from Administration. Very subdued . . . what the hell, this is Fairfax. As near as we can determine, he went out his back door at about twenty minutes past midnight. Carrying out garbage, we think; maybe just to get some air. He didn't come back. . . . A guard down the road came to the door, saying he'd heard a shot. No one else had. At least, not inside."

"That's unusual. These quarters are hardly soundproof."

"Someone had turned up the phonograph."

"I thought it was a subdued party."

Barden looked hard at Spaulding. His glare was not anger, it was his way of telegraphing his deep concern. "That record player was turned up for no more than thirty seconds. The rifle used—and ballistics confirms this—was a training weapon, .22 caliber."

"A sharp crack, no louder," said David.

"Exactly. The phonograph was a signal."

"Inside. At the party," added Spaulding.

"Yes. . . . McCleod here is the base psychiatrist. We've been going over everyone who was inside. . . ."

"Psychiatrist?" David was confused. It was a security problem, not medical.

"Ed was a hardnose, you know that as well as I do. He trained you. . . . I looked you up, Lisbon. It's one angle. We're covering the others."

"Look," interrupted the doctor, "you two want to talk, and I've got files to go over. I'll call you in the morning; later this morning, Ira. Nice to meet you, Spaulding. Wish it wasn't this way."

"Agreed," said Spaulding, shaking the man's hand.

The psychiatrist gathered up the twelve file folders on the colonel's desk and left.

The door closed. Barden indicated a chair to Spaulding. David sat down, rubbing his eyes. "One hell of a New Year's, isn't it?" said Barden.

"I've seen better," Spaulding replied.

"Do you want to go over what happened to you?"

"I don't think there's any point. I was stopped; I told you what was said. Ed Pace was obviously the 'Fairfax lesson.' It's tied to a brigadier named Swanson at DW."

"I'm afraid it isn't."

"It has to be."

"Negative. Pace wasn't involved with the DW thing. His only tie was recruiting you; a simple transfer."

David remembered Ed Pace's words: *I'm not cleared . . . how does it strike you? Have you met Swanson?* He looked at Barden. "Then someone thinks he was. Same motive. Related to the sabotage at Lajes. In the Azores."

"How?"

"The son of a bitch said so on Fifty-second Street! Five *hours* ago. . . . Look, Pace is dead; that gives you certain latitude under the circumstances. I want to check Ed's four-zero files. Everything connected to my transfer."

"I've already done that. After your call there was no point in waiting for an inspector general. Ed was about my closest friend. . . ."

"And?"

"There are no files. Nothing."

"There *has* to be! There's got to be a record for Lisbon. For *me*."

"There is. It states simple transfer to DW. No names. Just a word. A single word: 'Tortugas.' "

"What about the papers you prepared? The discharge, the medical record; Fifth Army, One Hundred and Twelfth Battalion? Italy? . . . Those papers aren't manufactured without a Fairfax file!"

"This is the first I've heard of them. There's nothing about them in Ed's vaults."

"A major—Winston, I think his name is—met me at Mitchell Field. I flew in from Newfoundland on a coastal patrol. He brought me the papers."

"He brought you a sealed envelope and gave you verbal instructions. That's all he knows."

"*Jesus!* What the hell happened to the so-called Fairfax efficiency?"

"You tell me. And while you're at it, who murdered Ed Pace?"

David looked over at Barden. The word *murder* hadn't occurred to him. One didn't commit *murder*; one killed, yes, that was part of it. But murder? Yet it *was* murder.

"I can't tell you that. But I can tell you where to start asking questions."

"Please do."

"Raise Lisbon. Find out what happened to a cryptographer named Marshall."

# JANUARY 1, 1944, WASHINGTON, D.C.

The news of Pace's murder reached Alan Swanson indirectly; the effect was numbing.

He had been in Arlington, at a small New Year's Eve dinner party given by the ranking general of Ordnance when the telephone call came. It was an emergency communication for another guest, a lieutenant general on the staff of the Joint Chiefs. Swanson had been near the library door when the man emerged; the staffer had been white, his voice incredulous.

"My God!" he had said to no one in particular. "Someone shot Pace over at Fairfax. He's dead!"

Those few in that small gathering in Arlington comprised the highest echelons of the military; there was no need for concealing the news; they would all, sooner or later, be told.

Swanson's hysterical first thoughts were of Buenos Aires. Was there *any possible connection?*

He listened as the brigadiers and the two- and three-stars joined in controlled but excited speculations. He heard the words . . . *infiltrators, hired assassins, double agents.* He was stunned by the wild theories . . . advanced rationally . . . that one of Pace's undercover agents had to be behind the murder. Somewhere a defector had been paid to make his way back to Fairfax; somewhere there was a weak link in a chain of Intelligence that had been bought.

Pace was not just a crack Intelligence man, he was one of the best in Allied Central. So much so that he twice had requested that his brigadier star be officially recorded but not issued, thus protecting his low profile.

But the profile was not low enough. An extraordinary man like Pace would have an extraordinary price on his head. From Shanghai to Berne; with Fairfax's rigid security the killing had to have been planned for months. Conceived as a long-range project, to be executed internally. There was no other way it could have been accomplished. And there were currently over five hundred personnel in the compound, including a rotating force of espionage units-in-training—nationals from many countries. No se-

curity system could be that absolute under the circumstances. All that was needed was one man to slip through.

*Planned for months . . . a defector who had made his
way back to Fairfax . . . a double agent . . . a weak
Intelligence link paid a fortune. Berne to Shanghai.*

*A long-range project!*

These were the specific words and terms and judgments
that Swanson heard clearly because he wanted to hear
them.

They removed the motive from Buenos Aires. Pace's
death had nothing to *do* with Buenos Aires because the
time element prohibited it.

The Rhinemann exchange had been conceived barely
three weeks ago; it was inconceivable that Pace's murder
was related. For it to be so would mean that he, himself,
had broken the silence.

No one else on earth knew of Pace's contribution. And
even Pace had known precious little.

Only fragments.

And all the background papers concerning the man in
Lisbon had been removed from Pace's vault. Only the War
Department transfer remained.

A fragment.

Then Alan Swanson thought of something and he marveled at his own cold sense of the devious. In a way, it was
chilling that it could escape the recesses of his mind. With
Edmund Pace's death, not even Fairfax could piece together the events leading up to Buenos Aires. The government of the United States was removed one step further.

As if abstractly seeking support, he ventured aloud to
the small group of his peers that he recently had been in
communication with Fairfax, with Pace as a matter of fact,
over a minor matter of clearance. It was insignificant
really, but he hoped to Christ . . .

He found his support instantly. The lieutenant general
from staff, two brigs and a three-star all volunteered that
they, too, had used Pace.

Frequently. Obviously more than he did.

"You could save a lot of time dealing directly with Ed,"
said the staffer. "He cut tape and shot you off a clearance
right away."

*One step further removed.*

Once back in his Washington apartment, Swanson experienced the doubts again. Doubts and opportunities alike. Pace's murder was potentially a problem because of the shock waves it would produce. There would be a major investigation, all avenues explored. On the other hand, the concentration would be on Fairfax. It would consume Allied Central Intelligence. At least for a while. He had to move now. Walter Kendall had to get to Buenos Aires and conclude the arrangements with Rhinemann.

The guidance designs from Peenemünde. Only the designs were important.

But first tonight, this morning. David Spaulding. It was time to give the former man in Lisbon his assignment.

Swanson picked up the telephone. His hand shook.

The guilt was becoming unbearable.


## JANUARY 1, 1944, FAIRFAX, VIRGINIA

"Marshall was killed several miles from a place called Valdero's. In the Basque province. It was an ambush."

"That's horseshit! Marsh never went into the north country! He wasn't trained, he wouldn't know what to do!" David was out of the chair, confronting Barden.

"Rules change. You're not the man in Lisbon now. . . . He went, he was killed."

"Source?"

"The ambassador himself."

"*His* source?"

"Your normal channels, I assume. He said it was confirmed. Identification was brought back."

"Meaningless!"

"What do you want? A body?"

"This may surprise you, Barden, but a hand or a finger isn't out of the question. *That's* identification. . . . Any photographs? Close shots, wounds, the eyes? Even those can be doctored."

"He didn't indicate any. What the hell's eating you? This is *confirmed*."

"Really?" David stared at Barden.

"For Christ's sake, Spaulding! What the hell is . . . 'Tortugas'? If it killed Ed Pace, I want to know! And I'm

going to goddamned well find out! I don't give a shit about
Lisbon cryps!"

The telephone rang on Barden's desk; the colonel looked
briefly at it, then pulled his eyes back to Spaulding.

"Answer it," said David. "One of those calls is going to
be Casualty. Pace has a family. . . . Had."

"Don't complicate my life any more than you have."
Barden crossed to his desk. "Ed was due for an escort leave
this Friday. I'm putting off calling—till morning. . . . Yes?"
The colonel listened to the phone for several seconds, then
looked at Spaulding. "It's the trip-line operator in New
York; the one we've got covering you. This General Swan-
son's been trying to reach you. He's got him holding now.
Do you want him to put the old man through?"

David remembered Pace's appraisal of the nervous
brigadier. "Do you have to tell him I'm here?"

"Hell, no."

"Then put him through."

Barden walked from behind the desk as Spaulding took
the phone and repeated the phrase "Yes, sir" a number of
times. Finally he replaced the instrument. "Swanson wants
me in his office this morning."

"I want to know why the hell they ripped you out of
Lisbon," Barden said.

David sat down in the chair without at first answering.
When he spoke he tried not to sound military or officious.
"I'm not sure it had anything to do with . . . anything. I
don't want to duck; on the other hand, in a way I have to.
But I want to keep a couple of options open. Call it in-
stinct, I don't know. . . . There's a man named Altmüller.
Franz Altmüller. . . . Who he is, where he is—I have no
idea. German, Swiss, I don't know. . . . Find out what you
can on a four-zero basis. Call me at the Hotel Montgomery
in New York. I'll be there for at least the rest of the week.
Then I go to Buenos Aires."

"I will if you flex the clearances . . . tell me what the hell
is going on."

"You won't like it. Because if I do, and if it *is* connected, it'll mean Fairfax has open code lines in Berlin."

# JANUARY 1, 1944, NEW YORK CITY

The commercial passenger plane began its descent toward La Guardia Airport. David looked at his watch. It was a little past noon. It had all happened in twelve hours: Cindy Bonner, the stranger on Fifty-second Street, Marshall, Pace's murder, Barden, the news from Valdero's . . . and finally the awkward conference with the amateur source control, Brigadier General Alan Swanson, DW.

Twelve hours.

He hadn't slept in nearly forty-eight. He needed sleep to find some kind of perspective, to piece together the elusive pattern. Not the one that was clear.

Erich Rhinemann was to be killed.

Of *course* he had to be killed. The only surprise for David was the bumbling manner in which the brigadier had given the order. It didn't require elaboration or apology. And it—at *last*—explained his transfer from Lisbon. It filled in the gaping hole of *why*. He was no gyroscope specialist; it hadn't made sense. But now it did. He was a good selection; Pace had made a thoroughly professional choice. It was a job for which he was suited—in addition to being a bilingual liaison between the mute gyroscopic scientist, Eugene Lyons, and Rhinemann's blueprint man.

*That* picture was clear; he was relieved to see it come into focus.

What bothered him was the unfocused picture.

The embassy's Marshall, the cryp who five days ago picked him up at a rain-soaked airfield outside of Lisbon. The man he *had* seen looking at him through the automobile window on Fifty-second Street; the man supposedly killed in an ambush in the north country, into which he never had ventured. Or would venture.

Leslie Jenner Hawkwood. The resourceful ex-lover who had lied and kept him away from his hotel room, who foolishly used the ploy of Cindy Bonner and the exchange of gifts for a dead husband she had stolen. Leslie was not an idiot. She *was* telling him something.

But what?

And Pace. Poor, humorless Ed Pace cut down within the most security-conscious enclosure in the United States.

The *lesson of Fairfax*, predicted with incredible accuracy—nearly to the moment—by a tall, sad-eyed man in shadows on Fifty-second Street.

That . . . *they* were the figures in the unfocused picture.

David had been harsh with the brigadier. He had demanded—professionally, of course—to know the exact date the decision had been reached to eliminate Erich Rhinemann. Who had arrived at it? How was the order transmitted? Did the general know a cryptographer named Marshall? Had Pace ever mentioned him? Had *anyone* ever mentioned him? And a man named Altmüller. Franz Altmüller. Did that name mean anything?

The answers were no help. And God knew Swanson wasn't lying. He wasn't pro enough to get away with it.

The names Marshall and Altmüller were unknown to him. The decision to execute Rhinemann was made within hours. There was absolutely no way Ed Pace could have known; he was not consulted, nor was anyone at Fairfax. It was a decision emanating from the cellars of the White House; no one at Fairfax or Lisbon could have been involved. For David that absence of involvement was the important factor. It meant simply that the whole unfocused picture had nothing to do with Erich Rhinemann. And thus, as far as could be determined, was unrelated to Buenos Aires. David made the quick decision not to confide in the nervous brigadier. Pace had been right: the man couldn't take any more complications. He'd use Fairfax, source control be damned.

The plane landed; Spaulding walked into the passenger terminal and looked for the signs that read Taxis. He went through the double doors to the platform and heard the porters shouting the various destinations of the unfilled cabs. It was funny, but the shared taxis were the only things that caused him to think La Guardia Airport knew there was a war going on somewhere.

Simultaneously he recognized the foolishness of his thoughts. And the pretentiousness of them.

A soldier with no legs was being helped into a cab. Porters and civilians were touched, helpful.

The soldier was drunk. What was left of him, unstable.

Spaulding shared a taxi with three other men, and they

talked of little but the latest reports out of Italy. David decided to forget his cover in case the inevitable questions came up. He wasn't about to discuss any mythical combat in Salerno. But the questions did not arise. And then he saw why.

The man next to him was blind; the man shifted his weight and the afternoon sun caused a reflection in his lapel. It was a tiny metal replica of a ribbon: South Pacific.

David considered again that he was terribly tired. He was about the most unobservant agent ever to have been given an operation, he thought.

He got out of the cab on Fifth Avenue, three blocks north of the Montgomery. He had overpaid his share; he hoped the other two men would apply it to the blind veteran whose clothes were one hell of a long way from Leslie Jenner's Rogers Peet.

Leslie Jenner . . . Hawkwood.

A cryptographer named Marshall.

The unfocused picture.

He had to put it all out of his mind. He had to sleep, forget; let everything settle before he thought again. Tomorrow morning he would meet Eugene Lyons and begin . . . again. He had to be ready for the man who'd burned his throat out with raw alcohol and had not had a conversation in ten years.

The elevator stopped at the sixth floor. His was the seventh. He was about to tell the elevator operator when he realized the doors were not opening.

Instead, the operator turned in place. In his hand he gripped a short-barreled Smith & Wesson revolver. He reached behind him to the lever control and pushed it to the left, the enclosed box jerked and edged itself up between floors.

"The lobby lights go out this way, Colonel Spaulding. We may hear buzzers, but there's a second elevator used in emergencies. We won't be disturbed."

The accent was the same, thought David. British overlay, Middle Europe. "I'm glad of that. I mean, Jesus, it's been so long."

"I don't find you amusing."

"Nor I, you . . . obviously."

"You've been to Fairfax, Virginia. Did you have a pleasant journey?"

"You've got an extraordinary pipeline." Spaulding wasn't only buying time with conversation. He and Ira Barden had taken the required precautions. Even if the Montgomery switchboard reported everything he said, there was no evidence that he had flown to Virginia. The arrangements were made from telephone booths, the flight from Mitchell to Andrews under an assumed name on a crew sheet. Even the Manhattan number he had left with the Montgomery desk had a New York address under constant surveillance. And *in* the Fairfax compound, only the security gate had his name; he had been seen by only four, perhaps five men.

"We have reliable sources of information. . . . Now you have learned firsthand the lesson of Fairfax, no?"

"I've learned that a good man was murdered. I imagine his wife and children have been told by now."

"There is no murder in war, colonel. A misapplication of the word. And don't speak to us. . . ."

A buzzer interrupted the man. It was short, a polite ring.

"Who is 'us'?" asked David.

"You'll know in time, if you cooperate. If you don't cooperate, it will make no difference; you'll be killed. . . . We don't make idle threats. Witness Fairfax."

The buzzer sounded again. This time prolonged, not quite polite.

"How am I supposed to cooperate? What about?"

"We must know the precise location of Tortugas."

Spaulding's mind raced back to five o'clock that morning. In Fairfax. Ira Barden had said that the name "Tortugas" was the single word opposite his transfer specification. No other data, nothing but the word "Tortugas." And it had been buried in Pace's "vaults." Cabinets kept behind steel doors, accessible only to the highest echelon Intelligence personnel.

"Tortugas is part of an island complex off the coast of Florida. It's usually referred to as the Dry Tortugas. It's on any map."

The buzzer again. Now repeated; in short, angry spurts.

"Don't be foolish, colonel."

"I'm not being anything. I don't know what you're talking about."

The man stared at Spaulding. David saw that he was unsure, controlling his anger. The elevator buzzer was incessant now; voices could be heard from above and below.

"I'd prefer not to have to kill you but I will. *Where is Tortugas?*"

Suddenly a loud male voice, no more than ten feet from the enclosure, on the sixth floor, shouted:

"*It's up here! It's stuck!* Are you all *right* up there?"

The man blinked, the shouting had unnerved him. It was the instant David was waiting for. He lashed his right hand out in a diagonal thrust and gripped the man's forearm, hammering it against the metal door. He slammed his body into the man's chest and brought his knee up in a single, crushing assault against the groin. The man screamed in agony; Spaulding grabbed the arched throat with his left hand and tore at the veins around the larynx. He hammered the man twice more in the groin, until the pain was so excruciating that no more screams could emerge, only low, wailing moans of anguish. The body went limp, the revolver fell to the floor, and the man slid downward against the wall.

Spaulding kicked the weapon away and gripped the man's neck with both hands, shaking the head back and forth to keep him conscious.

"Now, you tell *me*, you son of a bitch! What *is* 'Tortugas'?"

The shouting outside the elevator was now deafening. There was a cacophony of hysteria brought on by the screams of the battered operator. There were cries for the hotel management. For the police.

The man looked up at David, tears of terrible pain streaming from his eyes. "Why not kill me, pig," he said between agonizing chokes of breath. ". . . You've tried before."

David was bewildered. He'd never *seen* the man. The north country? Basque? Navarre?

There was no time to think.

"What is '*Tortugas*'?"

"Altmüller, pig. The pig Altmüller . . ." The man fell into unconsciousness.

There was the name again.

*Altmüller.*

Spaulding rose from the unconscious body and grabbed the control lever of the elevator. He swung it to the far left, accelerating the speed as fast as possible. There were ten floors in the Montgomery; the panel lights indicated that the first-, third-, and sixth-floor buttons had been activated. If he could reach the tenth before the hysterical voices followed him up the stairs, it was possible that he could get out of the elevator, race down the corridor to one of the corners, then double back into the crowd which surely would gather around the open elevator doors.

Around the unconscious man on the floor.

It *had* to be possible! This was no time for him to be involved with the New York police.

The man was carried away on a stretcher; the questions were brief.

*No, he didn't know the elevator operator. The man had dropped him off at his floor ten or twelve minutes ago. He'd been in his room and came out when he'd heard all the shouting.*

*The same as everyone else.*

*What was New York coming to?*

David reached his room on seven, closed the door and stared at the bed. Christ, he was exhausted! But his mind refused to stop racing.

He would postpone everything until he had rested, except for two items. He had to consider those now. They could not wait for sleep because a telephone might ring, or someone might come to his hotel room. And he had to make his decisions in advance. Be prepared.

The first item was that Fairfax no longer could be used as a source. It was riddled, infiltrated. He had to function without Fairfax, which, in a way, was akin to telling a cripple he had to walk without braces.

On the other hand, he was no cripple.

The second item was a man named Altmüller. He had to find a man named Franz Altmüller; find out who he was, what he meant to the unfocused picture.

David lay down on the bed; he didn't have the energy to remove his clothes, even his shoes. He brought his arm up to shade his eyes from the afternoon sun streaming in the hotel windows. The afternoon sun of the first day of the new year, 1944.

Suddenly, he opened his eyes in the black void of tweed cloth. There was a third item. Inextricably bound to the man named Altmüller.

What the hell did "Tortugas" mean?

# 21

*JANUARY 2, 1944, NEW YORK CITY*

Eugene Lyons sat at a drafting board in the bare office. He was in shirtsleeves. There were blueprints strewn about on tables. The bright morning sun bouncing off the white walls gave the room the antiseptic appearance of a large hospital cubicle.

And Eugene Lyons's face and body did nothing to discourage such thoughts.

David had followed Kendall through the door, apprehensive at the forthcoming introduction. He would have preferred not knowing anything about Lyons.

The scientist turned on the stool. He was among the thinnest men Spaulding had ever seen. The bones were surrounded by flesh, not protected by it. Light blue veins were in evidence throughout the hands, arms, neck and temples. The skin wasn't old, it was worn out. The eyes were deep-set but in no way dull or flat; they were alert and, in their own way, penetrating. His straight grey hair was thinned out before its time; he could have been any age within a twenty-year span.

There was, however, one quality about the man that seemed specific: disinterest. He acknowledged the intrusion, obviously knew who David was, but made no move to interrupt his concentration.

Kendall forced the break. "Eugene, this is Spaulding. You show him where to start."

And with those words Kendall turned on his heel and went out the door, closing it behind him.

David stood across the room from Lyons. He took the

necessary steps and extended his hand. He knew exactly what he was going to say.

"It's an honor to meet you, Dr. Lyons. I'm no expert in your field, but I've heard about your work at MIT. I'm lucky to have you spread the wealth, even if it's only for a short time."

There was a slight, momentary flicker of interest in the eyes. David had gambled on a simple greeting that told the emaciated scientist several things, among which was the fact that David was aware of Lyons's tragedy in Boston—thus, undoubtedly, the rest of his story—and was not inhibited by it.

Lyons's grip was limp; the disinterest quickly returned. Disinterest, not necessarily rudeness. On the borderline.

"I know we haven't much time and I'm a neophyte in gyroscopics," said Spaulding, releasing the hand, backing off to the side of the drafting board. "But I'm told I don't have to recognize much more than pretty basic stuff; be able to verbalize in German the terms and formulas you write out for me."

David emphasized—with the barest rise in his voice—the words *verbalize . . . you write out for me.* He watched Lyons to see if there was any reaction to his open acknowledgment of the scientist's vocal problem. He thought he detected a small hint of relief.

Lyons looked up at him. The thin lips flattened slightly against the teeth; there was a short extension at the corners of the mouth and the scientist nodded. There was even an infinitesimal glint of appreciation in the deep-set eyes. He got up from his stool and crossed to the nearest table where several books lay on blueprints. He picked up the top volume and handed it to Spaulding. The title on the cover was *Diagrammatics: Inertia and Precession.*

David knew it would be all right.

It was past six o'clock.

Kendall had gone; the receptionist had bolted at the stroke of five, asking David to close the doors if he was the last person to leave. If not, tell one of the others.

The "others" were Eugene Lyons and his two male nurses.

Spaulding met them—the male nurses—briefly in the reception room. Their names were Hal and Johnny. Both

were large men; the talkative one was Hal, the leader was
Johnny, an ex-marine.

"The old guy is on his real good behavior," said Hal.
"Nothing to worry about."

"It's time to get him back to St. Luke's," said Johnny.
"They get pissed off if he's too late for the night meal."

Together the men went into Lyons's office and brought
him out. They were polite with the cadaverous physicist,
but firm. Eugene Lyons looked indifferently at Spaulding,
shrugged and walked silently out the door with his two
keepers.

David waited until he heard the sound of the elevator in
the hallway. Then he put down the *Diagrammatics* volume
the physicist had given him on the receptionist's desk and
crossed to Walter Kendall's office.

The door was locked, which struck him as strange. Kendall was on his way to Buenos Aires, he might not be back
for several weeks. Spaulding withdrew a small object from
his pocket and knelt down. At first glance, the instrument
in David's hand appeared to be an expensive silver pocket
knife, the sort so often found at the end of an expensive
key chain, especially in very expensive men's clubs. It
wasn't. It was a locksmith's pick designed to give that
appearance. It had been made in London's Silver Vaults, a
gift from an MI-5 counterpart in Lisbon.

David spun out a tiny cylinder with a flat tip and inserted it into the lock housing. In less than thirty seconds
the appropriate clicks were heard and Spaulding opened
the door. He walked in, leaving it ajar.

Kendall's office had no file cabinets, no closets, no book-
shelves; no recesses whatsoever other than the desk
drawers. David turned on the fluorescent reading lamp at
the far edge of the blotter and opened the top center
drawer.

He had to stifle a genuine laugh. Surrounded by an odd
assortment of paper clips, toothpicks, loose Lifesavers, and
note paper were two pornographic magazines. Although
marked with dirty fingerprints, both were fairly new.

*Merry Christmas, Walter Kendall*, thought David a little
sadly.

The side drawers were empty, at least there was nothing
of interest. In the bottom drawer lay crumpled yellow

pages of note paper, meaningless doodles drawn with a hard pencil, piercing the pages.

He was about to get up and leave when he decided to look once more at the incoherent patterns on the crumpled paper. There was nothing else; Kendall had locked his office door out of reflex, not necessity. And again by reflex, perhaps, he had put the yellow pages—not in a waste-basket, which had only the contents of emptied ashtrays—but in a drawer. Out of sight.

David knew he was reaching. There was no choice; he wasn't sure what he was looking for, if anything.

He spread two of the pages on top of the blotter, press-ing the surfaces flat.

Nothing.

Well, something. Outlines of women's breasts and geni-talia. Assorted circles and arrows, diagrams: a psychoana-lyst's paradise.

He removed another single page and pressed it out. More circles, arrows, breasts. Then to one side, childlike outlines of clouds—billowy, shaded; diagonal marks that could be rain or multiple sheets of thin lightning.

Nothing.

Another page.

It caught David's eye. On the bottom of the soiled yellow page, barely distinguishable between criss-cross penciling, was the outline of a large swastika. He looked at it closely. The swastika had circles at the right-hand points of the insignia, circles that spun off as if the artist were duplicating the ovals of a Palmer writing exercise. And flowing out of these ovals were unmistakable initials. *JD.* Then *Joh D., J. Diet.* . . . The letters appeared at the end of each oval line. And beyond the final letters in each area were elaborately drawn *? ? ?*

*? ? ?*

David folded the paper carefully and put it in his jacket pocket.

There were two remaining pages, so he took them out simultaneously. The page to the left had only one large, indecipherable scribble—once more circular, now angry—and meaningless. But on the second paper, again toward the bottom of the page, was a series of scroll-like markings that could be interpreted as *J*s and *D*s. similar in flow to the letters after the swastika points on the other page.

And opposite the final *D* was a strange horizontal obelisk, its taper on the right. There were lines on the side as though they were edges. . . . A bullet, perhaps, with bore markings. Underneath, on the next line of the paper to the left, were the same oval motions that brought to mind the Palmer exercise. Only they were firmer here, pressed harder into the yellow paper.

Suddenly David realized what he was staring at.

Walter Kendall had subconsciously outlined an obscene caricature of an erect penis and testicles.

*Happy New Year, Mr. Kendall,* thought Spaulding.

He put the page carefully into his pocket with its partner, returned the others and shut the drawer. He switched off the lamp, walked to the open door, turning to see if he had left everything as it was, and crossed into the reception room. He pulled Kendall's door shut and considered briefly whether to lock the tumblers in place.

It would be pointless to waste the time. The lock was old, simple; janitorial personnel in just about any building in New York would have a key, and it was more difficult inserting tumblers than releasing them. To hell with it.

A half hour later it occurred to him—in an instant of reflection—that this decision probably saved his life. The sixty, or ninety, or one-hundred-odd seconds he eliminated from his departure placed him in the position of an observer, not a target.

He put on the Rogers Peet overcoat, turned off the lights, and walked into the corridor to the bank of elevators. It was nearly seven, the day after New Year's, and the building was practically deserted. A single elevator was working. It had passed his floor, ascending to the upper stories, where it seemed to linger. He was about to use the stairs—the offices were on the third floor, it might be quicker—when he heard rapid, multiple footsteps coming up the staircase. The sound was incongruous. Moments ago the elevator had been in the lobby; why would two—more than two?—people be racing up the stairs at seven at night? There could be a dozen reasonable explanations, but his instincts made him consider *un*reasonable ones.

Silently, he ran to the opposite end of the short floor, where an intersecting corridor led to additional offices on the south side of the building. He rounded the corner and pressed himself against the wall. Since the assault in the

Montgomery elevator, he carried a weapon—a small Beretta revolver—strapped to his chest, under his clothes. He flipped open his overcoat and undid the buttons of his jacket and shirt. Access to the pistol would be swift and efficient, should it be necessary.

It probably wouldn't be, he thought, as he heard the footsteps disappear.

Then he realized that they had not disappeared, they had faded, slowed down to a walk—a quiet, cautious walk. And then he heard the voices: whisper-like, indistinguishable. They came from around the edge of the wall, in the vicinity of the unmarked Meridian office, no more than thirty feet away.

He inched the flat of his face to the sharp, concrete corner and simultaneously reached his right hand under his shirt to the handle of the Beretta.

There were two men with their backs to him, facing the darkened glass of the unmarked office door. The shorter of the two put his face against the pane, hands to both temples to shut out the light from the corridor. He pulled back and looked at his partner, shaking his head negatively.

The taller man turned slightly, enough for Spaulding to recognize him.

It was the stranger in the recessed, darkened doorway on Fifty-second Street. The tall, sad-eyed man who spoke gently, in bastardized British-out-of-the-Balkans, and held him under the barrel of a thick, powerful weapon.

The man reached into his left overcoat pocket and gave a key to his friend. With his right hand he removed a pistol from his belt. It was a heavy-duty .45, army issue. At close range, David knew it would blow a person into the air and off the earth. The man nodded and spoke softly but clearly.

"He has to be. He didn't leave. I want him."

With these words the shorter man inserted the key and shoved at the door. It swung back slowly. Together, both men walked in.

At that precise moment the elevator grill could be heard opening, its metal frames ringing throughout the corridor. David could see the two men in the darkened reception room freeze, turn toward the open door and quickly shut it.

"*Chee-ryst Almighty!*" was the irate shout from the

angry elevator operator as the grill rang shut with a clamor.

David knew it was the instant to move. Within seconds one or both men inside the deserted Meridian offices would realize that the elevator had stopped on the third floor because someone had pushed the button. Someone not in evidence, someone they had not met on the stairs. Someone still on the floor.

He spun around the edge of the wall and raced down the corridor toward the staircase. He didn't look back; he didn't bother to muffle his steps—it would have reduced his speed. His only concern was to get down those steps and out of the building. He leaped down the right-angled staircase to the in-between landing and whipped around the corner.

And then he stopped.

Below him, leaning against the railing, was the third man. He *knew* he'd heard more than two sets of feet racing up the staircase minutes ago. The man was startled, his eyes widened in shocked recognition and his right hand jerked backwards toward his coat pocket. Spaulding didn't have to be told what he was reaching for.

David sprang off the landing straight down at the man, making contact in midair, his hands clawing for the man's throat and right arm. He gripped the skin on the neck below the left ear and tore at it, slamming the man's head into the concrete wall as he did so. David's heavier body crushed into the would-be sentry's chest; he twisted the right arm nearly out of its shoulder socket.

The man screamed and collapsed; the scalp was lacerated, blood flowing out of the section of his skull that had crashed into the wall.

David could hear the sounds of a door being thrown open and men running. Above him, of course; one floor above him.

He freed his entangled legs from the unconscious body and raced down the remaining flight of stairs to the lobby. The elevator had, moments ago, let out its cargo of passengers; the last few were going out the front entrance. If any had heard the prolonged scream from the battered man sixty feet away up the staircase, none acknowledged it.

David rushed into the stragglers, elbowing his way through the wide double doors and onto the sidewalk. He turned east and ran as fast as he could.

He had walked over forty city blocks—some two miles in Basque country, but here infinitely less pleasant.

He had come to several decisions. The problem was how to implement them.

He could not stay in New York; not without facing risks, palpably unacceptable. And he had to get to Buenos Aires at once, before any of those hunting him in New York knew he was gone.

For they were hunting him now; that much was clear.

It would be suicide to return to the Montgomery. Or for that matter, to the unmarked Meridian offices in the morning. He could handle both with telephone calls. He would tell the hotel that he had been suddenly transferred to Pennsylvania; could the Montgomery management pack and hold his things? He'd call later about his bill. . . .

Kendall was on his way to Argentina. It wouldn't make any difference what the Meridian office was told.

Suddenly, he thought of Eugene Lyons.

He was a little sad about Lyons. Not the man (of course the man, he reconsidered quickly, but not the man's affliction, in this instance), but the fact that he would have little chance to develop any sense of rapport before Buenos Aires. Lyons might take his sudden absence as one more rejection in a long series. And the scientist might really need his help in Buenos Aires, at least in the area of German translation. David decided that he had to have the books Lyons selected for him; he had to have as solid a grasp of Lyons's language as was possible.

And then David realized where his thoughts were leading him.

For the next few hours the safest places in New York were the Meridian offices and St. Luke's Hospital.

After his visits to both locations he'd get out to Mitchell Field and telephone Brigadier General Swanson.

The answer to the violent enigma of the past seven days —from the Azores to a staircase on Thirty-eighth Street and everything in between—was in Buenos Aires.

Swanson did not know it and could not help; Fairfax was infiltrated and could not be told. And *that* told *him* something.

He was on his own. A man had two choices in such a dilemma: take himself out of strategy, or dig for identities and blow the covers off.

The first choice would be denied him. The brigadier, Swanson, was paranoid on the subject of the gyroscopic designs. And Rhinemann. There'd be no out of strategy.

That left the second: the identity of those behind the enigma.

A feeling swept over him, one he had not experienced in several years: the fear of sudden inadequacy. He was confronted with an extraordinary problem for which there was no pat—or complicated—solution in the north country. No unraveling that came with moves or countermoves whose strategies he had mastered in Basque and Navarre.

He was suddenly in another war. One he was not familiar with; one that raised doubts about himself.

He saw an unoccupied taxi, its roof light dimly lit, as if embarrassed to announce its emptiness. He looked up at the street sign; he was on Sheridan Square—it accounted for the muted sounds of jazz that floated up from cellars and surged down crowded side streets. The Village was warming up for another evening.

He raised his hand for the taxi; the driver did not see him. He started running as the cab proceeded up the street to the corner traffic light. Suddenly he realized that someone else on the other side of the square was rushing toward the empty taxi; the man was closer to it than Spaulding, his right hand was gesturing.

It was now terribly important to David that he reach the car first. He gathered speed and ran into the street, dodging pedestrians, momentarily blocked by two automobiles that were bumper to bumper. He spread his hands from hood to trunk and jumped over into the middle of the street and continued racing toward his objective.

Objective.

He reached the taxi no more than half a second after the other man.

Goddamn it! It was the obstruction of the two automobiles!

Obstruction.

He slammed his hand on the door panel, preventing the other man from pulling it open. The man looked up at Spaulding's face, at Spaulding's eyes.

"Christ, fella. I'll wait for another one," the man said quickly.

David was embarrassed. What the hell was he *doing*?

The doubts? The goddamned doubts.

"No, really, I'm terribly sorry." He mumbled the words, smiling apologetically. "You take it. I'm in no hurry. . . . Sorry again."

He turned and walked rapidly across the street into the crowds of Sheridan Square.

He could have had the taxi. That was the important thing.

Jesus! The treadmill never let up.

# PART 2

## 1944, BUENOS AIRES, ARGENTINA

The Pan American Clipper left Tampa at eight in the morning, with scheduled coastline stops at Caracas, São Luís, Salvador, and Rio de Janeiro before the final twelve hundred miles to Buenos Aires. David was listed on the passenger invoice as Mr. Donald Scanlan of Cincinnati, Ohio; occupation: mining surveyor. It was a temporary cover for the journey only. "Donald Scanlan" would disappear after the clipper landed at the Aeroparque in Buenos Aires. The initials were the same as his own for the simple reason that it was so easy to forget a monogrammed gift or the first letter of a hastily written signature. Especially if one was preoccupied or tired . . . or afraid.

Swanson had been close to panic when David reached him from the Mitchell Field Operations Room in New York. As a source control, Swanson was about as decisive as a bewildered bird dog. Any deviation from Kendall's schedule—Kendall's instructions, really—was abhorrent to him. And Kendall wasn't even *leaving* for Buenos Aires until the following morning.

David had not wasted complicated explanations on the general. As far as he was concerned, three attempts had been made on his life—at least, they could be so interpreted—and if the general wanted his "services" in Buenos Aires, he'd better get down there while he was still in one piece and functioning.

Were the attempts—the attacks—related to Buenos Aires? Swanson had asked the question as though he were afraid to name the Argentine city.

David was honest: there was no way to tell. The answer

was in Buenos Aires. It was reasonable to consider the possibility, but not to assume it.

"That's what Pace said," had been Swanson's reply. "Consider, don't assume."

"Ed was generally right about such things."

"He said when you operated in Lisbon, you were often involved in messy situations in the field."

"True. I doubt that Ed knew the particulars, though. But he was right in what he was trying to tell you. There are a lot of people in Portugal and Spain who'd rather see me dead than alive. Or at least they think they would. They could never be sure. Standard procedure, general."

There had been a prolonged pause on the Washington line. Finally, Swanson had said the words. "You realize, Spaulding, that we may have to replace you."

"Of course. You can do so right now, if you like." David had been sincere. He wanted very much to return to Lisbon. To go into the north country. To Valdero's. To find out about a cryp named Marshall.

"No. . . . No, everything's too far along. The designs. They're the important thing. Nothing else matters."

The remainder of the conversation concerned the details of transportation, American and Argentine currency, replenishing of a basic wardrobe, and luggage. Logistics which were not in the general's frame of reference and for which David took responsibility. The final command—request—was delivered, not by the general, but by Spaulding.

Fairfax was not to be informed of his whereabouts. Nor was anyone else for that matter, except the embassy in Buenos Aires; but make every effort to keep the information from Fairfax.

Why? Did Spaulding think . . .

"There's a leak in Fairfax, general. You might pass that on to the White House cellars."

"That's impossible!"

"Tell that to Ed Pace's widow."

David looked out the Clipper window. The pilot, moments ago, had informed the passengers that they were passing over the huge coastal lake of Mirim in Uruguay. Soon they'd be over Montevideo, forty minutes from Buenos Aires.

Buenos Aires. The unfocused picture, the blurred figures

of Leslie Jenner Hawkwood, the cryptographer Marshall, a man named Franz Altmüller; strange but committed men on Fifty-second and Thirty-eighth streets—in a darkened doorway, in a building after office hours, on a staircase. A man in an elevator who was so unafraid to die. An enemy who displayed enormous courage . . . or misguided zealousness. A maniac.

The answer to the enigma was in Buenos Aires, less than an hour away. The city was an hour away, the answer much longer. But no more than three weeks if his instincts were right. By the time the gyroscopic designs were delivered.

He would begin slowly, as he always did with a new field problem. Trying first to melt into the surroundings, absorb his cover; be comfortable, facile in his relationships. It shouldn't be difficult. His cover was merely an extension of Lisbon's: the wealthy trilingual attaché whose background, parents, and prewar associations in the fashionable centers of Europe made him a desirable social buffer for any ambassador's dinner table. He was an attractive addition to the delicate world of a neutral capital; and if there were those who thought someone, somewhere, had used money and influence to secure him such combat-exempt employment, so be it. It was denied emphatically, but not vehemently; there was a difference.

The "extension" for Buenos Aires was direct and afforded him top-secret classification. He was acting as a liaison between New York-London banking circles and the German expatriate Erich Rhinemann. Washington approved, of course; postwar financing in areas of reconstruction and industrial rebuilding were going to be international problems. Rhinemann could not be overlooked, not in the civilized marble halls of Berne and Geneva.

David's thoughts returned to the book on his lap. It was the second of six volumes Eugene Lyons had chosen for him.

"Donald Scanlan" went through the Aeroparque customs without difficulty. Even the embassy liaison, who checked in all Americans, seemed unaware of his identity.

His single suitcase in hand, David walked to the taxi station and stood on the cement platform looking at the drivers standing beside their vehicles. He wasn't prepared

to assume the name of Spaulding or to be taken directly to
the embassy just yet. He wanted to assure himself that
"Donald Scanlan" was accepted for what he was—a mining surveyor, nothing more; that there was no unusual
interest in such a man. For if there were, it would point to
David Spaulding, Military Intelligence, Fairfax and Lisbon
graduate.

He selected an obese, pleasant-looking driver in the
fourth cab from the front of the line. There were protests
from those in front, but David pretended not to understand. "Donald Scanlan" might know a smattering of Spanish, but certainly not the epithets employed by the dis-
gruntled drivers cheated out of a fare.

Once inside he settled back and gave instructions to the
unctuous driver. He told the man he had nearly an hour to
waste before he was to be met—the meeting place not
mentioned—and asked if the driver would give him a short
tour of the city. The tour would serve two purposes: he
could position himself so that he could constantly check
for surveillance, and he would learn the main points of the
city.

The driver, impressed by David's educated, grammatical
Spanish, assumed the role of tour director and drove out of
the airport's winding lanes to the exit of the huge Parque 3
de Febrero in which the field was centered.

Thirty minutes later David had filled a dozen pages with
notes. The city was like a European insert on the southern
continent. It was a strange mixture of Paris, Rome and
middle Spain. The streets were not city streets, they were
boulevards: wide, lined with color. Fountains and statuary
everywhere. The Avenida 9 de Julio might have been a
larger Via Veneto or Saint-Germain-des-Prés. The sidewalk
cafes, profuse with brightly decorated awnings and green-
ery from hundreds of planter boxes, were doing a brisk
summer afternoon business. The fact that it *was* summer in
Argentina was emphasized for David by the perspiration
on his neck and shirt front. The driver admitted that the
day was inordinately warm, in the high seventies.

David asked to be driven—among other places—to a
district called San Telmo. The cab owner nodded apprecia-
tively, as if he had accurately assessed the rich American.
Soon Spaulding understood. San Telmo was as Kendall had
noted: elegant, secluded, beautifully kept old houses and

apartment buildings with wrought-iron balustrades and brilliantly blossoming flowers lining the spotless streets.

Lyons would be comfortable.

From San Telmo the driver doubled back into the inner city and began the tour from the banks of the Río de la Plata.

The Plaza de Mayo, the Cabildo, the Casa Rosada, Calle Rivadavia. The names filled David's notebook; these were the streets, the squares, the locations he would absorb quickly.

La Boca. The waterfront, south of the city; this, the driver said, was no place for the tourist.

The Calle Florida. Here was the finest shopping area in all South America. The driver could take his American to several store owners personally known to him and extraordinary purchases could be made.

Sorry, there was no time. But David wrote in his notebook that traffic was banned at the borders of the Calle Florida.

The driver then sped out the Avenida Santa Fé toward the Palermo. No sight in Buenos Aires was as beautiful as the Palermo.

What interested David more than the beauty was the huge park—or series of individual parks; the quiet, immense, artificial lake. The acres of botanical gardens; the enormous zoo complex with rows of cages and buildings.

Beauty, yes. Secure areas of contact, more so. The Palermo might come in handy.

An hour had passed; there were no automobiles following the taxi. "Donald Scanlan" had not been under surveillance; David Spaulding could emerge.

Quietly.

He instructed the driver to leave him off at the cabstand outside the entrance to the Palermo zoo. He was to meet his party there. The driver looked crestfallen. Was there no hotel? No place of residence?

Spaulding did not reply, he simply asked the fare and quickly held out the amount. No more questions were in order.

David spent an additional fifteen minutes inside the zoo, actually enjoying it. He bought an ice from a vendor, wandered past the cages of marmosets and orangutans— finding extraordinary resemblances to friends and enemies

—and when he felt comfortable (as only a field man can feel comfortable), walked out to the cabstand.

He waited another five minutes while mothers and governesses and children entered the available taxis. It was his turn.

"The American embassy, *por favor*."

Ambassador Henderson Granville allowed the new attaché a half hour. There would be other days when they could sit and chat at length, but Sundays were hectic. The rest of Buenos Aires might be at church or at play; the diplomatic corps was at work. He had two garden parties still to attend—telephone calls would be made detailing the departures and arrivals of the German and the Japanese guests; *his* arrivals and departures would be timed accordingly. And after the second garden-bore there was dinner at the Brazilian embassy. Neither German nor Japanese interference was anticipated. Brazil was close to an open break.

"The Italians, you realize," said Granville, smiling at David, "don't count any longer. Never did really; not down here. They spend most of their time cornering us in restaurants, or calling from public phones, explaining how Mussolini ruined the country."

"Not too different from Lisbon."

"I'm afraid they're the only pleasant similarity. . . . I won't bore you with a tedious account of the upheavals we've experienced here, but a quick sketch—and emphasis —will help you adjust. You've read up, I assume."

"I haven't had much time. I left Lisbon only a week ago. I know that the Castillo government was overthrown."

"Last June. Inevitable. . . . Ramón Castillo was as inept a president as Argentina ever had, and it's had its share of buffoons. The economy was disastrous: agriculture and industry came virtually to a halt; his cabinet never made provisions to fill the beef market void created by the British struggle, even though the lot of them figured John Bull was finished. He deserved to be thrown out. . . . Unfortunately, what came in the front door—marched in phalanx up the Rivadavia, to be more precise—hardly makes our lives easier."

"That's the military council, isn't it? The junta?"

Granville gestured with his delicate hands; the chiseled

features of his aging, aristocratic face formed a sardonic
grimace. "The Grupo de Oficiales Unidos! As unpleasant a
band of goose-stepping opportunists as you will meet . . . I
daresay, anywhere. You know, of course, the entire army
was trained by the Wehrmacht officer corps. Add to that
jovial premise the hot Latin temperament, economic chaos,
a neutrality that's enforced but not believed in, and what
have you got? A suspension of the political apparatus; no
checks and balances. A police state rife with corruption."

"What maintains the neutrality?"

"The infighting, primarily. The GOU—that's what we
call it—has more factions than the '29 Reichstag. They're
all jockeying for the power spots. And naturally, the cold
fear of an American fleet and air force right up the street,
so to speak. . . . The GOU has been reappraising its judgments during the past five months. The colonels are beginning to wonder about their mentors' thousand-year cru-
sade; extremely impressed by our supply and production
lines."

"They should be. We've . . ."

"And there's another aspect," interrupted Granville
thoughtfully. "There's a small, very wealthy community of
Jews here. Your Erich Rhinemann, for example. The GOU
isn't prepared to openly advocate the solutions of Julius
Streicher. . . . It's already used Jewish money to keep alive
lines of credit pretty well chewed up by Castillo. The colonels are afraid of financial manipulations, most military
people are. But there's a great deal of money to be made in
this war. The colonels intend to make it. . . . Do I sketch a
recognizable picture?"

"A complicated one."

"I daresay. . . . We have a maxim here that serves quite
well. Today's friend will probably be on the Axis payroll
tomorrow; conversely, yesterday's Berlin courier might be
for sale next week. Keep your options open and your
opinions private. And publicly . . . allow for a touch more
flexibility than might be approved of at another post. It's
tolerated."

"And expected?" asked David.

"Both."

David lit a cigarette. He wanted to shift the conversation; old Granville was one of those ambassadors, profes-
sorial by nature, who would go on analyzing the subtleties

of his station all day if someone listened. Such men were usually the best diplomats but not always the most desirable liaisons in times of active practicality. Henderson Granville was a good man, though; his concerns shone in his eyes, and they were fair concerns.

"I imagine Washington has outlined my purpose here."

"Yes. I wish I could say I approved. Not of you; you've got your instructions. And I suppose international finance will continue long after Herr Hitler has shrieked his last scream. . . . Perhaps I'm no better than the GOU. Money matters can be most distasteful."

"These in particular, I gather."

"Again, yes. Erich Rhinemann is a sworn companion of the wind. A powerful companion, make no mistake, but totally without conscience; a hurricane's morality. Unquestionably the least honorable man I've ever met. I think it's criminal that his resources make him acceptable to London and New York."

"Perhaps necessary is a more appropriate term."

"I'm sure that's the rationalization, at any rate."

"It's mine."

"Of course. Forgive an old man's obsolete limits of necessity. But we have no quarrel. You have an assignment. What can I do for you? I understand it's very little."

"Very little indeed, sir. Just have me listed on the embassy index; any kind of office space will do as long as it has a door and a telephone. And I'd like to meet your cryp. I'll have codes to send."

"My word, that sounds ominous," said Granville, smiling without humor.

"Routine, sir. Washington relay; simple Yes and Nos."

"Very well. Our head cryptographer is named Ballard. Nice fellow; speaks seven or eight languages and is an absolute whiz at parlor games. You'll meet him directly. What else?"

"I'd like an apartment. . . ."

"Yes, we know," interrupted Granville gently, snatching a brief look at the wall clock. "Mrs. Cameron has scouted one she thinks you'll approve. . . . Of course, Washington gave us no indication of your length of stay. So Mrs. Cameron took it for three months."

"That's far too long. I'll straighten it out. . . . I think

that's almost all, Mr. Ambassador. I know you're in a hurry."

"I'm afraid I am."

David got out of his chair, as did Granville. "Oh, one thing, sir. Would this Ballard have an embassy index? I'd like to learn the names here."

"There aren't that many," said Granville, leveling his gaze at David, a subtle note of disapproval in his voice. "Eight or ten would be those you'd normally come in contact with. And I can assure you we have our own security measures."

David accepted the rebuke. "That wasn't my point, sir. I really *do* like to familiarize myself with the names."

"Yes, of course." Granville came around the desk and walked Spaulding to the door. "Chat with my secretary for a few minutes. I'll get hold of Ballard; he'll show you around."

"Thank you, sir." Spaulding extended his hand to Granville, and as he did so he realized for the first time how tall the man was.

"You know," said the ambassador, releasing David's hand, "there was a question I wanted to ask you, but the answer will have to wait for another time. I'm late already."

"What was that?"

"I've been wondering why the boys on Wall Street and the Strand sent *you*. I can't imagine there being a dearth of experienced bankers in New York or London, can you?"

"There probably isn't. But then I'm only a liaison carrying messages; information best kept private, I gather. I *have* had experience in those areas . . . in a neutral country."

Granville smiled once more and once more there was no humor conveyed. "Yes, of course. I was sure there was a reason."

# 23

Ballard shared two traits common to most cryptographers, thought David. He was a casual cynic and a fount of information. Qualities, Spaulding believed, developed over years of deciphering other men's secrets only to find the great majority unimportant. He was also cursed with the first name of Robert, by itself acceptable but when followed by Ballard, invariably reduced to Bobby. Bobby Ballard. It had the ring of a 1920s socialite or the name in a cereal box cartoon.

He was neither. He was a linguist with a mathematical mind and a shock of red hair on top of a medium-sized, muscular body; a pleasant man.

"That's our home," Ballard was saying. "You've seen the working sections; big, rambling, baroque and goddamned hot this time of year. I hope you're smart and have your own apartment."

"Don't you? Do you live *here*?"

"It's easier. My dials are very inconsiderate, they hum at all hours. Better than scrambling down from Chacarita or Telmo. And it's not bad; we stay out of each other's way pretty much."

"Oh? A lot of you here?"

"No. They alternate. Six, usually. In the two wings, east and south. Granville has the north apartments. Besides him, Jean Cameron and I are the only permanents. You'll meet Jean tomorrow, unless we run into her on the way out with the old man. She generally goes with him to the diplobores."

"The what?"

"Diplo-bores. The old man's word . . . contraction. I'm surprised he didn't use it with you. He's proud of it.

Diplobore is an embassy duty bash." They were in a large, empty reception room; Ballard was opening a pair of French doors leading out onto a short balcony. In the distance could be seen the waters of the Río de la Plata and the estuary basin of the Puerto Nuevo, Buenos Aires' main port. "Nice view, isn't it?"

"Certainly is." David joined the cryptographer on the balcony. "Does this Jean Cameron and the ambassador . . . I mean, are they . . . ?"

"Jean and the old *man?*" Ballard laughed loud and good-naturedly. "Christ, no! . . . Come to think of it, I don't know why it strikes me so funny. I suppose there're a lot of people who think that. And *that's* funny."

"Why?"

"Sad-funny, I guess I should say," continued Ballard without interruption. "The old man and the Cameron family go back to the original Maryland money. Eastern Shore yacht clubs, blazer jackets, tennis in the morning—you know: diplomat territory. Jean's family was part of it, too. She married this Cameron; knew him since they could play doctor together in their Abercrombie pup tents. A rich-people romance, childhood sweethearts. They got married, the war came; he chucked his law books for a TBF—aircraft carrier pilot. He was killed in the Leyte Gulf. That was last year. She went a little crazy; maybe more than a little."

"So the . . . Granville brought her down here?"

"That's right."

"Nice therapy, if you can afford it."

"She'd probably agree with that." Ballard walked back into the reception room; Spaulding followed. "But most people will tell you she pays her dues for the treatment. She works damned hard and knows what she's doing. Has rotten hours, too; what with the diplobores."

"Where's *Mrs*. Granville?"

"No idea. She divorced the old man ten, fifteen years ago."

"I still say it's nice work if you can get it." David was thinking, in an offhand way, of several hundred thousand other women whose husbands had been killed, living with reminders every day. He dismissed his thoughts; they weren't his concerns.

"Well, she's qualified."

"What?" David was looking at a rococo-styled corner pillar in the wall, not really listening.

"Jean spent four years—off and on—down here as a kid. Her father was in Foreign Service; probably would have been an ambassador by now if he'd stuck with it. . . . Come on, I'll show you the office Granville assigned you. Maintenance should have it tidied up by now," Ballard smiled.

"You've been employing a diversion," laughed David, following the cryp out the door into another hallway.

"I had to. You've got a room in the back. So far back it's been used for storage, I think."

"Obviously I made points with Granville."

"You sure did. He can't figure you out. . . . Me? I don't try." Ballard turned left into still another intersecting hallway. "This is the south wing. Offices on the first and second floors; not many, three on each. Apartments on the third and fourth. The roof is great for sunbathing, if you like that sort of thing."

"Depends on the company, I suppose."

The two men approached a wide staircase, preparing to veer to the left beyond it, when a feminine voice called down from the second landing.

"Bobby, is that you?"

"It's Jean," said Ballard. "Yes," he called out. "I'm with Spaulding. Come on down and meet the new recruit with enough influence to get his own apartment right off."

"Wait'll he sees the apartment!"

Jean Cameron came into sight from around the corner landing. She was a moderately tall woman, slender and dressed in a floor-length cocktail gown at once vivid with color yet simple in design. Her light brown hair was shoulder length, full and casual. Her face was a combination of striking features blended into a soft whole: wide, alive blue eyes; a thin, sharply etched nose; lips medium full and set as if in a half-smile. Her very clear skin was bronzed by the Argentine sun.

David saw that Ballard was watching him, anticipating his reaction to the girl's loveliness. Ballard's expression was humorously sardonic, and Spaulding read the message: Ballard had been to the font and found it empty—for those seeking other than a few drops of cool water. Ballard was now a friend to the lady; he knew better than to try being anything else.

Jean Cameron seemed embarrassed by her introduction on the staircase. She descended rapidly, her lips parted into one of the most genuine smiles David had seen in years. Genuine and totally devoid of innuendo.

"Welcome," she said, extending her hand. "Thank heavens I have a chance to apologize before you walk into that place. You may change your mind and move right back here."

"It's that bad?" David saw that Jean wasn't quite as young at close range as she seemed on the staircase. She was past thirty; comfortably past. And she seemed aware of his inspection, the approbation—or lack of it—unimportant to her.

"Oh, it's all right for a limited stay. You can't get anything else on that basis, not if you're American. But it's small."

Her handshake was firm, almost masculine, thought Spaulding. "I appreciate your taking the trouble. I'm sorry to have caused it."

"No one else here could have gotten you anything but a hotel," said Ballard, touching the girl's shoulder; was the contact protective? wondered David. "The *porteños* trust Mother Cameron. Not the rest of us."

"*Porteños*," said Jean in response to Spaulding's questioning expression, "are the people who live in BA. . . ."

"And BA—don't tell me—stands for Montevideo," replied David.

"Aw, they sent us a *bright* one," said Ballard.

"You'll get used to it," continued Jean. "Everyone in the American and English settlements calls it BA. Montevideo, of course," she added, smiling. "I think we see it so often on reports, we just do it automatically."

"Wrong," interjected Ballard. "The vowel juxtaposition in 'Buenos Aires' is uncomfortable for British speech."

"That's something else you'll learn during your stay, Mr. Spaulding," said Jean Cameron, looking affectionately at Ballard. "Be careful offering opinions around Bobby. He has a penchant for disagreeing."

"Never so," answered the cryp. "I simply care enough for my fellow prisoners to want to enlighten them. Prepare them for the outside when they get paroled."

"Well, I've got a temporary pass right now, and if I don't get over to the ambassador's office, he'll start on that damned address system. . . . Welcome again, Mr. Spaulding."

"Please. The name's David."

"Mine's Jean. Bye," said the girl, dashing down the hallway, calling back to Ballard. "Bobby? You've got the address and the key? For . . . David's place?"

"Yep. Go get irresponsibly drunk, I'll handle everything."

Jean Cameron disappeared through a door in the right wall.

"She's very attractive," said Spaulding, "and you two are good friends. I should apologize for . . ."

"No, you shouldn't," interrupted Ballard. "Nothing to apologize for. You formed a quick judgment on isolated facts. I'd've done the same, thought the same. Not that you've changed your mind; no reason to, really."

"She's right. You disagree . . . before you know what you're disagreeing to; and then you debate your disagreement. And if you go on, you'll probably challenge your last position."

"You know what? I can follow that. Isn't it frightening?"

"You guys are a separate breed," said David, chuckling, following Ballard beyond the stairs into a smaller corridor.

"Let's take a quick look at your Siberian cubicle and then head over to your other cell. It's on Córdoba; we're on Corrientes. It's about ten minutes from here."

David thanked Bobby Ballard once again and shut the apartment door. He had pleaded exhaustion from the trip, preceded by too much welcome home in New York—and God knew that was the truth—and would Ballard take a raincheck for dinner?

Alone now, he inspected the apartment; it wasn't intolerable at all. It was small: a bedroom, a sitting room-kitchen, and a bath. But there was a dividend Jean Cameron hadn't mentioned. The rooms were on the first floor, and at the rear was a tiny brick-leveled patio surrounded by a tall concrete wall, profuse with hanging vines and drooping flowers from immense pots on the ledge. In the center of the enclosure was a gnarled fruit-bearing tree he could not identify; around the trunk were three rope-webbed chairs that had seen better days but looked extremely comfortable. As far as he was concerned, the dividend made the dwelling.

Ballard had pointed out that his section of the Avenida Córdoba was just over the borderline from the commercial area, the "downtown" complex of Buenos Aires. Quasi residential, yet near enough to stores and restaurants to be easy for a newcomer.

David picked up the telephone; the dial tone was delayed but eventually there. He replaced it and walked across the small room to the refrigerator, an American Sears Roebuck. He opened it and smiled. The Cameron girl had provided—or had somebody provide—several basic items: milk, butter, bread, eggs, coffee. Then happily he spotted two bottles of wine: an Orfila *tinto* and a Colón *blanco*. He closed the refrigerator and went back into the bedroom.

He unpacked his single suitcase, unwrapping a bottle of Scotch, and remembered that he'd have to buy additional clothes in the morning. Ballard had offered to go with him to a men's shop in the Calle Florida—if his goddamned dials weren't "humming." He placed the books Eugene Lyons had given him on the bedside table. He had gone through two of them; he was beginning to gain confidence in the aerophysicists' language. He would need comparable studies in German to be really secure. He would cruise around the bookshops in the German settlement tomorrow; he wasn't looking for definitive texts, just enough to understand the terms. It was really a minor part of his assignment, he understood that.

Suddenly, David remembered Walter Kendall. Kendall was either in Buenos Aires by now or would be arriving within hours. The accountant had left the United States at approximately the same time he had, but Kendall's flight from New York was more direct, with far fewer stopovers.

He wondered whether it would be feasible to go out to the airport and trace Kendall. If he hadn't arrived, he could wait for him; if he had, it would be simple enough to check the hotels—according to Ballard there were only three or four good ones.

On the other hand, any additional time—more than absolutely essential—spent with the manipulating accountant was not a pleasant prospect. Kendall would be upset at finding him in Buenos Aires before he'd given the order to

Swanson. Kendall, no doubt, would demand explanations beyond those David wished to give; probably send angry cables to an already strung-out brigadier general.

There were no benefits in hunting down Walter Kendall until Kendall expected to find him. Only liabilities.

He had other things to do: the unfocused picture. He could begin that search far better alone.

David walked back into the living room-kitchen carrying the Scotch and took out a tray of ice from the refrigerator. He made himself a drink and looked over at the double doors leading to his miniature patio. He would spend a few quiet twilight moments in the January summertime breeze of Buenos Aires.

The sun was fighting its final descent beyond the city; the last orange rays were filtering through the thick foliage of the unidentified fruit tree. Underneath, David stretched his legs and leaned back in the rope-webbed chair. He realized that if he kept his eyes closed for any length of time, they would not reopen for a number of hours. He had to watch that; long experience in the field had taught him to eat something before sleeping.

Eating had long since lost its pleasure for him—it was merely a necessity directly related to his energy level. He wondered if the pleasure would ever come back; whether so much he had put aside would return. Lisbon had probably the best accommodations—food, shelter, comfort—of all the major cities, excepting New York, on both continents. And now he was on a third continent, in a city that boasted undiluted luxury.

But for him it was the field—as much as was the north country in Spain. As much as Basque and Navarre, and the freezing nights in the Galician hills or the sweat-prone silences in ravines, waiting for patrols—waiting to kill.

So much. So alien.

He brought his head forward, took a long drink from the glass and let his neck arch back into the frame of the chair. A small bird was chattering away in the midsection of the tree, annoyed at his intrusion. It reminded David of how he would listen for such birds in the north country. They telegraphed the approach of men unseen, often falling into different rhythms that he began to identify—or thought he identified—with the numbers of the unseen, approaching patrols.

Then David realized that the small chattering bird was not concerned with him. It hopped upward, still screeching its harsh little screech, only faster now, more strident.

There was someone else.

Through half-closed eyes, David focused above, beyond the foliage. He did so without moving any part of his body or head, as if the last moments were approaching before sleep took over.

The apartment house had four stories and a roof that appeared to have a gentle slope covered in a terra-cotta tile of sorts—brownish pink in color. The windows of the rooms above him were mostly open to the breezes off the Río de la Plata. He could hear snatches of subdued conversation, nothing threatening, no loud vibrations. It was the Buenos Aires siesta hour, according to Ballard; quite different from Rome's afternoon or the Paris lunch. Dinner in BA was very late, by the rest of the world's schedule. Ten, ten thirty, even midnight was not out of the question.

The screeching bird was not bothered by the inhabitants of the Córdoba apartment house; yet still he kept up his strident alarms.

And then David saw why.

On the roof, obscured but not hidden by the branches of the fruit tree, were the outlines of two men.

They were crouched, staring downward; staring, he was sure, at him.

Spaulding judged the position of the main intersecting tree limb and rolled his head slightly, as if the long-awaited sleep were upon him, his neck resting in exhaustion on his right shoulder, the drink barely held by a relaxed hand, millimeters from the brick pavement.

It helped; he could see better, not well. Enough, however, to make out the sharp, straight silhouette of a rifle barrel, the orange sun careening off its black steel. It was stationary, in an arrest position under the arm of the man on the right. No movement was made to raise it, to aim it; it remained immobile, cradled.

Somehow, it was more ominous that way, thought Spaulding. As though in the arms of a killer guard who was sure his prisoner could not possibly vault the stockade; there was plenty of time to shoulder and fire.

David carried through his charade. He raised his hand slightly and let his drink fall. The sound of the minor crash "awakened" him; he shook the pretended sleep from his head and rubbed his eyes with his fingers. As he did so, he maneuvered his face casually upward. The figures on the roof had stepped back on the terra-cotta tiles. There would be no shots. Not directed at him.

He picked up a few pieces of the glass, rose from the chair and walked into the apartment as a tired man does when annoyed with his own carelessness. Slowly, with barely controlled irritation.

Once he crossed the saddle of the door, beneath the sightline of the roof, he threw the glass fragments into a wastebasket and walked rapidly into the bedroom. He opened the top drawer of the bureau, separated some handkerchiefs and withdrew his revolver.

He clamped it inside his belt and picked up his jacket from the chair into which he'd thrown it earlier. He put it on, satisfied that it concealed the weapon.

He crossed out into the living room, to the apartment door, and opened it silently.

The staircase was against the left wall and David swore to himself, cursing the architect of this particular Avenida Córdoba building—or the profuseness of lumber in Argentina. The stairs were made of wood, the brightly polished wax not concealing the obvious fact that they were ancient and probably squeaked like hell.

He closed his apartment door and approached the staircase, putting his feet on the first step.

It creaked the solid creak of antique shops.

He had four flights to go; the first three were unimportant. He took the steps two at a time, discovering that if he hugged the wall, the noise of his ascent was minimized.

Sixty seconds later he faced a closed door marked with a sign—in goddamned curlicued Castilian lettering:

*El Techo.*

The roof.

The door, as the stairs, was old. Decades of seasonal heat and humidity had caused the wood to swell about the hinges; the borders were forced into the frame.

It, too, would scream his arrival if he opened it slowly.

There was no other way: he slipped the weapon out of his belt and took one step back on the tiny platform. He judged the frame—the concrete walls—surrounding the old wooden door and with an adequate intake of breath, he pulled at the handle, yanked the door open and jumped diagonally into the right wall, slamming his back against the concrete.

The two men whirled around, stunned. They were thirty feet from David at the edge of the sloping roof. The man with the rifle hesitated, then raised the weapon into waist-firing position. Spaulding had his pistol aimed directly into the man's chest. However, the man with the gun did not have the look of one about to fire at a target; the hesitation was deliberate, not the result of panic or indecision.

The second man shouted in Spanish; David recognized the accent as southern Spain, not Argentine. *"Por favor, señor!"*

Spaulding replied in English to establish their understanding, or lack of it. "Lower that rifle. *Now!*"

The first man did so, holding it by the stock. "You are in error," he said in halting English. "There have been . . . how do you say, *ladrones* . . . thieves in the neighborhood."

David walked over the metal transom onto the roof, holding his pistol on the two men. "You're not very convincing. *Se dan corte, amigos.* You're not from Buenos Aires."

"There are a great many people in this neighborhood who are as we: displaced, *señor.* This is a community of . . . not the native born," said the second man.

"You're telling me you weren't up here for my benefit? You weren't watching me?"

"It was coincidental, I assure you," said the man with the rifle.

*"Es la verdad,"* added the other. "Two *habitaciones* have been broken into during the past week. The police do not help; we are . . . *extranjeros,* foreigners to them. We protect ourselves."

Spaulding watched the men closely. There was no waver in either man's expression, no hint of lies. No essential fear.

"I'm with the American embassy," said David curtly. There was no reaction from either *extranjero.* "I must ask you for identification."

*"Qué cosa?"* The man with the gun.

"Papers. Your names. . . . *Certificados.*"

*"Por cierto, en seguida."* The second man reached back

into his trousers pocket; Spaulding raised the pistol slightly,
in warning.

The man hesitated, now showing his fear. "Only a
*registro, señor*. We all must carry them. . . . Please. In my
*cartera*."

David held out his left hand as the second man gave him
a cheap leather wallet. He flipped it open with minor feelings of regret. There was a kind of helplessness about the
two *extranjeros*; he'd seen the look thousands of times.
Franco's Falangistas were experts at provoking it.

He looked quickly down at the cellophane window of
the billfold; it was cracked with age.

Suddenly, the barrel of the rifle came crashing across his
right wrist; the pain was excruciating. Then his hand was
being twisted expertly inward and down; he had no choice
but to release the weapon and try to kick it away on the
sloping roof. To hold it would mean breaking his wrist.

He did so as his left arm was being hammerlocked—
again expertly—up over his neck. He lashed his foot out at
the unarmed *extranjero*, who had hold of his hand. He
caught him in the stomach and as the man bent forward,
David crossed his weight and kicked again, sending the
man tumbling down on the tiled incline.

David fell in the thrust direction of the hammerlock—
downward, to his rear—and as the first man countered the
position, Spaulding brought his right elbow back up, crushing into the man's groin. The arm was released as the
*extranjero* tried to regain his balance.

He wasn't quick enough; Spaulding whipped to his left
and brought his knee up into the man's throat. The rifle
clattered on the tiles and rolled downward on the slope.
The man sank, blood dribbling from his mouth where his
teeth had punctured the skin.

Spaulding heard the sound behind him and turned.

He was too late. The second *extranjero* was over him,
and David could hear the whistling of his own pistol piercing the air above him, crashing down into his skull.

All was black. Void.


"They described the right attitude but the wrong section
of town," said Ballard, sitting across the room from David,
who held an ice pack to his head. "The *extranjeros* are
concentrated in the west areas of the La Boca district.

They've got a hell of a crime rate over there; the *policía* prefer strolling the parks rather than those streets. And the Grupo—the GOU—has no love for *extranjeros*."

"You're no help," said Spaulding, shifting the ice pack around in circles on the back of his head.

"Well, they weren't out to kill you. They could have thrown you off or just left you on the edge; five to one you'd've rolled over and down four flights."

"I knew they weren't intent on killing me. . . ."

"How?"

"They could have done that easily before. I think they were waiting for me to go out. I'd unpacked; they'd have the apartment to themselves."

"What for?"

"To search my things. They *have* done that before."

"Who?"

"Damned if I know."

"Now who's no help?"

"Sorry. . . . Tell me, Bobby, who exactly knew I was flying in? How was it handled?"

"First question: three people. I did, of course; I'm on the dials. Granville, obviously. And Jean Cameron; the old man asked her to follow up on an apartment . . . but you know that. Question two: very confidentially. Remember, your orders came through at night. From Washington. Jean was playing chess with Granville in his quarters when I brought him the eggs. . . ."

"The what?" interrupted David.

"The scrambler; it's marked. Washington had your sheet radioed in on a scrambler code. That means only myself or my head man can handle it, deliver it to the ambassador."

"O.K. Then what?"

"Nothing. I mean nothing you don't know about."

"Tell me anyway."

Ballard exhaled a long, condescending breath. "Well, the three of us were alone; what the hell, I'd read the scramble and the instructions were clear about the apartment. So Granville figured—apparently—that Jean was the logical one to scout one up. He told her you were coming in; to do what she could on such short notice." Ballard looked about the room and over at the patio doors. "She didn't do badly, either."

"Then that's it; they've got a network fanned out over

the city; nothing unusual. They keep tabs on unoccupied places: apartments, rooming houses; hotels are the easiest."

"I'm not sure I follow you," said Ballard, trying to.

"We can all be smart as whips, Bobby, but we can't change a couple of basics: we have to have a place to sleep and take a bath."

"Oh, I follow *that*, but you can't apply it here. Starting tomorrow you're no secret; until then you are. D.C. said you were coming down on your own; we had no idea precisely when or how. . . . Jean didn't get this apartment for *you*. Not in *your name*."

"Oh?" David was far more concerned than his expression indicated. The two *extranjeros* had to have been on the roof before he arrived. Or, at least, within minutes after he did so. "How did she lease it then? Whose name did she use? I didn't want a cover; we didn't ask for one."

"Jesus, I thought *I* talked fast. Sunday is *Sunday*, Monday is *Monday*. Sunday we don't know you; Monday we do. That's what Washington spelled out. They wanted no advance notice of your arrival and, incidentally, if *you* decided to stay out of sight, we were to adhere to your wishes. I'm sure Granville will ask you what you want to do in the morning. . . . How did Jean lease the place? Knowing her, she probably implied the ambassador had a girl on the side, or something. The *porteños* are very *simpático* with that sort of thing; the Paris of South America and all that. . . . One thing I *do* know, she wouldn't have used your name. Or any obvious cover. She'd use her own first."

"Oh, boy," said Spaulding wearily, removing the ice pack and feeling the back of his head. He looked at his fingers. Smudges of blood were apparent.

"I hope you're not going to play hero with that gash. You should see a doctor."

"No hero." David smiled. "I've got to have some sutures removed, anyway. Might as well be tonight, if you can arrange it."

"I can arrange it. Where did you get the stitches?"

"I had an accident in the Azores."

"Christ, you travel, don't you?"

"So does something ahead of me."

## 24

"Mrs. Cameron is here at my request, Spaulding. Come in. I've talked with Ballard and the doctor. Stitches taken out and new ones put in; you must feel like a pincushion."

Granville was behind his baroque desk, reclining comfortably in his highbacked chair. Jean Cameron sat on the couch against the left wall; one of the chairs in front of the desk was obviously meant for David. He decided to wait until Granville said so before sitting down. He remained standing; he wasn't sure he liked the ambassador. The office assigned to him was, indeed, far back and used for storage.

"Nothing serious, sir. If it was, I'd say so." Spaulding nodded to Jean and saw her concern. Or, at least, that's what he thought he read in her eyes.

"You'd be foolish not to. The doctor says the blow to the head fortunately fell between concussion areas. Otherwise, you'd be in rather bad shape."

"It was delivered by an experienced man."

"Yes, I see. . . . Our doctor didn't think much of the sutures he removed."

"That seems to be a general medical opinion. They served their purpose; the shoulder's fine. He strapped it."

"Yes. . . . Sit down, sit down."

David sat down. "Thank you, sir."

"I gather the two men who attacked you last evening were *provincianos*. Not *porteños*."

Spaulding gave a short, defeated smile and turned to Jean Cameron. "I got to *porteños*; I guess *provincianos* means what it says. The country folk? Outside the cities."

"Yes," said the girl softly. "*The* city. BA."

"Two entirely different cultures," continued Granville.

"The *provincianos* are hostile and with much legitimacy. They're really quite exploited; the resentments are flaring up. The GOU has done nothing to ease matters, it only conscripts them in the lowest ranks."

"The *provincianos* are native to Argentina, though, aren't they?"

"Certainly. From their point of view, much more so than Buenos Airens, *porteños*. Less Italian and German blood, to say nothing of Portuguese, Balkan and Jewish. There were waves of immigrations, you see. . . ."

"Then, Mr. Ambassador," interrupted David, hoping to stem another post analysis by the pedagogical diplomat, "these were not *provincianos*. They called themselves *extranjeros*. Displaced persons, I gathered."

"*Extranjero* is a rather sarcastic term. Inverse morbidity. As though employed by a reservation Indian in our Washington. A foreigner in his own native land, you see what I mean?"

"These men were not from Argentina," said David quietly, dismissing Granville's question. "Their speech pattern was considerably alien."

"Oh? Are you an expert?"

"Yes, I am. In these matters."

"I see." Granville leaned forward. "Do you ascribe the attack to embassy concerns? Allied concerns?"

"I'm not sure. It's my opinion I was the target. I'd like to know how they knew I was here."

Jean Cameron spoke from the couch. "I've gone over everything I said, David." She stopped and paused briefly, aware that the ambassador had shot her a look at her use of Spaulding's first name. "Your place was the fourth apartment I checked into. I started at ten in the morning and got there around two o'clock. And leased it immediately. I'm sorry to say it was the patio that convinced me."

David smiled at her.

"Anyway, I went to a real estate office at Viamonte. Geraldo Baldez is the owner; we all know him. He's partisan; has no use for Germans. I made it clear that I wanted to rent the apartment for one of our people who was living here and who, frankly, found the embassy restrictions too limiting. He laughed and said he was sure it was Bobby. I didn't disagree."

"But it was a short lease," said David.

"I used it as an excuse in case you didn't like the apartment. It's a standard three-month clause."

"Why wouldn't Bobby—or anyone else—get his own place?"

"Any number of reasons. Also standard . . . here." Jean smiled, a touch embarrassed, thought David. "I know the city better than most; I lived here for several years. Also there's a little matter of expense allowance; I'm a pretty good bargainer. And men like Bobby have urgent work to do. My hours are more flexible; I have the time."

"Mrs. Cameron is too modest, Spaulding. She's an enormous asset to our small community."

"I'm sure she is, sir. . . . Then you don't think anyone had reason to suspect you were finding a place for an incoming attaché."

"Absolutely not. It was all done in such a . . . light-hearted way, if you know what I mean."

"What about the owner of the building?" David asked.

"I never saw him. Most apartments are owned by wealthy people who live in the Telmo or Palermo districts. Everything's done through rental agencies."

David turned to Granville. "Have there been any calls for me? Messages?"

"No. Not that I'm aware of, and I'm sure I would be. You would have been contacted, of course."

"A man named Kendall. . . ."

"Kendall?" interrupted the ambassador. "I know that name. . . . Kendall. Yes, Kendall." Granville riffled through some papers on his desk. "Here. A Walter Kendall came in last night. Ten thirty flight. He's staying at the Alvear; that's near the Palermo Park. Fine old hotel." Granville suddenly looked over at Spaulding. "He's listed on the sheet as an industrial economist. Now that's a rather all-inclusive description, isn't it? Would he be the banker I referred to yesterday?"

"He'll make certain arrangements relative to my instructions." David did not conceal his reluctance to go into the matter of Walter Kendall. On the other hand, he instinctively found himself offering a token clarification to Jean Cameron. "My primary job here is to act as liaison between financial people in New York and London and banking interests here in Buenos . . . BA." David smiled; he

hoped as genuinely as Jean smiled. "I think it's a little silly.
I don't know a debit from an asset. But Washington
okayed me. The ambassador is worried that I'm too inexperienced."

Spaulding quickly shifted his gaze to Granville, reminding the old man that "banking interests" was the limit of
identities. The name of Erich Rhinemann was out of
bounds.

"Yes, I admit, I was. . . . But that's neither here nor
there. What do you wish to do about last night? I think we
should lodge a formal complaint with the police. Not that
it will do a damn bit of good."

David fell silent for a few moments, trying to consider
the pros and cons of Granville's suggestion. "Would we get
press coverage?"

"Very little, I'd think," answered Jean.

"Embassy attachés usually have money," said Granville.
"They've been robbed. It will be called an attempted robbery. Probably was."

"But the Grupo doesn't like that kind of news. It doesn't
fit in with the colonels' view of things, and they control the
press." Jean was thinking out loud, looking at David.
"They'll play it down."

"And if we don't complain—assuming it was not
robbery—we're admitting we think it was something else.
Which I'm not prepared to do," said Spaulding.

"Then by all means, a formal complaint will be registered this morning. Will you dictate a report of the incident
and sign it, please?" Obviously, Granville wished to terminate the meeting. "And to be frank with you, Spaulding,
unless I'm considerably in the dark, I believe it *was* an
attempt to rob a newly arrived rich American. I'm told the
airport taxi drivers have formed a veritable thieves' carni-
val. *Extranjeros* would be perfectly logical participants."

David stood up; he was pleased to see that Jean did the
same. "I'll accept that, Mr. Ambassador. The years in Lisbon have made me overly . . . concerned. I'll adjust."

"I daresay. Do write up the report."

"Yes, sir."

"I'll get him a stenographer," said Jean. "Bilingual."

"Not necessary. I'll dictate it in Spanish."

"I forgot." Jean smiled. "Bobby said they'd sent us a
bright one."

David supposed it began with that first lunch. Later she told him it was before, but he didn't believe her. She claimed it was when he said that BA stood for Montevideo; that was silly, it didn't make sense.

What made sense—and they both recognized it without any attempt to verbalize it—was the total relaxation each felt in the other's company. It was as simple as that. It was a splendid comfort; the silences never awkward, the laughter easy and based in communicated humor, not forced response.

It was remarkable. Made more so, David believed, because neither expected it, neither sought it. Both had good and sufficient reasons to avoid any relationships other than surface or slightly below. He was an impermanent man, hoping only to survive and start somewhere again with a clear head and suppressed memories. That was important to him. And he knew she still mourned a man so deeply she couldn't possibly—without intolerable guilt—push that man's face and body and mind behind her.

She told him partially why herself. Her husband had not been the image of the dashing carrier pilot so often depicted by navy public relations. He'd had an extraordinary fear—not for himself—but of taking lives. Were it not for the abuse he knew would have been directed at his Maryland wife and Maryland family, Cameron would have sought conscientious objector status. Then, too, perhaps he hadn't the courage of his own convictions.

Why a pilot?

Cameron had been flying since he was in his teens. It seemed natural and he believed his civilian training might lead to a Stateside instructor's berth. He rejected military law; too many of his fellow attorneys had gone after it and found themselves in the infantry and on the decks of battleships. The military had enough lawyers; they wanted pilots.

David thought he understood why Jean told him so much about her dead husband. There were two reasons. The first was that by doing so openly, she was adjusting to what she felt was happening between them; atoning, perhaps. The second was less clear but in no way less important. Jean Cameron hated the war; hated what it had taken away from her. She wanted him to know that.

Because—David realized—her instincts told her he was

very much involved. And she would have no part of that involvement; she owed that much to Cameron's memory.

They'd gone to lunch at a restaurant overlooking the waters of the Riachúelo Basin near the piers of Dársena Sud. She had suggested it—the restaurant and the lunch. She saw that he was still exhausted; what sleep he'd managed had been interrupted constantly with pain. She insisted that he needed a long, relaxing lunch, then home to bed and a day's recuperation.

She hadn't meant to go with him.

He hadn't meant for her to.

"Ballard's a nice guy," said Spaulding, pouring a clear white Colón.

"Bobby's a dear," she agreed. "He's a kind person."

"He's very fond of you."

"And I of him. . . . What you're speculating on is perfectly natural, and I'm sorry to spoil the wilder melody. Is melody right? Granville told me who your parents were. I'm impressed."

"I've refused to read music since the age of eight. But 'melody's' fine. I just wondered."

"Bobby gave me a thoroughly professional try, with enormous charm and good humor. A better girl would have responded. He had every right to be angry. . . . I wanted his company but gave very little in return for it."

"He accepted your terms," said David affirmatively.

"I said he was kind."

"There must be ten other fellows here. . . ."

"Plus the marine guard," interjected Jean, feigning a lovely, unmilitary salute. "Don't forget them."

"A hundred and ten, then. You're Deanna Durbin."

"Hardly. The marines rotate off the FMF base south of La Boca; the staff—those without wives and kinder—are plagued with the embassy syndrome."

"What's that?"

"State Department-eye-tis. . . . The quivers. You seem to be singularly lacking in them."

"I don't know whether I am or not. I don't know what they are."

"Which tells me something about you, doesn't it?"

"What does it tell you?"

"You're not a State Department climber. The 'eye-tis'

syndrome is treading lightly and making damned sure everybody above you—especially the ambassador—is happy with your *sincerest efforts*." Jean grimaced like a boxer puppy, her delicate chin forward, her eyebrows down—mocking the words. Spaulding broke out laughing; the girl had captured the embassy look and voice with devastating accuracy.

"Christ, I'm going to put you on the radio." He laughed again. "You've described the syndrome. I see it, Lord! I see it!"

"But you're not infected by it." Jean stopped her mimicry and looked into his eyes. "I watched you with Granville; you were just barely polite. You weren't looking for a fitness report, were you?"

He returned her gaze. "No, I wasn't. . . . To answer the question that's rattling around that lovely head of yours so loud it vibrates—I'm not a Foreign Service career officer. I'm strictly wartime. I *do* work out of embassies on a variety of related assignments for a couple of related reasons. I speak four languages and because of those parents that impressed you so, I have what is euphemistically described as access to important people in government, commerce, those areas. Since I'm not a complete idiot, I often circulate confidential information among corporations in various countries. The market place doesn't stop humming for such inconveniences as war. . . . That's my contribution. I'm not very proud of it, but it's what they handed me."

She smiled her genuine smile and reached for his hand. "*I* think you do whatever you do very intelligently and well. There aren't many people who can say that. And God knows you can't choose."

" 'What did you do in the war, daddy?' . . . 'Well, son,' " David tried his own caricature. " 'I went from place to place telling friends of the Chase Bank to sell high and buy low and clear a decent profit margin.' " He kept her hand in his.

"And got attacked on Argentine rooftops and . . . and what were those stitches in your shoulder?"

"The cargo plane I was on in the Azores made a rotten landing. I think the pilot and his whole crew were plastered."

"There. See? You live as dangerously as any man at the front. . . . If I meet that boy you're talking to, I'll tell him that."

Their eyes were locked; Jean withdrew her hand, embarrassed. But for Spaulding the important thing was that she believed him. She accepted his cover extension without question. It occurred to him that he was at once greatly relieved and yet, in a way, quite sorry. He found no professional pride in lying to her successfully.

"So now you know how I've avoided the State Department syndrome. I'm still not sure why it's relevant. What the hell, with a hundred and ten men and marines. . . ."

"The marines don't count. They have sundry interests down here in La Boca."

"Then the staff—those without the 'Wives and kinder'—they can't all be quivering."

"But they do and I've been grateful. They'd like to get to the Court of St. James's someday."

"Now you're playing mental gymnastics. I'm not following you."

"No, I'm not. I wanted to see if Bobby had told you. He hasn't. I said he was kind. . . . He was giving me the chance to tell you myself."

"Tell me what?"

"My husband was Henderson Granville's stepson. They were very close."

They left the restaurant shortly past four and walked around the docks of the Dársena Sud waterfront, breathing in the salt air. It seemed to David that Jean was enjoying herself in a way she hadn't in too long a time. That it was part of the instant comfort between them, he realized, but it went further. As if some splendid relief had swept over her.

Her loveliness had been evident from those first moments on the staircase, but as he thought back on that brief introduction, he knew what the difference was. Jean Cameron had been outgoing, good-natured . . . welcoming charm itself. But there'd been something else: a detachment born of self-control. Total control. A patina of authority that had nothing to do with her status at the embassy or whatever other benefits derived from her marriage to the ambassador's stepson. It was related solely to her own decisions, her own outlook.

He had seen that detached authority throughout the morning—when she introduced him to various embassy employees; when she gave directions to her secretary; when she answered her telephone and rendered quick instructions.

Even in the byplay with Bobby Ballard she glided firmly, with the assurance of knowing her own pattern. Ballard could shout humorously that she could "get irresponsibly drunk" because by no stretch of the imagination would she allow herself to do that.

Jean kept a tight rein on herself.

The rein was loosening now.

Yesterday he had looked at her closely, finding the years; and she was completely unconcerned, without vanity. Now, walking along the docks, holding his arm, she was pleasantly aware of the looks she received from the scores of waterfront *Bocamos*. Spaulding knew she hoped he was aware of those looks.

"Look, David," she said excitedly. "Those boats are going to crash head on."

Several hundred yards out in the bay, two trawlers were on a collision course, both steam whistles filling the air with aggressive warnings, both crews shouting at each other from port and starboard railings.

"The one on the right will veer."

It did. At the last moment, amid dozens of guttural oaths and gestures.

"How did you know?" she said.

"Simple right of way; the owner would get clobbered with damages. There'll be a brawl on one of these piers pretty soon, though."

"Let's not wait for it. You've had enough of that."

They walked out of the dock area into the narrow La Boca streets, teeming with small fish markets, profuse with fat merchants in bloodied aprons and shouting customers. The afternoon catch was in, the day's labor on the water over. The rest was selling and drinking and retelling the misadventures of the past twelve hours.

They reached a miniature square called—for no apparent reason—Plaza Ocho Calle; there was no street number

eight, no plaza to speak of. A taxi hesitantly came to a stop
at the corner, let out its fare and started up again, blocked
by pedestrians unconcerned with such vehicles. David
looked at Jean and she nodded, smiling. He shouted at the
driver.

Inside the taxi he gave his address. It didn't occur to him
to do otherwise.

They rode in silence for several minutes, their shoulders
touching, her hand underneath his arm.

"What are you thinking of?" David asked, seeing the
distant but happy expression on her face.

"Oh, the way I pictured you when Henderson read the
scramble the other night. . . . Yes, I call him Henderson; I
always have."

"I can't imagine anyone, even the president, calling him
Henderson."

"You don't know him. Underneath that Racquet Club
jacket is lovable Henderson."

"How did you picture me?"

"Very differently."

"From what?"

"You. . . . I thought you'd be terribly short, to begin
with. An attaché named David Spaulding who's some kind
of financial whiz and is going to have conferences with the
banks and the colonels about money things is short, at least
fifty years old and has *very* little hair. He also wears
spectacles—not glasses—and has a thin nose. Probably has
an allergy as well—he sneezes a lot and blows his nose all
the time. And he speaks in short, clipped sentences; very
precise and quite disagreeable."

"He chases secretaries, too; don't leave that out."

"My David Spaulding doesn't chase secretaries. He reads
dirty books."

David felt a twinge. Throw in an unkempt appearance, a
soiled handkerchief and replace the spectacles with glasses
—worn occasionally—and Jean was describing Walter
Kendall.

"Your Spaulding's an unpleasant fellow."

"Not the new one," she said, tightening her grip on his
arm.

The taxi drew up to the curb in front of the entrance on
Córdoba. Jean Cameron hesitated, staring momentarily at

the apartment house door. David spoke softly, without emphasis.

"Shall I take you to the embassy?"

She turned to him. "No."

He paid the driver and they went inside.

The field thread was invisibly protruding from the knob; he felt it.

He inserted the key in the lock and instinctively, gently shouldered her aside as he pushed the door open. The apartment was as he had left it that morning; he knew she felt his relief. He held the door for her. Jean entered and looked around.

"It really *isn't* so bad, is it?" she said.

"Humble but home." He left the door open and with a smile, a gesture—without words—he asked her to stay where she was. He walked rapidly into the bedroom, returned and went through the double doors onto his miniature, high-walled patio. He looked up, scanning the windows and the roof carefully. He smiled again at her from under the branches of the fruit tree. She understood, closed the door and came out to him.

"You did that very professionally, Mr. Spaulding."

"In the best traditions of extreme cowardice, Mrs. Cameron."

He realized his mistake the minute he'd made it. It was not the moment to use the married title. And yet, in some oblique way she seemed grateful that he had. She moved again and stood directly in front of him.

"Mrs. Cameron thanks you."

He reached out and held her by the waist. Her arms slowly, haltingly, went up to his shoulders; her hands cupped his face and she stared into his eyes.

He did not move. The decision, the first step, had to be hers; he understood that.

She brought her lips to his. The touch was soft and lovely and meant for earthbound angels. And then she trembled with an almost uncontrollable sense of urgency. Her lips parted and she pressed her body with extraordinary strength into his, her arms clutched about his neck.

She pulled her lips away from his and buried her face into his chest, holding him with fierce possession.

"Don't say anything," she whispered. "Don't say anything at all. . . . *Just take me.*"

He picked her up silently and carried her into the bedroom. She kept her face pressed into his chest, as if she were afraid to see light or even him. He lowered her gently onto the bed and closed the door.

In a few moments they were naked and he pulled the blankets over them. It was a moist and beautiful darkness. A splendid comfort.

"I want to say something," she said, tracing her finger over his lips, her face above his, her breasts innocently on his chest. And smiling her genuine smile.

"I know. You want the other Spaulding. The thin one with spectacles." He kissed her fingers.

"He disappeared in an explosion of sorts."

"You're positively descriptive, young lady."

"And not so young. . . . That's what I want to talk about."

"A pension. You're angling for Social Security. I'll see what I can do."

"Be serious, silly boy."

"And not so silly. . . ."

"There's no commitment, David," she said, interrupting him. "I want you to know that. . . . I don't know how else to say it. Everything happened so fast."

"Everything happened very naturally. Explanations aren't required."

"Well, I think some are. I didn't expect to be here."

"I didn't expect that you would be. I suppose I hoped, I'll admit that. . . . I didn't plan; neither of us did."

"I don't know; I think I did. I think I saw you yesterday and somewhere in the back of my mind I made a decision. Does that sound brazen of me?"

"If you did, the decision was long overdue."

"Yes, I imagine it was." She lay back, pulling the sheet over her. "I've been very selfish. Spoiled and selfish and behaving really quite badly."

"Because you haven't slept around?" It was his turn to roll over and touch her face. He kissed both her eyes, now open; the deep speckles of blue made bluer, deeper, by the late afternoon sun streaming through the blinds. She smiled; her perfect white teeth glistening with the moisture of her mouth, her lips curved in that genuine curve of humor.

"That's funny. I must be unpatriotic. I've withheld my charms only to deliver them to a noncombatant."

"The Visigoths wouldn't have approved. The warriors came first, I'm told."

"Let's not tell them." She reached up for his face. "Oh, David, David, *David*."

## 25

"I hope I didn't wake you. I wouldn't have troubled you but I thought you'd want me to."

Ambassador Granville's voice over the telephone was more solicitous than David expected it to be. He looked at his watch as he replied. It was three minutes of ten in the morning.

"Oh? . . . No, sir. I was just getting up. Sorry I overslept."

There was a note on the telephone table. It was from Jean.

"Your friend was in contact with us."

"Friend?" David unfolded the note. *My Darling—You fell into such a beautiful sleep it would have broken my heart to disturb you. Called a taxi. See you in the morning. At the Bastile. Your ex-regimented phoenix.* David smiled, remembering her smile.

". . . the details, I'm sure, aren't warranted." Granville had said something and he hadn't been listening.

"I'm sorry, Mr. Ambassador. This must be a poor connection; your voice fades in and out." All telephones beyond the Atlantic, north, middle and south, were temperamental instruments. An unassailable fact.

"Or something else, I'm afraid," said Granville with irritation, obviously referring to the possibility of a telephone tap. "When you get in, please come to see me."

"Yes, sir. I'll be there directly."

He picked up Jean's note and read it again.

She had said last night that he was complicating her life. But there were no commitments; she'd said that, too.

What the hell was a commitment? He didn't want to speculate. He didn't want to think about the awful discovery—the instant, splendid comfort they both recognized. It wasn't the time for it. . . .

Yet to deny it would be to reject an extraordinary reality. He was trained to deal with reality.

He didn't want to think about it.

His "friend" had been in contact with the embassy. Walter Kendall.

That was another reality. It couldn't wait.

He crushed out his cigarette angrily, watching his fingers stab the butt into the metal ashtray.

Why was he angry?

He didn't care to speculate on that, either. He had a job to do. He hoped he had the commitment for it.

"Jean said you barely made it through dinner. You needed a good night's sleep; I must say you look better." The ambassador had come from around his desk to greet him as he entered the large, ornate office. David was a little bewildered. The old diplomat was actually being solicitous, displaying a concern that belied his unconcealed disapproval of two days ago. Or was it his use of the name Jean instead of the forbidding Mrs. Cameron.

"She was very kind. I couldn't have found a decent restaurant without her."

"I daresay. . . . I won't detain you, you'd better get cracking with this Kendall."

"You said he's been in contact. . . ."

"Starting last night; early this morning to be accurate. He's at the Alvear and apparently quite agitated, according to the switchboard. At two thirty this morning he was shouting, demanding to know where you were. Naturally, we don't give out that information."

"I'm grateful. As you said, I needed the sleep; Kendall would have prevented it. Do you have his telephone number? Or shall I get it from the book?"

"No, right here." Granville walked to his desk and picked up a sheet of notepaper. David followed and took it from the ambassador's outstretched hand.

"Thank you, sir. I'll get on it." He turned and started for the door, Granville's voice stopping him.

"Spaulding?"

"Yes, sir?"

"I'm sure Mrs. Cameron would like to see you. Assess

your recovery, I daresay. Her office is in the south wing.
First door from the entrance, on the right. Do you know
where that is?"

"I'll find it, sir."

"I'm sure you will. See you later in the day."

David went out the heavy baroque door, closing it behind him. Was it his imagination or was Granville reluctantly giving an approval to his and Jean's sudden . . .
alliance? The words were approving, the tone of voice reluctant.

He walked down the connecting corridor toward the
south wing and reached her door. Her name was stamped
on a brass plate to the left of the doorframe. He had not
noticed it yesterday.

*Mrs. Andrew Cameron.*

So his name had been Andrew. Spaulding hadn't asked
his first name; she hadn't volunteered it.

As he looked at the brass plate he found himself experi-
encing a very strange reaction. He resented Andrew Cameron; resented his life, his death.

The door was open and he entered. Jean's secretary was
obviously an Argentine. A *porteña*. The black Spanish hair
was pulled back into a bun, her features Latin.

"Mrs. Cameron, please. David Spaulding."

"Please go in. She's expecting you." David approached
the door and turned the knob.

She was taken by surprise, he thought. She was at the
window looking out at the south lawn, a page of paper in
her hand, glasses pushed above her forehead, resting on top
of her light brown hair.

Startled, she removed her glasses from their perch and
stood immobile. Slowly, as if studying him first, she smiled.

He found himself afraid. More than afraid, for a moment. And then she spoke and the sudden anguish left him,
replaced by a deeply felt relief.

"I woke up this morning and reached for you. You
weren't there and I thought I might cry."

He walked rapidly to her and they held each other.
Neither spoke. The silence, the embrace, the splendid comfort returning.

"Granville acted like a procurer a little while ago," he
said finally, holding her by the shoulders, looking at her
blue speckled eyes that held such intelligent humor.

"I told you he was lovable. You wouldn't believe me."

"You didn't *tell* me we had dinner, though. Or that I could barely get through it."

"I was hoping you'd slip; give him more to think about."

"I don't understand him. Or you, maybe."

"Henderson has a problem. . . . Me. He's not sure how to handle it—me. He's overprotective because I've led him to believe I wanted that protection. I did; it was easier. But a man who's had three wives and at least twice that many mistresses over the years is no Victorian. . . . And he knows you're not going to be here long. As he would put it: do I sketch a reasonable picture?"

"I daresay," answered David in Granville's Anglicized manner.

"That's unkind." Jean laughed. "He probably doesn't approve of you, which makes his unspoken acceptance very difficult for him."

David released her. "I know damned well he doesn't approve. . . . Look, I have to make some calls; go out and meet someone. . . ."

"Just someone?"

"A ravishing beauty who'll introduce me to lots of other ravishing beauties. And between the two of us, I can't stand him. But I have to see him. . . . Will you have dinner with me?"

"Yes, I'll have dinner with you. I'd planned to. You didn't have a choice."

"You're right; you're brazen."

"I made that clear. You broke down the regimens; I'm flying up out of my own personal ash heap. . . . The air feels good."

"It was going to happen. . . . I was here." He wasn't sure why he said it but he had to.


Walter Kendall paced the hotel room as though it were a cage. Spaulding sat on the couch watching him, trying to decide which animal Kendall reminded him of; there were several that came to mind, none pets.

"You listen to *me*," Kendall said. "This is no military operation. You *take* orders, you don't give them."

"I'm sorry; I think you're misreading me." David was tempted to answer Kendall's anger in kind, but he decided not to.

"I misread, bullshit! You told Swanson you were in some trouble in New York. That's *your* problem, not *ours*."

"You can't be sure of that."

"Oh yes I can! You tried to sell that to Swanson and he bought it. You could have involved *us*!"

"Now just a minute." Spaulding felt he could object legitimately—within the boundaries he had mentally staked off for Kendall. "I told Swanson that in my opinion the 'trouble' in New York might have been related to Buenos Aires. I didn't say it *was*, I said it might have been."

"That's not possible!"

"How the hell can you be so sure?"

"Because I am." Kendall was not only agitated, thought David, he was impatient. "This is a business proposition. The deal's been made. There's no one trying to stop it. Stop *us*."

"Hostilities don't cease because a deal's been made. If the German command got wind of it they'd blow up Buenos Aires to stop it."

"Yeah . . . well, that's not possible."

"You *know* that?"

"We know it. . . . So don't go confusing that stupid bastard Swanson. I'll level with you. This is strictly a money-line negotiation. We could have completed it without any help from Washington, but they insisted—Swanson insisted—that they have a man here. O.K., you're him. You can be helpful; you can get the papers out and you speak the languages. But that's *all* you've got to do. Don't call attention to yourself. We don't want anyone upset."

Grudgingly, David began to understand the subtle clarity of Brigadier General Swanson's manipulation. Swanson had maneuvered him into a clean position. The killing of Erich Rhinemann—whether he did it himself or whether he bought the assassin—would be totally unexpected. Swanson wasn't by any means the "stupid bastard" Kendall thought he was. Or that David had considered.

Swanson was nervous. A neophyte. But he was pretty damned good.

"All right. My apologies," said Spaulding, indicating a sincerity he didn't feel. "Perhaps the New York thing was

exaggerated. I made enemies in Portugal, I can't deny that.
. . . I got out under cover, you know."

"What?"

"There's no way the people in New York could know I left the city."

"You're sure?"

"As sure as you are that no one's trying to stop your negotiations."

"Yeah. . . . O.K. Well, everything's set. I got a schedule."

"You've seen Rhinemann?"

"Yesterday. All day."

"What about Lyons?" asked David.

"Swanson's packing him off at the end of the week. With his nursemaids. Rhinemann figures the designs will be arriving Sunday or Monday."

"In steps or all together?"

"Probably two sets of prints. He's not sure. It doesn't make any difference; they'll be here in full by Tuesday. He guaranteed."

"Then we've moved up. You estimated three weeks." David felt a pain in his stomach. He knew it wasn't related to Walter Kendall or Eugene Lyons or designs for high-altitude gyroscopes. It was Jean Cameron and the simple fact that he'd have only one week with her.

It disturbed him greatly and he speculated—briefly—on the meaning of this disturbance.

And then he knew he could not allow himself the indulgence; the two entities had to remain separate, the worlds separate.

"Rhinemann's got good control," said Kendall, more than a hint of respect showing in his voice. "I'm impressed with his methods. Very precise."

"If you think that, you don't need me." David was buying a few seconds to steer their conversation to another area. His statement was rhetorical.

"We don't; that's what I said. But there's a lot of money involved and since the War Department—one way or another—is picking up a large share of the tab, Swanson wants his accounts covered. I don't sweat him on that. It's business."

Spaulding recognized his moment. "Then let's get to the

codes. I haven't wasted the three days down here. I've struck up a friendship of sorts with the embassy cryp."

"The what?"

"The head cryptographer. He'll send out the codes to Washington; the payment authorization."

"Oh. . . . Yeah, that." Kendall was squeezing a cigarette, prepared to insert it in his mouth. He was only half-concerned with codes and cryptographers, thought David. They were the wrap-up, the necessary details relegated to others. Or was it an act? wondered Spaulding.

He'd know in a moment or two.

"As you pointed out, it's a great deal of money. So we've decided to use a scrambler with code switches every twelve hours. We'll prepare the cryp schedule tonight and send it out by patrol courier to Washington tomorrow. The master plate will allow for fifteen letters. . . . Naturally, the prime word will be 'Tortugas.' "

Spaulding watched the disheveled accountant.

There was no reaction whatsoever.

"O.K. . . . Yeah, O.K." Kendall sat down in an easy chair. His mind seemed somewhere else.

"That meets with your approval, doesn't it?"

"Sure. Why not? Play any games you like. All I give a shit about is that Geneva radios the confirmation and you fly out of here."

"Yes, but I thought the reference had to include the . . . code factor."

"What the hell are you talking about?"

" 'Tortugas.' Hasn't it got to be 'Tortugas'?"

"Why? What's 'Tortugas'?"

The man wasn't acting. David was sure of that. "Perhaps I misunderstood. I thought 'Tortugas' was part of the authorization code."

"Christ! You and Swanson! All of you. Military geniuses! *Jesus!* If it doesn't sound like Dan Dunn, Secret Agent, it's not the real McCoy, huh? . . . Look. When Lyons tells you everything's in order, just say so. Then drive out to the airport . . . it's a small field called Mendarro . . . and Rhinemann's men will tell you when you can leave. O.K.? You got that?"

"Yes, I've got it," said Spaulding. But he wasn't sure.

Outside, David walked aimlessly down the Buenos Aires streets. He reached the huge park of the Plaza San Martín, with its fountains, its rows of white gravel paths, its calm disorder.

He sat down on a slatted bench and tried to define the elusive pieces of the increasingly complex puzzle.

Walter Kendall hadn't lied. "Tortugas" meant nothing to him.

Yet a man in an elevator in New York City had risked his life to learn about "Tortugas."

Ira Barden in Fairfax had told him there was only a single word opposite his name in the DW transfer in Ed Pace's vaults: "Tortugas."

There was an obvious answer, perhaps. Ed Pace's death prohibited any real knowledge, but the probability was genuine.

Berlin had gotten word of the Peenemünde negotiation —too late to prevent the theft of the designs—and was now committed to stopping the sale. Not only stopping it, but if possible tracing the involvement of everyone concerned. Trapping the entire Rhinemann network.

If this was the explanation—and what other plausible one existed?—Pace's code name, "Tortugas," had been leaked to Berlin by Fairfax infiltration. That there was a serious breach of security at Fairfax was clear; Pace's murder was proof.

His own role could be easily assessed by Berlin, thought David. The man in Lisbon suddenly transferred to Buenos Aires. The expert whose skill was proven in hundreds of espionage transactions, whose own network was the most ruthlessly efficient in southern Europe, did not walk out of his own creation unless his expertise was considered vital someplace else. He'd long ago accepted the fact that Berlin more than suspected him. In a way it was his protection; he'd by no means won every roll of the dice. If the enemy killed him, someone else would take his place. The enemy would have to start all over again. He was a known commodity . . . accept an existing devil.

Spaulding considered carefully, minutely, what he might do were he the enemy. What steps would he take at this specific juncture?

Barring panic or error, the enemy would not kill him.

Not now. Because he could *not* by himself inhibit the delivery of the designs. He could, however, lead his counterparts to the moment and place of delivery.

*What is the location of Tortugas!?*

The desperate . . . hysterical man in the Montgomery elevator had screamed the question, preferring to die rather than reveal those whose orders he followed. The Nazis reveled in such fanaticism. And so did others, for other reasons.

He—Spaulding—would therefore be placed under *äusserste Überwachung*—foolproof surveillance, three- to four-man teams, twenty-four hours a day. That would account for the recruitment of the extraterritorial personnel on the Berlin payroll. Agents who operated outside the borders of Germany, *had* operated—for profit—for years. The languages and dialects would vary; deep-cover operatives who could move with impunity in neutral capitals because they had no Gestapo or Gehlen or Nachrichtendienst histories.

The Balkans and the Middle East countries had such personnel for hire. They were expensive; they were among the best. Their only loyalty was to the pound sterling and the American dollar.

Along with this round-the-clock surveillance, Berlin would take extraordinary measures to prevent him from developing his own network in Buenos Aires. That would mean infiltrating the American embassy. Berlin would not overlook that possibility. A great deal of money would be offered.

Who at the embassy could be bought?

To attempt corrupting an individual too highly placed could backfire; give him, Spaulding, dangerous information. . . . Someone not too far up on the roster; someone who could gain access to doors and locks and desk-drawer vaults. And codes. . . . A middle-level attaché. A man who'd probably never make it to the Court of St. James's anyway; who'd settle for another kind of security. Negotiable at a very high price.

Someone at the embassy would be Spaulding's enemy.

Finally, Berlin would order him killed. Along with numerous others, of course. Killed at the moment of delivery; killed after the *äusserste Überwachung* had extracted everything it could.

David got up from the slatted green bench and stretched, observing the beauty that was the Plaza San Martín park. He wandered beyond the path onto the grass, to the edge of a pond whose dark waters reflected the surrounding trees like a black mirror. Two white swans paddled by in alabaster obliviousness. A little girl was kneeling by a rock on the tiny embankment, separating the petals from a yellow flower.

He was satisfied that he had adequately analyzed the immediate options of his counterparts. Options and probable courses of action. His gut feeling was positive—not in the sense of being enthusiastic, merely not negative.

He now had to evolve his own counterstrategy. He had to bring into play the lessons he had learned over the years in Lisbon. But there was so little time allowed him. And because of this fact, he understood that a misstep could be fatal here.

Nonchalantly—but with no feelings of nonchalance—he looked around at the scores of strollers on the paths, on the grass; the rowers and the passengers in the small boats on the small dark lake. Which of them were the enemy?

Who were the ones watching him, trying to think what he was thinking?

He would have to find them—one or two of them anyway—before the next few days were over.

That was the genesis of his counterstrategy.

Isolate and break.

David lit a cigarette and walked over the miniature bridge. He was primed. The hunter and the hunted were now one. There was the slightest straining throughout his entire body; the hands, the arms, the legs: there was a muscular tension, an awareness. He recognized it. He was back in the north country.

And he was good in that jungle. He was the best there was. It was here that he built his architectural monuments, his massive structures of concrete and steel. In his mind.

It was all he had sometimes.

## 26

He looked at his watch. It was five thirty; Jean had said she'd be at his apartment around six. He had walked for nearly two hours and now found himself at the corner of Viamonte, several blocks from his apartment. He crossed the street and walked to a newsstand under a storefront awning, where he bought a paper.

He glanced at the front pages, amused to see that the war news—what there was of it—was relegated to the bottom, surrounded by accounts of the Grupo de Oficiales' latest benefits to Argentina. He noted that the name of a particular colonel, one Juan Perón, was mentioned in three separate subheadlines.

He folded the paper under his arm and, because he realized he had been absently musing, looked once again at his watch.

It was not a deliberate move on David's part. That is to say, he did not calculate the abruptness of his turn; he simply turned because the angle of the sun caused a reflection on his wristwatch and he unconsciously shifted his body to the right, his left hand extended, covered by his own shadow.

But his attention was instantly diverted from his watch. Out of the corner of his eye he could discern a sudden, sharp break in the sidewalk's human traffic. Thirty feet away across the street two men had swiftly turned around, colliding with oncoming pedestrians, apologizing, stepping into the flow on the curbside.

The man on the left had not been quick enough; or he was too careless—too inexperienced, perhaps—to angle his shoulders, or hunch them imperceptibly so as to melt into the crowd.

He stood out and David recognized him.

He was one of the men from the roof of the Córdoba apartment. His companion David couldn't be sure of, but he *was* sure of that man. There was even the hint of a limp in his gait; David remembered the battering he'd given him.

He was being followed, then, and that was good.

His point of departure wasn't as remote as he'd thought.

He walked another ten yards, into a fairly large group approaching the corner of Córdoba. He sidestepped his way between arms and legs and packages, and entered a small jewelry store whose wares were gaudy, inexpensive. Inside, several office girls were trying to select a gift for a departing secretary. Spaulding smiled at the annoyed proprietor, indicating that he could wait, he was in no hurry. The proprietor made a gesture of helplessness.

Spaulding stood by the front window, his body concealed from outside by the frame of the door.

Before a minute was up he saw the two men again. They were still across the street; David had to follow their progress through the intermittent gaps in the crowd. The two men were talking heatedly, the second man annoyed with his limping companion. Both were trying to glance above the heads of the surrounding bodies, raising themselves up on their toes, looking foolish, amateur.

David figured they would turn right at the corner and walk east on Córdoba, toward his apartment. They did so and, as the owner of the jewelry store protested, Spaulding walked swiftly out into the crowds and ran across the Avenida Callao, dodging cars and angry drivers. He had to reach the other side, staying out of the sightlines of the two men. He could not use the crosswalks or the curbs. It would be too easy, too logical, for the men to look backward as men did when trying to spot someone they had lost in surveillance.

David knew his objective now. He had to separate the men and take the one with a limp. Take him and force answers.

If they had any experience, he considered, they would reach his apartment and divide, one man cautiously going inside to listen through the door, ascertaining the subject's presence, the other remaining outside, far enough from the entrance to be unobserved. And common sense would dic-

tate that the man unknown to David would be the one to
enter the apartment.

Spaulding removed his jacket and held up the newspaper
—not full but folded; not obviously but casually, as if he
were uncertain of the meaning of some awkwardly phrased
headline—and walked with the crowds to the north side of
Córdoba. He turned right and maintained a steady, unbroken pace east, remaining as far left on the sidewalk as
possible.

His apartment was less than a block and a half away
now. He could see the two men; intermittently they *did*
look back, but on their own side of the street.

Amateurs. If he taught surveillance, they'd fail his
course.

The men drew nearer to the apartment, their concentration on the entrance. David knew it was his moment to
move. The only moment of risk, really; the few split seconds when one or the other might turn and see him across
the street, only yards away. But it was a necessary gamble.
He had to get beyond the apartment entrance. That was
the essence of his trap.

Several lengths ahead was a middle-aged *porteña* housewife carrying groceries, hurrying, obviously anxious to get
home. Spaulding came alongside and without breaking
stride, keeping in step with her, he started asking directions
in his best, most elegant Castilian, starting among other
points that he knew this was the right street and he was
late. His head was tilted from the curb.

If anyone watched them, the housewife and the shirt-
sleeved man with a jacket under one arm and a newspaper
under the other looked like two friends hastening to a
mutual destination.

Twenty yards beyond the entrance on the other side,
Spaulding left the smiling *porteña* and ducked into a canopied doorway. He pressed himself into the wall and
looked back across the street. The two men stood by the
curb and, as he expected, they separated. The unknown
man went into his apartment house; the man with the limp
looked up and down the sidewalk, checked oncoming vehicles, and started across Córdoba to the north side.
David's side.

Spaulding knew it would be a matter of seconds before

the limping figure passed him. Logic, again; common sense. The man would continue east—he would not reverse direction—over traversed ground. He would station himself at a vantage point from which he could observe those approaching the apartment from the west. David's approach.

The man did not see him until David touched him, grabbed his left arm around the elbow, forced the arm into a horizontal position, and clamped the man's hand downward so that the slightest force on David's part caused an excruciating pain in the man's bent wrist.

"Just keep walking or I'll snap your hand off," said David in English, pushing the man to the right of the sidewalk to avoid the few pedestrians walking west on Córdoba.

The man's face grimaced in pain; David's accelerated walk caused him to partially stumble—his limp emphasized —and brought further agony to the wrist.

"You're breaking my arm. You're *breaking* it!" said the anguished man, hurrying his steps to relieve the pressure.

"Keep up with me or I will." David spoke calmly, even politely. They reached the corner of the Avenida Paraná and Spaulding swung left, propelling the man with him. There was a wide, recessed doorway of an old office building—the type that had few offices remaining within it. David spun the man around, keeping the arm locked, and slammed him into the wooden wall at the point farthest inside. He released the arm; the man grabbed for his strained wrist. Spaulding took the moment to flip open the man's jacket, forcing the arms downward, and removed a revolver strapped in a large holster above the man's left hip.

It was a Lüger. Issued less than a year ago.

David clamped it inside his belt and pushed a lateral forearm against the man's throat, crashing his head into the wood as he searched the pockets of the jacket. Inside he found a large rectangular European billfold. He slapped it open, removed his forearm from the man's throat, and shoved his left shoulder into the man's chest, pinning him unmercifully against the wall. With both hands, David removed identification papers.

A German driver's license; an Autobahn vehicle pass;

rationing cards countersigned by Oberführers, allowing the owner to utilize them throughout the Reich—a privilege granted to upper-level government personnel and above.

And then he found it.

An identity pass with a photograph affixed; for the ministries of Information, Armaments, Air and Supply.

*Gestapo.*

"You're about the most inept recruit Himmler's turned out," said David, meaning the judgment profoundly, putting the billfold in his back pocket. "You must have relatives. . . . *Was ist 'Tortugas'?*" Spaulding whispered harshly, suddenly. He removed his shoulder from the man's chest and thrust two extended knuckles into the Nazi's breastbone with such impact that the German coughed, the sharp blow nearly paralyzing him. "*Wer ist Altmüller? Was wissen Sie über Marshall?*" David repeatedly hammered the man's ribs with his knuckles, sending shock waves of pain throughout the Gestapo agent's rib cage. "*Sprechen Sie! Sofort!*"

"*Nein! Ich weiss nichts!*" the man answered between gasps. "*Nein!*"

Spaulding heard it again. The dialect. Nowhere near *Berliner*; not even a mountainized *Bavarian*. Something else.

What was it?

"*Noch 'mal! Again! Sprechen Sie!*"

And then the man did something quite out of the ordinary. In his pain, his fear, he stopped speaking German. He spoke in English. "I have not the information you want! I follow orders. . . . That is all!"

David shifted his stand to the left, covering the Nazi from the intermittent looks they both received from the passersby on the sidewalk. The doorway was deep, however, in shadows; no one stopped. The two men could have been acquaintances, one or both perhaps a little drunk.

Spaulding clenched his right fist, his left elbow against the wall, his left hand poised to clamp over the German's mouth. He leaned against the slatted wood and brought his fist crashing into the man's stomach with such force that the agent lurched forward, held only by David's hand, now gripping him by the hairline.

"I can keep this up until I rupture everything inside you. And when I'm finished I'll throw you in a taxi and drop you off at the German embassy with a note attached. You'll get it from both sides then, won't you? . . . Now, tell me what I want to know!" David brought his two bent knuckles up into the man's throat, jabbing twice.

"Stop. . . . *Mein Gott!* Stop!"

"Why don't you yell? You can scream your head off, you know. . . . Of course, then I'll have to put you to sleep and let your own people find you. Without your credentials, naturally. . . . Go on! Yell!" David knuckled the man once more in the throat. "Now, you start telling me. What's 'Tortugas'? Who's Altmüller? How did you get a cryp named Marshall?"

"I swear to God! I know nothing!"

David punched him again. The man collapsed; Spaulding pulled him up against the wall, leaning against him, hiding him, really. The Gestapo agent opened his lids, his eyes swimming uncontrollably.

"You've got five seconds. Then I'll rip your throat out."

"No! . . . Please! Altmüller. . . . Armaments. . . . Peenemünde. . . ."

"What about Peenemünde?"

"The tooling. . . . 'Tortugas.' "

"What does that *mean*!?" David showed the man his two bent fingers. The recollection of pain terrified the German. "What is 'Tortugas'?"

Suddenly the German's eyes flickered, trying to focus. Spaulding saw that the man was looking above his shoulder. It wasn't a ruse; the Nazi was too far gone for strategies.

And then David felt the presence behind him. It was an unmistakable feeling that had been developed over the recent years; it was never false.

He turned.

Coming into the dark shadows from the harsh Argentine sunlight was the second part of the surveillance team, the man who'd entered his apartment building. He was Spaulding's size, a large man and heavily muscular.

The light and the onrushing figure caused David to wince. He released the German, prepared to throw himself onto the opposite wall.

He couldn't!

The Gestapo agent—in a last surge of strength—held onto his arms!

Held his arms, threw his hands around David's chest and hung his full weight on him!

Spaulding lashed out with his foot at the man attacking, swung his elbows back, slamming the German back into the wood.

It was too late and David knew it.

He saw the huge hand—the long fingers spread—rushing into his face. It was as if a ghoulish film was being played before his eyes in slow motion. He felt the fingers clamp into his skin and realized that his head was being shoved with great strength into the wall.

The sensations of diving, crashing, spinning accompanied the shock of pain above his neck.

He shook his head; the first thing that struck him was the stench. It was all around him, sickening.

He was lying in the recessed doorway, curled up against the wall in a fetal position. He was wet, drenched around his face and shirt and in the crotch area of his trousers.

It was cheap whisky. Very cheap and very profuse.

His shirt had been ripped, collar to waist; one shoe was off, the sock removed. His belt was undone, his fly partially unzipped.

He was the perfect picture of a derelict.

He rose to a sitting position and remedied as best he could his appearance. He looked at his watch.

Or where his watch had been; it was gone.

His wallet, too. And money. And whatever else had been in his pockets.

He stood up. The sun was down, early night had begun; there were not so many people on the Avenida Paraná now.

He wondered what time it was. It couldn't be much more than an hour later, he supposed.

He wondered if Jean were still waiting for him.

She removed his clothes, pressed the back of his head with ice and insisted that he take a long, hot shower.

When he emerged from the bathroom, she fixed him a drink, then sat down next to him on the small couch.

"Henderson will insist on your moving into the embassy; you know that, don't you?"

"I can't."

"Well, you can't go on being beaten up every day. And don't tell me they were *thieves*. *You* wouldn't swallow that when Henderson and Bobby *both* tried to tell you that about the men on the roof!"

"This was different. For God's *sake*, Jean, I was robbed of everything on me!" David spoke sternly. It was important to him that she believe him now. And it was entirely possible that he'd find it necessary to avoid her from now on. That might be important, too. And terribly painful.

"People don't rob people and then douse them with whisky!"

"They do if they want to create sufficient time to get out of the area. It's not a new tactic. By the time a mark gets finished explaining to the police that he's a sober citizen, the hustlers are twenty miles away."

"I don't believe you. I don't even think you expect me to." She sat up and looked at him.

"I do expect you to because it's the truth. A man doesn't throw away his wallet, his money, his watch . . . in order to impress a girl with the validity of a lie. Come *on*, Jean! I'm very thirsty and my head still hurts."

She shrugged, obviously realizing it was futile to argue.

"You're just about out of Scotch, I'm afraid. I'll go buy a bottle for you. There's a liquor store on the corner of Talcahuano. It's not far. . . ."

"No," he said, interrupting, recalling the man with huge hands who'd entered his building. "I will. Lend me some money."

"We'll both go," she responded.

"Please? . . . Would you mind waiting? I may get a phone call; I'd like the person to know I'll be right back."

"Who?"

"A man named Kendall."

Out on the street, he asked the first man he saw where the nearest pay phone could be found. It was several blocks away, on Rodríguez Peña, in a newspaper store.

David ran as fast as he could.

The hotel page found Kendall in the dining room. When he got on the phone he spoke while chewing. Spaulding pictured the man, the doodled obscenities, the animal-like breathing. He controlled himself. Walter Kendall was sick.

"Lyons is coming in in three days," Kendall told him. "With his nurses. I got him a place in this San Telmo district. A quiet apartment, quiet street. I wired Swanson the address. He'll give it to the keepers and they'll get him set up. They'll be touch with you."

"I thought *I* was to get him settled."

"I figured you'd complicate things," interrupted Kendall. "No piss lost. They'll call you. Or I will. I'll be here for a while."

"I'm glad. . . . Because so's the Gestapo."

"*What?*"

"I said so's the Gestapo. You figured a little inaccurately, Kendall. Someone *is* trying to stop you. It doesn't surprise me."

"You're out of your fucking mind!"

"I'm not."

"What happened?"

So David told him, and for the first time in his brief association with the accountant, he detected fear.

"There was a break in Rhinemann's network. It doesn't mean the designs won't get here. It does mean we have obstacles—if Rhinemann's as good as you say. As I read it, Berlin found out the designs were stolen. They know they're filtering down or across or however Rhinemann's routing them out of Europe. The High Command got wind of the transactions. The Reichsführers aren't going to broadcast, they're going to try and intercept. With as little noise as possible. But you can bet your ass there's been a slew of executions in Peenemünde."

"It's crazy. . . ." Kendall could hardly be heard. And then he mumbled something; David could not understand the words.

"What did you say?"

"The address in this Telmo. For Lyons. It's three rooms. Back entrance." Kendall still kept his voice low, almost indistinct.

The man was close to panic, thought Spaulding. "I can barely hear you, Kendall. . . . Now, calm down! I think it's time I introduced myself to Rhinemann, don't you?"

"The Telmo address. It's Fifteen Terraza Verde . . . it's quiet."

"Who's the contact for Rhinemann?"

"The what?"

"Rhinemann's contact."

"I don't know. . . ."

"For Christ's sake, Kendall, you held a five-hour conference with him!"

"I'll be in touch. . . ."

David heard the click. He was stunned. Kendall had hung up on him. He considered calling again but in Kendall's state of anxiety it might only make matters worse.

Goddamned amateurs! What the hell did they expect? Albert Speer himself to get in touch with Washington and lend the army air corps a few designs because he heard they had problems!?

*Jesus!*

David walked angrily out of the telephone booth and the store and into the street.

Where the goddamned hell was he? Oh, yes, the Scotch. The store was back at Talcahuano, Jean said. Four blocks west. He looked at his watch and, of course, there was no watch.

*Goddamn.*

"I'm sorry I took so long. I got confused. I walked the wrong way for a couple of blocks." David put the package of Scotch and soda water on the sink. Jean was sitting on the sofa; disturbed about something, he thought. "Did I get the call?"

"Not the one you expected," said Jean softly. "Someone else. He said he'd phone you tomorrow."

"Oh? Did he leave a name?"

"Yes, he did." When she answered, David heard the questioning fear in her voice. "It was Heinrich Stoltz."

"Stoltz? Don't know him."

"You should. He's an undersecretary at the German embassy. . . . David, what are you doing?"

## 27

"Sorry, *señor*. Mister Kendall checked out last night. At ten thirty, according to the card."

"Did he leave any other address or telephone number here in Buenos Aires?"

"No, *señor*. I believe he was going back to the United States. There was a Pan American flight at midnight."

"Thank you." David put down the telephone and reached for his cigarettes.

It was incredible! Kendall had shot out at the first moment of difficulty.

Why?

The telephone rang, startling David.

"Hello?"

"Herr Spaulding?"

"Yes."

"Heinrich Stoltz. I called last night but you were out."

"Yes, I know. . . . I understand you're with the German embassy. I hope I don't have to tell you that I find your contacting me unorthodox. And not a little distasteful."

"Oh, come, Herr Spaulding. The man from *Lisbon? He* finds unorthodoxy?" Stoltz laughed quietly but not insultingly.

"I am an embassy attaché specializing in economics. Nothing more. If you know anything about me, surely you know that. . . . Now, I'm late. . . ."

"Please," interrupted Stoltz. "I call from a public telephone. Surely *that* tells *you* something."

It did, of course.

"I don't talk on telephones."

"Yours is clean, I checked thoroughly."

"If you want to meet, give me a time and an address. . . ."

Somewhere in the downtown area. With people around; no outside locations."

"There's a restaurant, Casa Langosta del Mar, several blocks north of the Parque Lezama. It's out of the way, not outside. There are back rooms. Curtains, no doors; no means of isolation. Only seclusion."

"Time?"

"Half past twelve."

"Do you smoke?" asked David sharply.

"Yes."

"Carry a pack of American cigarettes from the moment you get out of the car. In your left hand; the foil off one end of the top, two cigarettes removed."

"It's quite unnecessary. I know who you are. I'll recognize you."

"That's not my concern. I don't know you." David hung up the phone abruptly. As in all such rendezvous, he would arrive at the location early, through a delivery entrance if possible, and position himself as best he could to observe his contact's arrival. The cigarettes were nothing more than a psychological device: the contact was thrown off balance with the realization that he was an identified mark. A target. A marked contact was reluctant to bring trouble. And if trouble was his intent, he wouldn't show up.

Jean Cameron walked down the corridor toward the metal staircase that led to the cellars.

To the "Caves."

The "Caves"—a name given without affection by Foreign Service officers the world over—were those underground rooms housing file cabinets containing dossiers on just about everybody who had the slightest contact with an embassy, known and unknown, friend and adversary. They included exhaustive checks and counterchecks on all embassy personnel; service background, State Department evaluations, progress reports. Nothing was left out if it was obtainable.

Two signatures were required to gain entrance into the "Caves." The ambassador's and that of the senior attaché seeking information.

It was a regulation that was occasionally bypassed in the interests of haste and emergency. The marine officer of the guard generally could be convinced that an established attaché *had* to have immediate background material; the marine would list both the names of the embassy man and his subject on the check sheet, then stand in attendance while the file was removed. If there were repercussions, they were the attaché's responsibility.

There never were. Violations of this sort guaranteed a post in Uganda. The check sheet was sealed daily and sent only to the ambassador.

Jean rarely took advantage of her relationship to Henderson Granville in embassy matters. In truth, the occasion rarely arose, and when it did, the matter was always insignificant.

It was not insignificant now. And she intended to use fully her status as *family*, as well as a respected member of the staff. Granville had left for lunch; he would not return for several hours. She had made up her mind to tell the marine guard that her "father-in-law, the ambassador" had asked her to make a discreet inquiry regarding a new transfer.

Spaulding, David.

If Henderson wished to call her down for it, she would tell him the truth. She found herself very, *very* involved with the enigmatic Mr. Spaulding, and if Henderson did not realize it, he was a damn fool.

The marine officer of the guard was a young lieutenant from the FMF base south of La Boca. The personnel from FMF were sped in civilian clothes through the city to their posts at the embassy; the treaty that permitted the small, limited base did not condone uniformed men outside either territory. These restrictions tended to make the young officers sensitive to the functionary, faceless roles they were forced to play. So it was understandable that when the ambassador's daughter-in-law called him by name and spoke confidentially of a discreet matter, the marine complied without question.

Jean stared at David's file. It was frightening. It was not like any file she had ever seen. There was no dossier; no State Department records, no reports, no evaluations, no listing of post assignments.

There was only a single page.

It gave his description by sex, height, weight, coloring and visible markings.

Beneath this cursory data, separated by a three-line space, was the following:

> *War Dept. Transfer. Clandestine Operations. Finance.*
> *Tortugas.*

And nothing more.

"Finding what you need, Mrs. Cameron?" asked the marine lieutenant by the steel-grilled gate.

"Yes. . . . Thank you." Jean slipped David's thin folder back into place in the cabinet, smiled at the marine, and left.

She reached the staircase and walked slowly up the steps. She accepted the fact that David was involved with an undercover assignment—accepted it while hating it; loathing the secrecy, the obvious danger. But in a conscious way she had prepared herself, expecting the worst and finding it. She was not at all sure she could handle the knowledge, but she was willing to try. If she could not handle it she'd take what moments of selfish pleasure she could and kiss David Spaulding good-bye. She had made up her mind to that . . . unconsciously, really. She could not allow herself more pain.

And there was something else. It was only a dim shadow in a half-lit room but it kept falling across her eyes. It was the word.

"Tortugas."

She had seen it before. Recently. Only days ago.

It had caught her attention because she'd thought of the Dry Tortugas . . . and the few times she and Andrew had sailed there from the Keys.

Where was it? Yes. . . . Yes, she remembered.

It had been in a very mechanical paragraph within the context of an area surveillance report on Henderson Granville's desk. She had read it rather absently one morning . . . only a few days ago. But she hadn't read it closely. Area surveillance reports were composed of short, choppy informational sentences devoid of rhythm and color. Written by unimaginative men concerned only with what they could describe briefly, with data.

It had been down at La Boca.

Something about the captain of a trawler . . . and cargo.

Cargo that had a lading destination of Tortugas. A violation of coastal limits; said destination rescinded, called an obvious error by the trawler's captain.

Yet the lading papers had said Tortugas.

And David Spaulding's classified operation—*clandestine* operation—was coded "Tortugas."

And Heinrich Stoltz of the German embassy had called David.

And Jean Cameron was suddenly afraid.

Spaulding was convinced that Stoltz was alone. He signaled the German to follow him to the back of the restaurant, to the curtained cubicle David had arranged for with the waiter a half hour ago.

Stoltz entered carrying the pack of cigarettes in his left hand. Spaulding circled the round table and sat facing the curtain.

"Have a seat," said David, indicating the chair opposite him. Stoltz smiled, realizing that his back would be to the entrance.

"The man from Lisbon is a cautious man." The German pulled out the chair and sat down, placing the cigarettes on the table. "I can assure you I'm not armed."

"Good. I am."

"You are *too* cautious. The colonels look askance at belligerents carrying weapons in their neutral city. Your embassy should have told you."

"I understand they also arrest Americans quicker than they do you fellows."

Stoltz shrugged. "Why not? After all, we trained them. You only buy their beef."

"There'll be no lunch, incidentally. I paid the waiter for the table."

"I'm sorry. The langosta . . . the lobster here is excellent. Perhaps a drink?"

"No drinks. Just talk."

Stoltz spoke, his voice flat. "I bring a welcome to Buenos Aires. From Erich Rhinemann."

David stared at the man. "You?"

"Yes. I'm your contact."

"That's interesting."

"That's the way of Erich Rhinemann. He pays for allegiances."

"I'll want proof."

"By all means. From Rhinemann himself. . . . Acceptable?"

Spaulding nodded. "When? Where?"

"That's what I'm here to discuss. Rhinemann is as cautious as the man from Lisbon."

"I was attached to the diplomatic corps in Portugal. Don't try to make anything more of it than that."

"Unfortunately, I have to speak the truth. Herr Rhinemann is most upset that the men in Washington saw fit to send you as the liaison. Your presence in Buenos Aires could attract attention."

David reached for the cigarettes Stoltz had placed on the table. He lit one. . . . The German was right, of course; Rhinemann was right. The one liability in his having been chosen was the enemy's probable knowledge of his Lisbon operations. Ed Pace, he was sure, had considered that aspect, discarding it in favor of the overriding assets. Regardless, it was not a subject to discuss with Heinrich Stoltz. The German attaché was still an unproven factor.

"I have no idea what you're referring to. I'm in Buenos Aires to transmit preliminary recommendations from New York and London banking circles relative to postwar reconstruction negotiations. You see, we *do* believe we'll win. Rhinemann can't be overlooked in such projected discussions."

"The man from Lisbon is most professional."

"I wish you'd stop repeating that nonsense. . . ."

"And convincing," interrupted Stoltz. "The cover is one of your better ones. It has more stature than a cowardly American socialite. . . . Even Herr Kendall agrees with that."

David paused before replying. Stoltz was circling in, about to deliver his proof. "Describe Kendall," he said quietly.

"In short words?"

"It doesn't matter."

Stoltz laughed under his breath. "I'd prefer as few as possible. He's a most unattractive biped. He must be an extraordinary man with figures; there's no other earthly reason to stay in the same room with him."

"Have you stayed in the same room with him?"

"For hours, unfortunately. With Rhinemann. . . . Now. May we talk?"

"Go ahead."

"Your man Lyons will be here the day after tomorrow. We can accomplish everything very quickly. The designs will be delivered in one package, not two as Kendall believes."

"Does he believe that?"

"It's what he was told."

"Why?"

"Because until late last evening Herr Rhinemann thought it was so. I myself did not know of the change until this morning."

"Then why did you call me last night?"

"Instructions from Walter Kendall."

"Please explain that."

"Is it necessary? One has nothing to do with the other. Herr Kendall telephoned *me.* Apparently he had just spoken with you. He said he was called back to Washington suddenly; that I was to contact you immediately so there's no break in communications. He was most adamant."

"Did Kendall say why he was returning to the States?"

"No. And I saw no reason to inquire. His work here is finished. He's of no concern to us. You are the man with the codes, not him."

David crushed out his cigarette, staring at the tablecloth. "What's your rank at the embassy?"

Stoltz smiled. "Third . . . fourth in command would be a modest appraisal. My loyalty, however, is to the Rhinemann interests. Surely that's apparent."

"I'll know when I talk to Rhinemann, won't I?" David looked up at the German. "Why are the Gestapo here in Buenos Aires?"

"They're not. . . . Well, there's one man; no more than a clerk, really. As all Gestapo he thinks of himself as the personal spokesman for the Reich and overburdens the couriers—who, incidentally, cooperate with us. He is, as you *Amerikaner* say, a jackass. There is no one else."

"Are you sure?"

"Of course. I would be the first to know; before the ambassador, I assure you. This game is quite unnecessary, Herr Spaulding."

"You'd better set up that meeting with Rhinemann . . . *that's* necessary."

"Yes. Certainly. . . . Which brings us back to Herr Rhinemann's concerns. Why is the man from Lisbon in Buenos Aires?"

"I'm afraid he has to be. You said it. I'm cautious. I'm experienced. And I have the codes."

"But why *you*? To remove you from Lisbon is costly. I speak both as an enemy and as an objective neutral, allied with Rhinemann. Is there some side issue of which we're not aware?"

"If there is, I'm not aware of it, either," answered Spaulding, neutralizing Stoltz's inquisitorial look with one of his own. "Since we're talking plain, I want to get those designs okayed, send the codes for your goddamned money and get the hell out of here. Since a large share of that financing will come from the government, Washington obviously thinks I'm the best man to see we're not cheated."

Both men remained silent for several moments. Stoltz spoke.

"I believe you. You Americans always worry about being cheated, don't you?"

"Let's talk about Rhinemann. I want the meeting immediately. I won't be satisfied that Kendall's arrangements are solid until I hear it from him. And I won't organize a code schedule with Washington until I'm satisfied."

"There's no schedule?"

"There won't be any until I see Rhinemann."

Stoltz breathed deeply. "You are what they say, a thorough man. You'll see Rhinemann. . . . It will have to be after dark, two transfers of vehicles, his residence. He can't take the chance of anyone seeing you together. . . . Do these precautions disturb you?"

"Not a bit. Without the codes there's no money transferred in Switzerland. I think Herr Rhinemann will be most hospitable."

"Yes, I'm sure. . . . Very well. Our business is concluded. You'll be contacted this evening. Will you be at home?"

"If not, I'll leave word at the embassy switchboard."

"*Denn auf Wiedersehen, mein Herr.*" Stoltz got out of the chair and gave a diplomatic nod of his head. "*Heute Abend.*"

*"Heute Abend,"* replied Spaulding as the German parted the curtain and walked out of the cubicle. David saw that Stoltz had left his cigarettes on the table; a minor gift or a minor insult. He removed one and found himself squeezing the tip as he remembered Kendall doing—incessantly, with every cigarette the accountant prepared to smoke. David broke the paper around the tobacco and dropped it in the ashtray. Anything reminding him of Kendall was distasteful now. He couldn't think about Kendall and his sudden, fear-induced departure.

He had something else to think about.

Heinrich Stoltz, "third, fourth in command" at the German embassy, was not so highly placed as he believed. The Nazi had not been lying—he *did not* know the Gestapo was in Buenos Aires. And if he didn't know, that meant someone wasn't telling him.

It was ironic, thought David, that he and Erich Rhinemann would be working together after all. Before he killed Rhinemann, of course.

Heinrich Stoltz sat down at his desk and picked up the telephone. He spoke in his impeccable academic German.

"Get me Herr Rhinemann in Luján."

He replaced the phone, leaned back in his chair and smiled. Several moments later his buzzer hummed.

"Herr Rhinemann? . . . Heinrich Stoltz. . . . Yes, yes, everything went smoothly. Kendall spoke the truth. This Spaulding knows nothing about Koening or the diamonds; his only concerns are the designs. His only threat—that of withholding funds. He plays unimpressive games but we need the codes. The American fleet patrols could be ordered to seal off the harbor; the trawler will have to get out. . . . Can you imagine? All this Spaulding is interested in is not being cheated!"

## 28

At first he thought he was mistaken. . . . No, that wasn't quite right, he considered; that wasn't his first thought. He didn't have a first *thought*, he had only a *reaction*.

He was stunned.

*Leslie Hawkwood!*

He saw her from his taxi window talking with a man at the south end of the fountain in the Plaza de Mayo. The cab was slowly making its way through the traffic around the huge square; he ordered the driver to pull over and stop.

David paid the driver and got out. He was now directly opposite Leslie and the man; he could see the blurred figures through the spray of the fountain.

The man handed Leslie an envelope and bowed a European bow. He turned and went to the curb, his hand held up for a taxi. One stopped and the man got in; the cab entered the flow of traffic and Leslie went to the crosswalk, waiting for the pedestrian signal.

David made his way cautiously around the fountain and dashed to the curb just as the crosswalk light flashed.

He dodged the anxious vehicles, arousing horns and angry shouts, angling his path to the left in case she turned around at the commotion. She was at least fifty yards ahead of him; she couldn't spot him, he was sure of that.

On the boulevard, Leslie headed west toward Avenida 9 de Julio. David closed the gap between them but kept himself obscured by the crowds. She stopped briefly at several store windows, twice obviously trying to make up her mind whether to enter or not.

So like Leslie; she had always hated to give up the acquisition of something new.

She kept walking, however. Once she looked at her wristwatch; she turned north on Julio and checked the numbers of two storefront addresses, apparently to determine the directional sequence.

Leslie Hawkwood had never been to Buenos Aires.

She continued north at a leisurely pace, taking in the extraordinary color and size of the boulevard. She reached the corner of Corrientes, in the middle of the theater district, and wandered past the billboards, looking at the photographs of the performers.

Spaulding realized that the American embassy was less than two blocks away—between the Avenidas Supacha and Esmeralda. There was no point in wasting time.

She saw him before he spoke. Her eyes widened, her jaw fell, her whole body trembled visibly. The blood drained from her suntanned face.

"You have two alternatives, Leslie," said Spaulding as he came within a foot of her, looking down at her terrified face. "The embassy is right up there; it's United States territory. You'll be arrested as a citizen interfering with national security, if not espionage. Or you can come with me. . . . And answer questions. Which will it be?"

The taxi took them to the airport, where Spaulding rented a car with the papers identifying him as "Donald Scanlan, mining surveyor." They were the sort of identifications he carried when making contact with such men as Heinrich Stoltz.

He had held Leslie by the arm with sufficient pressure to warn her not to attempt running; she was his prisoner and he was deadly serious about the fact. She said nothing at all during the ride to the airport; she simply stared out the window, avoiding his eyes.

Her only words at the rental counter were, "Where are we going?"

His reply was succinct: "Out of Buenos Aires."

He followed the river road north toward the outskirts, into the hills above the city. A few miles into the Sante Fé province, the Río Luján curved westward, and he descended the steep inclines onto the highway paralleling the water's edge. It was the territory of the Argentine rich. Yachts were moored or cruising slowly; sailboats of all classes were lazily catching the upriver winds, tacking harmoniously among the tiny green islands which sprung out of the water

like lush gardens. Private roads veered off the highway—
now subtly curving west, away from the water. Enormous
villas dotted the banks; nothing was without visual effect.

He saw a road to his left that was the start of a hill. He
swung up into it, and after a mile there was a break in the
area.

*Vigía Tigre.*

A lookout. A courtesy for tourists.

He drove the car to the front of the parking ground and
pulled to a stop, next to the railing. It was a weekday; there
were no other automobiles.

Leslie had said nothing throughout the hour's ride. She
had smoked cigarettes, her hands trembling, her eyes refusing to make contact with his. And through experience,
David knew the benefits of silence under such conditions.

The girl was close to breaking.

"All right. Now come the questions." Spaulding turned
in the seat and faced her. "And please believe me, I won't
hesitate to run you into military arrest if you refuse."

She swung her head around and stared at him angrily—
yet still in fear. "Why didn't you do that an hour ago?"

"Two reasons," he answered simply. "Once the embassy
is involved, I'd be locked into a chain of command; the
decisions wouldn't be mine. I'm too curious to lose that
control. . . . And second, old friend, I think you're in way
the hell over your head. What is it, Leslie? What *are* you
into?"

She put the cigarette to her lips and inhaled as though
her life depended on the smoke. She closed her eyes briefly
and spoke barely above a whisper. "I can't tell you. Don't
force me to."

He sighed. "I don't think you understand. I'm an Intelligence officer assigned to Clandestine Operations—I'm not
telling you anything you don't know. You made it possible
for my hotel room to be searched; you lied; you went into
hiding; for all I know, you were responsible for several
assaults which nearly cost me my life. Now, you turn up in
Buenos Aires, four thousand miles away from that Park
Avenue apartment. You followed me four thousand miles!
. . . *Why?*"

"I can't *tell* you! I haven't been *told* what I can tell
you!"

"You haven't been . . . *Christ!* With what I can piece

together—and testify to—you could spend twenty years in prison!"

"I'd like to get out of the car. May I?" she said softly, snuffing out her cigarette in the ashtray.

"Sure. Go ahead." David opened his door and rapidly came around the automobile. Leslie walked to the railing, the waters of the Río Luján far below in the distance.

"It's very beautiful here, isn't it?"

"Yes. . . . Did you try to have me killed?"

"Oh, *God!*" She whirled on him, spitting out the words. "I tried to save your *life!* I'm here because I don't *want* you killed!"

It took David a few moments to recover from the girl's statement. Her hair had fallen carelessly around her face, her eyes blinking back tears, her lips trembling.

"I think you'd better explain that," he said in a quiet monotone.

She turned away from him and looked down at the river, the villas, the boats. "It's like the Riviera, isn't it?"

"*Stop it*, Leslie!"

"Why? It's part of it." She put her hands on the railing. "It used to be all there was. Nothing else mattered. *Where* next; *who* next? *What* a lovely party! . . . You were part of it."

"Not really. You're wrong if you thought that. Just as you're wrong now. . . . I won't be put off."

"I'm not putting you off." She gripped the railing harder; it was a physical gesture telegraphing her indecision with her words. "I'm trying to tell you something."

"That you followed me because you wanted to save my *life?*" He asked the question with incredulity. "You were filled with dramatics in New York, too, if I recall. You waited, how long was it? Five, six, eight years to get me on the boathouse floor again. You're a bitch."

"And *you're insignificant!*" She flung the words at him in heat. And then she subsided, controlling herself. "I don't mean you . . . *you*. Just compared to everything else. We're all insignificant in that sense."

"So the lady has a cause."

Leslie stared at him and spoke softly. "One she believes in very deeply."

"Then you should have no reservations explaining it to me."

"I *will*, I promise you. But I can't *now*. . . . Trust me!"

"Certainly," said David casually. And then he suddenly whipped out his hand, grabbing her purse, which hung from her shoulder by a leather strap. She started to resist; he looked at her. She stopped and breathed deeply.

He opened the purse and took out the envelope she had been given at the fountain in the Plaza de Mayo. As he did so, his eyes caught sight of a bulge at the bottom of the bag, covered by a silk scarf. He held the envelope between his fingers and reached down. He separated the scarf from the object and pulled out a small Remington revolver. Without saying anything, he checked the chamber and the safety and put the weapon in his jacket pocket.

"I've learned to use it," said Leslie tentatively.

"Good for you," replied Spaulding, opening the envelope.

"At least you'll see how efficient we are," she said, turning, looking down at the river.

There was no letterhead, no origin of writer or organization. The heading on the top of the paper read:

> *Spaulding, David. Lt. Col. Military Intelligence,*
> *U.S. Army. Classification 4-0. Fairfax.*

Beneath were five complicated paragraphs detailing every move he had made since he was picked up on Saturday afternoon entering the embassy. David was pleased to see that "Donald Scanlan" was not mentioned; he'd gotten through the airport and customs undetected.

Everything else was listed: his apartment, his telephone, his office at the embassy, the incident on the Córdoba roof, the lunch with Jean Cameron at La Boca, the meeting with Kendall at the hotel, the assault on the Avenida Paraná, his telephone call in the store on Rodríguez Peña.

Everything.

Even the "lunch" with Heinrich Stoltz at the Langosta del Mar, on the border of Lezama. The meeting with Stoltz was estimated to last "a minimum of one hour."

It was the explanation for her leisurely pace on the Avenida de Mayo. But David had cut the meeting short; there'd been no lunch. He wondered if he had been picked up after he'd left the restaurant. He had not been concerned. His thoughts had been on Heinrich Stoltz and the presence of a Gestapo Stoltz knew nothing about.

"Your people are *very* thorough. Now, who are they?"

"Men . . . and women who have a calling. A purpose. A *great* calling."

"That's not what I asked you. . . ."

There was the sound of an automobile coming up the hill below the parking area. Spaulding reached inside his jacket for his pistol. The car came into view and proceeded upward, past them. The people in the car were laughing. David turned his attention back to Leslie.

"I asked you to trust me," said the girl. "I was on my way to an address on that street, the boulevard called Julio. I was to be there at one thirty. They'll wonder where I am."

"You're not going to answer me, are you?"

"I'll answer you in one way. I'm here to convince you to get out of Buenos Aires."

"Why?"

"Whatever it is you're doing—and I don't *know* what it is, they haven't told me—it can't happen. We can't let it happen. It's wrong."

"Since you don't know what it is, how can you say it's wrong?"

"Because I've been told. That's enough!"

"*Ein Volk, ein Reich, ein Führer,*" said David quietly. "Get in the car!"

"No. You've got to listen to me! Get out of Buenos Aires! Tell your generals it can't be done!"

"Get in the car!"

There was the sound of another automobile, this time coming from the opposite direction, from above. David put his hand once more under his jacket, but then removed it casually. It was the same vehicle with the laughing tourists that had passed by moments ago. They were still laughing, still gesturing; probably drunk with luncheon wine.

"You can't take me to the embassy! You *can't!*"

"If you don't get in the car, you'll just wake up there! Go *on.*"

There was the screeching of tires on the gravel. The descending automobile had turned abruptly—at the last second—and swung sharply into the parking area and come to a stop.

David looked up and swore to himself, his hand immobile inside his jacket.

Two high-powered rifles protruded from the open windows of the car. They were aimed at him.

The heads of the three men inside were covered with silk stockings, the faces flattened, grotesque beyond the translucent masks. The rifles were held by one man next to the driver in the front seat and by another in the back.

The man in the rear opened the door, his rifle held steady. He gave his command in a calm voice. In English.

"Get in the car, Mrs. Hawkwood. . . . And you, colonel. Remove your weapon by the handle—with two fingers."

David did so.

"Walk to the railing," continued the man in the back seat, "and drop it over the side, into the woods."

David complied. The man got out of the car to let Leslie climb in. He then returned to his seat and closed the door.

There was the gunning of the powerful engine and the sound once more of spinning tires over the loose gravel. The car lurched forward out of the parking area and sped off down the hill.

David stood by the railing. He would go over it and find his pistol. There was no point in trying to follow the automobile with Leslie Hawkwood and three men in stocking masks. His rented car was no match for a Duesenberg.

# 29

The restaurant had been selected by Jean. It was out of the way in the north section of the city, beyond Palermo Park, a place for assignation. Telephone jacks were in the wall by the booths; waiters could be seen bringing phones to and from the secluded tables.

He was mildly surprised that Jean would know such a restaurant. Or would choose it for them.

"Where did you go this afternoon?" she asked, seeing him looking out over the dim room from their booth.

"A couple of conferences. Very dull. Bankers have a penchant for prolonging any meeting way beyond its finish. The Strand or Wall Street, makes no difference." He smiled at her.

"Yes. . . . Well perhaps they're always looking for ways to extract every last dollar."

"No 'perhaps.' That's it. . . . This is quite a place, by the way. Reminds me of Lisbon."

"Rome," she said. "It's more like Rome. Way out. Via Appia. Did you know that the Italians comprise over thirty per cent of the population in Buenos Aires?"

"I knew it was considerable."

"The Italian hand. . . . That's supposed to mean evil."

"Or clever. Not necessarily evil. The 'fine Italian hand' is usually envied."

"Bobby brought me here one night. . . . I think he brings lots of girls here."

"It's . . . discreet."

"I think he was worried that Henderson might find out he had dishonorable designs. And so he brought me here."

"Which confirmed his designs."

"Yes. . . . It's for lovers. But we weren't."

"I'm glad you chose it for us. It gives me a nice feeling of security."

"Oh, no! Don't look for that. No one's in the market for that this year. No. . . . Security's out of the question. And commitments. Those, too. No commitments for sale." She took a cigarette from his open pack; he lit it for her. Over the flame he saw her eyes staring at him. Caught, she glanced downward, at nothing.

"What's the matter?"

"Nothing. . . . Nothing at all." She smiled, but only the outlines were there; not the ingenuousness, not the humor. "Did you talk to that man Stoltz?"

"Good Lord, is that what's bothering you? . . . I'm sorry, I suppose I should have said something. Stoltz was selling fleet information; I'm in no position to buy. I told him to get in touch with Naval Intelligence. I made a report to the base commander at FMF this morning. If they want to use him, they will."

"Strange he should call you."

"That's what I thought. Apparently German surveillance picked me up the other day and the financial data was on their sheet. That was enough for Stoltz."

"He's a defector?"

"Or selling bad stuff. It's FMF's problem, not mine."

"You're very glib." She drank her coffee unsteadily.

"What's that supposed to mean?"

"Nothing. . . . Just that you're quick. Quick and facile. You must be very good at your work."

"And you're in a godawful mood. Does an excess of gin bring it on?"

"Oh, you think I'm drunk?"

"You're not sober. Not that it matters." He grinned. "You're hardly an alcoholic."

"Thanks for the vote of confidence. But don't speculate. That implies some kind of permanence. We must avoid that, mustn't we?"

"Must we? It seems to be a point with you tonight. It wasn't a problem I was considering."

"You just brushed it aside, I assume. I'm sure you have other, more pressing matters." In replacing her cup, Jean spilled coffee on the tablecloth. She was obviously annoyed with herself. "I'm doing it badly," she said after a moment of silence.

"You're doing it badly," he agreed.

"I'm frightened."

"Of what?"

"You're not here in Buenos Aires to talk to bankers, are you? It's much more than that. You won't tell me, I know. And in a few weeks, you'll be gone . . . if you're alive."

"You're letting your imagination take over." He took her hand; she crushed out her cigarette and put her other hand over his. She gripped him tightly.

"All right. Let's say you're right." She spoke quietly now; he had to strain to hear her. "I'm making everything up. I'm crazy and I drank too much. Indulge me. Play the game for a minute."

"If you want me to . . . O.K."

"It's hypothetical. My David isn't a State Department syndromer, you see. He's an agent. We've had a few here; I've met them. The colonels call them *provocarios.* . . . So, my David is an agent and being an agent is called . . . high-risk something-or-other because the rules are different. That is, the rules don't have any meaning. . . . There aren't any rules for these people . . . like my hypothetical David. Do you follow?"

"I follow," he replied simply. "I'm not sure what the object is or how a person scores."

"We'll get to that." She drank the last of her coffee, holding the cup firmly—too firmly; her fingers shook. "The point is, such a man as my . . . mythical David could be killed or crippled or have his face shot off. That's a horrible thought, isn't it?"

"Yes. I imagine that possibility has occurred to several hundred thousand men by now. It's horrible."

"But they're different. They have armies and uniforms and certain rules. Even in airplanes . . . their chances are better. And I say this with a certain expertise."

He looked at her intently. "Stop."

"Oh, not yet. Now, I'm going to tell you how you can score a goal. Why does my hypothetical David do what he does? . . . No, don't answer yet." She stopped and smiled weakly. "But you weren't about to answer, were you? It doesn't matter; there's a second part of the question. You get extra points for considering it."

"What's the second part?" He thought that Jean was

recapitulating an argument she had memorized. Her next words proved it.

"You see, I've thought about it over and over again . . . for this make-believe game . . . this make-believe agent. He's in a very unique position: he works alone . . . or at least with very, *very* few people. He's in a strange country and he's alone. . . . Do you understand the second part now?"

David watched her. She had made some abstract connection in her mind without verbalizing it. "No, I don't."

"If David is working alone and in a strange country and has to send codes to Washington . . . Henderson told me that . . . that means the people he's working for have to believe what he tells them. He can tell them anything he wants to. . . . So now we come back to the question. Knowing all this, why does the mythical David do what he does? He can't really believe that he'll influence the outcome of the whole war. He's only one among millions and millions."

"And . . . if I'm following you . . . this make-believe man can send word to his superiors that he's having difficulties. . . ."

"He has to stay on in Buenos Aires. For a long time," she interrupted, holding his hand fiercely.

"And if they say no, he can always hide out in the pampas."

"Don't make fun of me!" she said intensely.

"I'm not. I won't pretend that I can give you logical answers, but I don't think the man you're talking about has such a clear field. Tight reins are kept on such men, I believe. Other men could be sent into the area . . . would be sent, I'm sure. Your strategy is only a short-term gain; the penalties are long and damned stiff."

She withdrew her hands slowly, looking away from him. "It's a gamble that might be worth it, though. I love you very much. I don't want you hurt and I know there are people trying to hurt you." She stopped and turned her eyes back to him. "They're trying to kill you, aren't they? . . . One among so many millions . . . and I keep saying to myself, 'Not him. Oh, God, not him.' Don't you see? . . . Do we need them? Are those people—whoever they are—so important? To us? Haven't you done enough?"

He returned her stare and found himself understanding the profundity of her question. It wasn't a pleasant realization. . . . He *had* done enough. His whole life had been turned around until the alien was an everyday occurrence.

For what?

The amateurs? Alan Swanson? Walter Kendall?

A dead Ed Pace. A corrupt Fairfax.

One among so many millions.

"Señor Spaulding?" The words shocked him momentarily because they were so completely unexpected. A tuxedoed maître d' was standing by the edge of the booth, his voice low.

"Yes?"

"There's a telephone call for you."

David looked at the discreet man. "Can't you bring the telephone to the table?"

"Our sincere apologies. The instrument plug at this booth is not functioning."

A lie, of course, Spaulding knew.

"Very well." David got out of the booth. He turned to Jean. "I'll be right back. Have some more coffee."

"Suppose I wanted a drink?"

"Order it." He started to walk away.

"David?" She called out enough to be heard; not loudly.

"Yes." He turned back; she was staring at him again.

" 'Tortugas' isn't worth it," she said quietly.

It was as if he'd been hit a furious blow in the stomach. Acid formed in his throat, his breath stopped, his eyes pained him as he looked down at her.

"I'll be right back."


"Heinrich Stoltz here," the voice said.

"I've been expecting your call. I assume the switchboard gave you the number."

"It was not necessary to telephone. The arrangements have been made. In twenty minutes a green Packard automobile will be outside the restaurant. A man will have his left arm out the window, holding an open pack of German cigarettes this time. I thought you would appreciate the symbolic repetition."

"I'm touched. But you may have to alter the time and the car."

"There can be no changes. Herr Rhinemann is adamant."

"So am I. Something's come up."

"Sorry. Twenty minutes. A green Packard automobile."
The connection was severed.

Well, that was Stoltz's problem, thought David. There
was only one thought in mind. To get back to Jean.

He made his way out of the dimly lit corner and sidled
awkwardly past the bar patrons whose stools were blocking
the aisle. He was in a hurry; the human and inanimate
obstructions were frustrating, annoying. He reached the
arch into the dining area and walked rapidly through the
tables to the rear booth.

Jean Cameron was gone. There was a note on the table.

It was on the back of a cocktail napkin, the words
written in the heavy wax of an eyebrow pencil. Written
hastily, almost illegibly:

> David. I'm sure you have things to do—
> places to go—and I'm a bore tonight

Nothing else. As if she just stopped.

He crumpled the napkin in his pocket and raced back
across the dining room to the front entrance. The maître d'
stood by the door.

"*Señor?* Is there a problem?"

"The lady at the booth. Where did she go?!"

"Mrs. Cameron?"

*Christ!* thought David, looking at the calm *porteño*.
What was happening? The reservation was in *his* name.
Jean had indicated that she'd been to the restaurant only
once before.

"Yes! Mrs. Cameron! Goddamn you, where is she!?"

"She left a few minutes ago. She took the first taxi at the
curb."

"You *listen* to me. . . ."

"*Señor,*" interrupted the obsequious Argentine, "there is
a gentleman waiting for you outside. He will take care of
your bill. He has an account with us."

Spaulding looked out the large windowpanes in the
heavy front door. Through the glass he could see a man
standing on the sidewalk. He was dressed in a white Palm
Beach suit.

David pushed the door open and approached him.

"You want to see me?"

"I'm merely waiting for you, Herr Spaulding. To escort
you. The car should be here in fifteen minutes."

## 30

The green Packard sedan came to a stop across the street, directly in front of the restaurant. The driver's arm appeared through the open window, an indistinguishable pack of cigarettes in his hand. The man in the white Palm Beach suit gestured politely for Spaulding to accompany him.

As he drew nearer, David could see that the driver was a large man in a black knit, short-sleeved shirt that both revealed and accentuated his muscular arms. There was a stubble of beard, thick eyebrows; he looked like a mean-tempered longshoreman, the rough image intended, Spaulding was sure. The man walking beside him opened the car door and David climbed in.

No one spoke. The car headed south back toward the center of Buenos Aires; then northeast into the Aeroparque district. David was mildly surprised to realize that the driver had entered the wide highway paralleling the river. The same road he had taken that afternoon with Leslie Hawkwood. He wondered whether the route was chosen deliberately, if they expected him to make some remark about the coincidence.

He sat back, giving no indication that he recognized anything.

The Packard accelerated on the wide river road which now swung to the left, following the water into the hills of the northwest. The car did not, however, go up any of the offshoot roads as David had done hours ago. Instead the driver maintained a steady, high speed. A reflecting highway sign was caught momentarily in the glare of the headlights: *Tigre 12 kil.*

The traffic was mild; cars rushed past intermittently from the opposite direction; several were overtaken by the

Packard. The driver checked his rear- and side-view mirrors constantly.

In the middle of a long bend in the road, the Packard slowed down. The driver nodded his head to the man in the white Palm Beach suit beside David.

"We will exchange cars now, Herr Spaulding," said the man, reaching into his jacket, withdrawing a gun.

Ahead of them was a single building, an outskirts restaurant or an inn, with a circular drive that curved in front of an entrance and veered off into a large parking area on the side. Spotlights lit the entrance and the lawn in front.

The driver swung in; the man beside Spaulding tapped him.

"Get out here, please. Go directly inside."

David opened the door. He was surprised to see a uniformed doorman remain by the entrance, making no move toward the Packard. Instead, he crossed rapidly in front of the entrance and started walking on the graveled drive in the direction of the side parking lot. Spaulding opened the front door and stepped into the carpeted foyer of the restaurant; the man in the white suit was at his heels, his gun now in his pocket.

Instead of proceeding toward the entrance of the dining area, the man held David by the arm—politely—and knocked on what appeared to be the door of a small office in the foyer. The door opened and the two of them walked inside.

It was a tiny office but that fact made no impression on Spaulding. What fascinated him were the two men inside. One was dressed in a white Palm Beach suit; the other— and David instantly, involuntarily, had to smile—was in the identical clothes he himself was wearing. A light blue, striped cord jacket and dark trousers. The second man was his own height, the same general build, the same general coloring.

David had no time to observe further. The light in the small office—a desk lamp—was snapped off by the newly appeared white suit. The German who had accompanied Spaulding walked to the single window that looked out on the circular drive. He spoke softly.

*"Schnell. Beeilen Sie sich . . . Danke."*

The two men quickly walked to the door and let them-

selves out. The German by the window was silhouetted in
the filtered light of the front entrance. He beckoned David.

"*Kommen Sie her.*"

He went to the window and stood beside the man. Outside, their two counterparts were on the driveway, talking
and gesturing as if in an argument—a mild disagreement,
not violent. Both smoked cigarettes, their faces more often
covered by their hands than not. Their backs were to the
highway beyond.

Then an automobile came from the right, from the direction of the parking lot, and the two men got inside. The
car moved slowly to the left, to the entrance of the highway. It paused for several seconds, waiting for an oppor-
tune moment in the thinned-out night traffic. Suddenly it
lurched forward, crossed to the right of the highway and
sped off south, toward the city.

David wasn't sure why the elaborate ploy was considered
necessary; he was about to ask the man beside him. Before
he spoke, however, he noticed the smile on the man's face,
inches from his in the window. Spaulding looked out.

About fifty yards away, off the side of the river road,
headlights were snapped on. A vehicle, facing north, made
a fast U-turn on the wide highway and headed south in a
sudden burst of speed.

The German grinned. "*Amerikanische . . . Kinder.*"

David stepped back. The man crossed to the desk and
turned on the lamp.

"That was an interesting exercise," said Spaulding.

The man looked up. "Simply a—what are your words,
*eine Vorsichtsmassnahme*—a . . ."

"A precaution," said David.

"*Ja.* That's right, you speak German. . . . Come. Herr
Rhinemann must not be kept waiting longer than the . . .
*precautions* require."

Even in daylight, Spaulding realized, the dirt road would
be difficult to find. As it was, with no streetlamps and only
the misty illumination of the moon, it seemed as though
the Packard had swung off the hard pavement into a black
wall of towering overgrowth. Instead, there was the unmistakable sound of dirt beneath the wheels as the car
plunged forward, the driver secure in his knowledge of the
numerous turns and straightaways. A half mile into the

forest the dirt road suddenly widened and the surface became smooth and hard again.

There was an enormous parking area. Four stone
gateposts—wide, medieval in appearance—were spaced
equidistant from one another at the far end of the black-
topped field. Above each stone post was a massive flood-
lamp, the spills intersecting, throwing light over the entire
area and into the woods beyond. Between the huge posts
was a thick-grilled iron fence, in the center of which was a
webbed steel gate, obviously operated electrically.

Men dressed in dark shirts and trousers—quasi-military
in cut—stood around, several with dogs on leashes.

Dobermans. Massive, straining at their leather straps,
barking viciously.

Commands could be heard from the handlers and the
dogs subsided.

The man in the white Palm Beach suit opened the door
and got out. He walked to the main gatepost, where a
guard appeared at the fence from inside the compound.
The two men talked briefly; David could see that beyond
the guard stood a dark concrete or stucco enclosure, perhaps twenty feet in length, in which there were small windows with light showing through.

The guard returned to the miniature house; the man in
the white suit came back to the Packard.

"We will wait a few minutes," he said, climbing into the
rear seat.

"I thought we were in a hurry."

"To be here; to let Herr Rhinemann know we have
arrived. Not necessarily to be admitted."

"Accommodating fellow," said David.

"Herr Rhinemann can be what he likes."

Ten minutes later the steel-webbed gate swung slowly
open and the driver started the engine. The Packard
cruised by the gatehouse and the guards; the Dobermans
began their rapacious barking once again, only to be silenced by their masters. The road wound uphill, ending in
another huge parking area in front of an enormous white
mansion with wide marble steps leading to the largest pair
of oak doors David had ever seen. Here, too, floodlights
covered the whole area. Unlike the outside premises, there
was a fountain in the middle of the courtyard, the reflection of the lights bouncing off the spray of the water.

It was as if some extravagant plantation house from the antebellum South had been dismantled stone by stone, board by board, marble block by marble block, and rebuilt deep within an Argentine forest.

An extraordinary sight, and not a little frightening in its massive architectural concept. The construction engineer in David was provoked and stunned at the same time. The materials-logistics must have been staggering; the methods of leveling and transport incredible.

The cost unbelievable.

The German got out of the car and walked around to David's door. He opened it.

"We'll leave you now. It's been a pleasant trip. Go to the door; you'll be admitted. *Auf Wiedersehen.*"

David got out and stood on the hard surface before the marble steps. The green Packard started off down the winding descent.

Spaulding stood alone for nearly a minute. If he was being watched—and the thought crossed his mind—the observer might think he was an astonished caller overwhelmed by the magnificence in front of him. That judgment would have been partially accurate; his remaining concentration, however, was on the mansion's more mundane specifics: the windows, the roof, the grounds on both visible sides.

Ingress and egress were matters to be considered constantly; the unexpected was never to be projected as too unlikely.

He walked up the steps and approached the immense, thick wooden doors. There was no knocker, no bell; he hadn't thought there would be.

He turned and looked down at the floodlit area. Not a person in sight; neither guards nor servants. No one.

Quiet. Even the sounds of the forest seemed subdued. Only the splash of the fountain interrupted the stillness.

Which meant, of course, that there were eyes unseen and whispers unheard, directing their attention on him.

The door opened. Heinrich Stoltz stood in the frame.

"Welcome to Habichtsnest, Herr Spaulding. The Hawk's Lair; appropriately—if theatrically—named, is it not?"

David stepped inside. The foyer, as might be expected, was enormous; a marble staircase rose beyond a chandelier of several thousand crystal cones. The walls were covered with gold cloth; Renaissance paintings were hung beneath silver portrait lamps.

"It's not like any bird's nest I've ever seen."

"True. However, Habichtsnest, I think, loses something in your translation. Come with me, please. Herr Rhinemann is outside on the river balcony. It's a pleasant evening."

They walked underneath the grotesque yet beautiful chandelier, past the marble staircase to an archway at the end of the great hall. It led out to an enormous terrace that stretched the length of the building. There were white wrought-iron tables topped with spotless glass, chairs of varying sizes with brightly colored cushions. A series of large double doors could be seen on both sides of the arch; they presumably led to diverse sections of the huge house.

Bordering the terrace was a stone balustrade, waist high, with statuary and plants on the railing. Beyond the balcony, in the distance, were the waters of the Río Luján. At the left end of the terrace was a small platform, blocked by a gate. Enormously thick wires could be seen above. It was a dock for a cable car, the wires evidently extending down to the river.

David absorbed the splendor, expecting his first view of Rhinemann. There was no one; he walked to the railing and saw that beneath the balcony was another terrace perhaps twenty feet below. A large swimming pool—complete with racing lines in the tile—was illuminated by floodlights under the blue green water. Additional metal tables with sun umbrellas and deck chairs were dotted about the pool and the terrace. And surrounding it all was a manicured lawn that in the various reflections of light looked like the thickest, fullest putting green David had ever seen. Somewhat incongruously, there were the silhouettes of poles and wickets; a croquet course had been imposed on the smooth surface.

"I hope you'll come out one day and enjoy our simple pleasures, Colonel Spaulding."

David was startled by the strange, quiet voice. He turned. The figure of a man stood in shadows alongside the arch of the great hall.

Erich Rhinemann had been watching him, of course.

Rhinemann emerged from the darkened area. He was a moderately tall man with greying straight hair combed rigidly back—partless. He was somewhat stocky for his size—"powerful" would be the descriptive word, but his stomach girth might deny the term. His hands were large, beefy, yet somehow delicate, dwarfing the wineglass held between his fingers.

He came into a sufficient spill of light for David to see his face clearly. Spaulding wasn't sure why, but the face startled him. It was a broad face; a wide forehead above a wide expanse of lip beneath a rather wide, flat nose. He was deeply tanned, his eyebrows nearly white from the sun. And then David realized why he was startled.

Erich Rhinemann was an aging man. The deeply tanned skin was a cover for the myriad lines the years had given him; his eyes were narrow, surrounded by swollen folds of age; the faultlessly tailored sports jacket and trousers were cut for a much, much younger man.

Rhinemann was fighting a battle his wealth could not win for him.

"*Habichtsnest ist prächtig. Unglaublich*," said David politely but without commensurate enthusiasm.

"You are kind," replied Rhinemann, extending his hand. "And also courteous; but there is no reason not to speak English. . . . Come, sit down. May I offer you a drink?" The financier led the way to the nearest table.

"Thank you, no," said David, sitting across from Rhinemann. "I have urgent business in Buenos Aires. A fact I tried to make clear to Stoltz before he hung up."

Rhinemann looked over at an unperturbed Stoltz, who was leaning against the stone balustrade. "Was that necessary? Herr Spaulding is not to be so treated."

"I'm afraid it *was* necessary, *mein Herr*. For our American friend's own benefit. It was reported to us that he was followed; we were prepared for such an occurrence."

"If I was followed, you were doing the following."

"*After* the fact, colonel; I don't deny it. Before, we had no *reason*."

Rhinemann's narrow eyes pivoted to Spaulding. "This is disturbing. Who would have you followed?"

"May we talk privately?" David said, glancing at Heinrich Stoltz.

The financier smiled. "There's nothing in our arrangements that excludes the *Botschaftssekretär*. He is among my most valued associates in South America. Nothing should be withheld."

"I submit that you won't know unless we speak alone."

"Our American colonel is perhaps embarrassed," interrupted Stoltz, his voice laced with invective. "The man from Lisbon is not considered competent by his own government. He's placed under American surveillance."

David lit a cigarette; he did not reply to the German attaché. Rhinemann spoke, gesturing with his large, delicate hands.

"If this is so, there is no cause for exclusion. And obviously, there can be no other explanation."

"We're buying," said David with quiet emphasis. "You're selling. . . . Stolen property."

Stoltz was about to speak but Rhinemann held up his hand.

"What you are implying is not possible. Our arrangements were made in complete secrecy; they have been totally successful. And Herr Stoltz is a confidant of the High Command. More so than the ambassador."

"I don't like repeating myself." David spoke angrily. "Especially when I'm paying."

"Leave us, Heinrich," said Rhinemann, his eyes on Spaulding.

Stoltz bowed stiffly and walked rapidly, furiously, through the arch into the great hall.

"Thank you." David shifted his position in the chair and looked at up several small balconies on the second and third stories of the house. He wondered how many men were near the windows; watching, prepared to jump if he made a false move.

"We're alone as requested," said the German expatriate, hardly concealing his irritation. "What is it?"

"Stoltz is marked," said Spaulding. He paused to see what kind of reaction the financier would register at such news. As he might have expected, there was none. David continued, thinking perhaps that Rhinemann did not entirely understand. "He's not being given straight information at the embassy. He may do better at ours."

"Preposterous." Rhinemann remained immobile, his narrow eyelids half squinting, staring at David. "On what do you base such an opinion?"

"The Gestapo. Stoltz claims there's no active Gestapo in Buenos Aires. He's wrong. It's here. It's active. It's determined to stop you. Stop us."

Erich Rhinemann's composure cracked—if only infinitesimally. There was the slightest, tiny vibration within the rolls of flesh beneath his eyes, and his stare—if possible, thought David—was harder than before.

"Please clarify."

"I want questions answered first."

"*You want questions . . . ?*" Rhinemann's voice rose, his hand gripped the table; the veins were pronounced at his greying temples. He paused and continued as before. "Forgive me. I'm not used to conditions."

"I'm sure you're not. On the other hand, I'm not used to dealing with a contact like Stoltz who's blind to his own vulnerability. That kind of person annoys me . . . and worries me."

"These questions. What are they?"

"I assume the designs have been gotten out?"

"They have."

"En route?"

"They arrive tonight."

"You're early. Our man won't be here until the day after tomorrow."

"Now it is you who have been given erroneous information, Herr Colonel. The American scientist, Lyons, will be here tomorrow."

David was silent for several moments. He'd used such a ploy on too many others in the past to show surprise.

"He's expected in San Telmo the day *after* tomorrow," David said. "The change is insignificant but that's what Kendall told me."

"Before he boarded the Pan American Clipper. We spoke subsequently."

"Apparently he spoke to a lot of people. Is there a point to the change?"

"Schedules may be slowed or accelerated as the necessities dictate. . . ."

"Or altered to throw someone off balance," interrupted David.

"Such is not the case here. There would be no reason. As you phrased it—most succinctly—we're selling, you're buying."

"And, of course, there's no reason why the Gestapo's in Buenos Aires. . . ."

"May we *return* to that subject, please?" interjected Rhinemann.

"In a moment," answered Spaulding, aware that the German's temper was again stretched. "I need eighteen hours to get my codes to Washington. They have to go by courier, under chemical seal."

"Stoltz told me. You were foolish. The codes should have been sent."

"*Eine Vorsichtsmassnahme, mein Herr*," said David. "Put plainly, I don't know who's been bought at our embassy but I'm damned sure someone has. Codes have ways of getting sold. The authentic ones will be radioed only when Lyons verifies the designs."

"Then you must move quickly. You fly out your codes in the morning; I will bring the first set of prints to San Telmo tomorrow night. . . . *Eine Vorsichtsmassnahme.* You get the remaining set when you have assured us Washington is prepared to make payment in Switzerland . . . as a result of receiving your established code. You won't leave Argentina until I have word from Berne. There is a small airfield called Mendarro. Near here. My men control it. Your plane will be there."

"Agreed." David crushed out his cigarette. "Tomorrow evening, the first set of prints. The remaining within twenty-four hours. . . . Now we have a schedule. That's all I was interested in."

"*Gut!* And now we will return to this Gestapo business." Rhinemann leaned forward in his chair, the veins in his temples once more causing blue rivulets in his sun-drenched skin. "You said you would clarify!"

Spaulding did.

When he was finished, Erich Rhinemann was breathing deeply, steadily. Within the rolls of flesh, his narrow eyes were furious but controlled.

"Thank you. I'm sure there is an explanation. We'll proceed on schedule. . . . Now, it has been a long and complicated evening. You will be driven back to Córdoba. Good night."

"*Altmüller!*" Rhinemann roared. "An *idiot!* A *fool!*"

"I don't understand," Stoltz said.

"Altmüller. . . ." Rhinemann's voice subsided but the violence remained. He turned to the balcony, addressing the vast darkness and the river below. "In his insane attempts to *disassociate* the High Command from Buenos Aires . . . to *absolve* his precious ministry, he's *caught* by his own *Gestapo!*"

"There is *no Gestapo* in Buenos Aires, Herr Rhinemann," said Stoltz firmly. "The man from Lisbon lies."

Rhinemann turned and looked at the diplomat. His speech was ice. "I know when a man is lying, Herr Stoltz. This Lisbon told the truth; he'd have no reason to do otherwise. . . . So if Altmüller was *not* caught, he's betrayed me. He's sent in the Gestapo; he has no intention of going through with the exchange. He'll take the diamonds and destroy the designs. The Jew-haters have led me into a trap."

"I, myself, am the sole coordinator with Franz Altmüller." Stoltz spoke in his most persuasive tones, nurtured for decades in the Foreign Corps. "You, Herr Rhinemann, arranged for that. You have no cause to question me. The men at the warehouse in Ocho Calle have nearly finished. The Koening diamonds will be authenticated within a day or two; the courier will deliver the designs before the night is over. Everything is as we planned. The exchange will be made."

Rhinemann turned away again. He put his thick yet delicate hands on the railing and looked into the distance. "There is one way to be sure," he said quietly. "Radio Berlin. I want Altmüller in Buenos Aires. There will be no exchange otherwise."

## 31

The German in the white Palm Beach suit had changed into the paramilitary dress worn by the Rhinemann guards. The driver was not the same one as before. He was Argentine.

The automobile was different, too. It was a Bentley six-seater complete with mahogany dashboard, grey felt upholstery, and window curtains. It was a vehicle suited to the upper-level British diplomatic service, but not so high as to be ambassadorial; just eminently respectable. Another Rhinemann touch, David assumed.

The driver swung the car out onto the dark river highway from the darker confines of the hidden dirt road. He pressed the accelerator to the floor and the Bentley surged. The German beside Spaulding offered him a cigarette; David declined with a shake of his head.

"You say you wish to be driven to the American embassy, *señor?*" said the driver, turning his head slightly, not taking his eyes off the onrushing road. "I'm afraid I cannot do so. Señor Rhinemann's orders were to bring you to the apartment house on Córdoba. Forgive me."

"We may not deviate from instructions," added the German.

"Hope you never do. We win the wars that way."

"The insult is misdirected. I'm completely indifferent."

"I forgot. Habichtsnest is neutral." David ended the conversation by shifting in the seat, crossing his legs and staring in silence out the window. His only thought was to get to the embassy and to Jean. She had used the word "Tortugas."

Again the elusive "Tortugas"!

How could she know? Was it conceivable she was part of it? Part of the unfocused picture?

No.

*"Tortugas" isn't worth it.* Jean had said those words. She had pleaded.

Leslie Hawkwood had pleaded, too. Leslie had traveled four thousand miles to plead in defiance. Fanatically so.

*Get out of Buenos Aires, David!*

Was there a connection?

*Oh, Christ!* he thought. *Was there really a connection?*

"*Señores!*"

The driver spoke harshly, jolting David's thoughts. The German instantly—instinctively—whipped around in his seat and looked out the rear window. His question was two words.

"How long?"

"Too long for doubt. Have you watched?"

"No."

"I passed three automobiles. Without pattern. Then I slowed down, into the far right lane. He's with us. Moving up."

"We're in the Hill Two district, yes?" asked the German.

"*Sí.* . . . He's coming up rapidly. It's a powerful car; he'll take us on the highway."

"Head up into the Colinas Rojas! Take the next road on the right! Any one!" commanded Rhinemann's lieutenant, taking his pistol from inside his jacket as he spoke.

The Bentley skidded into a sudden turn, swerving diagonally to the right, throwing David and the German into the left section of the back seat. The Argentine gunned the engine, starting up a hill, slamming the gears into first position, reaching maximum speed in seconds. There was a slight leveling off, a connecting, flatter surface before a second hill, and the driver used it to race the motor in a higher gear for speed. The car pitched forward in a burst of acceleration, as if it were a huge bullet.

The second hill was steeper but the initial speed helped. They raced upward; the driver knew his machine, thought David.

"There are the lights!" yelled the German. "They follow!"

"There are flat stretches . . . I think," said the driver, concentrating on the road. "Beyond this section of hills. There are many side roads; we'll try to hide in one. Perhaps they'll pass."

"No." The German was still peering out the rear window. He checked the magazine of his pistol by touch; satisfied, he locked it in place. He then turned from the window and reached under the seat. The Bentley was pitching and vibrating on the uphill, back country road, and the German swore as he worked his hand furiously behind his legs.

Spaulding could hear the snap of metal latches. The German slipped the pistol into his belt and reached down with his free hand. He pulled up a thick-barreled automatic rifle that David recognized as the newest, most powerful front-line weapon the Third Reich had developed. The curved magazine, rapidly inserted by the German, held over forty rounds of .30 caliber ammunition.

Rhinemann's lieutenant spoke. "Reach your flat stretches. Let them close in."

David bolted up; he held onto the leather strap across the rear of the front seat and braced his left hand against the window frame. He spoke to the German harshly.

"Don't use that! You don't know who they are."

The man with the gun glanced briefly at Spaulding, dismissing him with a look: "I know my responsibilities." He reached over to the right of the rear window where there was a small metal ring imbedded in the felt. He inserted his forefinger, pulled it up, and yanked it toward him, revealing an open-air slot about ten inches wide, perhaps four inches high.

David looked at the left of the window. There was another ring, another opening.

Rhinemann's car was prepared for emergencies. Clean shots could be fired at any automobile pursuing it; the sightlines were clear and there was a minimum of awkwardness at high speeds over difficult terrain.

"Suppose it's American surveillance covering *me?*" David shouted as the German knelt on the seat, about to insert the rifle into the opening.

"It's not."

"You don't *know* that!"

"*Señores!*" shouted the driver. "We go down the hill; it's very long, a wide bend. I remember it! Below there are high-grass fields. Flat. . . . Roads. Hold *on!*"

The Bentley suddenly dipped as if it had sped off the edge of a precipice. There was an immediate, sustained

thrust of speed so abrupt that the German with the rifle
was thrown back, his body suspended for a fraction of a
second in midair. He crashed into the front seat support,
his weapon held up to break the fall.

David did not—could not—hesitate. He grabbed the
rifle, gripping his fingers around the trigger housing, twisting the stock inward and jerking it out of the German's
hands. Rhinemann's lieutenant was stunned by Spaulding's
action. He reached into his belt for his pistol.

The Bentley was now crashing down the steep incline at
an extraordinary speed. The wide bend referred to by the
Argentine was reached; the car entered a long, careening
pattern that seemed to be sustaining an engineering im-
probability: propelled by the wheels of a single side, the
other off the surface of the ground.

David and the German braced themselves with their
backs against opposite sides, their legs taut, their feet dug
into the felt carpet.

"Give me that *rifle!*" The German held his pistol on
David's chest. David had the rifle stock under his arm, his
finger on the trigger, the barrel of the monster weapon
leveled at the German's stomach.

"You fire, I fire," he shouted back. "I might come out of
it. You won't. You'll be all over the car!"

Spaulding saw that the driver had panicked. The action in
the back seat, coupled with the problems of the hill, the
speed and the curves created a crisis he was not capable of
handling.

"*Señores! Madre de Jesús!* . . . You'll *kill* us!"

The Bentley briefly struck the rocky shoulder of the
road; the jolt was staggering. The driver swung back toward the center line. The German spoke.

"You behave stupidly. Those men are after you, not
us!"

"I can't be sure of that. I don't kill people on speculation."

"You'll kill us, then? For what purpose?"

"I don't want anyone killed. . . . Now, put down that
gun! We both know the odds."

The German hesitated.

There was another jolt; the Bentley had struck a large
rock or a fallen limb. It was enough to convince Rhinemann's lieutenant. He placed the pistol on the seat.

The two adversaries braced themselves; David's eyes on the German's hand, the German's on the rifle.

"*Madre de Dios!*" The Argentine's shout conveyed relief, not further panic. Gradually the Bentley was slowing down.

David glanced through the windshield. They were coming out of the hill's curve; in the distance were flat blankets of fields, miniature pampas reflecting the dull moonlight. He reached over and took the German's pistol from the seat. It was an unexpected move; Rhinemann's lieutenant was annoyed with himself.

"Get your breath," said Spaulding to the driver. "Have a cigarette. And get me back to town."

"Colonel!" barked the German. "You may hold the weapons, but there's a car back there! If you won't follow my advice, at least let us get off the road!"

"I haven't the time to waste. I didn't tell him to slow down, just to relax."

The driver entered a level stretch of road and reaccelerated the Bentley. While doing so he took David's advice and lit a cigarette. The car was steady again.

"Sit back," ordered Spaulding, placing himself diagonally in the right corner, one knee on the floor—the rifle held casually, not carelessly.

The Argentine spoke in a frightened monotone. "There are the headlights again. They approach faster than I can drive this car. . . . What would you have me do?"

David considered the options. "Give them a chance to respond. . . . Is there enough moon to see the road? With your lights off?"

"For a while. Not long. I can't remember. . . ."

"Flick them on and off! Twice. . . . Now!"

The driver did as he was instructed. The effect was strange: the sudden darkness, the abrupt illumination—while the Bentley whipped past the tall grass on both sides of the road.

David watched the pursuing vehicle's lights through the rear window. There was no response to the signals. He wondered whether they'd been clear, whether they conveyed his message of accommodation.

"Flick them again," he commanded the driver. "Hold a couple of beats. . . . seconds. Now!"

The clicks were heard from the dashboard; the lights

remained off for three, four seconds. The clicks again; the darkness again.

And then it happened.

There was a burst of gunfire from the automobile in pursuit. The glass of the rear window was shattered; flying, imbedding itself into skin and upholstery. David could feel blood trickling down his cheek; the German screamed in pain, grasping his bleeding left hand.

The Bentley swerved; the driver swung the steering wheel back and forth, zigzagging the car in the road's path.

"There is your *reply!*" roared Rhinemann's lieutenant, his hand bloodied, his eyes a mixture of fury and panic.

Quickly, David handed the rifle to the German. "Use it!"

The German slipped the barrel into the opening; Spaulding sprang up into the seat and reached for the metal ring on the left side of the window, pulled it back and brought the pistol up.

There was another burst from the car behind. It was the volley of a submachine gun, scattershot, heavy caliber; spraying the rear of the Bentley. Bulges appeared throughout the felt top and sides, several bullets shattered the front windshield.

The German began firing the automatic; David aimed as best he could—the swerving, twisting Bentley kept pushing the pursuing car out of sightlines. Still he pulled the trigger, hoping only to spray the oncoming tires.

The roars from the German's weapon were thunderous; repeated crescendos of deafening *booms*, the shock waves of each discharge filling the small, elegant enclosure.

David could see the explosion the instant it happened. The hood of the onrushing automobile was suddenly a mass of smoke and steam.

But still the machine-gun volleys came *out* of the enveloping vapor.

"*Eeaagh!*" the driver screamed. David looked and saw blood flowing out of the man's head; the neck was half shot off. The Argentine's hands sprang back from the wheel.

Spaulding leaped forward, trying to reach the wheel, but he couldn't. The Bentley careened off the road, sideslipping into the tall grass.

The German took his automatic weapon from the opening. He smashed the side window with the barrel of the rifle and slammed in a second magazine as the Bentley came to a sharp, jolting stop in the grass.

The pursuing car—a cloud of smoke and spits of fire—was parallel now on the road. It braked twice, lurched once and locked into position, immobile.

Shots poured from the silhouetted vehicle. The German kicked the Bentley's door open and jumped out into the tall grass. David crouched against the left door, fingers searching for the handle, pushing his weight into the panel so that upon touch, the door would fly open and he could thrust himself into cover.

Suddenly the air was filled with the overpowering thunder of the automatic rifle held steady in a full-firing discharge.

Screams pierced the night; David sprung the door open, and as he leaped out he could see Rhinemann's lieutenant rising in the grass. *Rising* and *walking* through the shots, his finger depressing the automatic's trigger, his whole body shaking, staggering under the impact of the bullets entering his flesh.

He fell.

As he did so a second explosion came from the car on the road.

The gas tank burst from under the trunk, sending fire and metal into the air.

David sprang around the tail of the Bentley, his pistol steady.

The firing stopped. The roar of the flames, the hissing of steam was all there was.

He looked past the Bentley's trunk to the carnage on the road.

Then he recognized the automobile. It was the Duesenberg that had come for Leslie Hawkwood that afternoon.

Two dead bodies could be seen in the rear, rapidly being enveloped by fire. The driver was arched over the seat, his arms limp, his neck immobile, his eyes wide in death.

There was a fourth man, splayed out on the ground by the open right door.

The hand moved! Then the head!

He was alive!

Spaulding raced to the flaming Duesenberg and pulled the half-conscious man away from the wreckage.

He had seen too many men die to mistake the rapid ebbing of life. There was no point in trying to stem death; only to use it.

David crouched by the man. "Who are you? Why did you want to kill me?"

The man's eyes—swimming in their sockets—focused on David. A single headlight flickered from the smoke of the exploded Duesenberg; it was dying, too.

"Who *are* you? Tell me who you are!"

The man would not—or could not—speak. Instead, his lips moved, but not to whisper.

Spaulding bent down further.

The man died trying to spit in David's face. The phlegm and blood intermingled down the man's chin as his head went limp.

In the light of the spreading flames, Spaulding pulled the man's jacket open.

No identification.

Nor in the trousers.

He ripped at the lining in the coat, tore the shirt to the waist.

Then he stopped. Stunned, curious.

There were marks on the dead man's stomach. Wounds but not from bullets. David had seen those marks before.

He could not help himself. He lifted the man by the neck and yanked the coat off the left shoulder, tearing the shirt at the seams to expose the arm.

They were there. Deep in the skin. Never to be erased.

The tattooed numbers of a death camp.

*Ein Volk, ein Reich, ein Führer.*

The dead man was a Jew.

# 32

It was nearly five o'clock when Spaulding reached his apartment on Córdoba. He had taken the time to remove what obvious identification he could from the dead Argentine driver and Rhinemann's lieutenant. He found tools in the trunk and unfastened the Bentley's license plates; moved the dials of the dashboard clock forward, then smashed it. If nothing else, these details might slow police procedures —at least a few hours—giving him valuable time before facing Rhinemann.

Rhinemann would demand that confrontation.

And there was too much to learn, to piece together.

He had walked for nearly an hour back over the two hills—the Colinas Rojas—to the river highway. He had removed the fragments of window glass from his face, grateful they were few, the cuts minor. He had carried the awesome automatic rifle far from the scene of death, removed the chamber loading clip and smashed the trigger housing until the weapon was inoperable. Then he threw it into the woods.

A milk truck from the Tigre district picked him up; he told the driver an outrageous story of alcohol and sex— he'd been expertly rolled and had no one to blame but himself.

The driver admired the foreigner's spirit, his acceptance of risk and loss. The ride was made in laughter.

He knew it was pointless, even frivolous, to attempt sleep. There was too much to do. Instead he showered and made a large pot of coffee.

It was time. Daylight came up from the Atlantic. His head was clear; it was time to call Jean.

He told the astonished marine night operator on the

embassy switchboard that Mrs. Cameron expected the call;
actually he was late, he'd overslept. Mrs. Cameron had
made plans for deep-sea fishing; they were due at La Boca
at six.

"Hello? . . . Hello." Jean's voice was at first dazed, then
surprised.

"It's David. I haven't time to apologize. I've got to see
you right away."

"David? Oh, God! . . ."

"I'll meet you in your office in twenty minutes."

"*Please.* . . ."

"There's no *time!* Twenty minutes. Please, be there. . . .
I need you, Jean. *I need you!*"


The OD lieutenant at the embassy gate was cooperative,
if disagreeable. He consented to let the inside switchboard
ring Mrs. Cameron's office; if she came out and personally
vouched for him, the marine would let him pass.

Jean emerged on the front steps. She was vulnerable,
lovely. She walked around the driveway path to the gatehouse and saw him. The instant she did so, she stifled a
gasp.

He understood.

The styptic pencil could not eradicate the cuts from the
half dozen splinters of glass he had removed from his
cheeks and forehead. Partially conceal, perhaps; nothing
much more than that.

They did not speak as they walked down the corridor.
Instead, she held his arm with such force that he shifted to
her other side. She had been tugging at the shoulder not yet
healed from the Azores crash.

Inside her office she closed the door and rushed into his
arms. She was trembling.

"David, I'm *sorry, sorry, sorry.* I was dreadful. I behaved so badly."

He took her shoulders, holding her back very gently.
"You were coping with a problem."

"It seems to me I *can't* cope anymore. And I always
thought I was so good at it. . . . What happened to your
face?" She traced her fingers over his cheek. "It's swollen
here."

" 'Tortugas.' " He looked into her eyes. " 'Tortugas' happened."

"Oh, God." She whispered the words and buried her head in his chest. "I'm too disjointed; I can't say what I want to say. Don't. Please, don't . . . let anything more happen."

"Then you'll have to help me."

She pulled back. "*Me?* How can I?"

"Answer my questions. . . . I'll know if you're lying."

"*Lying?* . . . Don't joke. *I* haven't lied to *you.*"

He believed her . . . which didn't make his purpose any easier. Or clearer. "Where did you learn the name 'Tortugas'?"

She removed her arms from around his neck; he released her. She took several steps away from him but she was not retreating.

"I'm not proud of what I did; I've never done it before." She turned and faced him.

"I went down to the 'Caves' . . . without authorization . . . and read your file. I'm sure it's the briefest dossier in the history of the diplomatic corps."

"What did it say?"

She told him.

"So you see, my mythical David of last evening had a distinct basis in reality."

Spaulding walked to the window overlooking the west lawn of the embassy. The early sun was up, the grass flickered with dew; it brought to mind the manicured lawn seen in the night floodlights below Rhinemann's terrace. And that memory reminded him of the codes. He turned. "I have to talk to Ballard."

"Is that all you're going to say?"

"The not-so-mythical David has work to do. That doesn't change."

"I can't change it, you mean."

He walked back to her. "No, you can't. . . . I wish to God you could; I wish *I* could. I can't convince myself—to paraphrase a certain girl—that what I'm doing will make that much difference . . . but I react out of habit, I guess. Maybe ego; maybe it's as simple as that."

"I said you were good, didn't I?"

"Yes. And I am. . . . Do you know *what* I am?"

"An intelligence officer. An agent. A man who works with other men; in whispers and at night and with a great deal of money and lies. That's the way I think, you see."

"Not that. That's new. . . . What I *really* am. . . . I'm a construction engineer. I build buildings and bridges and dams and highways. I once built an extension for a zoo in Mexico; the best open-air enclosure for primates you ever saw. Unfortunately, we spent so much money the Zoological Society couldn't afford monkeys, but the space is there."

She laughed softly. "You're funny."

"I liked working on the bridges best. To cross a natural obstacle without marring it, without destroying its own purpose. . . ."

"I never thought of engineers as romantics."

"*Construction* engineers are. At least, the best ones. . . . But that's all long ago. When this mess is over I'll go back, of course, but I'm not a fool. I know the disadvantages I'll be faced with. . . . It's not the same as a lawyer putting down his books only to pick them up again; the law doesn't change that much. Or a stockbroker; the market solutions *can't* change."

"I'm not sure what you're driving at. . . ."

"Technology. It's the only real, civilized benefit war produces. In construction it's been revolutionary. In three years whole new techniques have been developed. . . . I've been out of it. My postwar references won't be the best."

"Good Lord, you're sorry for yourself."

"Christ, *yes!* In one way. . . . More to the point, I'm angry. Nobody held a gun to my head: I walked into this . . . this job for all the wrong reasons and without any foresight. . . . That's why I have to be good at it."

"What about us? Are we an 'us'?"

"I love you," he said simply. "I know that."

"After only a week? That's what I keep asking myself. We're not children."

"We're not children," he replied. "Children don't have access to State Department dossiers." He smiled, then grew serious. "I need your help."

She glanced at him sharply. "What is it?"

"What do you know about Erich Rhinemann?"

"He's a despicable man."

"He's a Jew."

"Then he's a despicable Jew. Race and religion notwithstanding, immaterial."

"Why is he despicable?"

"Because he uses people. Indiscriminately. Maliciously. He uses his money to corrupt whatever and whomever he can. He buys influence from the junta; that gets him land, government concessions, shipping rights. He forced a number of mining companies out of the Patagonia Basin; he took over a dozen or so oil fields at Comodoro Rivadavia. . . ."

"What are his politics?"

Jean thought for a second; she leaned back in the chair, looking for an instant at the window, then over to Spaulding. "Himself," she answered.

"I've heard he's openly pro-Axis."

"Only because he believed England would fall and terms would be made. He still owns a power base in Germany, I'm told."

"But he's a Jew."

"Temporary handicap. I don't think he's an elder at the synagogue. The Jewish community in Buenos Aires has no use for him."

David stood up. "Maybe that's it."

"What?"

"Rhinemann turned his back on the tribe, openly supports the creators of Auschwitz. Maybe they want him killed. Take out his guards first, then go after him."

"If by 'they' you mean the Jews here, I'd have to say no. The Argentine *judíos* tread lightly. The colonels' legions are awfully close to a goose step; Rhinemann has influence. Of course, nothing stops a fanatic or two. . . ."

"No. . . . They may be fanatics, but not one or two. They're organized; they've got backing—considerable amounts, I think."

"And they're after Rhinemann? The Jewish community would panic. Frankly, we'd be the first they'd come to."

David stopped his pacing. The words came back to him again: *there'll be no negotiations with Altmüller*. A darkened doorway on New York's Fifty-second Street.

"Have you ever heard the name Altmüller?"

"No. There's a plain Müller at the German embassy, I think, but that's like Smith or Jones. No Altmüller."

"What about Hawkwood? A woman named Leslie Jenner Hawkwood?"

"No again. But if these people are intelligence oriented, there'd be no reason for me to."

"They're Intelligence but I didn't think they were under-cover. At least not this Altmüller."

"What does that mean?"

"His name has been used in a context that assumes recognition. But I can't find him."

"Do you want to check the 'Caves'?" she asked.

"Yes. I'll do it directly with Granville. When do they open?"

"Eight thirty. Henderson's in his office by quarter to nine." She saw David hold up his wrist, forgetting he had no watch. She looked at her office clock. "A little over two hours. Remind me to buy you a watch."

"Thanks. . . . Ballard. I have to see him. How is he in the early morning? At this hour?"

"I trust that question's rhetorical. . . . He's used to being roused up for code problems. Shall I call him?"

"Please. Can you make coffee here?"

"There's a hotplate out there." Jean indicated the door to the anteroom. "Behind my secretary's chair. Sink's in the closet. . . . Never mind, I'll do it. Let me get Bobby first."

"I make a fine pot of coffee. You call, I'll cook. You look like such an executive, I'd hate to interfere."

He was emptying the grounds into the pot when he heard it. It was a footstep. A single footstep outside in the corridor. A footstep that should have been muffled but wasn't. A second step would ordinarily follow but didn't.

Spaulding put the pot on the desk, reached down and removed both his shoes without a sound. He crossed to the closed door and stood by the frame.

There it was again. Steps. Quiet; unnatural.

David opened his jacket, checking his weapon, and put his left hand on the knob. He turned it silently, then quickly opened the door and stepped out.

Fifteen feet away a man walking down the corridor spun around at the noise. The look on his face was one Spaulding had seen many times.

Fright.

"Oh, hello there, you must be the new man. We haven't met. . . . The name's Ellis. Bill Ellis. . . . I have a beastly conference at seven." The attaché was not convincing.

"Several of us were going fishing but the weather reports are uncertain. Care to come with us?"

"I'd love to except I have this damned ungodly hour meeting."

"Yes. That's what you said. How about coffee?"

"Thanks, old man. I really should bone up on some paperwork."

"O.K. Sorry."

"Yes, so am I. . . . Well, see you later." The man named Ellis smiled awkwardly, gestured a wave more awkwardly —which David returned—and continued on his way.

Spaulding went back into Jean's office and closed the door. She was standing by the secretary's desk.

"Who in heaven's name were you talking to at this hour?"

"He said his name was Ellis. He said he had a meeting with someone at seven o'clock. . . . He doesn't."

"What?"

"He was lying. What's Ellis's department?"

"Import-export clearances."

"That's handy. . . . What about Ballard?"

"He's on his way. He says you're a mean man. . . . What's 'handy' about Ellis?"

Spaulding went to the coffee pot on the desk, picked it up and started for the closet. Jean interrupted his movement, taking the pot from him. "What's Ellis's rating?" he asked.

"Excellent. Strictly the syndrome; he wants the Court of St. James's. You haven't answered me. What's 'handy'?"

"He's been bought. He's a funnel. It could be serious or just penny-ante waterfront stuff."

"Oh?" Jean, perplexed, opened the closet door where there was a washbasin. Suddenly, she stopped. She turned to Spaulding. "David. What does 'Tortugas' mean?"

"Oh, Christ, stop kidding."

"Which means you can't tell me."

"Which means I don't *know*. I wish to heaven I *did*."

"It's a code word, isn't it? That's what it says in your file."

"It's a code I've never been told about and I'm the one responsible!"

"Here, fill this; rinse it out first." Jean handed him the coffee pot and walked rapidly into her office, to the desk. David followed and stood in the doorway.

"What are you doing?"

"Attachés, even undersecretaries, if they have very early appointments, list them with the gate."

"Ellis?"

Jean nodded and spoke into the telephone; her conversation was brief. She replaced the instrument and looked over at Spaulding. "The first gate pass is listed for nine. Ellis has no meeting at seven thirty."

"I'm not surprised. Why are you?"

"I wanted to make sure. . . . You said you didn't know what 'Tortugas' meant. I might be able to tell you."

David, stunned, took several steps into the office. *"What?"*

"There was a surveillance report from La Boca—that's Ellis's district. His department must have cleared it up, given it a clean bill. It was dropped."

"What was dropped? What are you talking about?"

"A trawler in La Boca. It had cargo with a destination lading that violated coastal patrols . . . they called it an error. The destination was Tortugas."

The outer office door suddenly opened and Bobby Ballard walked in.

*"Jesus!"* he said. "The Munchkins go to work early in this wonderful world of Oz!"

# 33

The code schedules with Ballard took less than a half hour. David was amazed at the cryptographer's facile imagination. He developed—on the spot—a geometrical progress of numbers and corresponding letters that would take the best cryps Spaulding knew a week to break.

At maximum, all David needed was ninety-six hours.

Bobby placed Washington's copy in an official courier's envelope, sealed it chemically, placed it in a triple-locked pouch and called the FMF base for an officer—captain's rank or above—to get to the embassy within the hour. The codes would be on a coastal pursuit aircraft by nine; at Andrews Field by late afternoon; delivered to General Alan Swanson's office in the War Department by armored courier van shortly thereafter.

The confirmation message was simple; Spaulding had given Ballard two words: *Cable Tortugas*.

When the code was received in Washington, Swanson woud know that Eugene Lyons had authenticated the guidance designs. He could then radio the bank in Switzerland and payment would be made to Rhinemann's accounts. By using the name "Tortugas," David hoped that someone, somewhere, would understand his state of mind. His anger at being left with the full responsibility without all of the facts.

Spaulding was beginning to think that Erich Rhinemann was demanding more than he was entitled to. A possibility that would do him little good.

Rhinemann was to be killed.

And the outlines of a plan were coming into focus that would bring about that necessary death. The act itself might be the simplest part of his assignment.

There was no point in *not* telling Jean and Bobby Ballard about the guidance designs. Kendall had flown out of Buenos Aires—without explanation; David knew he might need assistance at a moment when there was no time to brief those helping him. His cover was superfluous now. He described minutely Rhinemann's schedule, the function of Eugene Lyons and Heinrich Stoltz's surfacing as a contact.

Ballard was astonished at Stoltz's inclusion. "*Stoltz!* That's a little bit of lightning. . . . I mean, he's a *believer*. Not the Hitler fire 'n' brimstone—he dismisses that, I'm told. But *Germany*. The Versailles motive, the reparations —bled giant, export or die—the whole thing. I figured him for the real Junker item. . . ."

David did not pay much attention.

The logistics of the morning were clear in Spaulding's mind and at eight forty-five he began.

His meeting with Henderson Granville was short and cordial. The ambassador was content not to know David's true purpose in Buenos Aires, as long as there was no diplomatic conflict. Spaulding assured him that to the best of his knowledge there was none; certainly less of a possibility if the ambassador remained outside the hard core of the assignment. Granville agreed. On the basis of David's direct request, he had the "Caves" checked for files on Franz Altmüller and Leslie Jenner Hawkwood.

Nothing.

Spaulding went from Granville's office back to Jean's. She had received the incoming passengers manifest from Aeroparque. Eugene Lyons was listed on clipper flight 101, arriving at two in the afternoon. His profession was given as "physicist"; the reason for entry, "industrial conferences."

David was annoyed with Walter Kendall. Or, he thought, should his annoyance be with the bewildered amateur, Brigadier General Alan Swanson? The least they could have done was term Lyons a "scientist"; "physicist" was stupid. A physicist in Buenos Aires was an open invitation to surveillance—even *Allied* surveillance.

He walked back to his own isolated, tiny office. To think.

He decided to meet Lyons himself. Walter Kendall had told him that Lyons's male nurses would settle the mute, sad man in San Telmo. Recalling the two men in question, David had premonitions of disaster. It wasn't beyond Johnny and Hal—those were the names, weren't they?—to deliver Lyons to the steps of the German embassy, thinking it was another hospital.

He would meet Pan Am Clipper 101. And proceed to take the three men on a complicated route to San Telmo.

Once he'd settled Lyons, David estimated that he would have about two, possibly three, hours before Rhinemann—or Stoltz—would make contact. Unless Rhinemann was hunting him now, in panic over the killings in the Colinas Rojas. If so, Spaulding had "built his shelter." His irrefutable alibi. . . . He hadn't been there. He'd been dropped off at Córdoba by two in the morning.

Who could dispute him?

So, he would have two or three hours in midafternoon. *La Boca.*

Discreetly, Jean had checked naval surveillance at FMF. The discretion came with her utterly routine, bored telephone call to the chief of operations. She had a "loose end" to tie up for a "dead file"; there was no significance, only a bureaucratic matter—someone was always looking for a good rating on the basis of closing out. Would the lieutenant mind filling in? . . . The trawler erroneously listed for Tortugas was moored by a warehouse complex in Ocho Calle. The error was checked and confirmed by the embassy attaché, Mr. William Ellis, Import-Export Clearance Division.

*Ocho Calle.*

David would spend an hour or so looking around. It could be a waste of time. What connection would a fishing trawler have with his assignment? There was none that he could see. But there *was* the name "Tortugas"; there *was* an attaché named Ellis who crept silently outside closed doors and lied about nonexistent conferences in the early morning.

Ocho Calle was worth looking into.

Afterward, he would stay by his telephone at Córdoba.

"Are you going to take me to lunch?" asked Jean, walking into his office. "Don't look at your watch; you haven't got one."

Spaulding's hand was in midair, his wrist turned. "I didn't realize it was so late."

"It's not. It's only eleven, but you haven't eaten—probably didn't sleep, either—and you said you were going to the airport shortly after one."

"I was right; you're a corporate executive. Your sense of organization is frightening."

"Nowhere near yours. We'll stop at a jewelry store first. I've already called. You have a present."

"I like presents. Let's go." Spaulding got out of his chair as the telephone rang. He looked down at it. "Do you know that's the first time that thing has made a sound?"

"It's probably for me. I told my secretary I was here. . . . I don't think I really *had* to tell her."

"Hello?" said David into the phone.

"Spaulding?"

David recognized the polished German of Heinrich Stoltz. His tension carried over the wire. "Isn't it a little foolish to call me here?"

"I have no choice. Our mutual friend is in a state of extreme anxiety. Everything is jeopardized."

"What are you talking about?"

"This is no time for foolishness! The situation is grave."

"It's no time for games, either. What the hell are you talking about?"

"Last night! This morning. What happened?"

"What happened where?"

"*Stop it!* You were *there!*"

"Where?"

Stoltz paused; David could hear his breath. The German was in panic, desperately trying to control himself. "The men were killed. We must know what happened!"

"Killed? . . . You're *crazy*. How?"

"I *warn* you. . . ."

"Now *you* cut it out! I'm *buying,* and don't you forget it. . . . I don't want to be mixed up in any organization problems. Those men dropped me off around one thirty. Incidentally, they met your other boys, the ones covering my apartment. And also incidentally, I don't like this round-the-clock surveillance!"

Stoltz was blanked—as David expected he would be. "The others? . . . What others?"

"Get off it! You know perfectly well." Spaulding let the inference hang.

"This is all most disturbing. . . ." Stoltz tried to compose himself.

"I'm sorry," said David noncommittally.

Exasperated, Stoltz interrupted. "I'll call you back."

"Not here. I'll be out most of the afternoon. . . . As a matter of fact," added Spaulding quickly, pleasantly, "I'll be in one of those sailboats our mutual friend looks down upon so majestically. I'm joining some diplomatic friends almost as rich as he is. Call me after five at Córdoba."

David hung up instantly, hearing the beginning of Stoltz's protest. Jean was watching him, fascinated.

"You did that very well," she said.

"I've had more practice than him."

"Stoltz?"

"Yes. Let's go into your office."

"I thought we were going to lunch."

"We are. Couple of things first. . . . There's a rear exit, isn't there?"

"Several. Back gate."

"I want to use an embassy vehicle. Any trouble?"

"No, of course not."

"Your secretary. Could you spare her for a long lunch?"

"You're sweet. I had the insane idea you were taking me."

"I am. Could she put her hair up and wear a floppy hat?"

"Any woman can."

"Good. Get that yellow coat you wore last night. And point out any man around here relatively my size. One that your secretary might enjoy that long lunch with. Preferably wearing dark trousers. He'll have my jacket."

"What are you doing?"

"Our friends are good at playing jokes on other people. Let's see how they take it when one's played on them."

Spaulding watched from the third-floor window, concealed by the full-length drapes. He held the binoculars to his eyes. Below, on the front steps, Jean's secretary—in a wide-brimmed hat and Jean's yellow coat—walked rapidly down to the curb of the driveway. Following her was one of Ballard's assistants, a tall man in dark trousers and David's jacket. Both wore sunglasses. Ballard's man paused momentarily on the top step, looking at an unfolded road map. His face was covered by the awkward mass of paper. He descended the stairs and together he and the girl climbed into the embassy limousine—an upper-level vehicle with curtains.

Spaulding scanned the Avenida Corrientes in front of the gates. As the limousine was passed through, a Mercedes coupe parked on the south side of the street pulled away from the curb and followed it. And then a second automobile on the north side made a cautious U-turn and took up its position several vehicles behind the Mercedes.

Satisfied, David put down the binoculars and went out of the room. In the corridor he turned left and walked swiftly past doors and around staircases toward the rear of the building, until he came to a room that corresponded to his observation post in front. Bobby Ballard sat in an armchair by the window; he turned around at the sound of David's footsteps, binoculars in his hands.

"Anything?" Spaulding asked.

"Two," answered the cryp. "Parked facing opposite directions. They just drove away."

"Same up front. They're in radio contact."

"Thorough, aren't they?"

"Not as much as they think," Spaulding said.

Ballard's sports coat was loose around the midsection and short in the sleeves, but it showed off David's new wristwatch. Jean was pleased about that. It was a very fine chronometer.

The restaurant was small, a virtual hole-in-the-wall on a side street near San Martín. The front was open; a short awning protected the few outside tables from the sun. Their table, however, was inside. Spaulding sat facing the entrance, able to see clearly the passersby on the sidewalk.

But he was not watching them now. He was looking at Jean. And what he saw in her face caused him to say the words without thinking.

"It's going to be over soon. I'm getting out."

She took his hand, searching his eyes. She did not reply for several moments. It was as if she wanted his words suspended, isolated, thought about. "That's a remarkable thing to say. I'm not sure what it means."

"It means I want to spend years and years with you. The

rest of my life. . . . I don't know any other way to put
it."

Jean closed her eyes briefly, for the duration of a single
breath of silence. "I think you've put it . . . very beautifully."

*How could he tell her? How could he explain? He had to
try. It was so damned important.* "Less than a month ago,"
he began softly, "something happened in a field. At night,
in Spain. By a campfire. . . . *To me.* The circumstances
aren't important, but what happened to me was . . . the
most frightening thing I could imagine. And it had nothing
to do with the calculated risks in my work; nothing to do
with being afraid—and I was always afraid, you can bet
your life on that. . . . But I suddenly found I had no
*feeling.* No feeling at all. I was given a report that should
have shaken me up—made me weep, or made me angry,
*goddamned angry.* But I didn't feel anything. I was numb.
I accepted the news and criticized the man for withholding
it. I told him not to make conditions. . . . You see, he
*rightfully* thought that I would." David stopped and put his
hand over Jean's. "What I'm trying to tell you is that
you've given me back something I thought I'd lost. I don't
ever want to take the chance of losing it again."

"You'll make me cry," she said quietly, her eyes moist,
her lips trembling to a smile. "Don't you know girls cry
when things like that are said to them? . . . I'll have to
teach you so much. . . . Oh, Lord," she whispered. "Please,
*please . . .* years."

David leaned over the small table; their lips touched and
as they held lightly together, he removed his hand from
hers and gently ran his fingers over the side of her face.

The tears were there.

He felt them, too. They would not come for him, but he
*felt* them.

"I'm going back with you, of course," she said.

Her words brought back the reality . . . the other reality,
the lesser one. "Not *with* me. But soon. I'm going to need a
couple of weeks to settle things. . . . And you'll have to
transfer your work down here."

She looked at him questioningly but did not ask a question. "There are . . . special arrangements for you to take
back the blueprints or designs or whatever they are."

"Yes."

"When?"

"If everything goes as we expect, in a day or two. At the most, three."

"Then why do you need a couple of weeks?"

He hesitated before answering. And then he realized he wanted to tell her the truth. It was part of the beginning for him. The truth. "There's a breach of security in a place called Fairfax. . . ."

"Fairfax," she interrupted. "That was in your file."

"It's an intelligence center in Virginia. Very classified. A man was killed there. He was a friend of mine. I purposely withheld information that might stop the leaks and, more important, find out who killed him."

"For heaven's sake, why?"

"In a way, I was forced to. The men in Fairfax weren't cleared for the information I had; the one man who was, is ineffectual . . . especially in something like this. He's not Intelligence oriented; he's a requisition general. He buys things."

"Like gyroscopic designs?"

"Yes. When I get back I'll force him to clear the data." David paused and then spoke as much to himself as to Jean. "Actually, I don't give a damn whether he does or not. I've got a long accumulated leave coming to me. I'll use a week or two of it in Fairfax. There's a German agent walking around in that compound with a four-zero rating. He killed a very good man."

"That frightens me."

"It shouldn't." David smiled, answering her with the truth. "I have no intention of risking those years we talked about. If I have to, I'll operate from a maximum security cell. . . . Don't worry."

She nodded. "I won't. I believe you. . . . I'll join you in, say, three weeks. I owe that to Henderson; there *will* be a lot of adjustments for him. Also, I'll have something done about Ellis."

"Don't touch him. We don't *know* anything yet. If we find out he's on an outside payroll he can be valuable right where he is. Reverse conduits are jewels. When we uncover one we make sure he's the healthiest man—or woman—around."

"What kind of a world do you live in?" Jean asked the question with concern, not humor.

"One that you'll help me leave. . . . After Fairfax, I'm finished."

Eugene Lyons edged into the back seat of the taxi between Spaulding and the male nurse named Hal. The other attendant, Johnny, sat in front with the driver. David gave his instructions in Spanish; the driver started out the long, smooth roadway of the Aeroparque.

David looked at Lyons; it wasn't easy to do so. The proximity of the sad, emaciated face emphasized the realization that what he saw was self-inflicted. Lyons's eyes were not responding; he was exhausted from the flight, suspicious of the new surroundings, annoyed by David's aggressive efficiency at hurrying them all out of the terminal.

"It's good to see you again," David told him.

Lyons blinked; Spaulding wasn't sure whether it was a greeting or not.

"We didn't expect you," said Johnny from the front seat. "We expected to get the professor set ourselves."

"We've got it all written down," added Hal, leaning forward on Lyons's right, taking a number of index cards out of his pocket. "Look. The address. Your telephone number. And the embassy's. And a wallet full of Argentine money."

Hal pronounced Argentine, "Argentyne." David wondered how he could be given a course in hypodermic injection; who would read the labels? On the other hand his partner Johnny—less talkative, more knowing somehow—was obviously the leader of the two.

"Well, these things are usually fouled up. Communications break down all the time. . . . Did you have a good flight down, doctor?"

"It wasn't bad," answered Hal. "But bumpy as a son of a bitch over Cuba."

"Those were probably heavy air masses coming up from the island," said David, watching Lyons out of the corner of his eye. The physicist responded now; a slight glance at Spaulding. And there was humor in the look.

"Yeah," replied Hal knowingly, "that's what the stewardess said."

Lyons smiled a thin smile.

David was about to capitalize on the small breakthrough

when he saw a disturbing sight in the driver's rear-view mirror—instinctively he'd been glancing at the glass.

It was the narrow grill of an automobile he'd previously spotted, though with no alarm. He had seen it twice: on the long curb in the taxi lineup and again on the turnout of the front park. Now it was there again, and David slowly shifted his position and looked out the taxi's rear window. Lyons seemed to sense that Spaulding was concerned; he moved to accommodate him.

The car was a 1937 La Salle, black, with rusted chrome on the grillwork and around the headlights. It remained fifty to sixty yards behind, but the driver—a blond-haired man—refused to let other vehicles come between them. He would accelerate each time his position was threatened. The blond-haired man, it appeared, was either inexperienced or careless. If he *was* following them.

David spoke to the taxi driver in urgent but quiet Spanish. He offered the man five dollars over the meter if he would reverse his direction and head away from San Telmo for the next several minutes. The *porteño* was less of an amateur than the driver of the La Salle; he understood immediately, with one look in his mirror. He nodded silently to Spaulding, made a sudden, awkwardly dangerous U-turn, and sped west. He kept the taxi on a fast zigzag course, weaving in and around the traffic, then turned abruptly to his right and accelerated the car south along the ocean drive. The sight of the water reminded David of Ocho Calle.

He wanted very much to deposit Eugene Lyons in San Telmo and get back to Ocho Calle.

The La Salle was no longer a problem.

"Christ!" said Hal. "What the hell was that?" And then he answered his own question. "We were being followed, right?"

"We weren't sure," said David.

Lyons was watching him, his look inexpressive. Johnny spoke from the front seat.

"Does that mean we can expect problems? You had this guy tooling pretty hard. Mr. Kendall didn't mention anything about trouble. . . . Just our job." Johnny did not turn around as he spoke.

"Would it bother you if there were?"

Johnny turned to face Spaulding; he was a very serious

fellow, thought David. "It depends," said the male nurse. "Our job is to watch out for the professor. Take care of him. If any trouble interfered with that, I don't think I'd like it."

"I see. What would you do?"

"Get him the hell out of here," answered Johnny simply.

"Dr. Lyons has a job to do in Buenos Aires. Kendall must have told you that."

Johnny's eyes leveled with Spaulding's. "I'll tell you straight, mister. That dirty pig can go screw. I never took so much shit from anyone in my life."

"Why don't you quit?"

"We don't work for Kendall," said Johnny, as if the thought was repulsive. "We're paid by the Research Center of Meridian Aircraft. That son of a bitch isn't even from Meridian. He's a lousy bookkeeper."

"You understand, Mr. Spaulding," said Hal, retreating from his partner's aggressiveness. "We have to do what's best for the professor. That's what the Research Center hires us for."

"I understand. I'm in constant touch with Meridian Research. The last thing anyone would wish is to harm Dr. Lyons. I can assure you of that." David lied convincingly. He couldn't give assurance because he himself was far from sure. His only course with Johnny and Hal was to turn this newfound liability into an asset. The key would be Meridian's Research Center and his fictional relationship to it; and a common repugnance for Kendall.

The taxi slowed down, turning a corner into a quiet San Telmo street. The driver pulled up to a narrow, three-storied, white stucco house with a sloping, rust-tiled roof. It was 15 Terraza Verde. The first floor was leased to Eugene Lyons and his "assistants."

"Here we are," said Spaulding, opening the door.

Lyons climbed out after David. He stood on the sidewalk and looked up at the quaint, colorful little house on the peaceful street. The trees by the curb were sculptured. Everything had a scrubbed look; there was an Old World serenity about the area. David had the feeling that Lyons had suddenly found something he'd been looking for.

And then he thought he saw what it was. Eugene Lyons was looking up at a lovely resting place. A final resting place. A grave.

## 34

There wasn't the time David thought there would be. He had told Stoltz to call him after five at Córdoba; it was nearly four now.

The first boats were coming into the piers, whistles blowing, men throwing and catching heavy ropes, nets everywhere, hanging out for the late drying rays of the sun.

Ocho Calle was in the Dársena Norte, east of the Retiro freight yards in a relatively secluded section of La Boca. Railroad tracks, long out of use, were implanted in the streets along the row of warehouses. Ocho Calle was not a prime storage or loading area. Its access to the sea channels wasn't as cumbersome as the inner units of the La Plata, but the facilities were outmoded. It was as if the management couldn't decide whether to sell its fair waterfront real estate or put it into good operating order. The indecision resulted in virtual abandonment.

Spaulding was in shirtsleeves; he had left Ballard's tan jacket at Terraza Verde. Over his shoulder was a large used net he had bought at an outdoor stall. The damn thing was rancid from rotting hemp and dead fish but it served its purpose. He could cover his face at will and move easily, comfortably among his surroundings—at one with them. David thought that should he ever—God forbid!—instruct recruits at Fairfax, he'd stress the factor of comfort. Psychological comfort. One could feel it immediately; just as swiftly as one felt the discomfort of artificiality.

He followed the sidewalk until it was no more. The final block of Ocho Calle was lined on the far side by a few old buildings and fenced-off abandoned lots once used for outside storage, now overgrown with tall weeds. On the water side were two huge warehouses connected to each other by a framed open area. The midships of a trawler could be seen moored between the two buildings. The next pier was across a stretch of water at least a quarter of a mile away. The Ocho Calle warehouses were secluded indeed.

David stopped. The block was like a miniature peninsula; there were few people on it. No side streets, no buildings beyond the row of houses on his left, only what appeared to be other lots behind the houses and further pilings that were sunk into the earth, holding back the water of a small channel.

The last stretch of Ocho Calle *was* a peninsula. The warehouses were not only secluded, they were isolated.

David swung the net off his right shoulder and hoisted it over his left. Two seamen walked out of a building; on the second floor a woman opened a window and shouted down, berating her husband about the projected hour of his return. An old man with dark Indian features sat in a wooden chair on a small, dilapidated stoop in front of a filthy bait store. Inside, through the glass stained with salt and dirt, other old men could be seen drinking from wine bottles. In the last house, a lone whore leaned out a first-floor window, saw David and opened her blouse, displaying a large, sagging breast. She squeezed it several times and pointed the nipple at Spaulding.

Ocho Calle was the end of a particular section of the earth.

He walked up to the old Indian, greeted him casually, and went into the bait store. The stench was overpowering, a combination of urine and rot. There were three men inside, more drunk than sober, nearer seventy than sixty.

The man behind the planked boards which served as a counter seemed startled to see a customer, not really sure what to do. Spaulding took a bill from his pocket—to the astonishment of all three surrounding him—and spoke in Spanish.

"Do you have squid?"

"No. . . . No, no squid. Very little supplies today," answered the owner, his eyes on the bill.

"What have you got?"

"Worms. Dog meat, some cat. Cat is very good."

"Give me a small container."

The man stumbled backward, picked up pieces of intes-

tine and wrapped them in a dirty newspaper. He put it on
the plank next to the money. "I have no change, señor. . . ."

"That's all right," replied Spaulding. "This money's for
you. And keep the bait."

The man grinned, bewildered. "*Señor? . . .*"

"You keep the money. Understand? . . . Tell me. Who
works over there?" David pointed at the barely translucent
front window. "In those big dock houses?"

"Hardly anybody. . . . A few men come and go . . . now
and then. A fishing boat . . . now and then."

"Have you been inside?"

"Oh yes. Three, four years ago, I work inside. Big business, three, four . . . five years ago. We all work." The
other two old men nodded, chattering old men's chatter.

"Not now?"

"No, no. . . . All closed down. Finished. Nobody goes
inside now. The owner is a very bad man. Watchmen break
heads."

"Watchmen?"

"Oh, yes. With guns. Many guns. Very bad."

"Do automobiles come here?"

"Oh, yes. Now and then. . . . One or two. . . . They don't
give us work."

"Thank you. You keep the money. Thank you, again."
David crossed to the filthy storefront window, rubbed a
small section of the glass and looked out at the block-long
stretch of warehouse. It appeared deserted except for the
men on the pier. And then he looked closer at those men.

At first he wasn't sure; the glass—though rubbed—still
had layers of film on the outside pane; it wasn't clear and
the men were moving about, in and out of the small transparent area.

Then he was sure. And suddenly very angry.

The men in the distance on the pier were wearing the
same paramilitary clothes the guards at Rhinemann's gate
had worn.

They were Rhinemann's men.

The telephone rang at precisely five thirty. The caller
was not Stoltz, and because it wasn't, David refused to
accept the instructions given him. He hung up and waited
less than two minutes for the phone to ring again.

"You are most obstinate," said Erich Rhinemann. "It is we who should be cautious, not you."

"That's a pointless statement. I have no intention of following the directions of someone I don't know. I don't expect airtight controls but that's too loose."

Rhinemann paused. Then he spoke harshly. "What happened last night?"

"I told Stoltz exactly what happened to *me*. I don't know anything else."

"I don't believe you." Rhinemann's voice was tense, sharp, his anger very close to the surface.

"I'm sorry," said David. "But that doesn't really concern me."

"Neither of those men would have left Córdoba! Impossible!"

"They left; take my word for it. . . . Look, I told Stoltz I don't want to get mixed up in your problems. . . ."

"How do you know you're not . . . mixed up?"

It was, of course, the logical question and Spaulding realized that. "Because I'm here in my apartment, talking to you. According to Stoltz, the others are dead; that's a condition I intend to avoid. I'm merely purchasing some papers from you. Let's concentrate on that."

"We'll talk further on this subject," said Rhinemann.

"Not now. We have business to transact."

Again the German Jew paused. "Do as the man told you. Go to the Casa Rosada on the Plaza de Mayo. South gate. If you take a taxi, get off at the Julio and walk."

"Your men will pick me up when I leave the apartment, I assume."

"Discreetly. To see if you're followed."

"Then I'll walk from here. It'll be easier."

"Very intelligent. A car will be waiting for you at the Rosada. The same automobile that brought you here last evening."

"Will you be there?" asked David.

"Of course not. But we'll meet shortly."

"I take the designs straight to Telmo?"

"If everything is clear, you may."

"I'll leave in five minutes. Will your men be ready?"

"They are ready now," answered Rhinemann. He hung up.

David strapped the Beretta to his chest and put on his jacket. He went into the bathroom, grabbed a towel from the rack and rubbed his shoes, removing the Aeroparque and La Boca dirt from the leather. He combed his hair and patted talcum powder over the scratches on his face.

He couldn't help but notice the dark crescents under his eyes. He needed sleep badly, but there was no time. For his own sake—survival, really—he knew he had to take the time.

He wondered when it would be.

He returned to the telephone. He had two calls to make before he left.

The first was to Jean. To ask her to stay in the embassy; he might have reason to call her. At any rate, he would talk to her when he returned. He said he would be with Eugene Lyons at Terraza Verde. And that he loved her.

The second call was to Henderson Granville.

"I told you I wouldn't involve the embassy or yourself in my work here, sir. If that's changed it's only because a man on your staff closed a naval surveillance file improperly. I'm afraid it directly affects me."

"How do you mean 'improperly'? That's a serious implication. If not a chargeable offense."

"Yes, sir. And for that reason it's imperative we raise no alarm, keep everything very quiet. It's an Intelligence matter."

"Who is this man?" asked Granville icily.

"An attaché named Ellis. William Ellis—please don't take *any* action, sir." Spaulding spoke rapidly, emphatically. "He may have been duped; he may *not* have been. Either way we can't have him alerted."

"Very well. I follow you. . . . Then why have you told me . . . if you want no action taken?"

"Not against Ellis, sir. We *do* need a clarification on the surveillance." David described the warehouses on Ocho Calle and the trawler moored between the two buildings.

Granville interrupted quietly. "I remember the report. Naval surveillance. It was a lading destination . . . let me think."

"Tortugas," supplied Spaulding.

"Yes, that was it. Coastal violations. An error, of course. No fishing boat would attempt such a trip. The actual destination was *Torugos*, a small port in northern Uruguay, I think."

David thought for a second. Jean hadn't mentioned the switch—or similarity—of names. "That may be, sir, but it would be advantageous to know the cargo."

"It was listed. Farm machinery, I believe."

"We don't think so," said Spaulding.

"Well, we have no right to inspect cargo. . . ."

"Mr. Ambassador?" David cut off the old gentleman. "Is there anyone in the junta we can trust, *completely* trust?"

Granville's reply was hesitant, cautious; Spaulding understood. "One. Two, perhaps."

"I won't ask you their names, sir. I *will* ask you to request their help. With priority security measures. Those warehouses are guarded . . . by Erich Rhinemann's men."

"*Rhinemann?*" The ambassador's distaste carried over the telephone. That was an asset, thought David.

"We have reason to believe he's aborting a negotiation or tying contraband into it. Smuggling, sir. We have to know what that cargo is." It was all David could think to say. A generalization without actual foundation. But if men were willing to kill and be killed for "Tortugas," perhaps that was foundation enough. If Fairfax could list the name on his transfer orders without telling him—that was *more* than enough.

"I'll do what I can, Spaulding. I can't promise anything, of course."

"Yes, sir. I realize. And thank you."


The Avenida de Mayo was jammed with traffic, the Plaza worse. At the end of the square the pinkish stone of Casa Rosada reflected the orange flood of the setting sun. Befitting a capital controlled by soldiers, thought David.

He crossed the Plaza, stopping at the fountain, recalling yesterday and Leslie Jenner Hawkwood. Where was she now? In Buenos Aires; but where? And more important, why?

The answer might lie in the name "Tortugas" and a trawler in Ocho Calle.

He circled the fountain twice, then reversed his steps once, testing himself, testing Erich Rhinemann. Where were the men watching him? Or were they women?

Were they in cars or taxis or small trucks? Circling as he was circling?

He spotted one. It wasn't hard to do. The man had seated himself on the edge of the fountain's pool, the tail of his jacket in the water. He'd sat down too quickly, trying to be inconspicuous.

David started across the pedestrian walk—the same pedestrian walk he'd used following Leslie Hawkwood—and at the first traffic island waited for a change of light. Instead of crossing, however, he walked back to the fountain. He stepped up his pace and sat down at the pool's edge and watched the crosswalk.

The man with the wet jacket emerged with the next contingent of pedestrians and looked anxiously around. Finally he saw Spaulding.

David waved.

The man turned and raced back across the street.

Spaulding ran after him, just making the light. The man did not look back; he seemed hell-bent to reach a contact, thought David; to have someone take over, perhaps. The man turned left at the Casa Rosada and Spaulding followed, keeping himself out of sight.

The man reached a corner and to David's surprise he slowed down, then stopped and entered a telephone booth.

It was a curiously amateurish thing to do, mused Spaulding. And it told him something about Erich Rhinemann's personnel: they weren't as good as they thought they were.

There was a long blasting of a horn that seemed louder than the normally jarring sounds of the Mayo's traffic. The single horn triggered other horns and in a few seconds a cacophony of strident honking filled the streets. David looked over. It was nothing; an irritated motorist had momentarily reached the end of his patience. Everything returned to normal chaos with the starting up of the automobiles at the crosswalk.

And then there was a scream. A woman's scream. And another; and still another.

A crowd gathered around the telephone booth.

David pushed his way through, yanking arms, pulling shoulders, shoving. He reached the edge of the booth and looked inside.

The man with the wet jacket was slumped awkwardly to the floor of the tiny glass enclosure, his legs buckled under him, his arms stretched above, one hand still gripping the telephone receiver so that the wire was taut. His head was sprung back from his neck. Blood was streaming down the back of his skull. Spaulding looked up at the walls of the booth. On the street side were three distinct holes surrounded by cracked glass.

He heard the piercing sounds of police whistles and pushed his way back through the crowd. He reached the iron fence that surrounded the Casa Rosada, turned right and started rapidly around the building to the south side.

To the south gate.

The Packard was parked in front of the entrance, its motor running. A man about his size approached him as David started for the automobile.

"Colonel Spaulding?"

"Yes?"

"If you'll hurry, please?" The man opened the back door and David climbed in quickly.

Heinrich Stoltz greeted him. "You've had a long walk. Sit. The ride will be relaxing."

"Not now." David pointed to the panels below the front dashboard. "Can you reach Rhinemann on that thing? Right away?"

"We're in constant contact. Why?"

"Get him. Your man was just killed."

"Our man?"

"The one following me. He was shot in a telephone booth."

"He wasn't our man, colonel. And *we* shot him," said Stoltz calmly.

"*What?*"

"The man was known to us. He was a hired killer out of Rio de Janeiro. You were his target."

Stoltz's explanation was succinct. They'd picked up the killer within moments after David left his apartment house. He was a Corsican, deported out of Marseilles before the war; a gun for the Unio Corso who had murdered one prefect too many under orders from the *contrabandistes* of southern France.

"We couldn't take a chance with the American who possesses the codes. A silencer in heavy traffic you'll agree is adequate."

"I don't think he was trying to kill me," said Spaulding. "I think you moved too soon."

"Then he was waiting for you to meet with *us*. Forgive me, but we couldn't permit that. You agree?"

"No. I could have taken him." David sat back and brought his hand to his forehead, tired and annoyed. "I was *going* to take him. Now we both lose."

Stoltz looked at David. He spoke cautiously; a question. "The same? You wonder also."

"Don't you? . . . You still think the Gestapo's not in Buenos Aires?"

"*Impossible!*" Stoltz whispered the word intensely through his teeth.

"That's what our mutual friend said about your men last night. . . . I don't know a goddamned thing about that, but I understand they're dead. So what's impossible?"

"The Gestapo *can't* be involved. We've learned that at the highest levels."

"Rhinemann's Jewish, isn't he?" David watched Stoltz as he asked the unexpected question.

The German turned and looked at Spaulding. There was a hint of embarrassment in his expression. "He practices no religion; his mother was Jewish. . . . Frankly, it's not pertinent. The racial theories of Rosenberg and Hitler are not shared unequivocally; far too much emphasis has been placed upon them. . . . It is—was—primarily an economic question. Distribution of banking controls, decentralization of financial hierarchies. . . . An unpleasant topic."

David was about to reply to the diplomat's evasions when he stopped himself. . . . Why did Stoltz find it necessary even to attempt a rationalization? To offer a weak explanation he himself knew was devoid of logic?

Heinrich Stoltz's loyalty was supposedly to Rhinemann, not the Third Reich.

Spaulding looked away and said nothing. He was, frankly, confused, but it was no time to betray that confusion. Stoltz continued.

"It's a curious question. Why did you bring it up?"

"A rumor. . . . I heard it at the embassy." And that was the truth, thought David. "I gathered that the Jewish community in Buenos Aires was hostile to Rhinemann."

"Mere speculation. The Jews here are like Jews elsewhere. They keep to themselves, have little to do with those outside. Perhaps the ghetto is less definable, but it's there. They have no argument with Rhinemann; there's no contact, really."

"Cross off one speculation," said Spaulding.

"There's another," said Stoltz. "Your own countrymen."

David turned slowly back to the German. "This is a good game. How did you arrive at that?"

"The purchase of the designs is being made by one aircraft corporation. There are five, six major companies in competition for your unending government contracts. Whoever possesses the gyroscope designs will have a powerful—I might even say irresistible—lever. All other guidance systems will be obsolete."

"Are you serious?"

"Most assuredly. We have discussed the situation at length . . . in depth. We are nearly convinced that this is the logical answer." Stoltz looked away from David and stared to the front. "There's no other. Those trying to stop us are American."

# 35

The green Packard made crisscross patterns over the Buenos Aires streets. The route was programmed aimlessness, and Spaulding recognized it for what it was: an extremely thorough surveillance check. Intermittently, the driver would pick up the microphone from beneath the dashboard and recite a prearranged series of numbers. The crackling response over the single speaker would repeat the numbers and the Packard would make yet another—seemingly aimless—turn.

Several times David spotted the corresponding vehicles making the visual checks. Rhinemann had a minimum of five automobiles involved. After three-quarters of an hour, it was certain beyond doubt that the trip to San Telmo was clean.

The driver spoke to Stoltz.

"We are clear. The others will take up their positions."

"Proceed," said Stoltz.

They swung northwest; the Packard accelerated toward San Telmo. David knew that at least three other cars were behind them; perhaps two in front. Rhinemann had set up his own transport column, and that meant the gyroscopic designs were in one of the automobiles.

"Have you got the merchandise?" he asked Stoltz.

"Part of it," replied the attaché, leaning forward, pressing a section of the felt backing in front of him. A latch sprung; Stoltz reached down and pulled out a tray from beneath the seat. Inside the concealed drawer was a thin metal box not unlike the containers used in libraries to protect rare manuscripts from possible loss by fire. The German picked it up, held it in his lap and pushed the drawer back with his foot. "We'll be there in a few minutes," he said.

The Packard pulled up to the curb in front of the white stucco house in San Telmo. Spaulding reached for the door handle but Stoltz touched his arm and shook his head. David withdrew his hand; he understood.

About fifty yards ahead, one of the checkpoint automobiles had parked and two men got out. One carried a thin metal container, the other an oblong leather case—a radio. They walked back toward the Packard.

David didn't have to look out the rear window to know what was happening behind him, but to confirm his thoughts he did so. Another automobile had parked. Two additional men were coming up the sidewalk; one, of course, carrying a container, the second, a leather-encased radio.

The four men met by the door of the Packard. Stoltz nodded to Spaulding; he got out of the car and walked around the vehicle, joining Rhinemann's contingent. He was about to start up the short path to the front entrance when Stoltz spoke through the automobile window.

"Please wait. Our men are not yet in position. They'll tell us."

Static could be heard over the radio beneath the Packard's dashboard. There followed a recitation of numbers; the driver picked up his microphone and repeated them.

Heinrich Stoltz nodded and got out of the car. David started toward the door.

Inside, two of Rhinemann's men remained in the hallway; two walked through the apartment to the kitchen and a rear door that opened onto a small, terraced back yard. Stoltz accompanied David into the living room where Eugene Lyons was seated at a large dining table. The table was cleared except for two note pads with a half dozen pencils.

The male nurses, Johnny and Hal, accepted Spaulding's terse commands. They stood at opposite ends of the room in front of a couch, in shirtsleeves, their pistols strapped in shoulder holsters emphasized by the white cloth of their shirts.

Stoltz had relieved one man of his metal case and told David to take the other. Together, Stoltz and Spaulding placed the three containers on the large table, and Stoltz

unlocked them. Lyons made no effort to greet his visitors
—his intruders—and only the most perfunctory salutation
came from Stoltz. It was apparent that Kendall had described the scientist's afflictions; the German diplomat conducted himself accordingly.

Stoltz spoke from across the table to the seated Lyons.
"From your left, the designs are in order of sequence. We
have prepared bilingual keys attached to each of the
schematics, and wherever processes are described, they
have been translated verbatim, utilizing English counterpart formulae or internationally recognized symbols, and
often both. . . . Not far from here, and easily contacted by
our automobile radio, is an aeronautical physicist from
Peenemünde. He is available for consultation at your request. . . . Finally, you understand that no photographs
may be taken."

Eugene Lyons picked up a pencil and wrote on a pad.
He tore off the page and handed it to Spaulding. It read:

*How long do I have? Are these complete?*

David handed the note to Stoltz, who replied.

"As long as you need, *Herr Doktor.* . . . There is one last
container. It will be brought to you later."

"Within twenty-four hours," interrupted Spaulding. "I
insist on that."

"When we receive confirmation that the codes have arrived in Washington."

"That message is undoubtedly at the embassy now."
David looked at his watch. "I'm sure it is."

"If you say it, I believe it," said Stoltz. "It would be
pointless to lie. You won't leave Argentina until *we* have
received word from . . . Switzerland."

Spaulding couldn't define why but there was something
questioning about the German's statement; a questioning
that didn't belong with such a pronouncement. David
began to think that Stoltz was far more nervous than he
wanted anyone to realize. "I'll confirm the codes when we
leave. . . . By the way, I also insist the designs remain here.
Just as Doctor Lyons has checked them."

"We anticipated your . . . request. You Americans are so
mistrustful. Two of our men will also remain. Others will
be outside."

"That's a waste of manpower. What good is three-
fourths of the merchandise?"

"Three-fourths better than you have," answered the German.

The next two and a half hours were marked by the scratches of Lyons's pencil; the incessant static of the radios from the hallway and the kitchen, over which came the incessant, irritating recitation of numbers; the pacing of Heinrich Stoltz—his eyes constantly riveting on the pages of notes taken by an exhausted Lyons, making sure the scientist did not try to pocket or hide them; the yawns of the male nurse, Hal; the silent, hostile stares of his partner, Johnny.

At ten thirty-five, Lyons rose from the chair. He placed the pile of notes to his left and wrote on a pad, tearing off the page and handing it to Spaulding.

*So far—authentic. I have no questions.*

David handed the note to an anxious Stoltz.

"Good," said the German. "Now, colonel, please explain to the doctor's companions that it will be necessary for us to relieve them of their weapons. They will be returned, of course."

David spoke to Johnny. "It's all right. Put them on the table."

"It's all right by who-says?" said Johnny, leaning against the wall, making no move to comply.

"I do," answered Spaulding. "Nothing will happen."

"These fuckers are Nazis! You want to put us in blindfolds, too?"

"They're German. Not Nazis."

"Horseshit!" Johnny pushed himself off the wall and stood erect. "I don't like the way they talk."

"Listen to me." David approached him. "A great many people have risked their lives to bring this thing off. For different reasons. You may not like them any more than I do, but we can't louse it up now. Please, do as I ask you."

Johnny stared angrily at Spaulding. "I hope to Christ you know what you're doing. . . ." He and his partner put down their guns.

"Thank you, gentlemen," said Stoltz, walking into the hallway. He spoke quietly in German to the two guards. The man with the radio walked rapidly through the sitting room into the kitchen; the other picked up the two weapons, placing one in his belt, the second in his jacket pocket. He then returned to the hallway without speaking.

Spaulding went to the table, joined by Stoltz. Lyons had replaced the designs in the manila envelopes; there were three. "I'd hate to think of the money our mutual friend is getting for these," said David.

"You wouldn't pay it if they weren't worth it."

"I suppose not. . . . No reason not to put them in one case. Along with the notes." Spaulding looked over at Lyons, who stood immobile at the end of the table. "Is that all right, doctor?"

Lyons nodded, his sad eyes half closed, his pallor accentuated.

"As you wish," said Stoltz. Picking up the envelopes and the notes, he put them in the first container, locked it, closed the other two and placed them on top of the first, as if he were performing a religious exercise in front of an altar.

Spaulding took several steps toward the two men by the window. "You've had a rough day. Doctor Lyons, too. Turn in and let your guests walk guard duty; I think they're on overtime."

Hal grinned. Johnny did not.

"Good evening, doctor. It's been a privilege meeting such a distinguished man of science." Across the room, Stoltz spoke in diplomatic tones, bowing a slight diplomatic bow.

The guard with the radio emerged from the kitchen and nodded to the German attaché. They left the room together. Spaulding smiled at Lyons; the scientist turned without acknowledging and walked into his bedroom to the right of the kitchen door.

Outside on the sidewalk, Stoltz held the car door for David. "A very strange man, your Doctor Lyons," he said as Spaulding got into the Packard.

"He may be, but he's one of the best in his field. . . . Ask your driver to stop at a pay phone. I'll check the embassy's radio room. You'll get your confirmation."

"Excellent idea. . . . Then, perhaps, you'll join me for dinner?"

David looked at the attaché who sat so confidently, so half-mockingly, beside him. Stoltz's nervousness had disappeared. "No, Herr Botschaftssekretär. I have another engagement."

"With the lovely Mrs. Cameron, no doubt. I defer."

Spaulding did not reply. Instead, he looked out the window in silence.

The Terraza Verde was peaceful. The streetlamps cast a soft glow on the quiet, darkened sidewalks; the sculptured trees in front of the picturesque Mediterranean houses were silhouetted against pastel-colored brick and stone. In windows beyond flower boxes, the yellow lamps of living rooms and bedrooms shone invitingly. A man in a business suit, a newspaper under his arm, walked up the steps to a door, taking a key from his pocket; a young couple were laughing quietly, leaning against a low wrought-iron fence. A little girl with a light brown cocker spaniel on a leash was skipping along the sidewalk, the dog jumping happily out of step.

Terraza Verde was a lovely place to live.

And David thought briefly of another block he'd seen that day. With old men who smelled of rot and urine; with a toothless whore who leaned on a filthy sill. With cat intestines and dirt-filmed windows. And with two huge warehouses that provided no work, and a trawler at anchor, recently destined for Tortugas.

The Packard turned the corner into another street. There were a few more lights, less sculptured trees, but the street was very much like Terraza Verde. It reminded David of those offshoot streets in Lisbon that approached the rich *caminos;* dotted with expensive shops, convenient for wealthy inhabitants a few hundred yards away.

There were shops here, too; with windows subtly lit, wares tastefully displayed.

Another block; the Packard slowed down at the intersecting street and then started across. More shops, less trees, more dogs—these often walked by maids. A group of teenagers were crowded around an Italian sportscar.

And then David saw the overcoat. It was just an overcoat at first; a light grey overcoat in a doorway.

A grey overcoat. A recessed doorway.

The man was tall and thin. A tall, thin man in a light grey overcoat. In a doorway!

My God! thought David. *The man on Fifty-second Street!*

The man was turned sideways, looking down into a dimly lit store window. Spaulding could not see them but he could picture the dark, hollow eyes; could hear the bastardized English out of somewhere in the Balkans; sense the desperation in the man's eyes:

*There are to be no negotiations with Franz Altmüller. . . . Heed the lesson of Fairfax!*

He had to get out of the Packard. Quickly!

He had to go back to Terraza Verde. Without Stoltz. He *had* to!

"There's a café in the next block," said Spaulding, pointing to an orange canopy with lights underneath, stretching across the sidewalk. "Stop there. I'll call the embassy."

"You seem anxious, colonel. It can wait. I believe you."

Spaulding turned to the German. "You want me to spell it out? O.K., I'll do that. . . . I don't like you, Stoltz. And I don't like Rhinemann; I don't like men who yell and bark orders and have me followed. . . . I'm buying from you, but I don't have to associate with you. I don't have to have dinner or ride in your automobile once our business for the day is over. Do I make myself clear?"

"You're clear. Though somewhat uncivilized. And ungrateful, if you don't mind my saying so. We saved your life earlier this evening."

"That's your opinion. Not mine. Just let me off, I'll telephone and come out with your confirmation. . . . As you said, there's no point in my lying. You go on your way, I'll grab a taxi."

Stoltz instructed the driver to pull up at the orange canopy. "Do as you please. And should your plans include Doctor Lyons, be advised we have men stationed about the area. Their orders are harsh. Those designs will stay where they are."

"I'm not paying for three-quarters of the merchandise regardless of what there is back home. And I have no intention of walking into that phalanx of robots."

The Packard drew up to the canopy. Spaulding opened the door quickly, slamming it angrily behind him. He walked swiftly into the lighted entrance and asked for the telephone.

"The ambassador has been trying to reach you for the past half-hour or so," said the night operator. "He says it's urgent. I'm to give you a telephone number." The operator drawled out the digits.

"Thank you," David said. "Now connect me with Mr. Ballard in Communications, please."

"O'Leary's Saloon," came the uninterested voice of Bobby Ballard over the wire.

"You're a funny man. I'll laugh next Tuesday."

"The 'switch' said it was you. You know Granville's trying to find you."

"I heard. Where's Jean?"

"In her room; pining away just like you ordered."

"Did you get word from D.C.?"

"All wrapped. Came in a couple of hours ago; your codes are cleared. How's the erector set?"

"The instructions—three-quarters of them—are in the box. But there are too many playmates."

"Terraza Verde?"

"Around there."

"Shall I send out a few FMF playground attendants?"

"I think I'd feel better," said Spaulding. "Tell them to cruise. Nothing else. I'll spot them and yell if I need them."

"It'll take a half-hour from the base."

"Thanks. No parades, please, Bobby."

"They'll be so quiet no one'll know but us Munchkins. Take care of yourself."

Spaulding held down the receiver with his finger, tempted to lift it, insert another coin and call Granville. . . . There wasn't time. He left the booth and walked out the restaurant door to the Packard. Stoltz was at the window; David saw that a trace of his previous nervousness had returned.

"You've got your confirmation. Deliver the rest of the goods and enjoy your money. . . . I don't know where you come from, Stoltz, but I'll find out and have it bombed off the map. I'll tell the Eighth Air Force to name the raid after you."

Stoltz seemed relieved at David's surliness—as David thought he might be. "The man from Lisbon is complicated. I suppose that's proper for a complicated assignment. . . . We'll call you by noon." Stoltz turned to the driver. "*Los, abfahren, machen Sie schnell!*"

The green Packard roared off down the street. Spaulding

waited under the canopy to see if it made any turns; should it do so, he would return to the cafe and wait.

It did not; it maintained a straight course. David watched until the taillights were infinitesimal red dots. Then he turned and walked as fast as he could without calling attention to himself toward Terraza Verde.

He reached the short block in which he'd seen the man in the light grey overcoat and stopped. His concerns made him want to rush on; his instincts forced him to wait, to look, to move cautiously.

The man was not on the block now; he was nowhere to be seen. David reversed his direction and walked to the end of the sidewalk. He turned left and raced down the street to the next corner, turning left again, now slowing down, walking casually. He wished to God he knew the area better, knew the buildings behind Lyons's white stucco house. Others did; others were positioned in dark recesses he knew nothing about.

Rhinemann's guards. The man in the light grey overcoat; how many more were with *him?*

He approached the intersection of Terraza Verde and crossed the road diagonally, away from the white stucco house. He stayed out of the spill of the lamps as best he could and continued down the pavement to the street behind the row of houses on Terraza Verde. It was, of course, a block lined with other houses; quaint, picturesque, quiet. Spaulding looked up at the vertical sign: *Terraza Amarilla.*

San Telmo fed upon itself.

He remained at the far end of the corner under a sculptured tree and looked toward the section of the adjacent street where he judged the rear of Lyons's house to be. He could barely make out the sloping tiled roof, but enough to pinpoint the building behind it—about 150 yards away.

He also saw Rhinemann's automobile, one of those he'd spotted during the long, security-conscious drive from the Casa Rosada. It was parked opposite a light-bricked Italian townhouse with large gates on both sides. David assumed those gates opened to stone paths leading to a wall or a fence separating Lyons's back terrace from the rear entrance of the townhouse. It had to be something like that; Rhinemann's guards were posted so that anyone emerging from those gates was equally in their sightlines.

And then Spaulding remembered the crackling static of the radios from the hallway and the kitchen and the incessant repetition of the German numbers. Those who carried the radios had weapons. He reached beneath his jacket to his holster and took out the Beretta. He knew the clip was filled; he unlatched the safety, shoved the weapon into his belt and started across the street toward the automobile.

Before he reached the opposite corner, he heard a car drive up behind him. He had no time to run, no moment to make a decision—good or bad. His hand went to his belt; he tried to assume a posture of indifference.

He heard the voice and was stunned.

"Get in, you goddamned *fool!*"

Leslie Hawkwood was behind the wheel of a small Renault coupe. She had reached over and unlatched the door. David caught it, his attention split between his shock and his concern that Rhinemann's guard—or guards—a hundred yards away might hear the noise. There were fewer than a dozen pedestrians within the two-block area. Rhinemann's men *had* to have been alerted.

He jumped into the Renault and with his left hand he grabbed Leslie's right leg above the knee, his grip a restraining vise, pressing on the nerve lines. He spoke softly but with unmistakable intensity.

"You back this car up as quietly as you can, and turn left down that street."

"Let *go!* Let . . ."

"Do as I say or I'll break your kneecap off!"

The Renault was short; there was no need to use the reverse gear. Leslie spun the wheel and the car veered into a sharp turn.

"Slowly!" commanded Spaulding, his eyes on Rhinemann's car. He could see a head turn—two heads. And then they were out of sight.

David took his hand off the girl's leg; she pulled it up and doubled her shoulders down in agony. Spaulding grabbed the wheel and forced the gears into neutral. The car came to a stop halfway down the block, at the curb.

"You bastard! You broke my leg!" Leslie's eyes were filled with tears of pain, not sorrow. She was close to fury but she did not shout. And that told David something about Leslie he had not known before.

"I'll break more than a leg if you don't start telling me

what you're doing here! How many others are there? I saw one; how many more?"

She snapped her head up, her long hair whipping back, her eyes defiant. "Did you think we couldn't find him?"

"Who?"

"Your *scientist*. This Lyons! We found him!"

"Leslie, for Christ's sake, what are you *doing?*"

"Stopping you!"

"*Me?*"

"You. Altmüller, Rhinemann. Koening! Those pigs in Washington. . . . Peenemünde! It's all over. They won't trust you anymore. 'Tortugas' is finished!"

The faceless name—Altmüller again. Tortugas. . . . Koening? Words, names . . . meaning and no meaning. The tunnels had no light.

There was no *time!*

Spaulding reached over and pulled the girl toward him. He clutched the hair above her forehead, yanking it taut, and with his other hand he circled his fingers high up under her throat, just below the jawbone. He applied pressure in swift, harsh spurts, each worse than the last.

*So much, so alien.*

"You want to play this game, you play it out! Now tell me! What's *happening? Now?*"

She tried to squirm, lashing out her arms, kicking at him; but each time she moved he ripped his fingers into her throat. Her eyes widened until the sockets were round. He spoke again.

"Say it, Leslie! I'll have to kill you if you don't. I don't have a choice! Not now. . . . For Christ's sake, don't *force* me!"

She slumped; her body went limp but not unconscious. Her head moved up and down; she sobbed deep-throated moans. He released her and gently held her face. She opened her eyes.

"Don't touch me! Oh, *God*, don't touch me!" She could barely whisper, much less scream. "Inside. . . . We're going inside. Kill the scientist; kill Rhinemann's men. . . ."

Before she finished, Spaulding clenched his fist and hammered a short, hard blow into the side of her chin. She slumped, unconscious.

He'd heard enough. There *was* no time.

He stretched her out in the small front seat, removing

the ignition keys as he did so. He looked for her purse; she
had none. He opened the door, closed it firmly and looked
up and down the street. There were two couples halfway
down the block; a car was parking at the corner; a window
was opened on the second floor of a building across the
way, music coming from within.

Except for these—nothing. San Telmo was at peace.

Spaulding ran to within yards of Terraza Amarilla. He
stopped and edged his way along an iron fence that bordered the corner, swearing at the spill of the streetlamp. He
looked through the black grillwork at Rhinemann's car less
than a hundred yards away. He tried to focus on the front
seat, on the two heads he'd seen moving minutes ago.
There was no movement now, no glow of cigarettes, no
shifting of shoulders.

Nothing.

Yet there was a break in the silhouette of the left window frame; an obstruction that filled the lower section of
the glass.

David rounded the sharp angle of the iron fence and
walked slowly toward the automobile, his hand clamped on
the Beretta, his finger steady over the trigger. *Seventy
yards, sixty, forty-five.*

The obstruction did not move.

*Thirty five, thirty . . .* he pulled the pistol from his belt,
prepared to fire.

Nothing.

He saw it clearly now. The obstruction was a head,
sprung back into the glass—not resting, but wrenched,
twisted from the neck; immobile.

Dead.

He raced across the street to the rear of the car and
crouched, his Beretta level with his shoulders. There was
no noise, no rustling from within.

The block was deserted now. The only sounds were the
muffled, blurred hums from a hundred lighted windows. A
latch could be heard far down the street; a small dog
barked; the wail of an infant was discernible in the distance.

David rose and looked through the automobile's rear
window.

He saw the figure of a second man sprawled over the felt
top of the front seat. The light of the streetlamps illumi-

nated the upper part of the man's back and shoulders. The whole area was a mass of blood and slashed cloth.

Spaulding slipped around the side of the car to the front right door. The window was open, the sight within sickening. The man behind the wheel had been shot through the side of his head, his companion knifed repeatedly.

The oblong, leather-cased radio was smashed, lying on the floor beneath the dashboard.

It had to have happened within the past five or six minutes, thought David. Leslie Hawkwood had rushed down the street in the Renault to intercept him—at the precise moment men with silenced pistols and long-bladed knives were heading for Rhinemann's guards.

The killings complete, the men with knives and pistols must have raced across the street into the gates toward Lyons's house. Raced without thought of cover or camouflage, knowing the radios were in constant contact with those inside 15 Terraza Verde.

Spaulding opened the car door, rolled up the window, and pulled the lifeless form off the top of the seat. He closed the door; the bodies were visible, but less so than before. It was no moment for alarms in the street if it could be avoided.

He looked over at the gates across the way on each side of the townhouse. The left one was slightly ajar.

He ran over to it and eased himself through the opening, touching nothing, his gun thrust laterally at his side, aiming forward. Beyond the gate was a cement passageway that stretched the length of the building to some sort of miniature patio bordered by a high brick wall.

He walked silently, rapidly to the end of the open alley; the patio was a combination of slate paths, plots of grass and small flower gardens. Alabaster statuary shone in the moonlight; vines crawled up the brick wall.

He judged the height of the wall: seven feet, perhaps seven and a half. Thickness: eight, ten inches—standard. Construction: new, within several years, strong. It was the construction with which he was most concerned. In 1942 he took a nine-foot wall in San Sebastián that collapsed under him. A month later it was amusing; at the time it nearly killed him.

He replaced the Beretta in his shoulder holster, locking the safety, shoving in the weapon securely. He bent down and rubbed his hands in the dry dirt at the edge of the cement, absorbing whatever sweat was on them. He stood up and raced toward the brick wall.

Spaulding leaped. Once on top of the wall, he held— silent, prone; his hands gripping the sides, his body motionless—a part of the stone. He remained immobile, his face toward Lyons's terrace, and waited several seconds. The back door to Lyons's flat was closed—no lights were on in the kitchen; the shades were drawn over the windows throughout the floor. No sounds from within.

He slid down from the wall, removed his gun and ran to the side of the kitchen door, pressing his back against the white stucco. To his astonishment he saw that the door was *not* closed; and then he saw why. At the base, barely visible in the darkness of the room beyond, was a section of a hand. It had gripped the bottom of the doorframe and been smashed into the saddle; the fingers were the fingers of a dead man.

Spaulding reached over and pressed the door. An inch. Two inches. Wood against dead weight; his elbow ached from the pressure.

Three, four, five inches. A foot.

Indistinguishable voices could be heard now; faint, male, excited.

He stepped swiftly in front of the door and pushed violently—as quietly as possible—against the fallen body that acted as a huge, soft, dead weight against the frame. He stepped over the corpse of Rhinemann's guard, noting that the oblong radio had been torn from its leather case, smashed on the floor. He closed the door silently.

The voices came from the sitting room. He edged his way against the wall, the Beretta poised, unlatched, ready to fire.

An open pantry against the opposite side of the room caught his eye. The single window, made of mass-produced stained glass, was high in the west wall, creating eerie shafts of colored light from the moon. Below, on the floor, was Rhinemann's second guard. The method of death he could not tell; the body was arched backward—probably a bullet from a small-caliber pistol had killed him. A pistol with a silencer attached. It would be very quiet. David felt the perspiration rolling down his forehead and over his neck.

How many were there? They'd immobilized a garrison. He had no commitment matching those odds.

Yet he had a strange commitment to Lyons. He had commitment enough for him at the moment. He dared not think beyond that instant.

And he was good; he could—should—never forget that. He was the best there was.

If it was important to anyone.

*So much, so alien.*

He pressed his cheek against the molding of the arch and what he saw sickened him. The revulsion, perhaps, was increased by the surroundings: a well-appointed flat with chairs and couches and tables meant for civilized people involved with civilized pursuits.

Not death.

The two male nurses—the hostile Johnny, the affable, dense Hal—were sprawled across the floor, their arms linked, their heads inches from each other. Their combined blood had formed a pool on the parquet surface. Johnny's eyes were wide, angry—dead; Hal's face composed, questioning, at rest.

Behind them were Rhinemann's two other guards, their bodies on the couch like slaughtered cattle.

*I hope you know what you're doing!*

Johnny's words vibrated painfully—in screams—in David's brain.

There were three other men in the room—standing, alive, in the same grotesque stocking masks that had been worn by those in the Duesenberg who had cut short the few moments he'd had alone with Leslie Hawkwood high in the hills of Luján.

The Duesenberg that had exploded in fire in the hills of Colinas Rojas.

The men were standing—none held weapons—over the spent figure of Eugene Lyons—seated gracefully, without fear, at the table. The look in the scientist's eyes told the truth, as Spaulding saw it: he welcomed death.

"You see what's around you!" The man in the light grey overcoat spoke to him. "We will not hesitate further! You're dead! . . . Give us the designs!"

*Jesus Christ!* thought David. Lyons had hidden the plans!

"There's no point in carrying on, please believe me," continued the man in the overcoat, the man with the hollow crescents under his eyes Spaulding remembered so well. "You may be spared, but only if you tell us! *Now!*"

Lyons did not move; he looked up at the man in the overcoat without shifting his head, his eyes calm. They touched David's.

"Write it!" said the man in the light grey overcoat.

It was the moment to move.

David spun around the molding, his pistol leveled.

"Don't reach for guns! *You!*" he yelled at the man nearest him. "Turn around!"

In shock, without thinking, the man obeyed. Spaulding took two steps forward and brought the barrel of the Beretta crashing down into the man's skull. He collapsed instantly.

David shouted at the man next to the interrogator in the grey overcoat. "Pick up that chair! *Now!*" He gestured with his pistol to a straight-backed chair several feet from the table. "*Now*, I said!"

The man reached over and did as he was told; he was immobilized. Spaulding continued. "You drop it and I'll kill you. . . . Doctor Lyons. Take their weapons. You'll find pistols and knives. Quickly, please."

It all happened so fast. David knew his only hope of avoiding gunfire was in the swiftness of the action, the rapid immobilization of one or two men, an instant reversal of the odds.

Lyons got out of the chair and went first to the man in the light grey overcoat. It was apparent that the scientist had observed where the man had put his pistol. He took it out of the overcoat pocket. He went to the man holding the chair and removed an identical gun, then searched the man and took a large knife from his jacket and a second, short revolver from a shoulder holster. He placed the weapons on the far side of the table and walked to the unconscious third man. He rolled him over and removed two guns and a switchblade knife.

"Take off your coats. *Now!*" Spaulding commanded both men. He took the chair from the one next to him and pushed him toward his companion. The men began removing their coats when Spaulding suddenly spoke, before either had completed their actions. "Stop right there! Hold it! . . . Doctor, please bring over two chairs and place them behind them."

Lyons did so.

"Sit down," said Spaulding to his captives.

They sat, coats half off their shoulders. David approached them and yanked the garments further—down to the elbows.

The two men in the grotesque stocking masks were seated now, their arms locked by their own clothes.

Standing in front of them, Spaulding reached down and ripped the silk masks off their faces. He moved back and leaned against the dining table, his pistol in his hand.

"All right," he said. "I estimate we've got about fifteen minutes before all hell breaks loose around here. . . . I have a few questions. You're going to give me the answers."

## 36

Spaulding listened in disbelief. The enormity of the charge
was so far-reaching it was—in a very real sense—beyond
his comprehension.

The man with the hollow eyes was Asher Feld, commander of the Provisional Wing of the Haganah operating
within the United States. He did the talking.

"The operation . . . the exchange of the guidance designs
for the industrial diamonds . . . was first given the name
'Tortugas' by the Americans—one American, to be exact.
He had decided that the transfer should be made in the
Dry Tortugas, but it was patently rejected by Berlin. It
was, however, kept as a code name by this man. The
misleading association dovetailed with his own panic at
being involved. It came—for him and for Fairfax—to
mean the activities of the man from Lisbon.

"When the War Department clearances were issued to
the Koening company's New York offices—an Allied
requisite—this man coded the clearance as 'Tortugas.' If
anyone checked, 'Tortugas' was a Fairfax operation. It
would not be questioned.

"The concept of the negotiation was first created by the
Nachrichtendienst. I'm sure you've heard of the Nachrichtendienst, colonel. . . ."

David did not reply. He could not speak. Feld continued.

"We of the Haganah learned of it in Geneva. We had
word of an unusual meeting between an American named
Kendall—a financial analyst for a major aircraft company
—and a very despised German businessman, a homosexual, who was sent to Switzerland by a leading administra-
tor in the Ministry of Armaments, Unterstaatssekretär

Franz Altmüller. . . . The Haganah is everywhere, colonel, including the outer offices of the ministry and in the Luft-waffe. . . ."

David continued to stare at the Jew, so matter of fact in his extraordinary . . . unbelievable . . . narrative.

"I think you'll agree that such a meeting was unusual. It was not difficult to maneuver these two messengers into a situation that gave us a wire recording. It was in an out-of-the-way restaurant and they were amateurs.

"We then knew the basics. The materials and the general location. But not the specific point of transfer. And that was the all-important factor. Buenos Aires is enormous, its harbor more so—stretching for miles. Where in this vast area of land and mountains and water was the transfer to take place?

"Then, of course, came word from Fairfax. The man in Lisbon was being recalled. A most unusual action. But then how well thought out. The finest network specialist in Europe, fluent German and Spanish, an expert in blueprint designs. How logical. Don't you agree?"

David started to speak, but stopped. Things were being said that triggered flashes of lightning in his mind. And unbelievable cracks of thunder . . . as unbelievable as the words he was hearing. He could only nod his head. Numbly.

Feld watched him closely. Then spoke.

"In New York I explained to you, albeit briefly, the sabotage at the airfield in Terceira. Zealots. The fact that the man in Lisbon could turn and be a part of the ex-change was too much for the hot-tempered Spanish Jews. No one was more relieved than we of the Provisional Wing when you escaped. We assumed your stopover in New York was for the purposes of refining the logistics in Buenos Aires. We proceeded on that assumption.

"Then quite abruptly there was no more time. Reports out of Johannesburg—unforgivably delayed—said that the diamonds had arrived in Buenos Aires. We took the neces-sary violent measures, including an attempt to kill you. Prevented, I presume, by Rhinemann's men." Asher Feld stopped. Then added wearily, "The rest you know."

*No! The rest he did not know! Nor any other part!*
*Insanity!*
*Madness!*

*Everything was nothing! Nothing was everything!*
*The years! The lives! . . . The terrible nightmares of fear*
*. . . the killing! Oh, my God, the killing!*
*For what?! . . . Oh, my God! For what?!*

"You're *lying!*" David crashed his hand down on the table. The steel of the pistol cracked against the wood with such force the vibration filled the room. "You're *lying!*" he cried; he did not shout. "I'm in Buenos Aires to buy gyroscopic designs! To have them authenticated! Confirmed by code so that son of a bitch gets paid in Switzerland! That's all. *Nothing else! Nothing else at all! Not this!*"

"Yes. . . ." Asher Feld spoke softly. "It is this."

David whirled around at nothing. He stretched his neck; the crashing thunder in his head would not stop, the blinding flashes of light in front of his eyes were causing a terrible pain. He saw the bodies on the floor, the blood . . . the corpses on the sofa, the blood.

Tableau of death.

*Death.*

His whole shadow world had been ripped out of orbit. A thousand gambles . . . pains, manipulations, death. And more death . . . all faded into a meaningless void. The betrayal—if it was a betrayal—was so immense . . . hundreds of thousands had been sacrificed for absolutely nothing.

He had to stop. He had to think. To concentrate.

He looked at the painfully gaunt Eugene Lyons, his face a sheet of white.

*The man's dying*, thought Spaulding.

*Death.*

*He had to concentrate.*

*Oh, Christ!* He had to *think*. Start *somewhere. Think. Concentrate.*

Or he would go out of his mind.

He turned to Feld. The Jew's eyes were compassionate. They might have been something else, but they were not. They were compassionate.

And yet, they were the eyes of a man who killed in calm deliberation.

As he, the man in Lisbon, had killed.

*Execution.*

*For what?*

There were questions. *Concentrate on the questions.*

*Listen.* Find error. *Find error*—if ever error was needed in this world it was *now!*

"I don't believe you," said David, trying as he had never tried in his life to be convincing.

"I think you do," replied Feld quietly. "The girl, Leslie Hawkwood, told us you didn't know. A judgment we found difficult to accept. . . . I accept it now."

David had to think for a moment. He did not, at first, recognize the name. *Leslie Hawkwood.* And then, of course, he did instantly. Painfully. "How is she involved with you?" he asked numbly.

"Herold Goldsmith is her uncle. By marriage, of course; she's not Jewish."

"Goldsmith? The name . . . doesn't mean anything to me." . . . *Concentrate!* He had to concentrate and speak rationally.

"It does to thousands of Jews. He's the man behind the Baruch and Lehman negotiations. He's done more to get our people out of the camps than any man in America. . . . He refused to have anything to do with us until the civilized, compassionate men in Washington, London and the Vatican turned their backs on him. Then he came to us . . . in fury. He created a hurricane; his niece was swept up in it. She's overly dramatic, perhaps, but committed, effective. She moves in circles barred to the Jew."

*"Why?"* . . . *Listen!* For God's sake, *listen.* Be *rational. Concentrate!*

Asher Feld paused for a moment, his dark, hollow eyes clouded with quiet hatred. "She met dozens . . . hundreds, perhaps, of those Herold Goldsmith got out. She saw the photographs, heard the stories. It was enough. She was ready."

The calm was beginning to return to David. Leslie was the springboard he needed to come back from the madness. There were questions. . . .

"I can't reject the premise that Rhinemann bought the designs. . . ."

"Oh, come!" interrupted Feld. "You were the man in Lisbon. How often did your own agents—your best men —find Peenemünde invulnerable. Has not the German underground itself given up penetration?"

"No one ever gives up. On either side. The German

underground is *part* of this!" *That was the error*, thought David.

"If that were so," said Feld, gesturing his head toward the dead Germans on the couch, "then those men were members of the underground. You know the Haganah, Lisbon. We don't kill such men."

Spaulding stared at the quiet-spoken Jew and knew he told the truth.

"The other evening," said Spaulding quickly, "on Paraná. I was followed, beaten up . . . but I saw the IDs. They were Gestapo!"

"They were Haganah," replied Feld. "The Gestapo is our best cover. If they had been Gestapo that would presume knowledge of your function. . . . Would they have let you live?"

Spaulding started to object. The Gestapo would not risk killing in a neutral country; not with identification on their persons. Then he realized the absurdity of his logic. Buenos Aires was not Lisbon. Of course, they would kill him. And then he recalled the words of Heinrich Stoltz.

*We've checked at the highest levels . . . not the Gestapo . . . impossible. . . .*

And the strangely inappropriate apologia: *the racial theories of Rosenberg and Hitler are not shared . . . primarily an economic . . .*

A defense of the indefensible offered by a man whose loyalty was purportedly *not* to the Third Reich but to *Erich Rhinemann. A Jew.*

Finally, Bobby Ballard:

*. . . he's a believer . . . the real Junker item. . . .*

"Oh, my God," said David under his breath.

"You have the advantage, colonel. What is your choice? We're prepared to die; I say this in no sense heroically, merely as a fact."

Spaulding stood motionless. He spoke softly, incredulously. "Do you understand the implications? . . ."

"We've understood them," interrupted Feld, "since that day in Geneva your Walter Kendall met with Johann Dietricht."

David reacted as though slapped. "Johann . . . *Dietricht?*"

"The expendable heir of Dietricht Fabriken."

"J.D.," whispered Spaulding, remembering the crumpled yellow pages in Walter Kendall's New York office. The breasts, the testicles, the swastikas . . . the obscene, nervous scribblings of an obscene, nervous man. "Johann Dietricht . . . *J.D.*"

"Altmüller had him killed. In a way that precluded any . . ."

"*Why?*" asked David.

"To remove any connection with the Ministry of Armaments, is our thought; any association with the High Command. Dietricht initiated the negotiations to the point where they could be shifted to Buenos Aires. To Rhinemann. With Dietricht's death the High Command was one more step removed."

The items raced through David's mind: Kendall had fled Buenos Aires in panic; something had gone wrong. The accountant would not allow himself to be trapped, to be killed. And he, David, was to kill—or have killed—Erich Rhinemann. Second to the designs, Rhinemann's death was termed paramount. And with his death, Washington, too, was "one more step removed" from the exchange.

Yet there was Edmund Pace.

Edmund *Pace.*

*Never.*

"A man was killed," said David. "A Colonel Pace. . . ."

"In Fairfax," completed Asher Feld. "A necessary death. He was being used as you are being used. We deal in pragmatics. . . . Without knowing the consequences—or refusing to admit them to himself—Colonel Pace was engineering 'Tortugas.' "

"You could have *told* him. Not kill him! You could have stopped it! You *bastards!*"

Asher Feld sighed. "I'm afraid you don't understand the hysteria among your industrialists. Or those of the Reich. He would have been eliminated. . . . By removing him ourselves, we neutralized Fairfax. And all its considerable facilities."

There was no point in dwelling on the *necessity* of Pace's death, thought David. Feld, the pragmatist, was right: Fairfax had been removed from "Tortugas."

"Then Fairfax doesn't know."

"Our man does. But not enough."

"Who is he? Who's your man in Fairfax?"

Feld gestured to his silent companion. "He doesn't know and I won't tell you. You may kill me but I won't tell you."

Spaulding knew the dark-eyed Jew spoke the truth. "If Pace was used . . . and me. Who's using us?"

"I can't answer that."

"You know this much. You must have . . . thoughts. Tell me."

"Whoever gives you orders, I imagine."

"One man. . . ."

"We know. He's not very good, is he? There are others."

"*Who?* Where does it *stop?* State? The War Department? *The White House? Where*, for Christ's sake!?"

"Such territories have no meaning in these transactions. They vanish."

"*Men don't!* Men don't vanish!"

"Then look for those who dealt with Koening. In South Africa. Kendall's men. They created 'Tortugas.' " Asher Feld's voice grew stronger. "That's your affair, Colonel Spaulding. We only wish to stop it. We'll gladly *die* to stop it."

David looked at the thin-faced, sad-faced man. "It means that much? With what you know, what you believe? Is either side worth it?"

"One must have priorities. Even in lessening descent. If Peenemünde is saved . . . put back on schedule . . . the Reich has a bargaining power that is unacceptable to us. Look to Dachau; look to Auschwitz, to Belsen. Unacceptable."

David walked around the table and stood in front of the Jews. He put his Beretta in his shoulder holster and looked at Asher Feld.

"If you've lied to me, I'll kill you. And then I'll go back to Lisbon, into the north country, and wipe out every Haganah fanatic in the hills. Those I don't kill, I'll expose. . . . Put on your coats and get out of here. Take a room at the Alvear under the name of . . . Pace. *E. Pace.* I'll be in touch."

"Our weapons?" asked Feld, pulling his light grey overcoat over his shoulders.

"I'll keep them. I'm sure you can afford others. . . . And don't wait for us outside. There's an FMF vehicle cruising for me."

"What about 'Tortugas'?" Asher Feld was pleading.

"I said I'll be in touch!" shouted Spaulding. "Now, get out of here! . . . Pick up the Hawkwood girl; she's around the corner in the Renault. Here are the keys." David reached in his pocket and threw the keys to Asher Feld's companion, who caught them effortlessly. "Send her back to California. Tonight, if you can. No later than tomorrow morning. Is that clear?"

"Yes. . . . You *will* be in touch?"

"Get out of here," said Spaulding in exhaustion.

The two Haganah agents rose from their chairs, the younger going to the unconscious third man and lifting him off the floor, onto his shoulders. Asher Feld stood in the front hallway and turned, his gaze resting momentarily on the dead bodies, then over to Spaulding.

"You and I. We must deal in priorities. . . . The man from Lisbon is an extraordinary man." He turned to the door and held it open as his companion carried out the third man. He went outside, closing the door behind him.

David turned to Lyons. "Get the designs."

## 37

When the assault on 15 Terraza Verde had begun, Eugene Lyons had done a remarkable thing. It was so simple it had a certain cleanliness to it, thought Spaulding. He had taken the metal container with the designs, opened his bedroom window and dropped the case five feet below into the row of tiger lilies that grew along the side of the house. The window shut, he had then run into his bathroom and locked the door.

All things considered—the shock, the panic, his own acknowledged incapacities—he had taken the least expected action: he had kept his head. He had removed the container, not tried to conceal it; he had transferred it to an *accessible* place, and that was not to be anticipated by the fanatic men who dealt in complicated tactics and convoluted deceits.

David followed Lyons out of the house through the kitchen door and around to the side. He took the container from the physicist's trembling hands and helped the near-helpless man over the small fence separating the adjacent property. Together they ran behind the next two houses and cautiously edged their way toward the street. Spaulding kept his left hand extended, gripping Lyon's shoulder, holding him against the wall, prepared to throw him to the ground at the first hint of hostilities.

Yet David was not really expecting hostilities; he was convinced the Haganah had eliminated whatever Rhinemann guards were posted in front, for the obvious reason that Asher Feld had left by the front door. What he did think was possible was a last-extremity attempt by Asher Feld to get the designs. Or the sudden emergence of a Rhinemann vehicle from some near location—a vehicle whose occupants were unable to raise a radio signal from 15 Terraza Verde.

Each possible; neither really expected.

It was too late and too soon.

What David profoundly hoped he would find, however, was a blue green sedan cruising slowly around the streets. A car with small orange insignias on the bumpers that designated the vehicle as U.S. property. Ballard's "playground attendants"; the men from the FMF base.

It wasn't cruising. It was stationary, on the far side of the street, its parking lights on. Three men inside were smoking cigarettes, the glows illuminating the interior. He turned to Lyons.

"Let's go. Walk slowly, casually. The car's over there."

The driver and the man next to him got out of the automobile the moment Spaulding and Lyons reached the curb. They stood awkwardly by the hood, dressed in civilian clothes. David crossed the street, addressing them.

"Get in that goddamned car and get us out of here! And while you're at it, why don't you paint bull's-eyes all over the vehicle? You wouldn't be any more of a target than you are now!"

"Take it easy, buddy," replied the driver. "We just got here." He opened the rear door as Spaulding helped Lyons inside.

"You were supposed to be cruising, not parked like watchdogs!" David climbed in beside Lyons; the man at the far window squeezed over. The driver got behind the wheel, closed his door and started the engine. The third man remained outside. "Get him in here!" barked Spaulding.

"He'll remain where he is, colonel," said the man in the back seat next to Lyons. "He stays here."

"Who the hell are you?"

"Colonel Daniel Meehan, Fleet Marine Force, Naval Intelligence. And we want to know what the fuck's going on."

The car started up.

"You have no control over this exercise," said David slowly, deliberately. "And I don't have time for bruised egos. Get us to the embassy, please."

"Screw egos! We'd like a little simple clarification! You know what the hell is going on down in our section of town? This side trip to Telmo's just a minor inconvenience! I wouldn't be here except your goddamned name was mentioned by that smart-ass cryp! . . . *Jesus!*"

Spaulding leaned forward on the seat, staring at Meehan. "You'd better tell me what's going on in your section of town. And why my name gets you to Telmo."

The marine returned the look, glancing once—with obvious distaste—at the ashen Lyons. "Why not? Your friend cleared?"

"He is now. No one more so."

"We have three cruisers patrolling the Buenos Aires coastal zone plus a destroyer and a carrier somewhere out there. . . . Five hours ago we get a blue alert: prepare for a radio-radar blackout, all sea and aircraft to hold to, no movement. Forty-five minutes later there's a scrambler from Fairfax, source four-zero. Intercept one Colonel David Spaulding, also four-zero. He's to make contact pronto."

"With Fairfax?"

"*Only* with Fairfax. . . . So we send a man to your address on Córdoba. He doesn't find you but he *does* find a weird son of a bitch tearing up your place. He tries to take him and gets laid out. . . . He gets back to us a couple of hours later with creases in his head and guess who calls? Right on an open-line telephone!"

"Ballard," answered David quietly. "The embassy cryp."

"The smart-ass! He makes jokes and tells us to play games out at Telmo! Wait for you to decide to show." The marine colonel shook his head in disgust.

"You said the blue alert was preparation for radar silence . . . and radio."

"And all ships and planes immobilized," interrupted Meehan. "What the hell's coming *in* here? The whole goddamned General *Staff? Roosevelt? Churchill? Rin-tin-tin?* And what are *we?* The *enemy!*"

"It's not what's coming in, colonel," said David softly. "It's what's going out. . . . What's the time of activation?"

"It's damn loose. Anytime during the next forty-eight hours. How's that for a tight schedule?"

"Who's my contact in Virginia?"

"Oh. . . . Here." Meehan shifted in his seat, proffering a sealed yellow envelope that was the mark of a scrambled message. David reached across Lyons and took it.

There was the crackling static of a radio from the front seat followed by the single word "Redbird!" out of the speaker. The driver quickly picked up the dashboard microphone.

"Redbird acknowledge," said the marine.

The static continued but the words were clear. "The Spaulding intercept. Pick him up and bring him in. Four-zero orders from Fairfax. No contact with the embassy."

"You heard the man," laughed Meehan. "No embassy tonight, colonel."

David was stunned. He started to object—angrily, furiously; then he stopped. . . . Fairfax. No Nazi, but Haganah. Asher Feld had said it. The Provisional Wing dealt in practicalities. And the most practical objective during the next forty-eight hours was to immobilize the man with the codes. Washington would not activate a radio-radar blackout without them; and an enemy submarine surfacing to rendezvous with a trawler would be picked up on the screens and blown out of the water. The Koening diamonds—the Peenemünde tools—would be sent to the bottom of the South Atlantic.

Christ! The *irony*, thought David. Fairfax—*someone* at Fairfax—was doing precisely what *should* be done, motivated by concerns Washington—and the aircraft companies—refused to acknowledge! It—they—had other concerns: three-quarters of them were at Spaulding's feet. High-altitude gyroscopic designs.

David pressed his arm into Lyons's shoulder. The emaciated scientist continued to stare straight ahead but responded to Spaulding's touch with a hesitant nudge of his left elbow.

David shook his head and sighed audibly. He held up the yellow envelope and shrugged, placing it into his jacket pocket.

When his hand emerged it held a gun.

"I'm afraid I can't accept those orders, Colonel Meehan." Spaulding pointed the automatic at the marine's head; Lyons leaned back into the seat.

"What the hell are you doing!?" Meehan jerked forward; David clicked the firing pin of the weapon into hair-release.

"Tell your man to drive where I say. I don't want to kill you, colonel, but I will. It's a matter of priorities."

"You're a goddamned double agent! That's what Fairfax was onto!"

David sighed. "I wish it were that simple."

Lyons's hands trembled as he tightened the knots around Meehan's wrists. The driver was a mile down the dirt road, bound securely, lying in the border of the tall grass. The area was rarely traveled at night. They were in the hills of Colinas Rojas.

Lyons stepped back and nodded to Spaulding.

"Get in the car."

Lyons nodded again and started toward the automobile. Meehan rolled over and looked up at David.

"You're dead, Spaulding. You got a firing squad on your duty sheet. You're stupid, too. Your Nazi friends are going to lose this war!"

"They'd better," answered David. "As to executions, there may be a number of them. Right in Washington. That's what this is all about, colonel. . . . Someone'll find you both tomorrow. If you like, you can start inching your way west. Your driver's a mile or so down the road. . . . I'm sorry."

Spaulding gave Meehan a half-felt shrug of apology and ran to the FMF automobile. Lyons sat in the front seat and when the door light spilled over his face, David saw his eyes. Was it possible that in that look there was an attempt to communicate a sense of gratitude? Or approval? There wasn't time to speculate, so David smiled gently and spoke quietly.

"This has been terrible for you, I know. . . . But I can't think what else to do. I don't know. If you like, I'll get you back to the embassy. You'll be safe there."

David started the car and drove up a steep incline—one of many—in the Colinas Rojas. He would double back on a parallel road and reach the highway within ten or fifteen minutes; he would take Lyons to an outskirts taxi and give the driver instructions to deliver the physicist to the American embassy. It wasn't really what he wanted to do; but what else was there?

Then the words came from beside him. *Words!* Whispered, muffled, barely audible but clear! From the recesses of a tortured throat.

"I . . . stay with . . . you. Together. . . ."

Spaulding had to grip the wheel harshly for fear of losing control. The shock of the pained speech—and it *was* a speech for Eugene Lyons—had nearly caused him to drop his hands. He turned and looked at the scientist. In the flashing shadows he saw Lyons return his stare; the lips were set firmly, the eyes steady. Lyons knew exactly what he was doing; what they both were doing—*had* to do.

"All right," said David, trying to remain calm and precise. "I read you clearly. God knows I need all the help I can get. We both do. It strikes me we've got two powerful enemies. Berlin *and* Washington."

"I don't want any interruptions, Stoltz!" David yelled into the mouthpiece of the telephone in the small booth near Ocho Calle. Lyons was now behind the wheel of the FMF car ten yards away on the street. The motor was running. The scientist hadn't driven in twelve years but with half-words and gestures he convinced Spaulding he would be capable in an emergency.

"You can't behave this way!" was the panicked reply.

"I'm Pavlov, you're the dog! Now shut up and listen! There's a mess in Terraza Verde, if you don't know it by now. Your men are dead; so are mine. I've got the designs *and* Lyons. . . . Your nonexistent Gestapo are carrying out a number of executions!"

"*Impossible!*" screamed Stoltz.

"Tell that to the corpses, you incompetent son of a bitch! While you clean up that mess! . . . I want the rest of those designs, Stoltz. Wait for my call!" David slammed down the receiver and bolted out of the booth to the car. It was time for the radio. After that the envelope from Fairfax. Then Ballard at the embassy. One step at a time.

Spaulding opened the door and slid into the seat beside Lyons. The physicist pointed to the dashboard.

"Again . . ." was the single, painful word.

"Good," said Spaulding. "They're anxious. They'll listen hard." David snapped the panel switch and lifted the microphone out of its cradle. He pressed his fingers against the tiny wire speaker with such pressure that the mesh was bent; he covered the instrument with his hand and held it against his jacket as he spoke, moving it in circles so as to further distort the sound.

"Redbird to base . . . Redbird to base."

The static began, the voice angry. "Christ, Redbird! We've been trying to raise you for damn near two hours! That Ballard keeps calling! Where the hell are you!?"

"Redbird. . . . Didn't you get our last transmission?"

"*Transmission?* Shit, man! I can hardly hear this one. Hold on; let me get the CO."

"Forget it! No sweat. You're fading here again. We're on Spaulding. We're following him; he's in a vehicle . . . twenty-seven, *twenty-eight miles north*. . . ." David abruptly stopped talking.

"Redbird! Redbird! . . . Christ, this frequency's puke! . . . Twenty-eight miles north *where?* . . . I'm not reading you, Redbird! Redbird, acknowledge!"

". . . bird, acknowledge," said David directly into the microphone. "This radio needs maintenance, pal. Repeat. No problems. Will *return to base in approximately*. . . ."

Spaulding reached down and snapped the switch into the off position.

He got out of the car and went back to the telephone booth.

One step at a time. No blurring, no overlapping—each action defined, handled with precision.

Now it was the scramble from Fairfax. The deciphered code that would tell him the name of the man who was having him intercepted; the source four-zero, whose priority rating allowed him to send such commands from the transmission core of the intelligence compound.

The agent who walked with impunity in the highest classified alleyways and killed a man named Ed Pace on New Year's Eve.

The Haganah infiltration.

He had been tempted to rip open the yellow envelope the moment the FMF officer had given it to him in San Telmo, but he had resisted the almost irresistible temptation. He knew that he would be stunned no matter who it was—whether known to him or not; and no *matter* who it was he would have a name to fit the revenge he planned for the killer of his friend.

Such thoughts were obstructions. Nothing could hinder their swift but cautious ride to Ocho Calle; nothing could interfere with his thought-out contact with Heinrich Stoltz.

He withdrew the yellow envelope and slid his finger across the flap.

At first, the name meant nothing.

Lieutenant Colonel Ira Barden.

Nothing.

Then he remembered.

New Year's Eve!

Oh, *Christ*, did he remember! The tough-talking hard-nose who was second in command at Fairfax. Ed Pace's "best friend" who had mourned his "best friend's" death with army anger; who secretly had arranged for David to be flown to the Virginia base and participate in the wake-investigation; who had used the tragic killing to enter his "best friend's" dossier vaults . . . only to find nothing.

The man who insisted a Lisbon cryptographer named Marshall had been killed in the Basque country; who said he would run a check on Franz Altmüller.

Which, of course, he never did.

The man who tried to convince David that it would be in everyone's interest if Spaulding would flex the clearance regulations and explain his War Department assignment.

Which David nearly did. And now wished he had.

Oh, God! Why hadn't Barden *trusted* him? On the other hand, he could not. For to do so would have raised specific, unwanted speculations on Pace's murder.

Ira Barden was no fool. A fanatic, perhaps, but not foolish. He knew the man from Lisbon would kill him if Pace's death was laid at his feet.

*Heed the lesson of Fairfax. . . .*

*Jesus!* thought David. We fight each other, kill each other . . . we don't know our enemies any longer.

For *what?*

There was now a second reason to call Ballard. A name was not enough; he needed more than just a name. He would confront Asher Feld.

He picked up the telephone's receiver off the hook, held his coin and dialed.

Ballard got on the line, no humor in evidence.

"*Look*, David." Ballard had not used his first name in conversation before. Ballard was suppressing a lot of anger. "I won't pretend to understand how you people turn your dials, but if you're going to use *my* set, keep me informed!"

"A number of people were killed; I wasn't one of them.

That was fortunate but the circumstances prohibited my contacting you. Does that answer your complaint?"

Ballard was silent for several seconds. The silence was not just his reaction to the news, thought David. There was someone with Bobby. When the cryp spoke, he was no longer angry; he was hesitant, afraid.

"You're all right?"

"Yes. Lyons is with me."

"The FMF were too late. . . ." Ballard seemed to regret his statement. "I keep phoning, they keep avoiding. I think their car's lost."

"Not really. I've got it. . . ."

"Oh, Christ!"

"They left one man at Telmo—for observation. There were two others. They're not hurt; they've disqualified."

"What the hell does *that* mean?"

"I haven't got time to explain. . . . There's an intercept order out for me. From Fairfax. The embassy's not supposed to know. It's a setup; I can't let them take me. Not for a while. . . ."

"Hey, we don't mess with Fairfax," said Ballard firmly.

"You can this time. I told Jean. There's a security breach in Fairfax. I'm not it, believe that. . . . I've *got* to have time. Maybe as much as forty-eight hours. I need questions answered. Lyons can help. For God's sake, trust me!"

"I can trust you but I'm no big deal here. . . . Wait a minute. Jean's with me. . . ."

"I thought so," interrupted Spaulding. It had been David's intention to ask Ballard for the help he needed. He suddenly realized that Jean could be far more helpful.

"Talk to her before she scratches the skin off my hand."

"Before you get off, Bobby. . . . Could you run a priority check on someone in Washington? In Fairfax, to be exact?"

"I'd have to have a reason. The subject—an Intelligence subject, *especially* Fairfax—would probably find out."

"I don't give a damn if he does. Say I demanded it. My rating's four-zero; G-2 has that in the records. I'll take the responsibility."

"Who is it?"

"A lieutenant colonel named Ira Barden. Got it?"

"Yes. Ira Barden. Fairfax."

"Right. Now let me talk to . . ."

Jean's words spilled over one another, a mixture of fury and love, desperation and relief.

"Jean," he said when she had finished a half-dozen questions he couldn't possibly answer, "the other night you made a suggestion I refused to take seriously. I'm taking it seriously now. That mythical David of yours needs a place to hide out. It can't be the pampas, but any place nearer will do. . . . Can you help me? Help us? For *God's sake!*"

# 38

He would call Jean later, before daybreak. He and Lyons had to move in darkness, wherever they were going. Wherever Jean could find them sanctuary.

There would be no codes sent to Washington, no clearance given for the obscene exchange, no radio or radar blackouts that would immobilize the fleet. David understood that; it was the simplest, surest way to abort "Tortugas."

But it was not enough.

There were the men behind "Tortugas." They had to be yanked up from the dark recesses of their filth and exposed to the sunlight. If there was any meaning left, if the years of pain and fear and death made any sense at all, they had to be given to the world in all their obscenity.

The world deserved that. Hundreds of thousands—on both sides—who would carry the scars of war throughout their lives, deserved it.

They had to understand the meaning of *For what*.

David accepted his role; he would face the men of "Tortugas." But he could not face them with the testimony of a fanatical Jew. The words of Asher Feld, leader of the Haganah's Provisional Wing, were no testimony at all. Fanatics were madmen; the world had seen enough of both, for both were one. And they were dismissed. Or killed. Or both.

David knew he had no choice.

When he faced the men of "Tortugas," it would not be with the words of Asher Feld. Or with deceptive codes and manipulations that were subject to a hundred interpretations.

*Deceits. Cover-ups. Removals.*

He would face them with what he saw. What he knew, because he had borne witness. He would present them with the irrefutable. And then he would destroy them.

To do this—all this—he had to get aboard the trawler in Ocho Calle. The trawler that would be blown out of the water should it attempt to run the harbor and rendezvous with a German submarine.

That it ultimately would attempt such a run was inevitable. The fanatic mind would demand it. Then there would be no evidence of things seen. Sworn to.

He had to get aboard that trawler now.

He gave his final instructions to Lyons and slid into the warm, oily waters of the Río de la Plata. Lyons would remain in the car—drive it, if necessary—and, if David did not return, allow ninety minutes to elapse before going to the FMF base and telling the commanding officer that David was being held prisoner aboard the trawler. An American agent held prisoner.

There was logic in the strategy. FMF had priority orders to bring in David; orders from Fairfax. It would be three thirty in the morning. Fairfax called for swift, bold action. Especially at three thirty in the morning in a neutral harbor.

It was the bridge David tried always to create for himself in times of high-risk infiltration. It was the trade-off; his life for a lesser loss. The lessons of the north country.

He did not want it to happen that way. There were too many ways to immobilize him; too many panicked men in Washington and Berlin to let him survive, perhaps. At best there would be compromise. At worst. . . . The collapse of "Tortugas" was not enough, the indictment was everything.

His pistol was tight against his head, tied with a strip of his shirt, the cloth running through his teeth. He breast-stroked toward the hull of the ship, keeping his head out of the water, the firing pin mechanism of his weapon as dry as possible. The price was mouthfuls of filthy, gasoline-polluted water, made further sickening by the touch of a large conger eel attracted, then repelled, by the moving white flesh.

He reached the hull. Waves slapped gently, unceasingly, against the hard expanse of darkness. He made his way to the stern of the ship, straining his eyes and his ears for evidence of life.

Nothing but the incessant lapping of water.

There was light from the deck but no movement, no shadows, no voices. Just the flat, colorless spill of naked bulbs strung on black wires, swaying in slow motion to the sluggish rhythm of the hull. On the port side of the ship—the dockside—were two lines looped over the aft and mid-ships pilings. Rat disks were placed every ten feet or so; the thick manila hemps were black with grease and oil slick. As he approached, David could see a single guard sitting in a chair by the huge loading doors, which were shut. The chair was tilted back against the warehouse wall; two wire-mesh lamps covered by metal shades were on both sides of the wide doorframe. Spaulding treaded backward to get a clearer view. The guard was dressed in the paramilitary clothes of Habichtsnest. He was reading a book; for some reason that fact struck David as odd.

Suddenly, there were footsteps at the west section of the warehouse dock. They were slow, steady; there was no attempt to muffle the noise.

The guard looked up from his book. Between the pilings David could see a second figure come into view. It was another guard wearing the Rhinemann uniform. He was carrying a leather case, the same radio case carried by the men—dead men—at 15 Terraza Verde.

The guard in the chair smiled and spoke to the standing sentry. The language was German.

"I'll trade places, if you wish," said the man in the chair. "Get off your feet for a while."

"No, thanks," replied the man with the radio. "I'd rather walk. Passes the time quicker."

"Anything new from Luján?"

"No change. Still a great deal of excitement. I can hear snatches of yelling now and then. Everybody's giving orders."

"I wonder what happened in Telmo."

"Bad trouble is all I know. They've blocked us off; they've sent men to the foot of Ocho Calle."

"You heard that?"

"No. I spoke with Geraldo. He and Luis are here. In front of the warehouse; in the street."

"I hope they don't wake up the whores."

The man with the radio laughed. "Even Geraldo can do better than those dogs."

"Don't bet good money on that," replied the guard in the chair.

The guard on foot laughed again and proceeded east on his solitary patrol around the building. The man in the chair returned to his book.

David sidestroked his way back toward the hull of the trawler.

His arms were getting tired; the foul-smelling waters of the harbor assaulted his nostrils. And now he had something else to consider: Eugene Lyons.

Lyons was a quarter of a mile away, diagonally across the water, four curving blocks from the foot of Ocho Calle. If Rhinemann's patrols began cruising the area, they would find the FMF vehicle with Lyons in it. It was a bridge he hadn't considered. He should have considered it.

But he couldn't think about that now.

He reached the starboard midships and held onto the waterline ledge, giving the muscles of his arms and shoulders a chance to throb in relief. The trawler was in the medium-craft classification, no more than seventy or eighty feet in length, perhaps a thirty-foot midship beam. By normal standards, and from what David could see as he approached the boat in darkness, the mid and aft cabins below the wheel shack were about fifteen and twenty feet long, respectively, with entrances at both ends and two portholes per cabin on the port and starboard sides. If the Koening diamonds *were* on board, it seemed logical that they'd be in the aft cabin, farthest away from the crew's normal activity. Too, aft cabins had more room and fewer distractions. And if Asher Feld was right, if two or three Peenemünde scientists were microscopically examining the Koening products, they would be under a pressured schedule and require isolation.

David found his breath coming easier. He'd know soon enough whether and where the diamonds were or were not. In moments.

He untied the cloth around his head, treading water as he did so, holding the pistol firmly. The shirt piece drifted away; he held onto the line ledge and looked above. The gunwale was six to seven feet out of the water; he would need both his hands to claw his way up the tiny ridges of the hull.

He spat out what harbor residue was in his mouth and clamped the barrel of the gun between his teeth. The only clothing he wore was his trousers; he plunged his hands beneath the water, rubbing them against the cloth in an effort to remove what estuary slick he could.

He gripped the line ledge once again and with his right hand extended, kicked his body out of the water and reached for the next tiny ridge along the hull. His fingers grasped the half-inch sprit; he pulled himself up, slapping his left hand next to his right, pushing his chest into the rough wood for leverage. His bare feet were near the water's surface, the gunwale no more than three feet above him now.

Slowly he raised his knees until the toes of both feet rested on the waterline ledge. He paused for breath, knowing that his fingers would not last long on the tiny ridge. He tensed the muscles of his stomach and pressed his aching toes against the ledge, pushing himself up as high as possible, whipping out his hands; knowing, again, that if he missed the gunwale he would plunge back into the water. The splash would raise alarms.

The left hand caught; the right slipped off. But it was enough.

He raised himself to the railing, his chest scraping against the rough, weathered hull until spots of blood emerged on his skin. He looped his left arm over the side and removed the pistol from his mouth. He was—as he hoped he would be—at the midpoint between the fore and aft cabins, the expanse of wall concealing him from the guards on the loading dock.

He silently rolled over the gunwale onto the narrow deck and took the necessary crouching steps to the cabin wall. He pressed his back into the wooden slats and slowly stood up. He inched his way toward the first aft porthole; the light from within was partially blocked by a primitive curtain of sorts, pulled back as if parted for the night air. The second porthole farther down had no such obstruction, but it was only feet from the edge of the wall; there was the possibility that a sentry—unseen from the water—might be stern watch there. He would see whatever there was to see in the first window.

His wet cheek against the rotted rubber surrounding the porthole, he looked inside. The "curtain" was a heavy sheet of black tarpaulin folded back at an angle. Beyond, the light was as he had pictured it: a single bulb suspended from the ceiling by a thick wire—a wire that ran out a port window to a pier outlet. Ship generators were not abused while at dock. There was an odd-shaped, flat piece of metal hanging on the side of the bulb, and at first David was not sure why it was there. And then he understood: the sheet of metal deflected the light of the bulb from the rear of the cabin, where he could make out—beyond the fold of the tarp—two bunk beds. Men were sleeping; the light remained on but they were in relative shadow.

On the far side of the cabin, butted against the wall, was a long table that had the incongruous appearance of a hospital laboratory workbench. It was covered by a taut, white, spotless oilcloth and on the cloth, equidistant from one another, were four powerful microscopes. Beside each instrument was a high-intensity lamp—all the wires leading to a twelve-volt utility battery under the table. On the floor in front of the microscopes were four high-backed stools— four white, spotless stools standing at clinical attention.

That was the effect, thought David. Clinical. This isolated section of the trawler was in counterpoint to the rest of the filthy ship: it was a small, clinical island surrounded by rotted sea waste and rat disks.

And then he saw them. In the corner.

Five steel crates, each with metal strips joined at the top edges and held in place with heavy vault locks. On the front of each crate was the clearly stenciled name: KOENING MINES, LTD.

He'd seen it now. The undeniable, the irrefutable.

*Tortugas.*

The obscene exchange funneled through Erich Rhinemann.

And he was so close, so near possession. The final indictment.

Within his fear—and he *was* afraid—furious anger and deep temptation converged. They were sufficient to suspend his anxiety, to force him to concentrate only on the objective. To believe—knowing the belief was false—in some mystical invulnerability, granted for only a few precious minutes.

That was enough.

He ducked under the first porthole and approached the second. He stood up and looked in; the door of the cabin was in his direct line of sight. It was a new door, not part of the trawler. It was steel and in the center was a bolt at least an inch thick, jammed into a bracket in the frame.

The Peenemünde scientists were not only clinically isolated, they were in a self-imposed prison.

That bolt, David realized, was his personal Alpine pass —to be crossed without rig.

He crouched and passed under the porthole to the edge of the cabin wall. He remained on his knees and, millimeter by millimeter, the side of his face against the wood, looked around the corner.

The guard was there, of course, standing his harbor watch in the tradition of such sentry duty: on deck, the inner line of defense; bored, irritated with his boredom, relaxed in his inactivity yet annoyed by its pointlessness.

But he was not in the paramilitary clothes of Habichtsnest. He was in a loose-fitting suit that did little to conceal a powerful—military—body. His hair was cut short, Wehrmacht style.

He was leaning against a large fishing net winch, smoking a thin cigar, blowing the smoke aimlessly into the night air. At his side was an automatic rifle, .30 caliber, the shoulder strap unbuckled, curled on the deck. The rifle had not been touched for quite some time; the strap had a film of moisture on the surface of the leather.

The strap. . . . David took the belt from his trousers. He stood up, inched back toward the porthole, reached underneath the railing and removed one of two gunwale spikes which were clamped against the inner hull for the fish nets. He tapped the railing softly twice; then twice again. He heard the shuffling of the guard's feet. No forward movement, just a change of position.

He tapped again. Twice. Then twice more. The quietly precise tapping—intentional, spaced evenly—was enough to arouse curiosity; insufficient to cause alarm.

He heard the guard's footsteps now. Still relaxed, the forward motion easy, not concerned with danger, only curious. A piece of harbor driftwood, perhaps, slapping against the hull, caught in the push-pull of the current.

The guard rounded the corner; Spaulding's belt whipped around his neck, instantly lashed taut, choking off the cry.

David twisted the leather as the guard sank to his knees, the face darkening perceptibly in the dim spill of light from the porthole, the lips pursed in strangled anguish.

David did not allow his victim to lose consciousness; he had the Alpine pass to cross. Instead, he wedged his pistol into his trousers, reached down to the scabbard on the guard's waist, and took out the carbine bayonet—a favorite knife of combat men, rarely used on the front of any rifle. He held the blade under the guard's eyes and whispered.

"*Español* or *Deutsch?*"

The man stared up in terror. Spaulding twisted the leather tighter; the guard choked a cough and struggled to raise two fingers. David whispered again, the blade pushing against the skin under the right eyeball.

"*Deutsch?*"

The man nodded.

Of course he was German, thought Spaulding. And Nazi. The clothes, the hair. Peenemünde *was* the Third Reich. Its scientists would be guarded by their own. He twisted the blade of the carbine bayonet so that a tiny laceration appeared under the eye. The guard's mouth opened in fright.

"You do exactly what I tell you," whispered David in German into the guard's ear, "or I'll carve out your sight. Understand?"

The man, nearly limp, nodded.

"Get up and call through the porthole. You have an urgent message from . . . Altmüller, Franz Altmüller! They must open the door and sign for it. . . . Do it! Now! And remember, this knife is inches from your eyes."

The guard, in shock, got up. Spaulding pushed the man's face to the open porthole, loosened the belt only slightly, and shifted his position to the side of the man and the window, his left hand holding the leather, his right the knife.

"*Now!*" whispered David, flicking the blade in half circles.

At first the guard's voice was strained, artificial. Spaulding moved in closer; the guard knew he had only seconds to live if he did not perform.

He performed.

There was stirring in the bunk beds within the cabin. Grumbling complaints to begin with, ceasing abruptly at the mention of Altmüller's name.

A small, middle-aged man got out of the left lower bunk and walked sleepily to the steel door. He was in undershorts, nothing else. David propelled the guard around the corner of the wall and reached the door at the sound of the sliding bolt.

He slammed the guard against the steel panel with the twisted belt; the door flung open, David grabbed the knob, preventing it from crashing into the bulkhead. He dropped the knife, yanked out his pistol, and crashed the barrel into the skull of the small scientist.

"*Schweigen!*" he whispered hoarsely. "*Wenn Ihnen Ihr Leben lieb ist!*"

The three men in the bunks—older men, one old man—stumbled out of their beds, trembling and speechless. The guard, choking still, began to focus around him and started to rise. Spaulding took two steps and slashed the pistol diagonally across the man's temple, splaying him out on the deck.

The old man, less afraid than his two companions, stared at David. For reasons Spaulding could not explain to himself, he felt ashamed. Violence was out of place in this antiseptic cabin.

"I have no quarrel with you," he whispered harshly in German. "You follow orders. But don't mistake me, I'll kill you if you make a sound!" He pointed to some papers next to a microscope; they were filled with numbers and columns. "You!" He gestured his pistol at the old man. "Give me those! Quickly!"

The old man trudged haltingly across the cabin to the clinical work area. He lifted the papers off the table and handed them to Spaulding, who stuffed them into his wet trousers pocket.

"Thanks. . . . Now!" He pointed his weapon at the other two. "Open one of those crates! Do it now!"

"No! . . . No! For God's sake!" said the taller of the middle-aged scientists, his voice low, filled with fear.

David grabbed the old man standing next to him. He clamped his arm around the loose flesh of the old neck and brought his pistol up to the head. He thumbed back the firing pin and spoke calmly. "You will open a crate or I

will kill this man. When he's dead, I'll turn my pistol on
you. Believe me, I have no alternative."

The shorter man whipped his head around, pleading silently with the taller one. The old man in David's grasp
was the leader; Spaulding knew that. An old . . . *alter-
Anführer*; always take the German leader.

The taller Peenemünde scientist walked—every step in
fear—to the far corner of the clinical workbench, where
there was a neat row of keys on the wall. He removed one
and hesitantly went to the first steel crate. He bent down
and inserted the key in the vault lock holding the metal
strip around the edge; the strip snapped apart in the center.

"Open the lid!" commanded Spaulding, his anxiety causing his whisper to become louder; too loud, he realized.

The cover of the steel crate was heavy; the German had
to lift it with both hands, the wrinkles around his eyes and
mouth betraying the effort required. Once at a ninety-
degree angle, chains on both sides became taut; there was a
click of a latch and the cover was locked in place.

Inside were dozens of identically matched compartments
in what appeared to be sliding trays—something akin to a
large, complicated fishing tackle box. Then David understood: the front of the steel case was on hinges; it too
could be opened—or lowered, to be exact—allowing the
trays to slide out.

In each compartment were two small, heavy, paper envelopes, apparently lined with layers of soft tissue. There
were dozens of envelopes on the top tray alone.

David released the old man, propelling him back toward
the bunk beds. He waved his pistol at the tall German who
had opened the crate, ordering him to join the other two.
He reached down into the steel crate, picked out a small
envelope and brought it to his mouth, tearing the edge with
his teeth. He shook it toward the ground; tiny translucent
nuggets spattered over the cabin deck.

The Koening diamonds.

He watched the German scientists as he crumpled the
envelope. They were staring at the stones on the floor.

Why not? thought David. In that cabin was the solution
for Peenemünde. In those crates were the tools to rain
death on untold thousands . . . as the gyroscopic designs
for which they were traded would make possible further
death, further massacre.

He was about to throw away the envelope in disgust and fill his pockets with others when his eyes caught sight of some lettering. He unwrinkled the envelope, his pistol steady on the Germans, and looked down. The single word:

# echt

True. Genuine. This envelope, this tray, this steel case had passed inspection.

He reached down and grabbed as many envelopes as his left hand could hold and stuffed them into his trousers pocket.

It was all he needed for the indictment.

It was everything. It was the meaning.

There was one thing more he could do. Of a more immediately practical nature. He crossed to the workbench and went down the line of four microscopes, crashing the barrel of his pistol up into each lens and down into the eyepieces. He looked for a laboratory case, the type which carried optical equipment. There had to be one!

It was on the floor beneath the long table. He kicked it out with his bare foot and reached down to open the hasp.

More slots and trays, only these filled with lenses and small black tubes in which to place them.

He bent down and overturned the case; dozens of circular lenses fell out onto the deck. As fast as he could he grabbed the nearest white stool and brought it down sideways into the piles of glass.

The destruction wasn't total, but the damage was enough, perhaps, for forty-eight hours.

He started to get up, his weapon still on the scientists, his ears and eyes alert.

He heard it! He sensed it! And simultaneously he understood that if he did not spin out of the way he would be dead!

He threw himself on the floor to the right; the hand above and behind him came down, the carbine bayonet slicing the air, aimed for the spot where his neck had been less than a second ago.

He had left the goddamned bayonet on the floor! He

had discarded the goddamned *bayonet!* The guard had revived and *taken* the goddamned *bayonet!*

The Nazi's single cry emerged before Spaulding leaped on his kneeling form, smashing his skull into the wood floor with such force that blood spewed out in tiny bursts throughout the head.

But the lone cry was enough.

"Is something wrong?" came a voice from outside, twenty yards away on the loading dock. "Heinrich! Did you call?"

There was no second, no instant, to throw away on hesitation.

David ran to the steel door, pulled it open and raced around the corner of the wall to the concealed section of the gunwale. As he did so, a guard—the sentry on the bow of the trawler—came into view. His rifle was waist high and he fired.

Spaulding fired back. But not before he realized he was hit. The Nazi's bullet had creased the side of his waist; he could feel the blood oozing down into his trousers.

He threw himself over the railing into the water; screams and shouts started from inside the cabin and farther away on the pier.

He thrashed against the dirty Río slime and tried to keep his head. Where was he? What direction! Where? For Christ's sake, *where!*

The shouts were louder now; searchlights were turned on all over the trawler, crisscrossing the harbor waters. He could hear men screaming into radios as only panicked men can scream. Accusing, helpless.

Suddenly, David realized there were no boats! No boats were coming out of the pier with the searchlights and high-powered rifles that would be his undoing!

No boats!

And he nearly laughed. The operation at Ocho Calle was so totally secretive they had allowed no small craft to put into the deserted area!

He held his side, going under water as often as he could, as fast as he could.

The trawler and the screaming Rhinemann-Altmüller guards were receding in the harbor mist. Spaulding kept bobbing his head up, hoping to God he was going in the right direction.

He was getting terribly tired, but he would not allow himself to grow weak. He *could not* allow that! Not now!

He had the "Tortugas" indictment!

He saw the pilings not far away. Perhaps two, three hundred yards. They *were* the right pilings, the right piers! They... it, *had* to be!

He felt the waters around him stir and then he saw the snakelike forms of the conger eels as they lashed blindly against his body. The blood from his wound was attracting them! A horrible mass of slashing giant worms were converging!

He thrashed and kicked and fought down a scream. He pulled at the waters in front of him, his hands in constant contact with the oily snakes of the harbor. His eyes were filled with flashing dots and streaks of yellow and white; his throat was dry in the water, his forehead pounded.

When it seemed at last the scream would come, *had* to come, he felt the hand in his hand. He felt his shoulders being lifted, heard the guttural cries of his own terrified voice—deep, frightened beyond his own endurance. He could look down and see, as his feet kept slipping off the ladder, the circles of swarming eels below.

Eugene Lyons carried him—*carried* him!—to the FMF automobile. He was aware—yet not aware—of the fact that Lyons pushed him gently into the back seat.

And then Lyons climbed in after him, and David understood—yet did not understand—that Lyons was slapping him. Hard. Harder.

Deliberately. Without rhythm but with a great deal of strength.

The slapping would not stop! He couldn't make it stop! He couldn't stop the half-destroyed, throatless Lyons from slapping him.

He could only cry. Weep as a child might weep.

And then suddenly he *could* make him stop. He took his hands from his face and grabbed Lyons's wrists, prepared, if need be, to break them.

He blinked and stared at the physicist.

Lyons smiled in the shadows. He spoke in his tortured whisper.

"I'm sorry. . . . You were . . . in temporary . . . shock. My friend."

## 39

An elaborate naval first aid kit was stored in the trunk of the FMF vehicle. Lyons filled David's wound with sulfa powder, laid on folded strips of gauze and pinched the skin together with three-inch adhesive. Since the wound was a gash, not a puncture, the bleeding stopped; it would hold until they reached a doctor. Even should the wait be a day or a day and a half, there would be no serious damage.

Lyons drove.

David watched the emaciated man behind the wheel. He was unsure but willing; that was the only way to describe him. Every now and then his foot pressed too hard on the accelerator, and the short bursts of speed frightened him— then annoyed him. Still, after a few minutes, he seemed to take a careful delight in manipulating the car around corners.

David knew he had to accomplish three things: reach Henderson Granville, talk to Jean and drive to that sanctuary he hoped to Christ Jean had found for them. If a doctor could be brought to him, fine. If not, he would sleep; he was beyond the point of functioning clearly without rest.

How often in the north country had he sought out isolated caves in the hills? How many times had he piled branches and limbs in front of small openings so his body and mind could restore the balance of objectivity that might save his life? He had to find such a resting place now.

And tomorrow he would make the final arrangements with Erich Rhinemann.

The final pages of the indictment.

"We have to find a telephone," said David. Lyons nodded as he drove.

David directed the physicist back into the center of Buenos Aires. By his guess they still had time before the FMF base sent out a search. The orange insignias on the bumpers would tend to dissuade the BA police from becoming too curious; the Americans were children of the night.

He remembered the telephone booth on the north side of the Casa Rosada. The telephone booth in which a hired gun from the Unio Corso—sent down from Rio de Janeiro —had taken his last breath.

They reached the Plaza de Mayo in fifteen minutes, taking a circular route, making sure they were not followed. The Plaza was not deserted. It was, as the prewar travel posters proclaimed, a Western Hemisphere Paris. Like Paris, there were dozens of early stragglers, dressed mainly in expensive clothes. Taxis stopped and started; prostitutes made their last attempts to find profitable beds; the streetlights illuminated the huge fountains; lovers dabbled their hands in the pools.

The Plaza de Mayo at three thirty in the morning was not a barren, dead place to be. And David was grateful for that.

Lyons pulled the car up to the telephone booth and Spaulding got out.

"Whatever it is, you've hit the rawest nerve in Buenos Aires." Granville's voice was hard and precise. "I must demand that you return to the embassy. For your own protection as well as the good of our diplomatic relations."

"You'll have to be clearer than that, I'm afraid," replied David.

Granville was.

The "one or two" contacts the ambassador felt he could reach in the Grupo were reduced, of course, to one. That man made inquiries as to the trawler in Ocho Calle and subsequently was taken from his home under guard. That was the information Granville gathered from a hysterical wife.

An hour later the ambassador received word from a GOU liaison that his "friend" had been killed in an automobile accident. The GOU wanted him to have the news. It was most unfortunate.

When Granville tried reaching the wife, an operator cut in, explaining that the telephone was disconnected.

"You've involved us, Spaulding! We can't function with Intelligence dead weight around our necks. The situation in Buenos Aires is extremely delicate."

"You *are* involved, sir. A couple of thousand miles away people are shooting at each other."

"Shit!" It was just about the most unexpected expletive David thought he could hear from Granville. "Learn your lines of demarcation! We all have jobs to do within the . . . artificial, if you like, parameters that are set for us! I repeat, sir. Return to the embassy and I'll expedite your immediate return to the United States. Or if you refuse, take yourself to FMF. *That's* beyond my jurisdiction; you will be no part of the embassy!"

*My God!* thought David. *Artificial parameters. Jurisdictions. Diplomatic nicetie*s. When men were dying, armies destroyed, cities obliterated! And men in high-ceilinged rooms played games with words and attitudes!

"I can't go to FMF. But I can give you something to think about. Within forty-eight hours all American ships and aircraft in the coastal zones are entering a radio and radar blackout! Everything grounded, immobilized. That's straight military holy writ. And I think you'd better find out why! Because I think I know, and if I'm right, your *diplomatic wreck* is filthier than anything you can imagine! Try a man named Swanson at the War Department. Brigadier Alan Swanson! And tell him I've found 'Tortugas'!"

David slammed down the receiver with such force that chips of Bakelite fell off the side of the telephone. He wanted to run. Open the door of the suffocating booth and race away.

But where to? There was nowhere.

He took several deep breaths and once more dialed the embassy.

Jean's voice was soft, filled with anxiety. But she had found a place!

He and Lyons were to drive due west on Rivadavia to the farthest outskirts of Buenos Aires. At the end of Rivadavia was a road bearing right—it could be spotted by a large statue of the Madonna at its beginning. The road led to the flat grass country, *provinciales* country. Thirty-six miles beyond the Madonna was another road—on the left—this marked by telephone junction wires converging into a transformer box on top of a double-strapped telephone pole. The road led to a ranch belonging to one Alfonso Quesarro. Señor Quesarro would not be there . . . under the circumstances. Neither would his wife. But a skeleton staff would be on; the remaining staff quarters would be available for Mrs. Cameron's unknown friends.

Jean would obey his orders: she would not leave the embassy.

And she loved him. Terribly.

Dawn came up over the grass country. The breezes were warm; David had to remind himself that it was January. The Argentine summer. A member of the skeleton staff of Estancia Quesarro met them several miles down the road past the telephone junction wires, on the property border, and escorted them to the *ranchería*—a cluster of small one-story cottages—near but not adjacent to the main buildings. They were led to an adobe farthest from the other houses; it was on the edge of a fenced grazing area, fields extending as far as the eye could see. The house was the residence of the *caporal*—the ranch foreman.

David understood as he looked up at the roof, at the single telephone line. Ranch foremen had to be able to use a telephone.

Their escort opened the door and stood in the frame, anxious to leave. He touched David's arm and spoke in a Spanish tempered with pampas Indian.

"The telephones out here are with operators. The service is poor; not like the city. I am to tell you this, *señor*."

But that information was not what the gaucho was telling him. He was telling him to be careful.

"I'll remember," said Spaulding. "Thank you."

The man left quickly and David closed the door. Lyons was standing across the room, in the center of a small monastery arch that led to some sort of sunlit enclosure. The metal case containing the gyroscopic designs was in his right hand; with his left he beckoned David.

Beyond the arch was a cubicle; in the center, underneath an oblong window overlooking the fields, there was a bed.

Spaulding undid the top of his trousers and peeled them off.

He fell with his full weight into the hard mattress and slept.

# 40

It seemed only seconds ago that he had walked through the small arch into the sunlit cubicle.

He felt the prodding fingers around his wound; he winced as a cold-hot liquid was applied about his waist and the adhesive ripped off.

He opened his eyes fiercely and saw the figure of a man bent over the bed. Lyons was standing beside him. At the edge of the hard mattress was the universal shape of a medical bag. The man bending over him was a doctor. He spoke in unusually clear English.

"You've slept nearly eight hours. That is the best prescription one could give you. . . . I'm going to suture this in three places; that should do it. There will be a degree of discomfort, but with the tape you'll be quite mobile."

"What time is it?" asked David.

Lyons looked at his watch. He whispered, and the words were clear. "Two . . . o'clock."

"Thank you for coming out here," said Spaulding, shifting his weight for the doctor's instruments.

"Wait until I'm back at my office in Palermo." The doctor laughed softly, sardonically. "I'm sure I'm on one of their lists." He inserted a suture, reassuring David with a tight smile. "I left word I was on a maternity call at an outback ranch. . . . There." He tied off the stitch and patted Spaulding's bare skin. "Two more and we're finished."

"Do you think you'll be questioned?"

"No. Not actually. The junta closes its eyes quite often. There's not an abundance of doctors here. . . . And amusingly enough, interrogators invariably seek free medical advice. I think it goes with their mentalities."

"And I think you're covering. I think it *was* dangerous."

The doctor held his hands in place as he looked at David. "Jean Cameron is a very special person. If the history of wartime Buenos Aires is written, she'll be prominently mentioned." He returned to the sutures without elaboration. David had the feeling that the doctor did not wish to talk further. He was in a hurry.

Twenty minutes later Spaulding was on his feet, the doctor at the door of the adobe hut. David shook the medical man's hand. "I'm afraid I can't pay you," he said.

"You already have, colonel. I'm a Jew."

Spaulding did not release the doctor's hand. Instead, he held it firmly—not in salutation. "Please explain."

"There's nothing to explain. The Jewish community is filled with rumors of an American officer who pits himself against the pig. . . . Rhinemann the pig."

"That's all?"

"It's enough." The doctor removed his hand from Spaulding's and walked out. David closed the door.

Rhinemann the pig. It was time for Rhinemann.


The teutonic, guttural voice screamed into the telephone. David could picture the blue-black veins protruding on the surface of the bloated, suntanned skin. He could see the narrow eyes bulging with fury.

"*It was you! It was you!*" The accusation was repeated over and over again, as if the repetition might provoke a denial.

"It was me," said David without emphasis.

"You are *dead!* You are a *dead man!*"

David spoke quietly, slowly. With precision. "If I'm dead, no codes are sent to Washington; no radar or radio blackout. The screens will pick up that trawler and the instant a submarine surfaces anywhere near it, it'll be blown out of the water."

Rhinemann was silent. Spaulding heard the German Jew's rhythmic breathing but said nothing. He let Rhinemann's thoughts dwell upon the implication. Finally Rhinemann spoke. With equal precision.

"Then you have something to say to me. Or you would not have telephoned."

"That's right," agreed David. "I have something to say. I

assume you're taking a broker's fee. I can't believe you arranged this exchange for nothing."

Rhinemann paused again. He replied cautiously, his breathing heavy, carried over the wire. "No. . . . It is a transaction. Accommodations must be paid for."

"But that payment comes later, doesn't it?" David kept his words calm, dispassionate. "You're in no hurry; you've got everyone where you want them. . . . There won't be any messages radioed out of Switzerland that accounts have been settled. The only message you'll get—or *won't* get—is from a submarine telling you the Koening diamonds have been transferred from the trawler. That's when I fly out of here with the designs. That's the signal." Spaulding laughed a brief, cold, quiet laugh. "It's very pro, Rhinemann. I congratulate you."

The financier's voice was suddenly low, circumspect. "What's your point?"

"It's also very pro . . . I'm the only one who can bring about that message from the U-boat. No one else. I have the codes that turn the lights off; that make the radar screens go dark. . . . But I expect to get paid for it."

"I see. . . ." Rhinemann hesitated, his breathing still audible. "It is a presumptuous demand. Your superiors expect the gyroscopic designs. Should you impede their delivery, your punishment, no doubt, will be execution. Not formally arrived at, of course, but the result will be the same. Surely you know that."

David laughed again, and again the laugh was brief—but now good-natured. "You're way off. *Way* off. There may be executions, but not mine. Until last night I only knew half the story. Now I know it *all*. . . . No, not *my* execution. On the other hand, you, *do* have a problem. I know *that;* four years in Lisbon teaches a man some things."

"What is my problem?"

"If the Koening merchandise in Ocho Calle is not delivered, Altmüller will send an undercover battalion into Buenos Aires. You won't survive it."

The silence again. And in that silence was Rhinemann's acknowledgment that David was right.

"Then we are allies," said Rhinemann. "In one night you've gone far. You took a dangerous risk and leaped many plateaus. I admire such aggressive ambitions. I'm sure arrangements can be made."

"I was sure you'd be sure."

"Shall we discuss figures?"

Again David laughed softly. "Payment from you is like . . . before last night. Only half the story. Make your half generous. In Switzerland. The second half will be paid in the States. A lifetime of *very* generous retainers." David suddenly spoke tersely. "I want names."

"I don't understand. . . ."

"*Think* about it. The men *behind* this operation. The Americans. Those are the names I want. Not an accountant, not a confused brigadier. The others. . . . Without those names there's no deal. No codes."

"The man from Lisbon is remarkably without conscience," said Rhinemann with a touch of respect. "You are . . . as you Americans say . . . quite a rotten fellow."

"I've watched the masters in action. I thought about it. . . . Why not?"

Rhinemann obviously had not listened to David's reply. His tone was abruptly suspicious. "If this . . . gain of personal wealth is the conclusion you arrived at, why did you do what you did last night? I must tell you that the damage is not irreparable, but why *did* you?"

"For the simplest of reasons. I hadn't thought about it last night. I hadn't arrived at this conclusion . . . last night." God knew, that was the truth, thought David.

"Yes. I think I understand," said the financier. "A very human reaction. . . ."

"I want the rest of these designs," broke in Spaulding. "And you want the codes sent out. To stay on schedule, we have thirty-six hours, give or take two or three. I'll call you at six o'clock. Be ready to move."

David hung up. He took a deep breath and realized he was perspiring . . . and the small concrete house was cool. The breezes from the fields were coming through the windows, billowing the curtains. He looked at Lyons, who sat watching him in a straight-backed wicker chair.

"How'd I do?" he asked.

The physicist swallowed and spoke, and it occurred to Spaulding that either he was getting used to Lyons's strained voice or Lyons's speech was improving.

"Very . . . convincing. Except for the . . . sweat on your
face and the expression . . . in your eyes." Lyons smiled;
then followed it instantly with a question he took seriously.
"Is there a chance . . . for the remaining blueprints?"

David held a match to a cigarette. He inhaled the
smoke, looked up at the gently swaying curtains of an open
window, then turned to the physicist. "I think we'd better
understand one another, doctor. I don't give a goddamn
about those designs. Perhaps I should, but I don't. And if
the way to get our hands on them is to risk that trawler
reaching a U-boat, it's out of the question. As far as I'm
concerned we're bringing out three-quarters more than
what we've got. And that's too goddamn much. . . . There's
only one thing I want: the names. . . . I've got the evidence; now I want the names."

"You want revenge," said Lyons softly.

"*Yes! . . . Jesus! Yes, I do!*" David crushed out his
barely touched cigarette, crossed to the open window and
looked out at the fields. "I'm sorry, I don't mean to yell at
you. Or maybe I should. You heard Feld; you saw what I
brought back from Ocho Calle. You know the whole
putrid . . . obscene thing."

"I know . . . the men who fly those planes . . . are not
responsible. . . . I know I believe that . . . Germany must
lose this war."

"For Christ's *sake!*" roared David, whirling from the
window. "You've *seen!* You've *got* to *understand!*"

"Are you saying . . . there's no difference? I don't believe
that. . . . I don't think you believe it."

"I don't know *what* I believe! . . . No. I *do* know. I know
what I object to; because it leaves no *room* for belief. . . .
And I know I want those names."

"You should have them. . . . Your questions are great . . .
moral ones. I think they will pain you . . . for years."
Lyons was finding it difficult to sustain his words now. "I
submit only . . . no matter what has happened . . . that
Asher Feld was right. This war must *not* be settled . . . it
must be won."

Lyons stopped talking and rubbed his throat. David
walked to a table where Lyons kept a pitcher of water and
poured a glass. He carried it over to the spent physicist and
handed it to him. It occurred to David, as he acknowledged the gesture of thanks, that it was strange. . . . Of all

men, the emaciated recluse in front of him would profit
least from the outcome of the war. Or the shortening of it.
Yet Eugene Lyons had been touched by the commitment
of Asher Feld. Perhaps, in his pain, Lyons understood the
simpler issues that his own anger had distorted.

*Asher Feld. The Alvear Hotel.*

"Listen to me," said Spaulding. "If there's a chance . . .
and there may be, we'll try for the blueprints. There's a
trade-off possible; a dangerous one . . . not for us, but for
your friend, Asher Feld. We'll see. No promises. The
names come first. . . . It's a parallel route; until I get the
names, Rhinemann has to believe I want the designs as
much as he wants the diamonds. . . . We'll see."

The weak, erratic bell of the country telephone spun out
its feeble ring. Spaulding picked it up.

"It's Ballard," said the voice anxiously.

"Yes, Bobby?"

"I hope to Christ you're clean, because there's a lot of
flak to the contrary. I'm going on the assumption that a
reasonable guy doesn't court-martial himself into a long
prison term for a few dollars."

"A reasonable assumption. What is it? Did you get the
information?"

"First things first. And the first thing is that the Fleet
Marine Force wants you dead or alive; the condition is
immaterial, and I think they'd prefer you dead."

"They found Meehan and the driver. . . ."

"You bet your ass they did! After they got rolled and
stripped to their skivvies by some wandering *vagos*. They're
mad as hell! They threw out the bullshit about not alerting
the embassy that Fairfax wants you picked up. Fairfax's
incidental; *they* want you. Assault, theft, et cetera."

"All right. That's to be expected."

"Expected? Oh, you're a pistol! I don't suppose I have to
tell you about Granville. You got him burning up my dials!
Washington's preparing a top-level scramble, so I'm
chained to my desk till it comes in."

"Then he doesn't know. They're covering," said Spaulding, annoyed.

"The hell he doesn't! The hell they *are!* This radio silence; you walked into a High Command *defection!* An
Allied Central project straight from the War Department."

"I'll bet it's from the War Department. I can tell you which office."

"It's true. . . . There's a U-boat bringing in a couple of very important Berliners. You're out of order; it's not your action. Granville will tell you that."

"Horseshit!" yelled David. "Pure horseshit! *Transparent* horseshit! Ask any network agent in Europe. You couldn't get a *Briefmarke* out of *any* German port! No one knows that better than me!"

"Interesting, ontologically speaking. Transparency isn't a quality one associates . . ."

"No jokes! My humor's strained!" And then suddenly David realized he had no cause to yell at the cryp. Ballard's frame of reference was essentially the same as it had been eighteen hours ago—with complications, perhaps, but not of death and survival. Ballard did not know about the carnage at San Telmo or the tools for Peenemünde in Ocho Calle; and a Haganah that reached into the most secret recesses of Military Intelligence. Nor would he be told just now. "I'm sorry. I've got a lot on my mind."

"Sure, sure." Ballard replied as if he were used to other people's tempers. Another trait common to most cryptographers, David reflected. "Jean said you were hurt; fell and cut yourself pretty badly. Did somebody push?"

"It's all right. The doctor was here. . . . Did you get the information? On Ira Barden."

"Yeah. . . . I used straight G-2 in Washington. A dossier Teletype request over your name. This Barden's going to know about it."

"That's O.K. What's it say?"

"The whole damn *thing?*"

"Whatever seems . . . unusual. Fairfax qualifications, probably."

"They don't use the name Fairfax. Just high-priority classification. . . . He's in the Reserves, not regular army. Family company's in importing. Spent a number of years in Europe and the Middle East; speaks five languages. . . ."

"And one of them's Hebrew," interrupted David quietly.

"That's right. How did . . . ? Never mind. He spent two years at the American University in Beirut while his father represented the firm in the Mediterranean area. The company was very big in Middle East textiles. Barden transferred to Harvard, then transferred again to a small college in New York State. . . . I don't know it. He majored in Near East studies, it says here. When he graduated he went into the family business until the war. . . . I guess it was the languages."

"Thanks," said David. "Burn the Teletype, Bobby."

"With pleasure. . . . When are you coming in? You better get here before the FMF finds you. Jean can probably convince old Henderson to cool things off."

"Pretty soon. How's Jean?"

"Huh? Fine. . . . Scared; nervous, I guess. You'll see. She's a strong girl, though."

"Tell her not to worry."

"Tell her yourself."

"She's there with you?"

"No. . . ." Ballard drew out the word, telegraphing a note of concern that had been absent. "No, she's not with me. She's on her way to see you. . . ."

*"What?"*

"The nurse. The doctor's nurse. She called about an hour ago. She said you wanted to see Jean." Ballard's voice suddenly became hard and loud. *"What the hell's going on, Spaulding?"*

# 41

"Surely the man from Lisbon expected countermeasures. I'm amazed he was so derelict." Heinrich Stoltz conveyed his arrogance over the telephone. "Mrs. Cameron was a flank you took for granted, yes? A summons from a loved one is difficult to resist, is it not?"

"Where is she?"

"She is on her way to Luján. She will be a guest at Habichtsnest. An honored guest, I can assure you. Herr Rhinemann will be immensely pleased; I was about to telephone him. I wanted to wait until the interception was made."

"You're out of line!" David said, trying to keep his voice calm. "You're asking for reprisals in every neutral area. Diplomatic hostages in a neutral . . ."

"A guest," interrupted the German with relish. "Hardly a prize; a *step*daughter-in-law; the husband *deceased*. With no official status. So complicated, these American social rituals."

"You know what I mean! You don't need diagrams!"

"I said she was a *guest!* Of an eminent financier you yourself were sent to contact . . . concerning international economic matters, I believe. A Jew expelled from his own country, that country your enemy. I see no cause for immediate alarm. . . . Although, perhaps, you should."

There was no reason to procrastinate. Jean was no part of the bargain, no part of the indictment. To hell with the indictment! To hell with a meaningless commitment! There *was* no meaning!

Only Jean.

"Call the moves," said David.

"I was sure you'd cooperate. What difference does it

make to you? Or to me, really. . . . You and I, we take orders. Leave the philosophy to men of great affairs. We survive."

"That doesn't sound like a true believer. I was told you were a believer." David spoke aimlessly; he needed time, only seconds. To think.

"Strangely enough, I am. In a world that passed, I'm afraid. Only partially in the one that's coming. . . . The remaining designs are at Habichtsnest. You and your aerophysicist will go there at once. I wish to conclude our negotiations this evening."

"Wait a minute!" David's mind raced over conjectures— his counterpart's options. "That's not the cleanest nest I've been in; the inhabitants leave something to be desired."

"So do the guests. . . ."

"Two conditions. One: I see Mrs. Cameron the minute I get there. Two: I don't send the codes—if they're to be sent—until she's back at the embassy. With Lyons."

"We'll discuss these points later. There is one prior condition, however." Stoltz paused. "Should you not be at Habichtsnest this afternoon, you will *never* see Mrs. Cameron. As you last saw her. . . . Habichtsnest has so many diversions; the guests enjoy them so. Unfortunately, there have been some frightful accidents in the past. On the river, in the pool . . . on horseback. . . ."

The foreman gave them a road map and filled the FMF automobile's gas tank with fuel from the ranch pump. Spaulding removed the orange medallions from the bumpers and blurred the numbers of the license plates by chipping away at the paint until the 7s looked like 1s, and 8s like 3s. Then he smashed the ornament off the tip of the hood, slapped black paint over the grill and removed all four hubcaps. Finally, he took a sledgehammer and, to the amazement of the silent gaucho, he crashed it into the side door panels, trunk and roof of the car.

When he had finished, the automobile from Fleet Marine Force looked like any number of back country wrecks.

They drove out the road to the primitive highway by the telephone junction box and turned east toward Buenos Aires. Spaulding pressed the accelerator; the vibrations caused the loose metal to rattle throughout the car. Lyons held the unfolded map on his knees; if it was correct, they could reach the Luján district without traveling the major highways, reducing the chances of discovery by the FMF patrols that were surely out by now.

The goddamned irony of it! thought David. Safety . . . safety for Jean, for him, too, really . . . lay in contact with the same enemy he had fought so viciously for over three years. An enemy made an ally by incredible events . . . treasons taking place in Washington and Berlin.

What had Stoltz said? *Leave the philosophy to men of great affairs.*

Meaning and no meaning at all.

David nearly missed the half-concealed entrance to Habichtsnest. He was approaching it from the opposite direction on the lonely stretch of road he had traveled only once, and at night. What caused him to slow down and look to his left, spotting the break in the woods, were sets of black tire marks on the light surface of the entrance. They had not been there long enough to be erased by the hot sun or succeeding traffic. And Spaulding recalled the words of the guard on the pier in Ocho Calle.

*. . . There is a lot of shouting.*

David could visualize Rhinemann screaming his orders, causing a column of racing Bentleys and Packards to come screeching out of the hidden road from Habichtsnest on its way to a quiet street in San Telmo.

And no doubt later—in the predawn hours—other automobiles, more sweating, frightened henchmen—racing to the small isolated peninsula that was Ocho Calle.

With a certain professional pride, Spaulding reflected that he had interdicted well.

Both enemies. All enemies.

A vague plan was coming into focus, but only the outlines. So much depended on what faced them at Habichtsnest.

And the soft-spoken words of hatred uttered by Asher Feld.

The guards in their paramilitary uniforms leveled their rifles at the approaching automobile. Others held dogs that were straining at leashes, teeth bared, barking viciously. The man behind the electric gate shouted orders to those in front; four guards ran to the car and yanked the smashed panels open. Spaulding and Lyons got out; they were pushed against the FMF vehicle and searched.

David kept turning his head, looking at the extended fence beyond both sides of the gate. He estimated the height and the tensile strength of the links, the points of electrical contact between the thick-poled sections. The angles of direction.

It was part of his plan.

Jean ran to him from across the terraced balcony. He held her, silently, for several moments. It was a brief span of sanity and he was grateful for it.

Rhinemann stood at the railing twenty feet away, Stoltz at his side. Rhinemann's narrow eyes stared at David from out of the folds of suntanned flesh. The look was one of despised respect, and David knew it.

There was a third man. A tall, blond-haired man in a white Palm Beach suit seated at a glass-topped table. Spaulding did not know him.

"David, *David*. What have I *done?*" Jean would not let him go; he stroked her soft brown hair, replying quietly.

"Saved my life among other things. . . ."

"The Third Reich has extraordinarily thorough surveillance, Mrs. Cameron," interrupted Stoltz, smiling. "We keep watch on all Jews. Especially professional men. We knew you were friendly with the doctor in Palermo; and that the colonel was wounded. It was all quite simple."

"Does your surveillance of Jews include the man beside you?" asked Spaulding in a monotone.

Stoltz paled slightly, his glance shifting unobtrusively from Rhinemann to the blond-haired man in the chair. "Herr Rhinemann understands my meaning. I speak pragmatically; of the necessary observation of hostile elements."

"Yes, I remember," said David, releasing Jean, putting his arm around her shoulders. "You were very clear yesterday about the regrettable necessity of certain practicalities. I'm sorry you missed the lecture, Rhinemann. It concerned the concentration of Jewish money. . . . We're here. Let's get on with it."

Rhinemann stepped away from the railing. "We shall. But first, so the . . . circle is complete, I wish to present to you an acquaintance who has flown in from Berlin. By way of neutral passage, of course. I want you to have the opportunity of knowing you deal *directly* with *him*. The exchange is more *genuine* this way."

Spaulding looked over at the blond-haired man in the white Palm Beach suit. Their eyes locked.

"Franz Altmüller, Ministry of Armaments. Berlin," said David.

"Colonel David Spaulding. Fairfax. Late of Portugal. The man in Lisbon," said Altmüller.

"You are jackals," added Rhinemann, "who fight as traitors fight and dishonor your houses. I say this to you both. For both to hear. . . . Now, as you say, colonel, we shall get on with it."

Stoltz took Lyons below to the manicured lawn by the pool. There, at a large, round table, a Rhinemann guard stood with a metal attaché case in his hand. Lyons sat down, his back to the balcony; the guard lifted the case onto the table.

"Open it," commanded Erich Rhinemann from above.

The guard did so; Lyons took out the plans and spread them on the table.

Altmüller spoke. "Remain with him, Stoltz."

Stoltz looked up, bewildered. However, he did not speak. He walked to the edge of the pool and sat in a deck chair, his eyes fixed on Lyons.

Altmüller turned to Jean. "May I have a word with the colonel, please?"

Jean looked at Spaulding. She took her hand from his and walked to the far end of the balcony. Rhinemann remained in the center, staring down at Lyons.

"For both our sakes," said Altmüller, "I think you should tell me what happened in San Telmo."

David watched the German closely. Altmüller was not lying; he was not trying to trap him. *He did not know about the Haganah. About Asher Feld.* It was Spaulding's only chance.

"Gestapo," said David, giving the lie the simplicity of conviction.

"*Impossible!*" Altmüller spat out the word. "You *know* that's impossible! *I* am here!"

"I've dealt with the Gestapo—in various forms—for

nearly four years. I know the enemy. . . . Grant me that much credit."

"You're wrong! There's *no possible way!*"

"You've spent too much time in the ministry, not enough in the field. Do you want a professional analysis?"

"What is it?"

David leaned against the railing. "You've been had."

"*What?*"

"Just as I've been had. By those who employ our considerable talents. In Berlin and Washington. There's a remarkable coincidence, too. . . . They both have the same initials. . . . A.S."

Altmüller stared at Spaulding, his blue eyes penetrating, his mouth parted slightly—in disbelief. He spoke the name under his breath.

"*Albert Speer. . . .*"

"*Alan Swanson,*" countered David softly.

"It can't *be,*" said Altmüller with less conviction than he wished to muster. "He doesn't know. . . ."

"Don't go into the field without some advanced training. You won't last. . . . Why do you think I offered to make a deal with Rhinemann?"

Altmüller was listening but not listening. He took his eyes from Spaulding, seemingly consumed with the pieces of an incredible puzzle. "If what you say is true—and by no means do I agree—the codes would not be sent, the transfer aborted. There would be no radio silence; your fleet cruising, radar and aircraft in operation. Everything lost!"

David folded his arms in front of him. It was the moment when the lie would either be bought or rejected out of hand. He knew it; he felt as he had felt scores of times in the north country when *the lie* was the keystone. "Your side plays rougher than mine. It goes with the New Order. My people won't kill me; they just want to make sure I don't know anything. All they care about are those designs. . . . With you it's different. Your people keep their options open."

David stopped and smiled at Rhinemann, who had turned from his sentry position by the balcony and was looking at them. Altmüller kept his eyes on Spaulding . . . the inexperienced "runner" being taught, thought David.

"And in your judgment, what are these options?"

"A couple I can think of," replied Spaulding. "Immobilize me, force in another code man at the last minute,
substitute faulty blueprints; or get the diamonds out from
Ocho Calle some other way than by water—difficult with
those crates, but not impossible."

"Then why should I not let these options be exercised?
You tempt me."

Spaulding had been glancing up, at nothing. Suddenly he
turned and looked at Altmüller. "Don't *ever* go into the
field; you won't last a day. Stay at your ministry."

"What does that mean?"

"Any alternate strategy used, you're dead. You're a
liability now. You 'dealt' with the enemy. Speer knows it,
the Gestapo knows it. Your only chance is to *use* what you
know. Just like me. You for your life; me for a great deal
of money. Christ knows, the aircraft companies will make a
pile; I deserve some of it."

Altmüller took two steps to the railing and stood alongside David, looking down at the distant river below. "It's
all so pointless."

"Not when you think about it," said Spaulding. "Something for nothing never is in this business."

David, staring straight ahead, could feel Altmüller's eyes
abruptly on him. He could sense the new thought coming
into focus in Altmüller's mind.

"Your generosity may be your undoing, colonel. . . . We
can still have something for nothing. And I, a hero's medal
from the Reich. We have you. Mrs. Cameron. The physicist's expendable, I'm sure. . . . You *will* send the codes.
You were willing to negotiate for money. Surely you'll
negotiate for your lives."

Like Altmüller, David stared straight ahead when he
replied. His arms still folded, he was irritatingly relaxed, as
he knew he had to be. "Those negotiations have been concluded. If Lyons approves the blueprints, I'll send the
codes when he and Mrs. Cameron are back at the embassy.
Not before."

"You'll send them when I *order* you to." Altmüller was
finding it difficult to keep his voice low. Rhinemann looked
over again but made no move to interfere. Spaulding
understood. Rhinemann was toying with his jackals.

"Sorry to disappoint you," said David.

"Then extremely unpleasant things will happen. To Mrs. Cameron first."

"Give it up." David sighed. "Play by the original rules. You haven't a chance."

"You talk confidently for a man alone."

Spaulding pushed himself off the railing and turned, facing the German. He spoke barely above a whisper. "You really are a goddamned fool. You wouldn't last an hour in Lisbon. . . . Do you think I drove in here without any backups? Do you think Rhinemann *expected* me to? . . . We men in the field are very cautious, very cowardly; we're not heroic at all. We don't blow up buildings if there's a chance we'll still be inside. We won't destroy an enemy bridge unless there's another way back to our side."

"You *are* alone. There are no bridges left for you!"

David looked at Altmüller as if appraising a bad cut of meat, then glanced at his watch. "Your Stoltz was a fool. If I don't make a call within fifteen minutes, there'll be a lot of busy telephones resulting in God knows how many very official automobiles driving out to Luján. I'm a military attaché stationed at the American embassy. I accompanied the ambassador's daughter to Luján. That's enough."

"That's preposterous! This is a neutral city. Rhinemann would . . ."

"*Rhinemann* would open the gates and throw the jackals out," interrupted Spaulding quietly and very calmly. "We're liabilities, both of us. 'Tortugas' could blow up in his postwar face. He's not going to allow that. Whatever he thinks of the systems, yours *or* mine, it doesn't matter. Only one thing matters to him: the cause of Erich Rhinemann. . . . I thought you knew that. You picked him."

Altmüller was breathing steadily, a bit too deeply, thought David. He was imposing a control on himself and he was only barely succeeding.

"You . . . have made arrangements to send the codes? From here?"

*The lie was bought. The keystone was now in place.*

"The rules are back in force. Radio and radar silence. No air strikes on surfacing submarines, no interceptions of trawlers . . . under Paraguayan flags entering the coastal zones. We both win. . . . Which do you want, jackal?"

Altmüller turned back to the railing and placed his
hands on the marble top. His fingers were rigid against the
stone. The tailored folds of his white Palm Beach suit were
starchly immobile. He looked down at the river and spoke.

"The rules of 'Tortugas' are reinstated."

"I have a telephone call to make," said David.

"I expected you would," replied Rhinemann, looking
contemptuously at Franz Altmüller. "I have no stomach
for an embassy kidnapping. It serves no one."

"Don't be too harsh," said Spaulding agreeably. "It got
me here in record time."

"Make your call." Rhinemann pointed to a telephone on
a table next to the archway. "Your conversation will be
amplified, of course."

"Of course," answered David, walking to the phone.

"Radio room . . . ," came the words from the unseen
speakers.

"This is Lieutenant Colonel Spaulding, military attaché,"
said David, interrupting Ballard's words.

There was the slightest pause before Ballard replied.

"Yes, sir, Colonel Spaulding?"

"I issued a directive of inquiry prior to my conference
this afternoon. You may void it now."

"Yes, sir. . . . Very good, sir."

"May I speak with the head cryptographer, please? A
Mr. Ballard, I believe."

"I'm . . . Ballard, sir."

"Sorry," said David curtly, "I didn't recognize you, Ballard. Be ready to send out the sealed code schedules I
prepared for you. The green envelope; open it and familiarize yourself with the progressions. When I give you the
word, I want it transmitted immediately. On a black-drape
priority."

"What . . . sir?"

"My authorization is black drape, Ballard. It's in the lex,
so clear all scrambler channels. You'll get no flak with that
priority. I'll call you back."

"Yes, sir. . . ."

David hung up, hoping to Christ that Ballard was as
good at his job as David thought he was. Or as good at
parlor games as Henderson Granville thought he was.

"You're very efficient," said Rhinemann.

"I try to be," said David.

Ballard stared at the telephone. What was Spaulding trying to tell him? Obviously that Jean was all right; that he and Lyons were all right, too. At least for the time being.

*Be ready to send out the sealed code schedules I prepared. . . .*

David had not prepared any codes. *He* had. Spaulding had memorized the progressions, that was true, but only as a contingency.

What goddamned *green envelope?*

There was no envelope, red, blue or green!

What the hell was that nonsense . . . *black-drape priority?*

What was a black drape? It didn't make sense!

But it *was* a key.

*It's in the lex. . . .*

*Lex. . . . Lexicon. The Lexicon of Cryptography!*

*Black drape. . . .* He recalled something . . . something very obscure, way in the past. *Black drape* was a very old term, long obsolete. But it *meant* something.

Ballard got out of his swivel chair and went to the bookshelf on the other side of the small radio room. He had not looked at *The Lexicon of Cryptography* in years. It was a useless, academic tome. . . . Obsolete.

It was on the top shelf with the other useless references and, like the others, had gathered dust.

He found the term on page 71. It was a single paragraph sandwiched between equally meaningless paragraphs. But it had meaning now.

"The Black Drape, otherwise known as *Schwarztuchchiffre,* for it was first employed by the German Imperial Army in 1916, is an entrapment device. It is hazardous for it cannot be repeated in a sector twice. It is a signal to proceed with a code, activating a given set of arrangements with intent to terminate, canceling said arrangements. The termination factor is expressed in minutes, specifically numbered. As a practice, it was abandoned in 1917 for it nullified . . ."

*Proceed . . . with intent to terminate.*

Ballard closed the book and returned to his chair in front of the dials.

Lyons kept turning the pages of the designs back and forth as if double-checking his calculations. Rhinemann called down twice from the balcony, inquiring if there were problems. Twice Lyons turned in his chair and shook his head. Stoltz remained in the deck chair by the pool, smoking cigarettes. Altmüller talked briefly with Rhinemann, the conversation obviously unsatisfactory to both. Altmüller returned to the chair by the glass-topped table and leafed through a Buenos Aires newspaper.

David and Jean remained at the far end of the terrace, talking quietly. Every once in a while Spaulding let his voice carry across; if Altmüller listened, he heard references to New York, to architectural firms, to vague postwar plans. Lovers' plans.

But these references were non sequiturs.

"At the Alvear Hotel," said David softly, holding Jean's hand, "there's a man registered under the name of E. Pace. *E. Pace.* His real name is Asher Feld. Identify yourself as the contact from me . . . and a Fairfax agent named Barden. Ira Barden. Nothing else. Tell him I'm calling his . . . priorities. In precisely two hours from . . . the minute you telephone from the embassy. . . . I *mean* the minute, Jean, he'll understand. . . ."

Only once did Jean Cameron gasp, an intake of breath that caused David to glare at her and press her hand. She covered her shock with artificial laughter.

Altmüller looked up from the newspaper. Contempt was in his eyes; beyond the contempt, and also obvious, was his anger.

Lyons got up from the chair and stretched his emaciated frame. He had spent three hours and ten minutes at the table; he turned and looked up at the balcony. At Spaulding.

He nodded.

"Good," said Rhinemann, crossing to Franz Altmüller. "We'll proceed. It will be dark soon; we'll conclude everything by early morning. No more delay! Stoltz! *Kommen Sie her! Bringen Sie die Aktenmappe!*"

Stoltz went to the table and began replacing the pages in the briefcase.

David took Jean's arm and guided her toward Rhinemann and Altmüller. The Nazi spoke.

"The plans comprise four hundred and sixty-odd pages of causal data and progressive equations. No man can retain such information; the absence of any part renders the designs useless. As soon as you contact the cryptographer and relay the codes, Mrs. Cameron and the physicist are free to leave."

"I'm sorry," said Spaulding. "My agreement was to send the codes when they were back at the embassy. That's the way it has to be."

"*Surely*," interjected Rhinemann angrily, "you don't think I would permit . . ."

"No, I don't," broke in David. "But I'm not sure what you can control outside the gates of Habichtsnest. This way, I know you'll try harder."

# 42

It was an hour and thirty-one minutes before the telephone rang. Nine fifteen exactly. The sun had descended behind the Luján hills; the light along the distant riverbank flickered in the enveloping darkness.

Rhinemann picked up the receiver, listened and nodded to David.

Spaulding got out of his chair and crossed to the financier, taking the receiver. Rhinemann flicked a switch on the wall. The speakers were activated.

"We're here, David." Jean's words were amplified on the terrace.

"Fine," answered Spaulding. "No problems then?"

"Not really. After five miles or so I thought Doctor Lyons was going to be sick. They drove so fast. . . ."

*After . . . five. . . .*

*Asher . . . Feld. . . .*

Jean had done it!

"But he's all right now?"

"He's resting. It'll take some time before he feels himself. . . ."

*Time.*

Jean had given Asher Feld the precise *time.*

"All right. . . ."

"*Genug! Genug!*" said Altmüller, standing by the balcony. "That's enough. You have your proof; they are there. The codes!"

David looked over at the Nazi. It was an unhurried look, not at all accommodating.

"Jean?"

"Yes?"

"You're in the radio room?"

"Yes."

"Let me speak to that Ballard fellow."

"Here he is."

Ballard's voice was impersonal, efficient. "Colonel Spaulding?"

"Ballard, have you cleared all scrambler channels?"

"Yes, sir. Along with your priority. The drape's confirmed, sir."

"Very good. Stand by for my call. It shouldn't be more than a few minutes." David quickly hung up the phone.

"What are you doing?!" yelled Altmüller furiously. "The *codes! Send them!*"

"He's *betraying* us!" screamed Stoltz, jumping up from his chair.

"I think you should explain yourself." Rhinemann spoke softly, his voice conveying the punishment he intended to inflict.

"Just last-minute details," said Spaulding, lighting a cigarette. "Only a few minutes. . . . Shall we talk alone, Rhinemann?"

"That is unnecessary. What is it?" asked the financier.

"Your method of departure? It's arranged. You'll be driven to the Mendarro field with the designs. It's less than ten minutes from here. You won't be airborne, however, until we have confirmation of the Koening transfer."

"How long will that be?"

"What difference does it make?"

"Once the blackout starts I have no protection, *that's* the difference."

"*Ach!*" Rhinemann was impatient. "For four hours you'll have the best protection in the world. I have no stomach for offending the men in Washington!"

"You see?" said David to Franz Altmüller. "I told you we were liabilities." He turned back to Rhinemann. "All right. I accept that. You've got too much to lose. Detail number one, crossed off. Now detail number two. My payment from you."

Rhinemann squinted his eyes. "You *are* a man of details. . . . The sum of five hundred thousand American dollars will be transferred to the Banque Louis Quatorze in Zürich. It's a nonnegotiable figure and a generous one."

"Extremely. More than I would have asked for. . . . What's my guarantee?"

"Come, colonel. We're not *salesmen*. You know where I live; your abilities are proven. I don't wish the specter of the man from Lisbon on my personal horizon."

"You flatter me."

"The money will be deposited, the proper papers held in Zürich for you. At the bank; normal procedures."

David crushed out his cigarette. "All right. Zürich. . . . Now the last detail. Those generous payments I'm going to receive right at home. . . . The names, please. Write them on a piece of paper."

"Are you so sure I possess these names?"

"It's the only thing I'm really sure of. It's the one opportunity you wouldn't miss."

Rhinemann took a small black leather notebook from his jacket pocket and wrote hastily on a page. He tore it out and handed it to Spaulding.

David read the names:

*Kendall, Walter*
*Swanson, A*. U.S. Army
*Oliver, H*. Meridian Aircraft
*Craft, J*. Packard

"Thank you," said Spaulding. He put the page in his pocket and reached for the telephone. "Get me the American embassy, please."

Ballard read the sequence of the code progressions David had recited to him. They were not perfect but they were not far off, either; Spaulding had confused a vowel equation, but the message was clear.

And David's emphasis on the "frequency megacycle of 120 for all subsequent scrambles" was meaningless gibberish. But it, too, was very clear.

120 minutes.

*Black Drape.*

The original code allowed for thirteen characters:

CABLE TORTUGAS

The code Spaulding had recited, however, had fifteen characters.

Ballard stared at the words.

## DESTROY TORTUGAS

In two hours.

David had a final "detail" which none could fault professionally, but all found objectionable. Since there were four hours—more or less—before he'd be driven to the Mendarro airfield, and there were any number of reasons during this period why he might be out of sight of the designs—or Rhinemann might be out of sight of the designs—he insisted that they be placed in a single locked metal case and chained to any permanent structure, the chain held by a new padlock, the keys given to him. Further, he would also hold the keys to the case and thread the hasps. If the designs were tampered with, he'd know it.

"Your precautions are now obsessive," said Rhinemann disagreeably. "I should ignore you. The codes have been sent."

"Then humor me. I'm a Fairfax four-zero. We might work again."

Rhinemann smiled. "That is always the way, is it not? So be it."

Rhinemann sent for a chain and a padlock, which he took a minor delight in showing to David in its original box. The ritual was over in several minutes, the metal case chained to the banister of the stairway in the great hall. The four men settled in the huge living room, to the right of the hall, an enormous archway affording a view of the staircase . . . and the metal briefcase.

The financier became genial host. He offered brandies; only Spaulding accepted at first, then Heinrich Stoltz followed. Altmüller would not drink.

A guard, his paramilitary uniform pressed into starched creases, came through the archway.

"Our operators confirm radio silence, sir. Throughout the entire coastal zone."

"Thank you," said Rhinemann. "Stand by on all frequencies."

The guard nodded. He turned and left the room as quickly as he had entered.

"Your men are efficient," observed David.

"They're paid to be," answered Rhinemann, looking at his watch. "Now, we wait. Everything progresses and we have merely to wait. I'll order a buffet. Canapes are hardly filling . . . and we have the time."

"You're hospitable," said Spaulding, carrying his brandy to a chair next to Altmüller.

"And generous. Don't forget that."

"It would be hard to. . . . I was wondering, however, if I might impose further?" David placed his brandy glass on the side table and gestured at his rumpled, ill-fitting clothes. "These were borrowed from a ranch hand. God knows when they were last washed. Or me. . . . I'd appreciate a shower, a shave; perhaps a pair of trousers and a shirt, or a sweater. . . ."

"I'm sure your army personnel can accommodate you," said Altmüller, watching David suspiciously.

"For Christ's sake, Altmüller, I'm not *going* anywhere! Except to a shower. The designs are over there!" Spaulding pointed angrily through the archway to the metal case chained to the banister of the stairway. "If you think I'm leaving without *that*, you're retarded."

The insult infuriated the Nazi; he gripped the arms of his chair, controlling himself. Rhinemann laughed and spoke to Altmüller.

"The colonel has had a tiresome few days. His request is minor; and I can assure you he is going nowhere but to the Mendarro airfield. . . . I wish he were. He'd save me a half million dollars."

David responded to Rhinemann's laugh with one of his own. "A man with that kind of money in Zürich should at least *feel* clean." He rose from the chair. "And you're right about the last few days. I'm bushed. And sore all over. If the bed is soft I'll grab a nap." He looked over at Altmüller. "With a battalion of armed guards at the door if it'll ease the little boy's concerns."

Altmüller shot up, his voice harsh and loud. *"Enough!"*

"Oh sit down," said David. "You look foolish."

Rhinemann's guard brought him a pair of trousers, a lightweight turtleneck sweater and a tan suede jacket. David saw that each was expensive and he knew each would fit. Shaving equipment was in the bathroom; if there was anything else he needed, all he had to do was open the door and ask. The man would be outside in the hall. Actually, there would be two men.

David understood.

He told the guard—a *porteño*—that he would sleep for an hour, then shower and shave for his journey. Would the guard be so considerate as to make sure he was awake by eleven o'clock?

The guard would do so.

It was five minutes past ten on David's watch. Jean had phoned at precisely nine fifteen. Asher Feld had exactly two hours from nine fifteen.

David had one hour and six minutes.

Eleven fifteen.

If Asher Feld really believed in his priorities.

The room was large, had a high ceiling and two double-casement windows three stories above the ground, and was in the east wing of the house. That was all Spaulding could tell—or wanted to study—while the lights were on.

He turned them off and went back to the windows. He opened the left casement quietly, peering out from behind the drapes.

The roof was slate; that wasn't good. It had a wide gutter; that was better. The gutter led to a drainpipe about twenty feet away. That was satisfactory.

Directly beneath, on the second floor, were four small balconies that probably led to four bedrooms. The farthest balcony was no more than five feet from the drainpipe. Possibly relevant; probably not.

Below, the lawn like all the grounds at Habichtsnest: manicured, greenish black in the moonlight, full; with white wrought-iron outdoor furniture dotted about, and flagstone walks bordered by rows of flowers. Curving away from the area beneath his windows was a wide, raked path that disappeared into the darkness and the trees. He remembered seeing that path from the far right end of the terrace overlooking the pool; he remembered the intermittent, unraked hoofprints. The path was for horses; it had to lead to stables somewhere beyond the trees.

That *was* relevant; relevancy, at this point, being relative.

And then Spaulding saw the cupped glow of a cigarette behind a latticed arbor thirty-odd feet from the perimeter of the wrought-iron furniture. Rhinemann may have expressed confidence that he, David, would be on his way to

Mendarro in a couple of hours, but that confidence was backed up by men on watch.

No surprise; the surprise would have been the absence of such patrols. It was one of the reasons he counted on Asher Feld's priorities.

He let the drapes fall back into place, stepped away from the window and went to the canopied bed. He pulled down the blankets and stripped to his shorts—coarse underdrawers he had found in the adobe hut to replace his own bloodstained ones. He lay down and closed his eyes with no intention of sleeping. Instead, he pictured the high, electrified fence down at the gate of Habichtsnest. As he had seen it while Rhinemann's guards searched him against the battered FMF automobile.

To the right of the huge gate. To the east.

The floodlights had thrown sufficient illumination for him to see the slightly angling curvature of the fence line as it receded into the woods. Not much but definite.

North by northeast.

He visualized once again the balcony above the pool. Beyond the railing at the far right end of the terrace where he had talked quietly with Jean. He concentrated on the area below—in front, to the right.

North by northeast.

He saw it clearly. The grounds to the right of the croquet course and the tables sloped gently downhill until they were met by the tall trees of the surrounding woods. It was into these woods that the bridle path below him now entered. And as the ground descended—ultimately a mile down to the river banks—he remembered the breaks in the patterns of the far off treetops. Again to the right.

Fields.

If there were horses—and there *were* horses—and stables—and there *had* to be stables—then there were fields. For the animals to graze and race off the frustrations of the wooded, confining bridle paths.

The spaces between the descending trees were carved-out pasture lands, there was no other explanation.

North by northeast.

He shifted his thoughts to the highway two miles south of the marble steps of Habichtsnest, the highway that cut through the outskirts of Luján toward Buenos Aires. He remembered: the road, although high above the river at the

Habichtsnest intersection, curved to the *left* and went *downhill* into the Tigre district. He tried to recall precisely the first minutes of the nightmare ride in the Bentley that ended in smoke and fire and death in the Colinas Rojas. The car had swung out of the hidden entrance and for several miles sped east *and* down *and* slightly north. It finally paralleled the shoreline of the river.

North by northeast.

And then he pictured the river below the terraced balcony, dotted with white sails and cabin cruisers. It flowed diagonally away . . . to the right.

North by northeast.

That was his escape.

Down the bridle path into the protective cover of the dark woods and northeast toward the breaks in the trees—the fields. Across the fields, always heading to the right—east, and downhill, north. Back into the sloping forest, following the line of the river, until he found the electrified fence bordering the enormous compound that was Habichtsnest.

Beyond that fence was the highway to Buenos Aires. And the embassy.

And Jean.

David let his body go limp, let the ache of his wound run around in circles on his torn skin. He breathed steadily, deeply. He had to remain calm; that was the hardest part.

He looked at his watch—his gift from Jean. It was nearly eleven o'clock. He got out of the bed and put on the trousers and the sweater. He slipped into his shoes and pulled the laces as tight as he could, until the leather pinched his feet, then reached for the pillow and wrapped the soiled shirt from the outback ranch around it. He replaced the pillow at the top of the bed and pulled the blanket partially over it. He lifted the sheets, bunched them, inserted the ranch hand's trousers and let the blankets fall back in place.

He stood up. In the darkness, and with what light would come from the hallway, the bed looked sufficiently full at least for his immediate purpose.

He crossed to the door and pressed his back into the wall beside it.

His watch read one minute to eleven.

The tapping was loud; the guard was not subtle.

The door opened.

"Señor? . . . Señor?"

The door opened further.

"Señor, it's time. It's eleven o'clock."

The guard stood in the frame, looking at the bed. "*El duerme*," he said casually over his shoulder.

"*Señor Spaulding!*" The guard walked into the darkened room.

The instant the man cleared the door panel, David took a single step and with both hands clasped the guard's neck from behind. He crushed his fingers into the throat and yanked the man diagonally into him.

No cry emerged; the guard's windpipe was choked of all air supply. He went down, limp.

Spaulding closed the door slowly and snapped on the wall switch.

"*Thanks very much*," he said loudly. "Give me a hand, will you please? My stomach hurts like *hell*. . . ."

It was no secret at Habichtsnest that the American had been wounded.

David bent over the collapsed guard. He massaged his throat, pinched his nostrils, put his lips to the man's mouth and blew air into the damaged windpipe.

The guard responded; conscious but not conscious. In semishock.

Spaulding removed the man's Lüger from his belt holster and a large hunting knife from a scabbard beside it. He put the blade underneath the man's jaw and drew blood with the sharp point. He whispered. In Spanish.

"Understand me! I want you to laugh! You start laughing *now!* If you don't, this goes home. Right up through your neck! . . . Now. *Laugh!*"

The guard's crazed eyes carried his total lack of comprehension. He seemed to know only that he was dealing with a maniac. A madman who would kill him.

Feebly at first, then with growing volume and panic, the man laughed.

Spaulding laughed with him.

The laughter grew; David kept staring at the guard, gesturing for louder, more enthusiastic merriment. The man—perplexed beyond reason and totally frightened—roared hysterically.

Spaulding heard the click of the doorknob two feet from his ear. He crashed the barrel of the Lüger into the guard's head and stood up as the second man entered.

"*Qué pasa, Antonio? Tu re——*"

The Lüger's handle smashed into the Argentine's skull with such force that the guard's expulsion of breath was as loud as his voice as he fell.

David looked at his watch. It was eight minutes past eleven. Seven minutes to go.

If the man named Asher Feld believed the words he spoke with such commitment.

Spaulding removed the second guard's weapons, putting the additional Lüger into his belt. He searched both men's pockets, removing whatever paper currency he could find. And a few coins.

He had no money whatsoever. He might well need money.

He ran into the bathroom and turned on the shower to the hottest position on the dial. He returned to the hallway door and locked it. Then he turned off all lights and went to the left casement window, closing his eyes to adjust to the darkness outside. He opened them and blinked several times, trying to blur out the white spots of anxiety.

It was nine minutes past eleven.

He rubbed his perspiring hands over the expensive turtleneck sweater; he took deep breaths and waited.

The waiting was nearly unendurable.

Because he could not know.

And then he heard it! And he knew.

Two thunderous explosions! So loud, so stunning, so totally without warning that he found himself trembling, his breathing stopped.

There followed bursts of machine-gun fire that ripped through the silent night.

Below him on the ground, men were screaming at one another, racing toward the sounds that were filling the perimeter of the compound with growing ferocity.

David watched the hysteria below. There were five guards beneath his windows, all running now out of their concealed stations. He could see the spill of additional floodlights being turned on to his right, in the elegant front courtyard of Habichtsnest. He could hear the roar of powerful automobile engines and the increasing frequency of panicked commands.

He eased himself out of the casement window, holding onto the sill until his feet touched the gutter.

Both Lügers were in his belt, the knife between his teeth. He could not chance a blade next to his body; he could always spit it out if necessary. He sidestepped his way along the slate roof. The drainpipe was only feet away.

The explosions and the gunfire from the gate increased. David marveled—not only at Asher Feld's commitment, but at his logistics. The Haganah leader must have brought a small, well-supplied army into Habichtsnest.

He lowered his body cautiously against the slate roof; he reached out, gripped the gutter on the far side of the drainpipe with his right hand and slowly, carefully crouched sideways, inching his feet into a support position. He pushed against the outside rim of the gutter, testing its strength, and in a quick-springing short jump, he leaped over the side, holding the rim with both hands, his feet against the wall, straddling the drainpipe.

He began his descent, hand-below-hand on the pipe.

Amid the sounds of the gunfire, he suddenly heard loud crashing above him. There were shouts in both German and Spanish and the unmistakable smashing of wood.

The room he had just left had been broken into.

The extreme north second-floor balcony was parallel with him now. He reached out with his left hand, gripped the edge, whipped his right hand across for support and swung underneath, his body dangling thirty feet above the ground but out of sight.

Men were at the casement windows above. They forced the lead frames open without regard to the handles; the glass smashed; metal screeched against metal.

There was another thunderous explosion from the battle-ground a quarter of a mile away in the black-topped field cut out of the forest. A far-off weapon caused a detonation in the front courtyard; the spill of floodlight suddenly disappeared. Asher Feld was moving up. The crossfire would be murderous. Suicidal.

The shouts above Spaulding receded from the window, and he kicked his feet out twice to get sufficient swing to lash his hands once more across and around the drainpipe.

He did so, the blade between his teeth making his jaws ache.

He slid to the ground, scraping his hands against the weathered metal, insensitive to the cuts on his palms and fingers.

He removed the knife from his mouth, a Lüger from his belt and raced along the edge of the raked bridle path toward the darkness of the trees. He ran into the pitch-black, tree-lined corridor, skirting the trunks, prepared to plunge between them at the first sound of nearby shots.

They came; four in succession, the bullets thumping with terrible finality into the surrounding tall shafts of wood.

He whipped around a thick trunk and looked toward the house. The man firing was alone, standing by the drain-pipe. Then a second guard joined him, racing from the area of the croquet course, a giant Doberman straining at its leash in his hand. The men shouted at one another, each trying to assert command, the dog barking savagely.

As they stood yelling, two bursts of machine-gun fire came from within the front courtyard; two more flood-lights exploded.

David saw the men freeze, their concentration shifted to the front. The guard with the dog yanked at the straps, forcing the animal back into the side of the house. The second man crouched, then rose and started sidestepping his way rapidly along the building toward the courtyard, ordering his associate to follow.

And then David saw him. Above. To the right. Through foliage. On the terrace overlooking the lawn and the pool.

Erich Rhinemann had burst through the doors, scream-ing commands in fury, but not in panic. He was marshal-ing his forces, implementing his defenses . . . somehow in the pitch of the assault, he was the messianic Caesar order-ing his battalions to attack, attack, *attack*. Three men came into view behind him; he roared at them and two of the three raced back into Habichtsnest. The third man argued; Rhinemann shot him without the slightest hesitation. The body collapsed out of David's sight. Then Rhinemann ran to the wall, partially obscured by the railing, but not en-tirely. He seemed to be yelling into the wall.

Screeching *into the wall*.

Through the bursts of gunfire, David heard the muted, steady whirring and he realized what Rhinemann was doing.

The cable car from the riverbank was being sent up for him.

While the battle was engaged, this Caesar would escape the fire.

Rhinemann the pig. The ultimate manipulator. Corruptor of all things, honoring nothing.

*We may work again. . . .*

*That is always the way, is it not?*

David sprang out of his recessed sanctuary and ran back on the path to the point where the gardens and woods joined the lawn below the balcony. He raced to a white metal table with the wrought-iron legs—the same table at which Lyons had sat, his frail body bent over the blueprints. Rhinemann was nowhere in sight.

*He had to be there!*

It was suddenly . . . inordinately clear to Spaulding that the one meaningful aspect of his having been ripped out of Lisbon and transported half a world away—through the fire and the pain—was the man above him now, concealed on the balcony.

"Rhinemann! . . . Rhinemann! *I'm here!*"

The immense figure of the financier came rushing to the railing. In his hand was a Sternlicht automatic. Powerful, murderous.

"*You. You are a dead man!*" He began firing; David threw himself to the ground behind the table, overturning it, erecting a shield. Bullets thumped into the earth and ricocheted off the metal. Rhinemann continued screaming. "Your tricks are *suicide*, Lisbon! My men come from everywhere! *Hundreds!* In minutes! . . . Come, Lisbon! Show yourself. You merely move up your death! You think I would have let *you live? Never!* Show yourself! You're *dead!*"

David understood. The manipulator would not offend the men in Washington, but neither would he allow the man from Lisbon to remain on his *personal horizon.* The designs would have gone to Mendarro. Not the man from Lisbon.

He would have been killed on his way to Mendarro.

It was *so* clear.

David raised his Lüger; he would have only an instant. A diversion, then an instant.

It would be enough. . . .

The lessons of the north country.

He reached down and clawed at the ground, gathering chunks of earth and lawn with his left hand. When he had a large fistful, he lobbed it into the air, to the *left* of the rim of metal. Black dirt and blades of grass floated up, magnified in the dim spills of light and the furious activity growing nearer.

There was a steady burst of fire from the Sternlicht. Spaulding sprang to the *right* of the table and squeezed the trigger of the Lüger five times in rapid succession.

Erich Rhinemann's face exploded in blood. The Sternlicht fell as his hands sprang up in the spasm of death. The immense body snapped backward, then forward; then lurched over the railing.

Rhinemann plummeted down from the balcony.

David heard the screams of the guards above and raced back to the darkness of the bridle path. He ran with all his strength down the twisting black corridor, his shoes sinking intermittently into the soft, raked edges.

The path abruptly curved. To the *left*.

*Goddamn it!*

And then he heard the whinnies of frightened horses. His nostrils picked up their smells and to his right he saw the one-story structure that housed the series of stalls that was the stables. He could hear the bewildered shouts of a groom somewhere within trying to calm his charges.

For a split second, David toyed with an idea, then rejected it. A horse would be swift, but possibly unmanageable.

He ran to the far end of the stables, turned the corner and stopped for breath, for a moment of orientation. He thought he knew where he was; he tried to picture an aerial view of the compound.

The fields! The fields had to be nearby.

He ran to the opposite end of the one-story structure and saw the pastures beyond. As he had visualized, the ground sloped gently downward—north—but not so much as to make grazing or running difficult. In the distance past the fields, he could see the wooded hills rise in the moonlight. To the right—east.

Between the slope of the fields and the rise of the hills was the line he had to follow. It was the most direct, concealed route to the electrified fence.

North by northeast.

He sped to the high post-and-rail fence that bordered the pasture, slipped through and began racing across the field. The volleys and salvos of gunfire continued behind him— in the distance now, but seemingly no less brutal. He reached a ridge in the field that gave him a line of sight to the river a half mile below. It, too, was bordered by a high post-and-rail, used to protect the animals from plummeting down the steeper inclines. He could see lights being turned on along the river; the incessant crescendos of death were being carried by the summer winds to the elegant communities below.

He spun in shock. A bullet whined above him. It had been *aimed* at him! He had been spotted!

He threw himself into the pasture grass and scrambled away. There was a slight incline and he let himself roll down it, over and over again, until his body hit the hard wood of a post. He had reached the opposite border of the field; beyond, the woods continued.

He heard the fierce howling of the dogs, and knew it was directed at him.

On his knees, he could see the outlines of a huge animal streaking toward him across the grass. His Lüger was poised, level, but he understood that by firing it, he would betray his position. He shifted the weapon to his left hand and pulled the hunting knife out of his belt.

The black monstrosity leaped through the air, honed by the scent into his target of human flesh. Spaulding lashed out his left hand with the Lüger, feeling the impact of the hard, muscular fur of the Doberman on his upper body, watching the ugly head whip sideways, the bared teeth tearing at the loose sweater and into his arm.

He swung his right hand upward, the knife gripped with all the strength he had, into the soft stomach of the animal. Warm blood erupted from the dog's lacerated belly; the swallowed sound of a savage roar burst from the animal's throat as it died.

David grabbed his arm. The Doberman's teeth had ripped into his skin below the shoulder. And the wrenching, rolling, twisting movements of his body had broken at least one of the stitches in his stomach wound.

He held onto the rail of the pasture fence and crawled east.

*North* by northeast! *Not east*, goddamn it!

In his momentary shock, he suddenly realized there was a perceptible reduction of the distant gunfire. How many minutes had it *not* been there? The explosions seemed to continue but the small-arms fire was subsiding.

Considerably.

There were shouts now; from across the field by the stables. He looked between and over the grass. Men were running with flashlights, the beams darting about in shifting diagonals. David could hear shouted commands.

What he saw made him stop all movement and stare incredulously. The flashlights of the men across the wide pasture were focused on a figure coming out of the stable —on horseback! The spill of a dozen beams picked up the glaring reflection of a white Palm Beach suit.

Franz Altmüller!

Altmüller had chosen the madness he, David, had rejected.

But, of course, their roles were different.

Spaulding knew he was the quarry now. Altmüller, the hunter.

There would be others following, but Altmüller would not, *could* not wait. He kicked at the animal's flanks and burst through the opened gate.

Spaulding understood again. Franz Altmüller was a dead man if David lived. His only means of survival in Berlin was to produce the corpse of the man from Lisbon. The Fairfax agent who had crippled "Tortugas"; the body of the man the patrols and the scientists in Ocho Calle could identify. The man the "Gestapo" had unearthed and provoked.

So much, so alien.

Horse and rider came racing across the field. David stayed prone and felt the hard earth to the east. He could not stand; Altmüller held a powerful, wide-beamed flashlight. If he rolled under the railing, the tall weeds and taller grass beyond might conceal him but just as easily might bend, breaking the pattern.

*If . . . might.*

He knew he was rationalizing. The tall grass would be best; out of sight. But also out of strategy. And he knew why that bothered him.

He wanted to be the hunter. Not the quarry.

He wanted Altmüller dead.

Franz Altmüller was not an enemy one left alive. Altmüller was every bit as lethal in a tranquil monastery during a time of peace as he was on a battlefield in war. He was the absolute enemy; it was in his eyes. Not related to the cause of Germany, but from deep within the man's arrogance: Altmüller had watched his masterful creation collapse, had seen "Tortugas" destroyed. By another man who had told him he was inferior.

That, Altmüller could not tolerate.

He would be scorned in the aftermath.

*Unacceptable!*

Altmüller would lie in wait. In Buenos Aires, in New York, in London; no matter where. And his first target would be Jean. In a rifle sight, or a knife in a crowd, or a concealed pistol at night. Altmüller would make him pay. It was in his eyes.

Spaulding hugged the earth as the galloping horse reached the midpoint of the field, plunging forward, directed by the searchlight beam from the patrols back at the stables a quarter of a mile away. They were directed at the area where the Doberman was last seen.

Altmüller reined in the animal, slowing it, not stopping it. He scanned the ground in front with his beam, approaching cautiously, a gun in his hand, holding the straps but prepared to fire.

Without warning, there was a sudden, deafening explosion from the stables. The beams of light that had come from the opposite side of the field were no more; men who had started out across the pasture after Altmüller stopped and turned back to the panic that was growing furiously at the bordering fence. Fires had broken out.

Altmüller continued; if he was aware of the alarms behind him he did not show it. He kicked his horse and urged it forward.

The horse halted, snorted; it pranced its front legs awkwardly and backstepped in spite of Altmüller's commands. The Nazi was in a frenzy; he screamed at the animal, but the shouts were in vain. The horse had come upon the dead Doberman; the scent of the fresh blood repelled it.

Altmüller saw the dog in the grass. He swung the light first to the left, then to the right, the beam piercing the space above David's head. Altmüller made his decision instinctively—or so it seemed to Spaulding. He whipped the reins of the horse to his right, toward David. He walked the horse; he did not run it.

Then David saw why. Altmüller was following the stains of the Doberman's blood in the grass.

David crawled as fast as he could in front of the spill of Altmüller's slow-moving beam. Once in relative darkness, he turned abruptly to his right and ran close to the ground back toward the *center* of the field. He waited until horse and rider were between him and the bordering post-and-rail, then inched his way toward the Nazi. He was tempted to take a clean shot with the Lüger, but he knew that had to be the last extremity. He had several miles to go over unfamiliar terrain, with a dark forest that others knew better. The loud report of a heavy-caliber pistol shot would force men out of the pandemonium a quarter of a mile away.

Nevertheless, it might be necessary.

He was within ten feet now, the Lüger in his left hand, his right free. . . . A little closer, just a bit closer. Altmuller's flashlight slowed to a near stop. He had approached the point where he, David, had lain in the grass immobile.

Then Spaulding felt the slight breeze from behind and knew—in a terrible instant of recognition—that it was the moment to move.

The horse's head yanked up, the wide eyes bulged. The scent of David's blood-drenched clothing had reached its nostrils.

Spaulding sprang out of the grass, his right hand aimed at Altmüller's wrist. He clasped his fingers over the barrel of the gun—it was a Colt! a U.S. Army issue Colt .45!—and forced his thumb into the trigger housing. Altmüller whipped around in shock, stunned by the totally unexpected attack. He pulled his arms back and lashed out with his feet. The horse reared high on its hind legs; Spaulding held on, forcing Altmüller's hand down, *down*. He yanked with every ounce of strength he had and literally ripped Altmüller off of the horse into the grass. He slammed the

Nazi's wrist into the ground again and again, until flesh hit rock and the Colt sprang loose. As it did so, he crashed his Lüger into Altmüller's face.

The German fought back. He clawed at Spaulding's eyes with his free left hand, kicked furiously with his knees and feet at David's testicles and legs and rocked violently, his shoulders and head pinned by Spaulding's body. He screamed.

"*You!* You and . . . *Rhinemann! Betrayal!*"

The Nazi saw the blood beneath David's shoulder and tore at the wound, ripping the already torn flesh until Spaulding thought he could not endure the pain.

Altmüller heaved his shoulder up into David's stomach, and yanked at David's bleeding arm, sending him sprawling off to the side. The Nazi leaped up on his feet, then threw himself back down on the grass where the Colt .45 had been pried loose. He worked his hands furiously over the ground.

He found the weapon.

Spaulding pulled the hunting knife from the back of his belt and sprang across the short distance that separated him from Altmüller. The Colt's barrel was coming into level position, the small black opening in front of his eyes.

As the blade entered the flesh, the ear-shattering fire of the heavy revolver exploded at the side of David's face, burning his skin, but missing its mark.

Spaulding tore the knife downward into Altmüller's chest and left it there.

The absolute enemy was dead.

David knew there was no instant to lose, or he was lost. There would be other men, other horses . . . many dogs.

He raced to the bordering pasture fence, over it and into the darkness of the woods. He ran blindly, trying desperately to swing partially to his left. North.

North by northeast.

Escape!

He fell over rocks and fallen branches, then at last penetrated deepening foliage, lashing his arms for a path, any kind of a path. His left shoulder was numb, both a danger and a blessing.

There was no gunfire in the distance now; only darkness and the hum of the night forest and the wild, rhythmic pounding of his chest. The fighting by the stables had stopped. Rhinemann's men were free to come after him now.

He had lost blood; how much and how severely he could not tell. Except that his eyes were growing tired, as his body was tired. The branches became heavy, coarse tentacles; the inclines, steep mountains. The slopes were enormous ravines that had to be crossed without ropes. His legs buckled and he had to force them taut again.

The fence! There was the fence!

At the bottom of a small hill, between the trees.

He began running, stumbling, clawing at the ground, pushing forward to the base of the hill.

He was there. *It* was there.

The fence.

Yet he could not touch it. But, perhaps. . . .

He picked up a dry stick from the ground and lobbed it into the wire.

Sparks and crackling static. To touch the fence meant death.

He looked up at the trees. The sweat from his scalp and forehead stung his eyes, blurring his already blurred vision. There had to be a tree.

*A* tree. The *right* tree.

He couldn't be sure. The darkness played tricks on the leaves, the limbs. There were shadows in the moonlight where substance should be.

There were no limbs! No limbs hanging over the fence whose touch meant oblivion. Rhinemann had severed—on both sides—whatever growths approached the high, linked steel wires!

He ran as best he could to his left—north. The river was perhaps a mile away. Perhaps.

Perhaps the water.

But the river, if he could reach it down the steep inclines barred to horses, would slow him up, would rob him of the time he needed desperately. And Rhinemann would have patrols on the river banks.

Then he saw it.

Perhaps.

A sheared limb several feet above the taut wires, coming to within a few feet of the fence! It was thick, widening into suddenly greater thickness as it joined the trunk. A laborer had taken the means of least resistance and had angled his chain saw just before the final thickness. He would not be criticized; the limb was too high, too far away, for all practical purposes.

But Spaulding knew it was his last chance. The only one left. And that fact was made indelibly clear to him with the distant sounds of men and dogs. They were coming after him now.

He removed one of the Lügers from his belt and threw it over the fence. One bulging impediment in his belt was enough.

He jumped twice before gripping a gnarled stub; his left arm aching, no longer numb, no longer a blessing. He scraped his legs up the wide trunk until his right hand grasped a higher branch. He struggled against the sharp bolts of pain in his shoulder and stomach and pulled himself up.

The sawed-off limb was just above.

He dug the sides of his shoes into the bark, jabbing them repeatedly to make tiny ridges. He strained his neck, pushing his chin into the calloused wood, and whipped both arms over his head, forcing his left elbow over the limb, pulling maniacally with his right hand. He hugged the amputated limb, pedaling his feet against the tree until the momentum allowed him the force to throw his right leg over it. He pressed his arms downward and thrust himself into a sitting position, his back against the trunk.

He had managed it. Part of it.

He took several deep breaths and tried to focus his sweat-filled, stinging eyes. He looked down at the electrified barbed wire on top of the fence. It was less than four feet below him but nearly three feet in front. From the crest of the ground, about eight. If he was going to clear the wire, he had to twist and jack his body into a lateral vault. And should he be able to do that, he was not at all sure his body could take the punishment of the fall.

But he could hear the dogs and the men clearly now. They had entered the woods beyond the fields. He turned his head and saw dim shafts of light piercing the dense foliage.

The other punishment was death.

There was no point in thinking further. Thoughts were out of place now. Only motion counted.

He reached above with both hands, refusing to acknowledge the silent screams from his shoulder, grabbed at the thin branches, pulled up his legs until his feet touched the top of the thick limb, and lunged, hurling himself straight out above the taut wires until he could see their blurred image. At that split-instant, he twisted his body violently to the right and down, jackknifing his legs under him.

It was a strange, fleeting sensation: disparate feelings of final desperation and, in a very real sense, clinical objectivity. He had done all he could do. There wasn't any more.

He hit the earth, absorbing the shock with his right shoulder, rolling forward, his knees tucked under him—rolling, rolling, not permitting the roll to stop; distributing the impact throughout his body.

He was propelled over a tangle of sharp roots and collided with the base of a tree. He grabbed his stomach; the surge of pain told him the wound was open now. He would have to hold it, clutch it . . . blot it. The cloth of the turtleneck sweater was drenched with sweat and blood—his own and the Doberman's—and torn in shreds from the scores of falls and stumbles.

But he had made it.

Or nearly.

He was out of the compound. He was free from Habichtsnest.

He looked around and saw the second Lüger on the ground in the moonlight. . . . The one in his belt would be enough. If it wasn't, a second wouldn't help him; he let it stay there.

The highway was no more than half a mile away now. He crawled into the underbrush to catch his spent breath, to temporarily restore what little strength he had left. He would need it for the remainder of his journey.

The dogs were louder now; the shouts of the patrols could be heard no more than several hundred yards away. And suddenly the panic returned. What in God's name had he been *thinking* of!? What was he *doing!?*

What *was* he doing?

He was lying in the underbrush assuming—*assuming* he was *free!*

But *was* he?

There were men with guns and savage—viciously savage —animals within the sound of his voice and the sight of his running body.

Then suddenly he heard the words, the commands, shouted—screamed in anticipation. In rage.

*"Freilassen! Die Hunde freilassen!"*

The dogs were being released! The handlers thought their quarry was cornered! The dogs were unleashed to tear the quarry apart!

He saw the beams of light come over the small hill before he saw the animals. Then the dogs were silhouetted as they streaked over the ridge and down the incline. Five, eight, a dozen racing, monstrous forms stampeding toward the hated object of their nostrils; growing nearer, panicked into wanting, needing the wild conclusion of teeth into flesh.

David was mesmerized—and sickened—by the terrible sight that followed.

The whole area lit up like a flashing diadem; crackling, hissing sounds of electricity filled the air. Dog after dog crashed into the high wire fence. Short fur caught fire; horrible, prolonged, screeching yelps of animal death shattered the night.

In alarm or terror or both, shots were fired from the ridge. Men ran in all directions—some to the dogs and the fence, some to the flanks, most away in retreat.

David crawled out of the brush and started running into the forest.

He *was* free!

The prison that was Habichtsnest confined his pursuers. . . . but *he* was free!

He held his stomach and ran into the darkness.


The highway was bordered by sand and loose gravel. He stumbled out of the woods and fell on the sharp, tiny stones. His vision blurred; nothing stayed level; his throat was dry, his mouth rancid with the vomit of fear. He realized that he could not get up. He could not stand.

He saw an automobile far in the distance, to his right. West. It was traveling at high speed; the headlights kept flashing. Off . . . on, off . . . on. On, on, on . . . off, off, off, interspersed.

It was a signal!

But he could not stand! He could not rise!

And then he heard his name. Shouted in unison through

open windows, by several voices. In unison! As a chant might be sung!

". . . Spaulding, Spaulding, Spaulding. . . ."

The car was about to pass him! He could not get up!

He reached into his belt and yanked out the Lüger.

He fired it twice, barely possessing the strength to pull the trigger.

With the second shot . . . all was blackness.

He felt the gentle fingers around his wound, felt the vibrations of the moving automobile.

He opened his eyes.

Asher Feld was looking down at him; his head was in Feld's lap. The Jew smiled.

"Everything will be answered. Let the doctor sew you up. We must patch you together quickly."

David raised his head as Feld held his neck. A second man, a young man, was also in the back seat, bending over his stomach; Spaulding's legs were stretched over the young man's knees. The man held gauze and pincers in his hands.

"There will be only minor pain," he said in that same bastardized British accent David had heard so often. "I think you've had enough of that. You're localized."

"I'm what?"

"Simple Novocain," replied the doctor. "I'll retie the stitches here; your arm is filled with an antibiotic—refined in a Jerusalem laboratory, incidentally." The young man smiled.

"What? Where . . ."

"There isn't time," interrupted Feld quietly, urgently. "We're on our way to Mendarro. The plane is waiting. There'll be no interference."

"You got the designs?"

"Chained to the staircase, Lisbon. We did not expect such accommodation. We thought probably the balcony, perhaps an upper floor. Our invasion was swift, thanks be to God. Rhinemann's troops came swiftly. Not swiftly enough. . . . Good work, that staircase. How did you manage it?"

David smiled through the "minor pain." It was difficult to talk. "Because . . . no one wanted the blueprints out of his sight. Isn't that funny?"

"I'm glad you think so. You'll need that quality."

"*What? . . . Jean?*" Spaulding started to rise from the awkward position. Feld restrained his shoulders, the doctor his midsection.

"No, colonel. There are no concerns for Mrs. Cameron or the physicist. They will, no doubt, be flown out of Buenos Aires in the morning. . . . And the coastal blackout will be terminated within minutes. The radar screens will pick up the trawler. . . ."

David held up his hand, stopping the Jew. He took several breaths in order to speak. "Reach FMF. Tell them the rendezvous is scheduled for approximately . . . four hours . . . from the time the trawler left Ocho Calle. Estimate the maximum speed of the trawler . . . semicircle the diameter . . . follow that line."

"Well done," said Asher Feld. "We'll get word to them."

The young doctor had finished. He leaned over and spoke pleasantly.

"All things considered, these patches are as good as you'd get at Bethesda. Better than the job someone did on your right shoulder; that was awful. You can sit up. Easy, now."

David had forgotten. The British medic in the Azores— centuries ago—had taken a lot of criticism from his professional brothers. Misdirected; his orders had been to get the American officer out of Lajes Field within the hour.

Spaulding inched his way stiffly into a sitting position, aided gently by the two Haganah men.

"Rhinemann is dead," he said simply. "Rhinemann the pig is gone. There'll be no more negotiations. Tell your people."

"Thank you," said Asher Feld.

They drove in silence for several minutes. The searchlights of the small airfield could be seen now; they were shafting their beams into the night sky.

Feld spoke. "The designs are in the aircraft. Our men are standing guard. . . . I'm sorry you have to fly out tonight. It would be simpler if the pilot were alone. But that's not possible."

"It's what I was sent down here for."

"It's a bit more complicated, I'm afraid. You've been through a great deal, you've been wounded severely. By all rights, you should be hospitalized. . . . But that will have to wait."

"Oh?" David understood that Feld had something to say that even this pragmatic Jew found difficult to put into words. "You'd better tell me. . . ."

"You'll have to deal with this in your *own* way, colonel," interrupted Feld. "You see . . . the men in Washington do not expect you on that plane. They've ordered your execution."

# 43

Brigadier General Alan Swanson, lately of the War Department, had committed suicide. Those who knew him said the pressures of his job, the immense logistics he was called upon to expedite daily, had become too much for this dedicated, patriotic officer. They also served who, far behind the lines, primed the machinery of war with all the selfless energy they possessed.

In Fairfax, Virginia, at the huge, security-conscious compound that held the secrets of Allied Central Intelligence, a lieutenant colonel named Ira Barden disappeared. Simply disappeared; substance one day, vapor the next. With him went a number of highly classified files from the vaults. What bewildered those who knew about them was the information these files contained. In the main they were personal dossiers of ranking Nazis involved with the concentration camps. Not the sort of intelligence data a defector would steal. Ira Barden's own dossier was pulled and placed in the archives. Regrets were sent to his family; Lieutenant Colonel Barden was MOA. Missing while on assignment. Strange, but the family never insisted upon an investigation. Which was their right, after all. . . . Strange.

A cryptographer in Lisbon, a man named Marshall, was found in the hills of the Basque country. He had been wounded in a border skirmish and nursed back to health by partisans. The reports of his death had been greatly exaggerated as intended. German Intelligence was onto him. For the time being, however, he was confined to the embassy and returned to duty. He had sent a personal message to an old friend he thought might be concerned; to Colonel David Spaulding. The message was amusing, in an oddly phrased way. He wanted Spaulding to know there were no hard feelings about the colonel's vacation in South America. The cryp had taken a vacation, too. There were codes that had to be broken—if they could be found. They both should plan better in the future; they should get together on vacations. Good friends should always do that.

There was another cryptographer. In Buenos Aires. One Robert Ballard. The State Department was very high on Ballard these days. The Buenos Aires cryptographer had spotted an enormous error in a scrambler and had taken the personal initiative to not only question it, but to refuse to *authenticate* it. Through a series of grave misunderstandings and faulty intelligence, an order for the on-sight execution of Colonel Spaulding had been issued by the War Department. Code: treason. Defection to the enemy while on assignment. It took a great deal of courage on Ballard's part to refuse to acknowledge so high priority a command. And State was never averse to embarrassing the Department of War.

The aerophysicist, Eugene Lyons, Ph.D., was flown back to Pasadena. Things . . . things had happened to Doctor Lyons. He was offered and accepted a lucrative, meaningful contract with Sperry Rand's Pacific laboratories, the finest in the country. He had entered a Los Angeles hospital for throat surgery—prognosis: sixty-forty in his favor, if the will was there. . . . It was. And there was something else about Lyons. On the strength of his contract he had secured a bank loan and was building an oddly shaped, Mediterranean-style house in a peaceful section of the San Fernando Valley.

Mrs. Jean Cameron returned to the Eastern Shore of Maryland—for two days. The State Department, at the personal behest of Ambassador Henderson Granville in Buenos Aires, issued a letter of commendation to Mrs. Cameron. Although her status was not official, her presence at the embassy had been most valuable. She had kept open lines of communication with diverse factions within the neutral city; lines of communication often jeopardized by diplomatic necessities. Officials at State decided to present Mrs. Cameron with the letter in a small ceremony, presided over by a prominent undersecretary. State was somewhat surprised to learn that Mrs. Cameron could not be reached at her family home on Maryland's Eastern Shore. She was in Washington. At the Shoreham Hotel.

The Shoreham was where Colonel David Spaulding was registered. . . . More than a coincidence, perhaps, but in no way would it interfere with the letter of commendation. Not these days. Not in Washington.

Colonel David Spaulding looked up at the light brown stone and square pillars of the War Department. He pulled at his army overcoat, adjusting the heavy cloth over the sling on his arm underneath. It was the last time he would wear a uniform or enter this building. He started up the steps.

It was curious, he mused. He had been back for nearly three weeks, and every day, every night he had thought about the words he was going to say this afternoon. The fury, the revulsion . . . the waste. Resentments for a lifetime. But life would go on and in some curious way the violent emotions had crested. He felt only a weariness now, an exhaustion that demanded that he get it over with and return to something of value. Somewhere.

With Jean.

He knew the men of "Tortugas" could not be reached with words. Words of conscience had lost meaning for such men. As they had so often lost meaning for him. That, too, was one of their crimes: they had stolen . . . decency. From so many. For so little.

Spaulding left his overcoat in the outer office and walked into the small conference room. They were there, the men of "Tortugas."

Walter Kendall.

Howard Oliver.

Jonathan Craft.

None got up from the table. All were silent. Each stared at him. The looks were mixtures of hate and fear—so often inseparable.

They were prepared to fight, to protest . . . to salvage. They had held their *discussions*, they had arrived at *strategies*.

They were so obvious, thought David.

He stood at the end of the table, reached into his pocket and took out a handful of carbonado diamonds. He threw them on the hard surface of the table; the tiny nuggets clattered and rolled.

The men of "Tortugas" remained silent. They shifted their eyes to the stones, then back to Spaulding.

"The Koening transfer," said David. "The tools for Peenemünde. I wanted you to see them."

Howard Oliver exhaled a loud, impatient breath and spoke in practiced condescension. "We have no idea what . . ."

"I know," interrupted Spaulding firmly. "You're busy men. So let's dispense with unnecessary conversation; as a matter of fact, there's no reason for you to talk at all. Just listen. I'll be quick. And you'll always know where to reach me."

David put his left hand into his arm sling and pulled out an envelope. It was an ordinary business envelope; sealed, thick. He placed it carefully on the table and continued.

"This is the history of 'Tortugas.' From Geneva to Buenos Aires. From Peenemünde to a place called Ocho Calle. From Pasadena to a street . . . Terraza Verde. It's an ugly story. It raises questions I'm not sure should be raised right now. Perhaps ever. For the sake of so much sanity . . . everywhere.

"But that's up to you here at this table. . . . There are several copies of this . . . this indictment. I won't tell you where and you'll never be able to find out. But they exist. And they'll be released in a way that will result in simultaneous headlines in New York and London and Berlin. Unless you do exactly as I say. . . .

"Don't protest, Mr. Kendall. It's useless. . . . This war is won. The killing will go on for a while but we've won it. Peenemünde hasn't been idle; they've scoured the earth. A few thousand rockets will be built, a few thousand killed. Nowhere near what they conceived of. Or needed. And our aircraft will blow up half of Germany; we'll be the victors now. And that's how it should be. What must come after the killing is the healing. And you gentlemen will dedicate the rest of your natural lives to it. You will sever all connections with your companies; you will sell all your holdings above a bare subsistence level—as defined by the national economic guidelines—donating the proceeds to charities—anonymously but with substantiation. And you will offer your considerable talents to a grateful government—in exchange for government salaries.

"For the rest of your lives you will be skilled government clerks. And that is all you'll be.

"You have sixty days to comply with these demands. Incidentally, since you ordered my execution once, you should know that part of our contract is my well-being. And the well-being of those close to me, of course.

"Lastly, because it occurred to me that you might wish to recruit others under this contract, the indictment makes it clear that you could not have created 'Tortugas' alone. . . . Name who you will. The world is in a sorry state, gentlemen. It needs all the help it can get."

Spaulding reached down for the envelope, picked it up and dropped it on the table. The slap of paper against wood drew all eyes to the spot.

"Consider *everything*," said David.

The men of "Tortugas" stared in silence at the envelope. David turned, walked to the door and let himself out.

March in Washington. The air was chilly, the winds were of winter but the snows would not come.

Lieutenant Colonel David Spaulding dodged the cars as he crossed Wisconsin Avenue to the Shoreham Hotel. He was unaware that his overcoat was open; he was oblivious to the cold.

It was over! He was finished! There would be scars—deep scars—but with time. . . .

With Jean. . . .